W9-BMF-621

FAMILY BLOOD

BY DAVID RITZ

NOVELS

Search for Happiness

The Man Who Brought the Dodgers Back to Brooklyn

Dreams

Blue Notes Under a Green Felt Hat

Barbells and Saxophones

Family Blood

BIOGRAPHIES

Brother Ray (with Ray Charles)

Divided Soul: The Life of Marvin Gaye

Smokey: Inside My Life (with Smokey Robinson)

LYRICS

"*Sexual Healing*" (Recorded by Marvin Gaye)

"*Love Is the Light*" (Recorded by Smokey Robinson)

"*Brothers in the Night*" (Theme Song to film, *Uncommon Valor*)

"*Release Your Love*" (Recorded by the Isley Brothers)

"*Eye on You*" (Recorded by Howard Hewett)

"*Get It While It's Hot*" (Recorded by Eddie Kendricks and Dennis Edwards)

"*Power*" (Recorded by Tramaine Hawkins)

"*Velvet Nights*" (Recorded by Leon Ware)

FAMILY BLOOD

by
David
Ritz

DONALD I. FINE, INC. *New York*

Library of Congress Cataloging-in-Publication Data

Ritz, David.
Family blood : a novel / David Ritz.
p. cm.
ISBN 1-55611-176-2
I. Title.
PS3568.I828F26 1991
813'.54—dc20 90-55023
CIP

Designed by Irving Perkins Associates

This novel is a work of fiction. Names, characters, places and incidents are either the product of the author's imagination or are used fictitiously. Any resemblance to actual events, locales, organizations or persons, living or dead, is entirely coincidental and beyond the intent of either the author or publisher.

Manufactured in the United States of America

10 9 8 7 6 5 4 3 2 1

For Don Fine,
Literary Godfather

HERE'S TO MY FAMILY—Roberta, Jessica, Alison, Mom, Dad, Esther, Elizabeth, Brad, Marc, Jennifer, Gabriel, Sarah, Julia, Mom Florence M. Plitt—my agent, Aaron Priest, lifelong friends Richard Freed, Phil Maxwell, Richard Cohen, and my extensive support group, including, among many others, Erina Siciliani, Dave Simmons, Steve Summi, Ray Baradat, Herb Boyd, Frieda and Mussimo dalla Torre, Ron Lockett and Jerry Wexler. God's been good to me.

FAMILY BLOOD

PART ONE

KENNEDY AIRPORT

AS THE STRIKINGLY HANDSOME couple—the white man and black woman—strode into the first-class cabin and took their seats in the first row, an elderly matron sitting across the aisle scrutinized them with disapproval.

She wondered whether the woman, whose smooth *café au lait* skin radiated a reddish glow, was a model or actress. Was the man, with pale blue eyes and longish brown hair, also some sort of celebrity? Was he the woman's husband or lover? They were both impeccably dressed—he in a camel-colored cashmere overcoat, she in a flowing dove-grey velvet cape. Their physical appeal seemed to infuse them with power. At the same time, they did not appear entirely comfortable in one another's company.

The man was David Crossman, twenty-seven, second-year attorney in the Wall Street establishment of Crossman, Croft and Snowden, a prestigious 150-lawyer firm managed by his father, Ralph Crossman.

The woman was Rita Moses, twenty-five, a promising jazz singer in the tradition of Billie Holiday, Sarah Vaughan and Ella Fitzgerald.

At six feet, David was only slightly taller than Rita whose slim statuesque figure was covered by a loose-fitting outfit, collarless white blouse and long fitted sage green flannel skirt.

Rita's beauty was subtle; her charcoal eyes narrow, her nose thin, her mouth broad, her teeth even and unblemished. Her hair was cropped short and worn naturally—no softener, no permanent—closely following the shape of her skull. Her high forehead seemed sculpted. Great silver hoops dangled from her ears. As she crossed her long legs and flipped through Essence magazine, David leaned over and said, "We're going to be late."

"No problem," she commented calmly. "Your meeting's not till tomorrow."

"Just anxious to get there," he said, thinking of how, after a half-dozen dates, he and Rita had yet to make love.

David saw the upcoming weekend as an intriguing adventure. Not only was he stealing away with a woman who fascinated him, but one whom his father would find outrageously unacceptable. What's more, he was traveling to a business meeting, shrouded in mystery, which his father had forbidden him to attend. In fact, just minutes before leaving for the airport, David and Ralph had locked horns.

"It makes no sense to fly off to Miami Beach," Ralph had claimed, "on the basis of a single phone call."

"Not one call, but three," answered David, always at a disadvantage in his father's office. The wood-paneled room, with its majestic floor-to-ceiling bookcases and original examples of the Hudson River School of nineteenth century landscape painting, was the size of a small ballroom. Prominently placed, so that no visitor could miss them, were gold-framed photographs of Ralph Crossman at formal functions with Henry Kissinger and Beverly Sills. Behind the stately Georgian desk, once used by Alexander Hamilton, was a wall of windows looking toward the twin towers of the World Trade Center.

Ralph rose from his desk like a tower. His eyes were a darker blue than David's—icier, far more focused. He stood two inches taller than his son. An avid horseback rider and Class-A squash player, Crossman, at fifty-four, had reached the peak of his political and financial power. Each Friday, a stylist came to trim his silver-gray hair while a manicurist cut, buffed and polished his nails. On Monday and Wednesday, at precisely seven A.M. a personal trainer propelled him through fifty minutes of vigorous cardiovascular weight training.

Ralph had never hit David as a child; he never had to. One frozen stare was enough to fill the young boy's heart with fear and reduce him to tears. Now standing before his father, David fought those old fears, feeling like an angry little boy, helpless, controlled, as though his life—his choices, his destiny—were not his own.

"My whole life," he said, "I've heard you preach how the lifeblood of a law firm is new business. So what happens? I'm on the brink of bringing in my first piece of new business and you won't allow it. That doesn't make sense."

"Who is this man in Miami Beach?" Ralph wanted to know, speaking in the accusatory tone of a relentless litigator. "What's his business? What's his background? How can you possibly consider taking a trip with absolutely no information."

"He sent me a round-trip ticket and a five thousand dollar advance against future fees. The check's cleared the bank. I thought that was good enough for starters. Look, Ralph," said David, who, even as a child, could never refer to his father as Dad, "what more could you want?"

"Discretion. Caution. Scrutiny. I might remind you that, as a firm, we do not tolerate ambulance chasers. Nor do we deal with common criminals."

"Just uncommon criminals—white-collar corporate raiders, green-mailers, crooked chairmen of the board."

"This firm has never—do you understand me?—*never* represented a crooked client," Ralph insisted, raising his voice in an uncharacteristic display of emotion. "Nor do we intend to begin now—"

"The guy in Miami said he wanted a will—

"Drew McKenzie is our specialist in wills and trusts. Why didn't he contact Drew?"

"He said he wanted someone young. He saw the article about my record collection in Goldmine magazine."

"Who is this man—a record collector, a manager, a musician? You still haven't given me the data I require."

"I'll fill you in when I get back."

"That article on you, by the way, was completely unnecessary. I would remind you that the wise attorney never seeks publicity for himself. That serves neither him nor his clients. Besides, why is a man in Florida interested in a New York lawyer?"

"He said he has business interests in New York."

"What business?"

"I said I don't know!"

"I'll need a better explanation than that."

"I need to get out of here. This conversation's boring. I'm on my way to the airport. My date's waiting," said David, showing more bravado than he felt.

"So you're bringing a girl on the trip."

"A woman."

"Have I met her?"

"Only if you've been following me to the jazz clubs."

"Confusing business with pleasure . . ."

"I'd rather be confused than miserable."

"I don't follow."

"Good. I'm gone."

Ralph moved to within inches of where his son was standing.

"Understand this, David. I am *not,* under any circumstances, authorizing the trip."

David stared back at his father, sucking in a deep breath before replying. "I don't care what you authorize."

"You and your downtown crowd consider vulgarity fashionable," Ralph shot back, narrowing his ice-blue eyes. "I find it vulgar."

"You seem a little edgy," Rita observed, breaking David's train of thought as the pilot fired up the engines. "Are you a nervous flyer?"

"Can't wait to fly away," said David, touching Rita's hand. "Just been a rough day."

"New suit?" Rita asked David, gently stroking the smooth dark fabric. "Have I seen you wear it before?"

"Brand new. Bought it just for the trip. Bought it just to impress you."

She liked David's clipped speech patterns, liked his sharp, chiseled chin and his overactive mind. At first she hadn't been sure. After all, he was a lawyer and, as a rule, lawyers were stiffs. When he'd kept coming back to see her at Mondrian Club on Madison Avenue, she'd written him off as another Upper East Side psuedosophisticate. But little by little she began to feel his energy—impetuous, unpredictable—and found it appealing. His unusually deep appreciation of her talent added to his charm. His speaking voice was alternately tender and tough, and she soon sensed other puzzling contradictions in his character. He was a rebel in conservative clothing, a man with a job he was reluctant to discuss. He said it was dull. He seemed far more interested in her than in himself, a quality she found especially rare in men. She liked the way he spent money freely—first-row seats for Miles Davis at Carnegie Hall, dinner at Lutece, The Four Seasons—and while he made it clear that he wanted to sleep with her, he qualified his persistence with eager patience. He was sexy.

She was enigmatic. At first, David thought he had pegged Rita—member of the new black middle class, college graduate, gifted vocalist with a strong sense of taste and tradition. But he quickly learned he was wrong: her background was blue-collar; she was a high school dropout and mostly she was self-taught. Her feelings for high fashion and literature—Ralph Ellison, James Baldwin, Toni Morrison—were seemingly innate. She lived alone in a small apartment not far from her parents in Greenwich Village. Her black mother, originally from Mississippi, earned excellent tips working as a waitress at the Second Avenue Delicatessen. Her father, a white Jewish man from Baltimore, was a twenty-five-year veteran of the post office in Chinatown.

"I don't impress too easily," she told David as she removed her hand from the arm of his suit.

"I've noticed," he said. "But you can't blame me for trying."

The 727 taxied to the runway, the noise from the engines growing louder.

"I've bought you a gift," she announced, fishing a cassette out of her Museum of Modern Art tote bag.

"What is it?"

"A demo I recorded the other day. I'd like your opinion."

Flattered, David took the tape, planting a soft thank-you kiss on Rita's cheek. Noticing, the matron across the aisle felt sick to her stomach.

David found his Walkman at the bottom of his attaché case, slipped on the earphones and slid in the cassette. Soft seductive music muffled the thunder of the jet roaring down the runway. Rita's voice had a thin top and rich bottom, a beguiling vibrato, an edge of hunger, a hopeful lilt, experience beyond her years.

"*My heart has been too shy . . .* " she sang as the plane lifted off, its huge wings cutting through sheets of winter sleet and freezing rain. "*I've whispered in my sleep . . . afraid to say the words . . . afraid to go too deep . . .* "

David felt the breath of her voice in his ear. It felt good to be quitting New York in nasty November, good to be forgetting his father's righteous anger, good to be soaring through storm clouds, good above all to be sitting next to Rita.

"*If my courage came too late . . .* " she said in song, "*I've only myself to blame . . . but today is the day . . . I'm revealing my motive and my aim . . .* "

What is your aim?"

"To learn your opinion of my song."

"I like it. Did you write it?"

"Only the lyrics."

"*Only*? The lyrics are everything. Who's it about?"

"No one I know."

"Not you? Not me?"

"I don't know you that well, David."

"That's what you said the first time we went out—and the second—and the sixth."

"This is only the fifth time."

"You're counting?"

She smiled. "What about adding a string section?"

"What about a good agent?"

"Are you volunteering."

"I'm not that kind of lawyer."

"Why not?"

"Present circumstances prohibit it." Sounded like Ralph.

"Would you be happier as an agent?"

"Strings might have you sounding like Whitney Houston," he said, avoiding her question. "Would you be happy being Whitney?"

"Her banker's happy."

"So you want a hit record."

"I want a banker."

David laughed. "The truth is, I don't think you know what you want. I don't think you're prepared to reveal your 'motive and your aim.' I think you're playing with me."

"Isn't this supposed to be playtime? Aren't we heading for the fun-and-sun capital of America? Look out there and see what's happening."

David turned his head just as the jet pierced the last layer of dark into a sky of brilliant blue.

"Illumination," said Rita. "Can you see the light?"

"I won't be diverted. I'm really interested in those lyrics, Rita. What are you afraid to reveal?"

"Look here, David," she said, turning to a sassier style. "If, as you suggest, the song's about you, then maybe you're the one who shies away from revelation. For the past two months, you've asked me a million questions while I've learned diddley about you."

"What's there to learn? I'm a lawyer. You said you find lawyers boring, so I figured I'd increase my chances by shutting up."

"Chances of what?"

"Of winning your heart." At least he held back on the "fair lady" part.

"Is my heart the body part that really interests you?"

"Among others, yes. But the best part is being alone with you, outside the city, up in the air."

"Everything's up in the air."

"And that bothers you?"

"It pleases me. I'm an improviser—remember?—I make it up as I go along . . . songs, life, trips with strangers."

"You still see me as a stranger."

"I don't have a very good sense of you yet. I don't even know where you live."

"Sixty-sixth between Madison and Fifth. I've repeatedly invited you over, you've repeatedly refused."

"Do you have roommates?" asked Rita.

"Only my father."

"You live with your father?"

"Separate entrances, same brownstone."

"Cozy."

"I also work for him."

"You never told me. So you two must be very close."

"In a perverse sort of way, we can't seem to get away from each other."

"And what about Mom?"

"Died when I was three."

"I'm sorry . . ."

"Don't worry about it. I can't remember that far back."

"Any brothers and sisters?"

"Only child. Spoiled rotten. Product of the Dalton School, Princeton and Columbia Law. Nearly flunked out of all of them. I was a little wild."

"I wasn't exactly tame myself."

"Tell me more about it."

"Don't want to interrupt you. Tell more," Rita urged.

"Well, I was a sort of fighter. I loved taking on brutes bigger than me. Always proving something. Discipline came late, such as it is. At school I always felt out of place, like I was born to the wrong woman or the wrong man, living in the wrong neighborhood, doing the wrong things. Somehow I wound up hanging out with bands in Harlem or Brooklyn."

"You were slumming."

"You call it that. I call it feeling good, like in a way I belonged. I hated my schools and most of my teachers, but something always got me through."

"Daddy's money?"

"Mean but close to the truth."

"Are you from one of those blue-blood families with their own crests and summer homes in Hyannis Port?"

"Martha's Vineyard. And no crest that I know of. My family history is a big blank. My mother was an orphan and Ralph's parents died before I was born. So it was just me, him and his ladies."

"You call your father 'Ralph'?"

"That's his name."

"And these ladies, he never married any of them?"

"He married his work, a match made in heaven."

"I'd like to meet him."

"No you wouldn't."

"Is he a bigot?"

"He's a stalwart of liberalism. He'd be horrified to hear the word 'bigot' applied to him."

"But is he?"

"Deep down, who knows what he is? Feelings aren't his strong suit. Lawsuits are. As managing partner, he specializes in making grown men cry."

"But he loves you . . ."

"He employs me. That's his kind of love."

"And you love him?"

"What is this, true confessions?"

"I'm doing the interviewing. Please answer all questions."

"As much as I love being interviewed by you, Rita, I love your singing even more. Let me drink this martini and see if I can understand the secret of your song. I want to hear it again."

The lobby of the Fontainebleau was a puffy plush affair, a sea of green-leaf carpeting, a sky of satellite-sized chandeliers.

"Feels like the fifties," said Rita.

"Or the sixties," David added, approaching the reception desk. "Either way, before our time."

"You've never been here before?" asked Rita.

"Too garish for Ralph. The Hamptons are more his style," David said, pulling out his Crossman, Croft and Snowden American Express credit card and explaining to the clerk that the reservation had been made by a Mr. Nathan Silver.

"The penthouse suite is reserved for you, sir."

David and Rita, watching moonlit waves wash over the beach, stood on the veranda. In contrast to frigid New York, the air was fresh, the ocean breeze a gentle caress. Up the coast, towering hotels, apartment buildings and stately palm trees lined the shore like sentries.

"Interested in going out for dinner?" he asked.

"What do you feel like doing?"

"Staying here. Let's call room service."

Cracked crab and chilled champagne. Flutes and flowers. From the stereo, a lilting refrain, a soft and silky Sade samba. Birds of paradise bursting from a sculpted porcelain vase. Bedroom filled with tuber roses, blue gardenias, white freesias. Velvet bedspread. Satin sheets.

Rita called to him from the bathroom, fragrant with jasmine incense. She stepped out of the tub, her lithe body—small, high breasts, dark pubis, gleaming legs—beaded with water.

"Would you hand me the kimono on the door?"

She stepped into it, into his arms. He held her for a few seconds, then watched her dry her hair with a large fluffy towel, all the while leaving the kimono open at the waist. He approached her again, standing behind her, stroking her thighs. She turned and opened her mouth to his kiss.

The bedroom opened onto a balcony; the sliding door opened to the night winds, brisker than before, cooling the skins of their naked bodies as the heat rose.

Her heat was overwhelming. She was a flower on fire, a Venus flytrap, a snapdragon, a hothouse of orchids. Her petals, lips, moisture, pumping heart. Slowly, he ventured into her heart—swaying samba, insistent flute, penetrating and probing, and delighting each other.

"Thank you," she whispered in his ear afterward as he drifted off to sleep, dreaming of her song.

* * *

In the morning he couldn't remember his dream, although the old Tropical Deco district of Miami Beach, drenched in golden sunlight, looked like a dream. He'd left Rita sleeping at the hotel and driven the rented Lincoln Town Car to Ocean Drive. Feeling warmth for the world—his skin still tingled from last night's afterglow—David saw clusters of white-haired retirees sitting on benches under palm trees in Lummus Park. They seemed at peace with themselves. The whitewashed bungalows and sun-soaked apartments seemed at peace with the quiet sea. Glass bricks, porthole windows, ships' railings—David was surrounded by the nautilus streamlined modernity of the 1930s—one hotel gone to seed, another freshly refurbished. Pastels pleased his eye, yellow and turquoise, ocean azure, salmon pink. This morning he found charm in everything, even the name of his mystery client's modest retirement hotel: the Atlantic Arms.

A seafoam green mural with pink flamingos drinking from a Byzantine fountain graced the lobby. He saw on the building directory that Nathan Silver lived in apartment 6C. Because his client was putting him up at the penthouse of the Fontainebleau, David was surprised by the seediness of the Atlantic Arms. The elevator creaked. The hallway smelled of sour cabbage and boiled potatoes. A handwritten note on the door, in flowery scrawl—was it a woman's writing?—read, "We are by the pool. In the back."

Outside, the recreation area, an interior courtyard, was deserted except for a couple slowly walking around the bug-littered pool. A tall white man wearing dark glasses was being led by a large, light-skinned black woman in her early forties dressed in nurse's white. The man clutched the woman's arm as though he were blind. Bald except for a ring of wispy snow-white hair, he walked tentatively, his arms frail, his body bird-like. As David approached, he took a better look. The man's pinched face had a tawny complexion, husky nose, large lips, oversized mouth. A small dark mole punctuated the center of his chin. He wore gray trousers hoisted by black suspenders and a gaudy Hawaiian sport shirt opened at his wrinkled throat. He looked near eighty.

"Mr. Silver?" David asked when the man and the woman walked near him.

"Yes?"

"I'm David Crossman, from New York."

The old gent stopped dead in his tracks. Sensing his desire, the woman directed him to David. He reached up, his arm extended toward David.

David moved in, allowing the man's hand to slowly trace the features of his face. His fingertips were boney and warm and David, uneasy, stood there in silence until the man withdrew his hand.

"You are Mr. Silver, aren't you?" David finally said.

"Much more than that," answered the stranger in a Yiddish-flavored accent, "I'm your grandfather."

DETROIT

1940

RUBEN "THE GENT" GINZBURG steered his sleek white-and-silver Hudson into Paradise Valley. He parked the roadster in a back alley behind John R Street, the entertainment strip of this black section of the city just east of downtown.

Getting out of his car, Ginzburg immediately heard the music, wailing joyful honky-tonk music. He snapped down the brim of his summer straw, pulled on the French cuffs of his custom-made silk shirt, straightened his wide white-on-white tie, brushed off his blue serge double-breasted suit and headed around the corner.

The June night was sticky, but the Gent, in a hurry, hardly noticed. The thick aroma of smoldering barbecue ribs floated over the midnight air, the hour when Paradise Valley began to swing.

On John R, Ruben slowly passed by all the hot spots—the Plantation Club, Mirror Ballroom, Alabam, E-Z Way Lounge. A white man in a black world, he felt at home. Beyond the music the people put him at ease. He liked the style. Ginzburg hadn't made it past the sixth grade, but at twenty-nine, with a wife and two small boys, he took his responsibilities seriously. He thought in terms of business opportunities. And his sharp ears told him that he was in the middle of a musical goldmine.

The street was crowded and the dress was sharp, women in black-and-white polka-dot dresses, men in yellow suits, hats of every shape and size, high heels and suspenders, big-seamed nylons and blood-red lipsticks, potent perfumes, the stink of whiskey, the buzz of neon, jazz and blues, boogie-woogie and swing, old music blending into new—the McKinney Cotton Pickers, Levy Mann at the organ, Savannah Churchill, Lucky Thompson, Little Walter, Wyonnie Harris and the Gent's favorite, John Lee Hooker, Mississippi free-verse poet in from Cincinnati to sing his salty country blues.

Ruben stopped for a minute to listen to John Lee, his voice crawling all over the street, "I'm a kingsnake, baby, gonna crawl all over you." The Gent would have gone in and listened for a while except for the business at hand.

A couple of doors away, flanked by a pawnshop and shoeshine stand, stood Pino's Place, the most lavish nightclub in Paradise Valley.

"Pino around?" Ginzburg asked the burly bouncer.

The guy grunted "yeah" as Ruben pushed open the plush red doors.

The place was done in clashing reds—burgundy red, cherry red, orangey tomato red—from the bar to the tufted banquettes. Ventilation was poor and smoke clouded the air. On the bandstand, Jefferson Thunder, barrelhouse pianist from Memphis, was putting on a show, grunting, grinning and winning over the capacity crowd with a rousing rendition of "Beale Street Blues."

The Gent nodded to a couple of women he knew but kept moving through the room to the kitchen which led to a suite of private offices in the back. The outer office was manned by Fingers Markowitz, the big guy who always stood between Pino Feldman and the rest of the world.

"The boss busy?" Ruben wanted to know.

"He's just talking to some nigger," said Fingers. "Go on in."

The inner office was done up like a throne room—gold carpeting, gold drapes, huge semi-circular desk raised on a platform. Lying on the desk was tomorrow's edition of the Detroit *News*, the headlines screaming, "Germans Occupy Paris. Press on South!" Behind the desk was Pino Feldman, at only five foot two a man women liked to call "devilishly handsome." His Latin-looking slick-black hair was thick and shiny, his dark eyes darting, his manner high-strung.

"You're just in time, Ruby," Feldman told Ginzburg. "Listen to this bitch's story. Tell me what you think."

The woman standing in front of Pino's desk seemed unafraid. She was attractive but stout, solid and strongly built, average height. Her skin was dark. She wore a close-clinging butterfly-patterned dress displaying wide shoulders, broad hips and extraordinary breasts. Her large unblinking eyes were fixed on Pino. Gent guessed she was no older than eighteen, twenty years younger than Feldman. He also guessed what was up—Pino was about to put her through the ringer—and Ginzburg wanted out.

"Don't wanna interrupt, boss," said Ruben. "Just brought over the receipts from Black Bottom. Thought you'd wanna know we had a hell of a week. Over ten K." Ginzburg put a pile of cash on the desk.

"See," a smiling Feldman said to the woman as he fingered the money. "This Gent is one smart guy. He works his territory. He takes care of his people. He keeps his nose clean and always looks like he just stepped out of the shower. He knows what side his bread's buttered on. Ain't that right, Ruby?"

"I'll check in with you tomorrow, boss."

"Stick around, Gent. I want you to hear what this broad's got to say."

"Got nothing to say," the woman said defiantly. "Don't need to say nothing."

"You do if you wanna work for me," Pino Feldman said.

"I work for myself, always have. Always will."

"You nuts or something?" asked Pino. "You own clubs like me? You own a record company and theaters like me? You run the numbers in this city? You run the game clubs? You have any idea who you're talking to? You know what I could do for you? Make you a goddamn star or break your fat ass"—he snapped a match in half—"just like that."

"You don't gotta tell me," she told him. "I been knowing about you for a long time."

"Ever hear this bitch sing?" Feldman asked Ruben who'd moved next to the door in the back of the office.

"Nope."

"She calls herself Eve Silk. She's been singing around Buffalo and Marty Strazo over there, Marty says she's starting to draw a crowd and do I want her for a week? Okay. I'll do her a favor, I'll bring her in and, if she's such hot shit, I'll put her in my own club, I'll let her sing with Thunder. Thunder's the best draw since Fats Waller, but Thunder's getting tired, and maybe Thunder could use a little pussy to spice up his act. So she starts in on Wednesday and now it's Saturday and all I got is aggravation—do you understand me, Gent?—all I got is complaints that she ain't singing songs my customers wanna hear. She ain't singing to the kinda music Thunder's playing. And she's got an attitude, insulting one coon and now she's whacking another coon in the face and he goes after her with a razor and she cuts him with hers—this broad carries a blade with her wherever she goes—and suddenly I got a club full of screaming animals and it's this bitch's fault. That was last night."

"The man grabbed me," said Eve. "He hurt me. I'll bust any man who hurts me."

"You fuckin' aggravated him," screamed Pino, getting up from his desk, "just the way you aggravate me! I bring you in cause Strazo says you can sing—"

"You heard me sing. You know I can sing."

"Weird singing. It ain't like the blues, it ain't like you hear on the radio, it ain't like nothing . . ."

"It's me."

"Well, if you wanna sing," said Feldman, coming around his desk to stand toe-to-toe with Eve, who was a good head taller, "you better fuckin' change your ways and change your high-falutin' attitude cause those people out there are paying me hard-earned cash and I'm paying you and if some guy like me wants to get a handful of tit from you, just like this—"

Suddenly Pino grabbed her left breast, wedging her nipple between his thumb and forefinger, squeezing with all his might.

She tried to push him off but he just smiled. Then she came at him with a right fist, striking his chin and stunning him for a split second. The blow was not light. Ruben considered his options but didn't have time to react before Feldman, pulling a Browning High Power GP35 from his shoulder holster, clubbed Eve in the head with the stub of the steel revolver. She fell to the floor. Pino bent down and pistol-whipped her again, this time in her temple. Blood oozed from her ear. Feldman kicked her in the side. She groaned out a "fuck you." He kicked her again, she passed out.

"I don't wanna look at this cunt. Get her outta here!" Feldman screamed to Fingers.

Fingers dragged her out the rear exit, into the alley, dumping her by the overflowing trash cans.

"See the crap I gotta put up with?" Pino asked Ginzburg back in the office.

"I see," Ruby said.

Ten minutes later he quietly drove his Hudson, headlights off, down the dark alley where he carefully picked up Eve Silk, lifted her onto the backseat and rushed her to Herman Keeper General Hospital.

When she came to and focused her eyes, the first thing she noticed was the small dark mole sitting in the center of Ginzburg's chin. Savior with a mole.

MIAMI BEACH

DAVID FOUND THE APARTMENT depressing. The furniture had a Sears Roebuck feeling—gold corduroy couch, blue shag carpeting, a painting of a circus clown in a fake-wood frame. There was a big-screen television which, with the sound turned down, played a rerun of "Lifestyles of the Rich and Famous" featuring the homes of Zsa Zsa Gabor and Wayne Newton.

Nathan Silver sat on the couch while the black woman chopped celery for a batch of tuna fish in the kitchenette. David sat in an overstuffed E-Z-Boy recliner chair close to the old man whose eyes were hidden behind coal-black sunglasses. In a nearby apartment someone was listening to the soundtrack from *Mary Poppins*.

"Every day she puts on that crap," said Nathan. "She's half deaf. She doesn't even know what she's listening to, and she drives me crazy. I tell her but she won't listen. She won't listen to anyone because she can't hear. Go next store and tell her to turn it down, Gert," he instructed the woman. "Bang on her door until she hears you. We can wait for lunch until later. You aren't hungry, David, are you?"

"Not at all."

"Good. Come get us in a couple of hours, Gert. By then we'll be hungry. Do you like tuna fish, David?"

"Tuna fish is fine."

"Gert makes it with celery. Very finely chopped. Delicious."

The black woman retired to the back bedroom where she sat on the bed and knitted.

"Look," David finally said to Silver, "is this some kind of joke?"

"Would I send you a ticket and money and put you up at a fancy hotel if this was a joke?"

"I don't understand. My father said his parents died years before I was born."

"Your grandmother died. She was a wonderful woman, my Reba. You would have loved her, David. I could feel her features on your face. I know you look like her. She was one of a kind. Not like the women of today—pushy and self-centered. No, my Reba was a pearl. She understood what it meant to love a man—and to stick by him."

"I've never seen a picture of her, I've never even heard her name.

Why would my father have hid this from me? Why would he have lied? Why should I believe you?"

"How can I blame you for being angry, David? I'd be angry too. The story I have to tell you is not so pretty."

"What *is* the story?"

"Come over here, David. Sit next to me. I'd rather not strain my voice. I'm not used to talking for long. These days I hardly talk at all. What's there to talk about? Maybe I'll tell Gert that the orange juice is too pulpy or the baked apple too sweet. Come close to me."

David moved to the couch, sitting only a few inches away from the old man whose long thin body smelled of baby powder. The collar of his Hawaiian shirt was frayed.

"Do you have any idea what brought us together, David?"

"No."

"Music."

"What music?"

"The music they mentioned in that article that Gert found for me. Someone had left the magazine out by the pool, and she picked it up, just like that. It was all about your record collection. David, I want to ask you a question. Do you believe in fate?"

"I don't know."

"I believe. I believe we each have a path, but sometimes those paths meet. When, we never know. For us, it happened at that moment by the pool—when was it, a month ago? I could feel our paths meeting. You ask me why, and I'm telling you. Music. You collect the music of the colored. The newspaper said you have thousands of records. But not just records of today. The article said you collect the old ones too. Records from before you were born. *Why is that?* I wanted to know. You see, I always ask myself questions. *Why does this boy have such a feeling for the colored music? Where does he get this from?* The answer is as plain as your grandmother's features on your face. *It's in the blood. The music is in his blood,* I told myself. I also told Gert, but who else could I tell? As far as the world is concerned I'm no longer alive. I'm a dead man. I could show you my death certificate. It says heart failure. There, in black and white, you will read that I no longer exist. It'll be four years in January. That was the second time I died. The first time was when your father, my Miltie—"

"My father's name is Ralph."

"He changed it, just as I changed my name—to hide. That was many years ago. The sad part is that we're still hiding, him and me both."

"I don't *believe* any of this."

"Seeing is believing, and soon you will see. Meanwhile, there are only two people who know I'm alive—Gert and your cousin in California . . ."

"What cousin?"

"Ira. He's the only one I could trust with this information. But now I'm trusting you, David, because of the music. Am I making sense?"

"No."

"There's something I want you to listen to. Have you heard of Eve Silk, a singer they called the Duchess?"

"My girlfriend knows about her. There was a big biography—"

"A piece of shit. Written by some hack who didn't even know her. Never even met her. Lies. Stupid lies. Got my name wrong. Never even mentioned all the things I did for Eve. It has nothing to do with who she was. Do you have any of her records?"

"My collection doesn't really start till the fifties with early rhythm-and-blues and—"

"The thirties and the forties. That's when it *all* started. Those were golden years. Go over to the cabinet by the clock and open the bottom drawer. You'll find an album of 78's. Have you ever *seen* 78's before, David? They're made of shellac, so be careful. They break easily. During the war it was hard to get shellac. The demand was great. I've lost so many shellacs. Take out the first record and put it on the victrola. You know how it works. Make sure the needle and the speed are set for 78. Don't make it too loud. When it's soft, it's soothing. The Duchess liked to sing softly. They told her to belt it out, but she never listened. Silk, she had her own style. After you put it on, come back to the couch. We'll sit and listen together. The song is called 'Morning After.' You'll hear how she does it. She wrote it herself. No training, no schooling, no nothing, except she was a genius, and this was her song."

BUFFALO

1940

FROM THE BACK OF the half-filled nightclub—the Wander Inn—Ruben the Gent Ginzburg slouched back in his chair and watched her sing:

The fussin' and cussin'
Lasted way too long
. . . Gee, baby,
Why couldn't we get along?
You said, "Silk,
You built for speed"
And I said, "Poppa,
You got what I need
. . . Do it slow, and I'll
Do it faster,"
And before you know
It's the morning after . . .
    Morning after
        Sun peeping through
    Morning after
        Lord, what didn't we do . . .
    Morning after
        Black coffee smells so nice
    Morning after
        Night of paradise

She floated on a cloud; she sang through a mist, now tough, now tender. Teasing, her voice cut through a fog of feelings. Her sound was small—little-girllike—young, old, worldly, naive, salted with pleasure, peppered with pain. She swung without effort. Rhythm was her servant, a toy, a puppy on a leash. Her enunciation was only slightly southern. She drawled, crawled her way through the lyrics, sliding behind the beat, telling the story at her own personal pace. She slurred but never shouted, cried but never wept. She was an instrument, a throaty saxophone, a feline trumpet, a bittersweet flute. Her white store-bought dress might have been cheap, but the royal-blue silk scarf tied loosely around her neck gave her a regal air. The Duchess.

Ginzburg just sat there, mesmerized by her half-closed eyes, her girlish face, her womanly body. As a result of her hospitalization, she'd shed thirty pounds. Her thinner waist emphasized the size and thrust of her breasts. Once, while helping her out of bed at the hospital, Ruben had watched her dressing gown slip from her shoulders. The large circumference of her dark nipples took his breath away. She saw him looking and was slow—very slow—to cover herself. Her head was still bandaged, and he dared not touch her, but the erotic image haunted his imagination. Tonight, five months after her incident with Pino Feldman, he still hadn't touched her.

"Ginzy!" she said, joining him at his table after closing her set with a light-hearted up-tempo "Cash for Your Trash," "You made it to the gig."

"Didn't I say I would?"

"It's a long drive. I wasn't sure."

"You got no reason to doubt me, Silky."

"I don't trust no one, Jack," she said, leaning over and kissing him on the cheek. Her lips were warm. "But I'm glad you're here."

"I ain't ever heard you sing before. You know that?"

"And?"

"You sing like a fuckin' angel, pardon my French."

"I'm rusty. Been laid up too long. And I lost that crowd that was coming 'round here before I went to Detroit. I'm telling you, Ginzy, this place is dead."

"Don't matter. You sound swell."

"I got me another set to sing. You ain't running back to Detroit tonight, are you?"

"I thought I'd stick around."

"Good. Stay close," she said, stroking his thigh with her fingernails.

Her second set kept him hard. Her voice seduced his soul. "With Thee I Swing," she swung, her head tilted to one side, smiling, promising.

"Silky web," she sang, "when I start weaving, there'll be no leaving . . ."

He thought of the night he had taken her to the hospital—blood dripping from her ear, her moans, the concern on the doctor's face, the waiting, the pessimistic prognosis, then her sudden rally and finally, after three weeks, her full recovery. Ruby had paid for the whole thing—no questions asked, no strings attached.

"Never mention it to Pino Feldman," is all he told her.
"Think I'm stupid, Ginzy?"
"I'm the stupid one."
"You've made yourself a friend—for life."

The day she checked out of the hospital he gave her bus fare to Cleveland where she lived with a great-aunt. "You're on your own now," he said.

"What else is new?"

Ruby had thought about collecting on his favor, but it didn't seem right. He'd helped her out of instinct, not because he wanted something. He'd never done anything like this before. Altruism was new to the Gent. Eve Silk made him act differently. She acted differently. She had guts. When the doctor said she'd never pull through she must have heard, because the second she'd regained consciousness she called him in and said, "Sold me short, motherfucker, didn't you?" He had no answer.

Now the Gent was watching her sway, watching the swish of her thighs and the swing of her breasts. She spoke with her body in slight tight ways while Ruby imagined her on the bed back in the hotel. He could taste her mouth, feel her moisture. "Silky web," she kept singing, "wanna pull you into my silky web."

It was one A.M., her last song—"Time on My Hands"—had been sung and she was back at Ginzburg's table, smoking a Chesterfield and nursing a cognac.

"You hungry, Silky?" he asked.

"Marty's on his way with some food."

Marty Strazo owned the Wander Inn. He had prematurely gray hair, a smashed-in nose, crooked smile and deep dimples. His eyes were beady and hard and his cocky gait suggested a brawler. To the Gent, Strazo's green worsted suit and purple grenadine tie were a miserable mismatch. But as Marty approached the table, pulling on his diamond cufflinks, he seemed pleased with his appearance. He was followed by a white-coated waiter carrying a plate of piping-hot spaghetti.

"For the Duchess," said Marty.

"You know Ruby Ginzburg?" asked Eve.

"Ginzburg?" Marty asked out loud. "You're outta Detroit, ain't you?"

"Yeah."

"What are you doing around here?"

"Spur of the moment thing."

"Ginzy's my friend," Silk asserted.

Acting a little jumpy, Strazo said, "You know Pino, don't you?"

"Pino who?"

"I didn't know there was more than one. Pino Feldman, that's who."

"Oh, *that* Pino. I know him."

"Haven't talked to him in a while. Give 'em my regards when you go back. You driving back tonight?"

"Don't know what I'm going to do . . ."

"Well, if you're hungry . . ."

"Already ate."

Eve ate ravenously as the two men watched.

"Once they hear you're back," Strazo told her, "the crowds will be in again."

"I ain't worried," said Eve, washing down her meal with a tall glass of red wine.

"The only thing is, they wanna hear those blues songs about you grinding the meat and hot jellyrolls and sugar bowls and all that nasty shit. Your songs are cute and everything, but the people paying, they wanna see you shakin' your titties . . ."

"I ain't no stripper," said Silk. "I'm a singer."

"You get too uppity, baby, and you lose . . ."

"She's an artist," Ginzburg interrupted.

"Who asked you?" Strazo said.

"You ain't showing her no respect," said Ruby. "She's unique. You gotta respect that . . ."

"I don't gotta respect shit . . ."

"And I don't gotta sit here, Strazo, and listen to you talk to a lady like she's some sort of . . ."

"Look, Ginzy," said Silk, "you're getting into something that you shouldn't. You mean well and all, but I ain't no kid. Besides, Marty and me go back a long ways and I can deal with the guy . . ."

"Well," the Gent said, "if you're through eating, Silky, I'll give you a ride to wherever you're staying."

"I got that covered," Strazo said.

"Got my car right out front," Ginzburg countered.

"I said, *I got that covered.*"

"Whatever you wanna do, Duchess," Ruby said coolly.

"Call me tomorrow," she told Ginzburg, scribbling a number on the back of a matchbook before stroking his cheek with the palm of her hand. "Let's go, Marty."

He wanted to kill her, wanted to slap her right then and there. But that wasn't the Gent's way. Instead, he waited until they left, then hurried off to pick up their trail in his white-and-silver Hudson.

It was November and the city was iced. The streets were deserted. Light snowflakes flickered down from a moonless sky. Strazo was driving a Packard and Eve was sitting close to him. They turned off Main Street, onto Oxford Avenue, with Ginzburg a block-and-a-half behind. When Marty got to Delaware he took a right and drove until he reached the Victor Hugo, a fancy mock-French apartment building. He and Silk went through the back entrance. Not long afterward, Ruby looked up and saw lights go on in the penthouse apartment. Ten minutes later the lights went out.

The Gent drove back to his hotel, but couldn't sleep. He kept thinking of Silk, thinking of Strazo, imagining them together. He hadn't counted on this. He'd seen her as a different person. Not that she owed him—but, well, hell, she *did* owe him her goddamn life. Besides, Strazo was scum. He owned this one crummy nightclub, a brewery and a couple of pool halls in Niagara Falls. Strictly small-time. Didn't Duchess know? Couldn't she tell class from trash? Why was she doing this? Was she scared of the guy? She couldn't be attracted to him. He looked like a train wreck. Ruby couldn't stop thinking, couldn't stay still.

He left his hotel room, got back in his car and drove off. Didn't matter where. The snow was thicker. A storm was brewing; the city was being blanketed in white. Even Buffalo looks pretty in white. Driving past windshield wiper factories, past sprawling steel plants and small Polish bars, past dark Gothic churches, their strange soot-caked spires stabbing the frozen sky—Ruby drove on, boiling, thinking . . . Didn't Eve see Strazo for what he was?—a two-bit nothing, a tone-deaf punk who didn't even appreciate her style. A guy with no style. He wore green with purple and stripes with checks. He dressed like a clown. In contrast, Gent's fur-lined topcoat, a gun-metal tweed, was custom-cut by a tailor in New York City who made suits for Mayor La Guardia. Hadn't the Duchess noticed Ruby's otter collar? What was wrong with her? Now it was the middle of the night—three A.M., four A.M.—but who cared? Ruby kept driving, over the bridge into Canada, speeding along the Niagara River, deeper into the night, until he found himself next to the mighty Falls. He got out to look. Tons of cascading water, roaring like lions, reflected his own rage. Inside he was seething, still seeing things between Silk and Strazo he didn't want to see. His eyes were bloodshot as he watched the sky go from black to gray. Daylight looked dirty. The storm subsided. The snow stopped. Ginzburg drove back to Buffalo.

He stopped in a downtown coffee shop, sitting at the counter, dipping his donut in a cup of steaming java. His anger hadn't softened. The paper said it was election day. Wilkie didn't stand a chance against FDR. FDR was going to win a third term. No president had ever won a third term. FDR was king. Across the street a man was putting up letters on the big marquee for a movie-and-vaudeville show—*The Road to Singapore* with Bing Crosby, Bob Hope and Dorothy Lamour, plus Al Jolson live on stage with an all-star revue. Ginzburg couldn't think about any of that. He could only think of Silk.

He went to the hotel, changed clothes and then drove back to the Victor Hugo, where he pulled behind the building and waited. Just waited. The wait lasted two hours. By now Ruby's fix was absolute, his patience unshakable. He had a wish. At ten A.M. his wish came true. Marty Strazo, wearing a black overcoat, left by the back door, alone. He walked to his Packard parked in a nearby alleyway. Gent surveyed the scene. No one in sight. Quickly, he opened his trunk, picked up the blow torch and headed for Marty.

"Hey!" Ruby yelled.

When Strazo turned around, he was knocked over by the force of shooting flames. Ginzburg stood directly over him, torch in hand. He aimed the fire at Strazo's lower body. He watched as the flames burned through the fabric of Strazo's overcoat and trousers before scorching flesh. As Marty began to scream, Ruby tilted the torch upward, which stopped all sound. The Gent watched while Strazo's skin turned to rubber, changing colors. Ginzburg watched him writhe until the snow surrounding the dead man turned blood red.

* * *

"Get the job done in Buffalo?" Pino Feldman asked when Ruby returned to Detroit.

"Clean as a whistle," Ginzburg assured him.

"No problems?"

"A pleasure."

MIAMI BEACH

"WOULD YOU MIND PASSING the salt?" asked Nathan Silver. "I shouldn't use salt, but every once in a while, when Gert's not looking, I cheat. What's life without a little spice? Do you like the tuna, David?"

"I want to know about all your deaths. When you say that you've already died twice, what does that mean? Look, you're making me crazy. I want to know who you are. I want to know what the hell you're talking about . . ."

"I'm talking about a lifetime, David. My lifetime. That is not a short amount of time. In my lifetime I have seen and learned many things. It's good to be curious. I'm glad you want to know. I could tell you appreciated the Duchess when she sang. That's also good. This morning, around this little table, our lives are changing. For an old man like me, this is an exciting thing. For a young man like you, you're finally learning about your family. Eat, then I'll show you proof. I have everything in black and white."

After lunch, growing more impatient by the minute, David followed as the old man stutter-stepped his way into his bedroom where another television, set on a bureau, was tuned to a muted "General Hospital." On the walls were travel posters of Israel, Italy and Puerto Rico.

"You'll sit on the bed," said Nathan. "I'll give you something to look at."

The pink chenille bedspread, like the old man, smelled of baby powder. David looked at his watch. He'd been here over two hours and still had no idea who this lunatic really was. He would have left long ago were it not for the fact that there did seem to be some facial resemblance between Nathan and Ralph. Or was it just David's imagination?

Nathan's hands felt their way up the wall behind his bed. There, behind a five-and-dime seascape reproduction, was a small safe. He turned the combination, opened the door and fished out two newspaper clippings, handing them to David.

"I've talked enough," he said. "Read."

The first item was an article from the New York *Times* of August 16, 1952. The headline read: "Target of Kefauver Probe Found Dead." The story said, "Ruby 'The Gent' Ginzburg, famed music manager with reputed ties to organized crime, was the victim of an apparent mob-style execution. A week before he was due to face questioning by Senator Estes Kefauver, Mr. Ginzburg's life ended violently while he was attending morning services at the Shearith Israel sanctuary in the South Shore section of Chicago."

The second item was a simple obituary from the Miami *Herald*: "January 3, 1986. Bernard Crossman, retired businessman, died of heart failure at age 75. He is survived by his son, Ralph Crossman, an attorney in New York City and two grandsons, David and Ira."

"What am I supposed to make of these things?" David asked. "What am I supposed to think?"

"You have a temper. I once had a temper. That's not all bad, David. If you live in a jungle, I say it's better to be a tiger than a pussycat. I must tell you—these articles saved my life. The one from the Miami *Herald* was printed just the way I wrote it."

"You wrote your own obituary?"

"Is my grammar correct? I'm a good speller but I don't know from grammar. You've been to college. You went to Princeton and Columbia, just like Miltie. I never graduated from grade school but I've read my whole life. I like stories. This man, Michener, I've read every one of his books. Nothing dirty, no four-letter words. He tells a beautiful story. I've tried to educate myself as best I could. Nathan Silver wasn't educated. He had no living relatives. He was a simple man. We went to the same eye doctor. We had the same disease. Glaucoma. He lost his sight a year before me. After his unfortunate accident, when I changed places with him, no one was the wiser, not even your father."

"How do I know that you didn't make all this up? Maybe you heard of my father somewhere—read about him in some magazine—and just dreamed up all this—."

"Why should I do that?"

"Blackmail . . . I don't know."

"You aren't making sense, David. I haven't asked you for a nickel, and I never will. Money, I got. I've paid *you* money. And I'm going to pay you even more. You see, I have an opportunity for you. That's why I sent for you. Believe me, your grandfather will never be a burden to you. I've never been a burden to anyone. Not even your father. I've left him alone because I know how he feels. Shame is a terrible thing. He drowns in shame. That's how his mind works. But now that you're grown up, you have a mind of your own. You can see the truth for yourself."

"What *you* call the truth."

"In law school they teach you to doubt, yes? It's a wonderful thing to have the intelligence to be a lawyer. Lawyers want proof. You want proof. That's fine with me. I have the proof."

The old man went back to the safe and produced a third document, a birth certificate for Milton Ginzburg marked Detroit, Michigan, April 8, 1935.

"If what you say is true, you're my grandfather Bernie."

"No—you must always call me Nathan. Ruby Ginzburg and Bernard Crossman are dead. They couldn't afford to be alive. They couldn't take the aggravation."

"And what about this mob-related business?"

"That's a long story, David, and today I'm too tired to tell it. It's time for my nap. I get cranky if I don't take a good nap every day at this time. You want to be with your girlfriend, so go. Come back in the morning. We'll sit by the pool. We'll have time to talk tomorrow."

"But what about—"

"I've given you enough to think about for one day. A nap wouldn't hurt you either."

"And what's my father going to think about all this?"

"He won't believe you. I can't tell you what to do. You're a big boy, David, but if your father believes I'm alive, I'll soon be dead."

"Why . . . ?"

"In the morning. All your questions will be answered in the morning."

In early evening, David and Rita were sitting on the balcony of their hotel room as the sun fell slowly into the ocean. The sky was ablaze, streaks of hot pink burning through a backdrop of glowing orange. The darkening sea was still. The breeze had picked up, but it was still warm enough for Rita to wear a loose-fitting T-shirt displaying Picasso's *Three Musicians*. David was in a robe and still in a fog.

"It didn't look like you had much of a nap," said Rita.

"What do you mean?"

"You were tossing and turning like crazy."

"Dreams."

"About what?"

"Don't remember."

"Nightmares?"

"I said I don't remember."

"Sorry. You must have had a hell of a meeting."

"It was little strange."

"Anything you want to talk about?"

"No."

"Why don't you go back to sleep?"

"Because I don't want to go back to sleep. If you don't mind, I'd just like to sit here and look."

"Look all you like," said Rita, getting up and leaving him alone.

The pompano was especially succulent, the angel hair pasta *al dente*, the Chardonnay chilled and buttery.

"Sorry," said David, sitting across from Rita at a corner table where candlelight flickered over white azaleas. "I wasn't too civil when I got up from my nap."

"Second thoughts about the weekend?"

"And third and fourth."

"About me?"

"No, it's this client . . ."

"Tell me about him."

David sighed before sipping his wine. Rita thought he looked especially handsome in his oversized cream-colored silk suit and collarless black shirt opened at the throat. She liked the fact that he paid attention to fashion.

"What do you think of Eve Silk?" he asked her.

"Where does that question come from?"

"I don't know. What do you think of her?"

"She was amazing. She was a great artist and a sad victim."

"A victim of what?"

"Her times. Her men."

"What makes you say that?"

"I hear it in her music. Why are you asking about Eve Silk?"

"Are you influenced by her?"

"No jazz singer isn't. She bent everyone out of shape. She rewrote the rules."

"How?"

"You're finally getting into jazz."

"I've always liked jazz. It just never hit me between the eyes like R & B."

"Until I came along."

"You could say that. Tell me more about Eve Silk."

"The best way to learn is to listen. Listen to the records."

"Let's buy some."

"Tonight?"

"Now."

Rita liked to see David in this sort of mood. Impetuous, exciting. And it didn't hurt that he was a well-heeled lawyer. She was tired of the hyper-hip artists, the Tribeca bohemians, the passionate but starving painters who had dotted her past.

There'd been a jazz drummer, an older man, whom she had nearly married. He was also a poet, a follower of Langston Hughes and Malcolm X, but when he refused to give up his lifelong mistress, a married woman, Rita refused to marry him. David was different. The idea that he was hurrying to an all-night record store at midnight to find Eve Silk tapes was a nice whimsy.

Under glaring fluorescent, she helped him make his selection. "Is 'Morning After' included?" David asked.

"I thought you said you didn't know her stuff."

"I'm starting to learn."

On the cassette tape back in the hotel suite, the singer sounded shockingly personal, as if she were singing about them, their weekend, their deepening relationship.

David's mind was on Nathan Silver, Ruby Ginzburg, Bernard Crossman. He was tempted to call his father, but he relished the mystery too much to betray the secret. If that's what it actually was. Either way, Ralph wouldn't believe the story. Chances were, he'd use the information to further his own accusation—that his son's trip was ill-advised. Besides, Nathan's warning that Ralph would hurt him rang true. Anyway, it was too soon to do anything. David wanted more information.

Rita sensed David's distance. His mind was wandering, but maybe that had nothing to do with her. Eve Silk was singing and he was lost in her song. In some faraway sense he related Rita to Silk. Rita was the first black woman he had dated seriously.

Rita understood. She realized all this was new for David. She liked the Fontainebleau, liked the penthouse suite, liked the fact that he found music—her kind of music—an erotic bond between them. Singers seduced. It was that simple. When Rita was out of work and stopped singing for any length of time, her desire dwindled. She felt less alive. The more open she became—the more vulnerable, the more sexually available—the more powerful her song. To make love to an audience was, at once, something staged, safe, yet thrillingly real. Rita heard this in Silk. You reach out, you offer, and sometimes you connect outside the lyric, inside the soul of the listener. You sing yourself into someone's life.

Am I in your life for more than a weekend? Rita wanted to ask David but knew the moment was wrong as they slowly danced around the room, she in panties and bra, he in briefs. The thick pile carpet felt good under their bare feet. When Silk had finished singing, Rita continued the song, whispering the melody in David's ear. When he lifted her off her feet, she was surprised by the strength of his arms. She felt so light. She unhooked her bra, let him slip off her panties. When he stepped out of his briefs, when he eased himself inside her, she was stirred beyond the boundaries of music. She called his name. His thrusts were filled with the hardened blood of need—need to please, need to release, need to know.

David needed to know.

CHICAGO
1941

JUST AS THE SAXOPHONIST stepped off the makeshift bandstand, Gent slipped him a twenty.

"That song," said Ruby, eyes filled with admiration, "it's real catchy."

The light-skinned black, who at six feet six inches was a half-foot taller than Ginzburg, checked the bill over twice. "Man, are you looking to buy the song?" His voice, like his sax, dripped like honey.

"You own the song?" asked the Gent.

"I wrote it."

"Is it for sale?"

The musician looked at the bill again. "It ain't for sale—not at twenty bucks."

"That's just a token of my appreciation. I want you to record it."

"You got a record company?"

"I got friends. What's the song called?"

"Southside Velvet."

"Sounds like the name of some nag."

"It is. You should have seen him, man. He was a long shot. Beautiful animal, long stride, easy rhythm. He looked like jazz. Talk about poetry in motion, that was Southside Velvet. Right away I read his mind when he was parading toward the gate. Cool, but on top of his shit. You dig? Then he winked at me. I wouldn't lie. Just like that, he winked, and when I saw his name, and me being from Chicago, I laid it all on the line. He breezed in and I breezed off with five G's. Stayed in Florida for the rest of the winter and when I came back, I had me a fine tan and a sweet song. What else could I call it?"

Ginzburg looked up at the man whose high forehead, deep-set eyes and thick-framed glasses gave him an improbably scholarly look. On the top of his head sat an authentic English derby.

"You got words to the song?" asked the Gent.

"It don't need words."

"I ain't sure."

"I am," said the saxist.

"Yeah, well maybe it needs a singer. I'm looking for a singer. You ever hear of Eve Silk?"

"The Duchess." He enunciated her name like a Londoner.

"I heard she was playing around here."

"She was. Around the corner. You missed her by a day."

"You know where she's staying?"

"I don't think she knows."

"What does that mean?"

"We make it up as we go along."

"Look, pal, can you help me find her?"

"Can you help me record that song?"

"I told you I would. You'll come to Detroit. We'll do it there. Southside Velvet. That's our lucky number."

"When can we do it?"

"Next week if you want. Here's my number. Call me when you get to town. I'm Ruby Ginzburg."

"The Gent?"

"How'd you hear about me?"

"Perhaps 'twas the Duchess," he said with a smile and Ronald Colman accent.

"Bring her with you. Tell her to come to Detroit."

"If I see the lady, I shall certainly do so."

Leaving the club, Ginzburg took one last glance at the handwritten sign on the window. "'Lord' Lowell Foreman," it read. "Tonight only."

Tonight reminded Ruby of that night in Buffalo two months earlier. Tonight was cold and snowy and he hadn't seen or heard from Silk since he'd iced Strazo. He'd gone looking for her here and there but no luck. This was a busy season for the Gent. Pino Feldman had sent him on the road, on personal assignments, and no matter where Ruby traveled—Providence, Syracuse, Cincy—he always wound up at the jazz spots, listening to the music and making inquiries.

"You're clean," Pino told him. "That's why I like your work. You ain't messy and you ain't got no big mouth. You get the job done and I don't get no excuses."

"Trying my best, boss," Ruby would reply, always careful to work around Feldman's moods while hiding his resentment.

The Gent went back to his hotel in the Loop, still thinking about Lord's tune. Even before Foreman had explained it, Ruby sensed a great story behind the song. Lowell's sound was different, just like Silk sang different. Ginzburg liked that. He took notice when someone had a different voice. Silk was salty, Lord was smooth, and he wondered whether they had ever played together. The Gent could tell everything about a jazz musician just by listening to the sound. Most of them were honest, he deduced, because they played honestly, their hearts open. They blew and talked the way they felt. Unlike his colleagues, they harbored no hidden agendas, no secret schemes, no dangerous subtexts. The only time Ruby could relax and let his guard down was with jazz musicians.

"NEVER CLOSED" the blue neon sign buzzed in the window of Aronstein's Delicatessen. By the time Gent arrived it was midnight and he was famished. He'd been looking forward to this all day. Nat Aronstein had been in business since the early twenties. He was famous for his knishes—potato, meat and kasha. Seated at the counter, the Gent ordered one of each. He broke open the flakey crust and smeared a generous glob of mustard over the piping hot insides. The rye bread had an equally fresh, crisp crust. The pastrami was lean, the chopped liver exactly the right consistency, neither moist nor dry. The rich Russian coffee cake, along with a cup of good strong coffee, set off what Ginzburg considered the perfect meal. Reading over the early edition of tomorrow's paper, he turned past the headlines about Hitler to a story on Joe Louis. Who the hell was ever going to beat Joe Louis?

A quick coffee refill and Ginzburg was gone. He walked out into the freezing cold, behind the restaurant, took a few steps into the alley and saw the light in the office behind the kitchen. It was Saturday night and, as usual, Nat Aronstein was doing the weekly bookkeeping. This was his ironclad routine. Ruby knocked twice. When Aronstein, a large clumsy man, opened the door, Ginzburg said, "You make a wonderful knish, I really mean it," before grabbing the man and slitting his throat with a seven-inch switchblade. The incision was lightning-fast and lethal, reminding Ruby of when as a boy he'd slit the throats of chickens behind his uncle's butchershop. Nat never knew what hit him. There was no sound, no protest. He simply collapsed on the floor, eyes wide open, blood oozing from his mouth and nose. Gent checked to see that his cashmere overcoat wasn't stained. Fortunately, it wasn't.

The next day Ginzburg was back in Detroit.

"Problems?" Pino wanted to know.

"Nope," Ruby assured him.

"The Aronsteins get the message?"

"They couldn't miss it."

"Now they'll know. They got no more business putting their people in Detroit than I got putting people in Chicago. Greed, Ruby. It's greed that fucks up this world."

The Gent nodded.

"I just want you to know," said Pino, "that I appreciate the swell job you're doing. And if there's something special you need . . ."

"There is, boss."

"Name it."

"You know that little record company you got?"

"Pino Records, sure. It's a nice little business. No one thinks the niggers got money for records, but I know better."

"I want to make a record."

"You kidding?"

"I know it sounds nuts but—"

"What do you know about nigger music?"

"Nothing, except I got this hunch."

MIAMI BEACH

"WHAT HAVE YOU LEARNED about Nathan Silver?" asked Ralph Crossman in his steely authoritative voice.

The phone call rattled David. Saturday morning and Rita was still asleep. The curtains were drawn, their suite pitch black, and David, stirred from a chaotic and violent dream, for a moment didn't know where he was.

"Who?" he said to his father.

"Your client. Nathan Silver. Who is he?"

"What time is it?"

"Eight."

"It's a little early to be calling, isn't it?"

"I've been in the office since six. Tell me about Silver."

"Your timing isn't terrific, Ralph. I was sleeping."

"What was the will problem?"

"Will problem?"

"You said Silver had a will problem."

"Oh yeah . . . we're just getting into it."

"You're meeting with him again? You've scheduled another meeting?"

David's head started clearing when the call-waiting signal beeped in his ear. "Let me see who this is," he said.

"I hope I'm not calling too early," said Nathan Silver on the other line. "But I'm up and I thought maybe we could get started earlier today. Do you want to come over now?"

"I have to shower and dress first," said David, wondering what Ralph would say if he knew his father . . . if it *was* his father . . . was on the other line.

"Good," Nathan replied, "I'll see you when you get here. Don't eat. Gertrude's cooking breakfast."

"Who was that?" asked Ralph.

"What do you mean, 'who was that?'" said David. "It was another call. Are you monitoring my calls?"

"It appears as if you're conducting a great deal of business in Florida. The firm must be kept abreast—"

"I had a meeting on Friday. Today's Saturday. I hardly think my report is overdue."

"Either way, you'll need to be back here first thing Monday morning. You'll meet with Drew McKenzie to go over your Nathan Silver situation and then—"

"I may not be back Monday."

"Why not?"

"I may take off a day, I may—"

"It was not my understanding that you were on vacation."

"I'm not talking about a vacation, I'm talking about an extra day. This Silver matter may need more time."

"Look, David, I'm going to phone McKenzie at home right now and conference him in on our call . . ."

"What for?"

"McKenzie's our wills and trusts man. You can apprise him of Silver's situation and he can advise you—"

"I don't need any advice, I just need a little more sleep."

"You'll also remember that Tuesday evening is our reception for Calvino Bari, the Italian financier. We're representing him in that buyout bid of Northwestern Trust. Margo's arranged a private recital back at our place, a string quartet. Bari's crazy about chamber music. He's also the father of Carla Bari, who recently won Best Actress at Cannes. She'll be coming along. I understand she's a delightful—"

"Why don't you propose to her for me? Why don't you go ahead and arrange the marriage? Have Margo choose the caterer. Tell Margo to go to Tiffany's and pick out our China pattern." Margo was Ralph's current lady friend.

"I don't find that in the least bit funny."

"Look, I'll call you tomorrow and let you know when I'm coming back." With that, David hung up.

"Who was that?" asked Rita, moving her warm, naked body against David's.

"My boss."

"Checking up on you?"

"I'm checking out for a while."

"Back to the mystery client?"

"I'll be back by early afternoon. Maybe it'll be warm enough to go swimming. Wait for me."

"Do you really think you're worth it?" Rita asked, a small smile across her lips.

He looked at the stunning woman now sitting straight up in bed, the nipples of her delicate breasts taut, her dark eyes still sleepy, her arms raised above her head, stretching, yawning.

"Who knows what I'm worth?" he said honestly before getting dressed and heading out.

Driving down Collins Avenue, past the diners and delis, David clicked on the radio. Dance music—Bobby Brown, Babyface, Prince—nervous modern supercharged fired-up funky dance music was David's speed. These were the sounds he grew up with, the rhythms to which he related, the grooves that kept him moving. Now, as always, music was a way to wipe out thoughts of Ralph, and the firm, and his business as a lawyer—mergers, dissolutions, employee contracts, shareholder agreements.

David's thoughts started dancing . . . tonight he would take Rita dancing. He loved to dance, found it freeing. Dancing enabled him to jump from one personality to another. On the dance floor he was nearly a wild man, not stuffy Ralph's overprotected only child. On the dance floor he felt black—uninhibited, instinctive, open. Even as a little boy he danced crazy dances to the hits of the Temptations and Supremes, the phonograph blasting, his father scowling. Now the Minneapolis maestros, Jimmy Jam and Terry Lewis, were pumping the prime of the Rhythm Nation, the radio in the rented Town Car cranked to the max, the Miami morning breezy and mild.

Suddenly, in the middle of a song, he remembered the stark images from last night's dream—men fighting, blood spurting, dogs howling. He felt frightened, felt like a little boy, vulnerable and confused.

"Start cooking the eggs, Gertrude," said Nathan Silver. He and David were sitting around the yellow formica table in the kitchenette. "I know the boy is hungry. I have a feeling he didn't sleep well. Tell me, what are you wearing, David?"

"What do you mean what am I wearing?"

"Your clothes. I want to know about your clothes. Clothes are important. You can tell about a man by his clothes. I'll show you how. We'll start with your jacket. Are you wearing a suit? A sports jacket? What?"

"I don't feel comfortable."

"What do you mean? Your clothes are uncomfortable?"

"I don't feel comfortable describing my outfit. It's crazy. This whole thing is crazy. Here I am, telling some man I don't even know about my sports jacket—"

"What color is it?"

"Blue."

"Double-breasted? Single-breasted?"

"A double-breasted blazer."

"What fabric?"

"Cashmere."

Nathan smiled. "My favorite," he said. "Cashmere is my favorite. Topcoats, sports jackets, scarves, sweaters—I was well-known for wearing nothing but cashmere. Do you own a lot of cashmere, David?"

"Sure, I like cashmere."

"And what about your trousers?"

"Levis."

"What's that?" asked Nathan.

"Jeans. Blue jeans."

"I don't understand. You're wearing a beautiful cashmere blazer with dungarees. What's that supposed to mean?"

"It doesn't mean anything. I like jeans."

"You're confused. Part of you is dressed up for business, and another part isn't. Didn't I say you can tell about a man by his clothes?"

"Then what am I supposed to make of your outfit? You've got on this powder-blue polyester leisure suit with twelve-inch collars that went out of style fifteen years ago."

"I wouldn't argue with you. To tell the truth, I look like a schmuck. But that's how Nathan Silver dresses. See, I got no choice in the matter. And believe me, it hurts me worse than you. All my life I took pride in what I wore. Now look at me. What about your shoes? Are you wearing lace-ups or loafers?"

"Loafers."

"Come. Let me feel."

David, feeling eerie, walked over to the old man, who bent to touch the shoes. "Beautiful. Very nice leather. And the tassels. I like the tassels. Italian?"

"Swiss. Bally."

"I know Bally. What does a pair of shoes like this cost these days?"

"Three hundred fifty. Stop this."

"Your father's law business must be very good."

"Look, Nathan, I didn't come here to have you critique my damn wardrobe. I'm here for answers."

"Here are the eggs. Eat your eggs."

After the meal—omelette, bagels and coffee—David was still on edge. "How and why did Ruben Ginzburg become Bernard Crossman?" he asked. "And why did Crossman become Nathan Silver?"

"The right questions. In law school they taught you to ask the right questions. Gertrude is pulling the car out of the garage. She'll drive us. I have a place where I've taken no one else except your cousin Ira. This is a place with many answers. Give me your arm. You'll help me downstairs."

Nathan held on to David's arm. The grasp, neither desperate nor helpless, was firm. "I need your eyes," the old man said. "I need you." David had never heard his father make such a statement.

Downstairs David led Nathan outside the main entrance of the Atlantic Arms. Gertrude was sitting behind the wheel of a great-finned 1957 black Cadillac. "This is Nathan's car," said Silver, getting in front while David slipped in the back. "If it was up to me, I'd get something new. But Nathan, he lived modestly."

"Where are we going?"

"Into my past," said Silver. "Isn't that what you want to know about?"

A half-hour later, in an industrial section of Miami dotted with concrete-block single-level office buildings, they pulled up to a nondescript warehouse that said, "Silver Printing Company."

"Silver is a printer," said Nathan. "Promotional flyers, travel posters, that sort of thing. Small potatoes. I thought about selling the business when Bernie died, but it was a buyer's market so I figured, why bother? I shut down the operation, but kept the equipment. I like the machinery. Maybe someday I'll find use for it. Who knows? Meanwhile, I come here to do different little things. You'll see."

The sprawling warehouse was dark and bleak, a series of printing presses, some antiquated, others computerized. The air was musty as David followed Nathan, who held Gertrude's hand. A back door, protected by a heavy steel bolt, opened into another world.

Inside was a cavernous music library the likes of which David had never seen before. Held in utilitarian steel bookcases were hundreds of rows—whole walls—of 78's, 45's and LP's. Compared to this, David's own collection paled.

"Go look if you like," said Nathan.

Each row was neatly labeled by year. The recordings began in the twenties and stretched to the early fifties, ending roughly where David's collection began. Bessie Smith and Kid Ory, Andy Kirk, Chick Webb, Erskine Hawkins, Goodman and Shaw; the sweet bands—"Swing and Sway with Sammy Kaye"—Paul Whiteman, the Dorseys, Andrew Sisters, Mills Brothers, Ziggy Elman and Harry James, Jimmy Rushing and Jimmy Durante, Louis Jordan and Louis Prima, mountains of Ellington, miles of Basie, an endless string of popular music, sentimental and artistic. The faces and designs of the album covers transported David back to another time and place. The romanticism of the past seduced him like an exotic drug. Excitedly, his eyes running over the record labels, he knew that somewhere in the grooves of this music was a story—his grandfather's story, his father's story?—he had to know.

"Why do you keep it all hidden back here?" he asked.

"Of course, like Mr. Hearst, I'd like my own castle. I'd like my own museum. But Nathan Silver is a simple man who leads a simple life. Anything else would raise suspicions which is something, David—listen to me now—something we never want to do."

Nathan walked around the massive room without Gertrude's help. He knew every step, every shelf. While he ran his hand over the albums, searching for one in particular, Gertrude sat in a corner knitting a wool sweater.

"This," he said, "this is the one."

"Which one?"

"The best one."

"Who's it by?"

"Before you listen, I want to tell you a story. Sit. There's a comfortable chair next to the phonograph. I'll stand. It'll do me good. All I do all day is sit."

Nathan leaned on his long cane as he told the story, his thin frame bobbing back and forth in the manner of the old men in the synagogue.

"I was living in Detroit. This was back in the forties when Detroit was still a liveable city. Today, nothing is liveable. Today is drugs and kicks and crack and God knows what else. Back then you lived by honor, and respect. Now these musicians, these two people, they respected me because never once in my life did I betray that trust. I respected them. I knew they were geniuses, not just talented people, mind you, but geniuses. They were artists. Do you understand this, David, because this is the most important part? If I promised to pay them a dollar, I paid them a dollar. If I told them I'd pay them a thousand dollars, that's what I paid. My word was my bond, never to be broken.

"Now there was a song called 'Southside Velvet' which was written by a man named Lowell Foreman, the greatest saxophonist of his or any day. He was the one they called 'Lord.' I heard him play this song one night in Chicago and I thought, *This is a gorgeous melody. People will love this melody.* So I told him, I said, 'Lord, I want to make a record of you playing this song if you'll think about only one thing. Words. It needs words.' 'No words,' he said. 'It isn't that kind of song.' 'Come to Detroit and we'll see,' I said. I didn't argue. What good is arguing, David? When he came, I was ready for him. That was my first day in a recording studio and I didn't come alone. I came with Eve Silk and four fiddlers. 'What's the Duchess doing here?' Lowell wanted to know. 'She came to sing your song,' I said. 'Who are these guys?' he asked. 'The Detroit String Quartet. You'll tell them what to play.' 'What are you talking about?' 'You'll hear what they should play and you'll tell them.' 'I don't read music.' 'Who cares? You'll hum what you hear. Then they'll play what you hum. Why should you read music? You're better than that.'

"Anyway, to make a long story short, David, it worked like a charm. Things happened none of us dreamed possible. For the first time, Lord sang. I told him to. I said if he could play like that—like a person talking—then he could sing the same way. He was a natural, an original. He was sandpaper and Eve was silk. They had a musical conversation—you can put it like that. What did I do? I helped them with a word here and a word there. If I was Irving Mills I would have put my name on the song. That's what Irving Mills did with Duke Ellington. But I didn't. You see, I didn't want to be Benny Goodman taking advantage of Fletcher Henderson. Or Joe Glaser with Louis Armstrong. Not that Benny didn't help Fletcher, and of course Joe was good for Pops, but I didn't want to be bossy. See, I had a boss. His name was Pino Feldman. He was a dangerous man. Moody like you wouldn't believe. Deep-down rotten. A bad man, an evil man. Others feared him, but I understood him. I'd watch, I'd listen—nothing is more important than being a good listener, David—and I'd study him. If you know a man, there's no reason to fear him. You fear the unknown, but I knew every side of Pino Feldman. I knew what to expect and what to avoid. I kept my distance.

"With Lord and Duchess, there was never fear. With them I could be sincere. I didn't have to hide my feelings. I didn't have to be on guard. I let them know that I loved their music so much I wanted violins behind them. They appreciated that. The fiddlers made them sing more beautifully. It gave the record class. The fiddlers were my idea. Getting Lord to sing was my idea. The duet with Silky was my idea. 'Southside Velvet' was my first record. It sold a half-million copies. To me it's a masterpiece. Now put it on. Listen."

Duchess sings:

You hung up on your looks
You think you got it made
But when it comes to lovin'
You ain't made the grade

But look here, Southside Velvet,
If what I hear is true
You ain't taking care of business
Like you oughta do

Lord sings:

You're signifyin', woman,
And staking out your claim
But if you don't understand me
Let me make it plain

Southside Velvet's sure to win
I'm your lucky charm
Southside Velvet's coming in
Straight into your arms

"You had to be there, David, because the whole time they were smiling. Now maybe they were drinking that night. I don't remember. Maybe they did something stronger. I didn't look, I didn't ask. Whatever they did, it worked. The fiddlers made them a pretty bed of strings to lay on, and then they made love with the music, and they only had to sing it twice to get it right, once for practice and another time for real. You hear the harmony? Well, they made up that harmony as they went along. No one had to tell them. I didn't say nothing. Just paid the bills. That was my part. And I made sure the song got out to the public. That's the hardest part. I'll tell you the most important thing in the record business. You worry about this, you worry about that, but your main worry is getting your song played. Believe me, it wasn't easy."

"Was Pino Feldman in the record business?"

"Why do you ask that?"

"You said he was your boss."

"He had a company that made records, but in the end I didn't want no part of it. I didn't like the way he treated his artists. And I didn't agree with his sales approach. He thought it was colored music for colored people. I thought it was colored music for everyone. But I never argued. I told you I don't argue."

"And Pino didn't object to your going off on your own?"

"Pino didn't know what I was doing, even though he thought he did."

"But you knew it was a conflict of interest."

"That's how they talk in the colleges, on Wall Street and in Washington, D.C. Remember, David, I wasn't on that level. I was down on the streets, in the colored neighborhoods of Detroit and Chicago."

"Did Pino ever find out?"

"You're getting ahead of the story."

"The record was made after my father was born. Why hasn't he ever mentioned this music to me?"

"Even when Miltie was a baby he didn't like the music. It made him cry. When he got older he said the colored sang like savages. It hurt me to hear that. That's why Miltie said it. He liked hurting me."

David shook his head, his mind reeling. Who to believe? What to think of this library, these stories, this Nathan Silver?

"Tell me about my . . . father as a little boy," he said, still somewhat skeptical. "Tell me what he was like."

DALLAS, TEXAS
1953

BERNARD CROSSMAN, HIS WIFE Lillian and their two teenage sons, Ralph and Steven, pulled their Nash Rambler into the twenty-dollar-a-night Sweetwater Motor Court on Harry Hines Boulevard in the anonymous-looking industrial district of Dallas.

A year ago they would have stayed at the poshest hotel in the city. They were used to the good life. Their swanky South Shore Chicago home was swimming with security. But they were different people then. They were Ruben the Gent Ginzburg, his wife Reba, and their sons, Milton and Irving. Names had been changed. In a three-week session in Arizona, the family had been indoctrinated into the Witness Protection Program, which, with Ginzburg's cooperation, had staged the Gent's public "execution." Ruben, not content to simply disappear—he was convinced Pino would search him out and kill him—wanted Feldman to believe he was already dead. Ginzburg's cooperation with the government put Pino behind bars.

Reba, an accomodating wife, went along with anything her husband wanted. Irving, the younger son, worshipped and obeyed his father. Only Miltie was the problem. He challenged Ruby. He asked questions. Even during the orientation program, he was unwilling to follow the party line. Miltie always wanted to know why.

"Because that's the way it is," Ruby would say. "I'm the father."

"What did you do wrong?"
"Why would I do wrong?"
"Then why are we hiding?"
"Business."
"Dirty business."
"Shut your mouth."
"Crime business."
"I said shut your mouth!"
"You made a deal with the FBI."

With that, Ruby whacked Miltie across the face, knocking him to the floor. The boy's lip cut, his nose filled with blood and he ran from the room.

"You don't got the guts to hit me back!" Ruby called after him.

Miltie ran all the way to the library. The library was his refuge. The library let him forget who he was. He found comfort in books, liked looking through magazines with photos of sprawling English country estates, gentlemen riding to hounds, the idle rich dressed in Harris tweeds. He dreamed of polo matches in East Hampton, Long Island, read F. Scott Fitzgerald. Alexander the Great and Madame Bovary were among his favorites. The music in Ruby's house drove him mad. Miltie preferred Mozart. He read the great musician's biography, fascinated to see that Wolfgang Amadeus also had a maniacally dominating father.

But instead of a lord's mansion in London, Miltie had to live in one-horse Dallas, in a nine-thousand-dollar house west of Marsh Lane and north of Love Field airport, where, night and day, planes roared overhead. Miltie resented their nouveau-riche Chicago home with its Chinese modern decor, but this was worse. He resented his father for being, well, low-class, resented his mother for loving his father, resented his brother for being bigger and better than he was in what seemed to matter most to Ruby—brawn. He did not resent his new name; he much preferred Ralph to Miltie. He also liked Crossman, whose advertisements for fine pens appeared regularly in the New Yorker.

Despite his new name, Ralph never adjusted to the move. The household was charged with the fear of a family in deep disguise. He was ashamed of the fact that his father managed a corner liquor store in South Dallas, the black part of town.

The flat city itself had no culture, he felt. The heat was brutal, the air-cooler in the Crossman home inadequate. Ralph felt disconnected from the rest of the world, worried that here in the wilds of Texas cockroaches, rattlesnakes and black widows would actually crawl into his bed.

Alone, Ralph would ride the bus on Saturday mornings. He'd read the paper about Joe McCarthy and Roy Cohn, convinced life was more exciting anywhere but desolate downtown Dallas. There he'd study in the library before walking a few blocks across Commerce to Neiman-Marcus, a fashionable oasis on the Texas prairie, where wildcatters bought their mistresses the priciest furs west of Bergdorf Goodman.

Ralph had no friends. A stranger in his own home, he spent Saturday nights reading. One Sunday, Bernie drove his sons down to the liquor store. Steve was happy to help his father take inventory. Ralph was miserable. Afterward Bernie took the two boys to an afternoon jazz session at the corner of Oakland and Carpenter in the American Woodmen Center. They were the only white people there.

Bernie loved the music.

This was Bernie's only entertainment. By necessity his life was low-key, low-profile. He needed the anonymity of South Dallas. He liked the scene at the Woodmen Center, the all-black after-church crowd dressed in yellows, pinks and Kool-Aid green, cats carrying whiskey and wine in paper bags, ladies slowly drifting in until five or five-thirty when the place was packed, the air thick with smoke, people drinking Scotch and soda, vodka and milk, long tables joined together, friends, neighbors, husbands, wives and lovers visiting one another, laughing and growing louder, and the music, the hard bop flowing from the stand, the sounds of David "Fathead" Newman and Leroy "Hog" Cooper—just off the road with Ray Charles—Willie T. Albert, Eugene "Worm" Halton, Charles Scott, Claude Johnson, Sol Samuels, A.D. Washington, Red King, Roger Boykin and the great James "Heavy" Clay.

Ralph felt frightened and out of place. At any moment he expected someone to pull a knife or gun. He didn't trust these people. Their crazy way of dressing, their slurred speech, their emotional extravagance—everything about blacks made Ralph uneasy.

The following morning he was even unhappier at the prospect of having to walk to high school with his kid brother. Bernie had refused to buy them a car.

"I can't afford it," he had said.

"I don't believe that," said Ralph. "You're hiding money in Switzerland."

"How do you know that?"

"I see the mail when it arrives. I see the postmarks."

"You don't know what you see."

"I know you can afford to buy us a car."

"Maybe Ruby could afford it. But not Bernie. Bernie's barely making a living. He can't afford cars for his kids."

So Steve and Ralph walked the two miles to an all-white high school filled with jocks and rednecks and tight-sweatered girls pining for the star quarterback. In an atmosphere where physical prowess ruled, Steven fit in. He ran track. Ralph read Henry James.

Ralph could relate to neither the students nor teachers. The football coach was his geometry instructor, the basketball coach taught English. Ralph excelled in all subjects, especially French, where he discussed Flaubert and Proust. But that only made his classmates resent him more. Physical Education was a nightmare. He was taunted for being gawky and slow; he felt inadequate and humiliated. Until . . .

It was three P.M. and school was over. Waiting for Steven, Ralph ignored the guys with black leather jackets and ducktails who burned off in their customized cars, tail pipes roaring. Steven was late. Impatiently glancing at his watch, Ralph was irritated. He didn't notice the baby-blue lowered and louvered Impala convertible pulling up to the curb.

"There's that Yankee with his head up his ass!" yelled one of the guys from the car.

"He wants your dick up his ass," someone else said from the back seat.

As the taunting continued, a crowd formed. And just as a nervous Ralph started to back away, Steven arrived on the scene.

"Fuck you," he told the carload of tough guys who immediately piled out and faced the brothers Crossman. It was five against two. Ralph ran. Steven stayed and got mauled.

That night, when Bernie heard the story, he told Steven that he was proud of him. Then he beat Ralph with his belt buckle until welts formed on the older boy's backside.

The next few months were quiet. But later in the term, just before the Christmas holidays, there was a terrible accident: the Impala, carrying the five boys, was found in a deserted ditch in Farmer's Branch. The police speculated that a truck had run them off the road. The car had flipped and the students were crushed, bodies mangled. All five DOA. No witnesses. The truck driver was never found. And never again were Ralph and Steven bothered by anyone at school.

NEW YORK CITY

RALPH CROSSMAN WAS UPSET. The caterers were late. His son David hadn't yet returned from Miami.

"Margo," he called to his lady friend. "The maid's used the wrong crystal. The Waterford is inappropriate. Why aren't we using the Baccarat? And where's the Wedgwood? Where's the string quartet? I thought you had this party organized . . ."

Unruffled, Margo Cunningham entered the dining room, smiling. A tall striking forty-year-old blond with slate-gray eyes and slender figure, she moved about the brownstone as though it were her own. She slept there, in fact, only on weekends and special occasions. Her own penthouse on Sutton Place had recently been featured in House and Gardens. Like Ralph, she cultivated a high profile. Also like Ralph, she had a hidden past that she revealed to no one, not even him.

Crossman thought Margo was a Bostonian who'd gone to Radcliffe. In truth she was from Iowa and had never gone to college. Her real name was Muriel Smith and her parents, Henrietta and Wilbur, were farmers. At age eighteen, she'd gone to Boston and worked in the bargain basement at Filene's. Soon after she came to New York, where she snuck into fashion shows and auctions, read Town and Country as though it were the Bible and finally landed a job at Bergdorf Goodman in the millinery department.

She could sell. She could sell hats to women, and herself to men. She did so subtly. She was feminine and demure and, in bed, creatively uninhibited, the opposite of the appearance she gave in public. Several men paid her good money on a regular basis. One man, a married interior decorator twenty years her senior, took her into his business, set her up in an apartment and insisted she give up all other customers. As his mistress and assistant she learned his trade in under a year. Her mind was quick and she had a feeling for fine furniture and unusual fabric like she was born to them. When her mentor died two years later she was in a position to start a business of her own. She was a worker, a climber, a strong-minded entrepreneur every bit as determined as Ralph. Her goal was to redefine herself, to be born again into a life of cultivation and wealth. She became her own mother and father. It wasn't surprising, then, that when Ralph met her at a dinner party a few seasons earlier

gave off an energy, a tension Ralph
confirmed bachelor didn't bother her.
ed his privacy—especially the privacy
y about her own background she knew

rphans.
that Ralph displayed unerring taste and
gs like tonight, fancy dinner parties, made
hey feared exposure, they helped each other
into each other's image.
said Margo. "The table looks fine. The pat-
n the Birds of Paradise . . ."
of Paradise?"
are the musicians. Everything will be perfect . . ."
ph, at times mothered him. She admired his in-
g. She knew his reputation, but she also saw that,
ng the field, he was getting tired of such romances.
He ... ow, when David was still a baby, he'd lost his wife
to cancer. Marg... nsed his fear of being hurt again and expertly tiptoed
around his quirks, providing companionship he found difficult to resist.

Ralph liked it that Margo was a decorator whose clients included prominent figures in New York society. He saw her taste as even more refined than his. Working with an architect, she'd renovated his brownstone in warm woods and English greens and muted rose hues, giving it a richer, more self-assured feeling. Only David's rooms on the top floor, where he slept and housed his records, were off-limits.

By seven, the recital had begun. In a corner in the mahogany-walled library the trio—violin, viola and cello—played Mozart's Divertimento in E-Flat Major, K. 563. The sound of the strings—civilized, ordered, perfectly attuned—brought pleasure to Ralph. Looking around the room he noted the group he had brought together. The two dozen guests included a former Secretary of State, the curator of the Museum of Metropolitan Art, a leading antiquarian, an internationally acclaimed fashion designer, the District Attorney of Manhattan and to make Calvino Bari and his daughter Carla feel at home, the Italian Ambassador to the United Nations.

In his mid-fifties, Bari was of medium height, with broad shoulders and the hint of a paunch hidden under an impeccably-tailored double-breasted black flannel suit. His bald pate added to the intensity of his presence; his small dark eyes seemed to focus about the room in rhythm with Mozart. Was he surveying the women or just excited by the music? There was something nearly sensuous about his small pink mouth. On his left hand a thin gold watch, encrusted with diamonds, matched his cufflinks. Standing beside him, swaying slightly to the "Allegro," his twenty-nine-year-old daughter Carla wore an outfit that defied observers not to stare.

Beneath her multi-colored shawl was a sheer black blouse through which her breasts were visible. She wore no bra—she required none—and due to a slight chill in the room, her nipples had stiffened. Carla's energy paralleled her father's. Her midnight-black eyes were bright, intense. She appeared restless, somewhat distracted, as though she were looking for someone or something she could not quite find. Her coal-colored hair, cropped fashionably short, and green lizard boots peeping from beneath her long black skirt added to the drama . . . there could be no doubt that she was an actress.

The post-recital spread was sturgeon, caviar, Perrier-Jouet Fleur de Champagne. The trio switched from Mozart to Schubert as the guests exchanged views on the European Common Market, the photography of Robert Mapplethorpe, the latest profile of Mrs. Onassis in Vanity Fair.

Ralph was especially attentive to Calvino Bari and his daughter. Meanwhile, Margo could not help but notice that Carla, whose Swiss education was responsible for her excellent English, seemed engrossed by Ralph's opinions on everything from nineteenth-century painting (favorable) to American rock 'n roll (unfavorable).

"I'm afraid my musical preferences are somewhat old-fashioned," said Ralph, struggling to keep his eyes off her breasts. "You'll have to ask my son about the rock 'n roll."

"Here's your opportunity, Carla," noted Margo as David, accompanied by Rita Moses, entered the room.

Stunned by the presence of the black woman, Ralph fought the shock while he and his son made the proper introductions. It did not help matters that beneath his cashmere blazer David wore faded jeans.

"Your boots!" said Carla, pointing to David's feet. "We buy our boots at the same place. The Big Kick in Soho. A fabulous shop. Giancarlo, the owner, is from Rome."

"Giancarlo's a friend of mine," said David, his eyes moving from Carla's breasts to her boots. "Were you at his birthday party?"

"I was in Paris. The Stones started their tour that same night."

"I think David has little use for the Rolling Stones," said Rita, who in a high white turtleneck was easily the most beautiful woman in the room.

"Why?" asked Carla.

"I agree," said Calvino Bari. "That group, they only scream. Tell me, *por favore*—where is their melody? Where is the beauty of their lyrics?"

"A man after my own heart," said Ralph. "I must say, Calvino, we think alike."

"It's not about thinking," said Carla. "It's about, as we say in Milano, *scopando*."

"What does that mean?" asked Rita.

"Screwing."

The conversation stopped cold. "Carla," Bari said, "is an expert at the art of surprise. She was raised without the benefit of a mother, and therefore lacks the proper manners."

"Our family situation is similar," Ralph said.

"Well," said Margo, taking a deep sigh, "perhaps David and Miss Moses would like something to eat."

"If you don't like the Stones," Carla asked David, before he had a chance to move toward the food, "who *do* you like?"

"Me," Rita replied. "He seems to like the way I sing."

"You sing rock 'n roll?"

"Jazz."

"I adore jazz, but does anyone listen to it anymore? I thought that when God died, this jazz died too."

"Here in America, it's alive and kicking," Rita said.

"What about hip hop, rap, house music?" David asked Carla.

"I adore it. Bobby Brown, he's marvelous. Very adorable. Very sexy. Do you know him?"

"Tell us about your new movie," said Margo, who knew little about pop music, much about film, and the right moment to step in.

"*La Bella Confusione*," said Carla. "Very controversial."

"Surely your public is used to your nude scenes by now," Margo said, straight-faced.

"I haven't seen any of them," David admitted.

"Except for tonight," Rita added, somewhere above a *sotto voce*.

"With your name, Miss Moses, I think you must go to church every day," said Carla.

"Without fail . . . Right now I'm going to get something to eat," Rita announced, leaving David with the actress.

Margo accompanied Rita to the food table as Ralph returned to speak to Carla and his son.

"The Cannes prize must have been very satisfying to you, Carla," said Ralph.

"I am Catholic and Catholics must confess," she said. "I confess that one of the judges, he is a former lover. He knows how good I am."

"How was the weather in Miami, David?" asked Margo, delivering a glass of champagne to Ralph.

"Miami?" said Carla. "I go there next month. They cast me as a drug dealer. My agent says the director is a genius. He's from Egypt, an Egyptian Jew. The script is marvelous. But do I look like a drug dealer?"

"I'd say," said Rita in between bites of caviar.

"You are so honest," the actress replied. "Honesty can bring great trouble. Have you been to Miami?"

"Just got back with David here."

"I see," said Carla. "A honeymoon?"

"Another Mozart piece," Ralph interrupted. "The trio is about to play again. Shall we return to the library?"

"You still haven't said what you thought of the place," David said to Rita in the back of the yellow cab. The reception was over, and the driver was streaking down Fifth Avenue, the windswept city flying by. No one seemed to care. The quicker this evening was over, the better. It was freezing.

"Your home is gorgeous," she said, obviously angry, sitting far from David. "*Exquisite* taste. *Exquisite* manners. Well-heeled crowd. Your father's a duke. His lady friend is a duchess. What more do you want me to say?"

"You were the one who insisted on seeing the place."

"Great. Now I've seen it. Now you've seen me. Now you'll see me home and that's it. We'll see each other around."

"Look, I know that Italian actress got you crazy . . ."

"Who's even thinking about her? Who cares about her? You're the one who's got me crazy, David, not her. We go to Florida for a fun weekend and you wind up going through some personal crisis that turns you into a basket case. You call that fun? You're on an emotional roller coaster and I'm supposed to act the part of understanding lover while I don't have the foggiest notion of what's going on between you and this client, who if I didn't know any better, I'd suspect was your lover, judging by the impact this man has had on you. Then, to top it off, you take me to meet your father on the very night and at the very moment that's sure to shock him most—when he's surrounded by his high-society pals. You used me. Don't you see that? You used me all weekend and you used me tonight."

"You wouldn't even come up to see my record collection," he said weakly, trying feeble humor.

"Don't give me the little-boy-blue act, David."

"This is sort of a tough time for me—"

"You kept saying that in Miami but I still don't know *why*. I still don't know what the hell's going on. How am I supposed to react? How am I supposed to help?"

"You helped, Rita. You helped a great deal."

"How?"

"By being there."

"And where were you?"

"I know I was far away. It's something I have to work out."

"Oh God . . . So what's the 'something'?"

"Look, I want to help you too."

"What are you talking about?"

"Your career. Your recording."

"We've had this talk before. You said you'd never represent a singer."

"Well, things are changing, I may have a new world of contacts."

"Based on the Miami trip?"

"Based on my opinion of your talent. You're a wonderful singer and you deserve to be recorded right."

"Is this your way of making up?"

"No, this is . . ." said David, taking Rita in his arms and kissing her on her mouth, their tongues slowly caressing.

"Couldn't you see that she was making a play for you?" said Margo from the bathroom, washing off her make-up while Ralph, in blue-striped Brooks Brothers pajamas, sat up in bed reading legal papers for an early-morning meeting.

"Who?" he asked, peering over his half-lensed reading glasses.

"Carla Bari."

Ralph smiled. "Thank you, Margo, but you mistake me for my son."

"You're the one who's mistaken. I could see it in her eyes. She likes mature men."

"She likes to be looked at—that's all."

"And you didn't look?"

"I'd be abnormal if I didn't."

"I think she's a slut."

"She's an artist."

"What's to prevent an artist from being a slut?"

"Their art, I guess."

"You're talking foolishly, Ralph," said Margo, slipping into bed.

"Her father is anything but foolish. David Rockefeller called him the sharpest financial mind in the Western world. Tomorrow we close the deal on his buy-out of Northwestern Trust. I'm pleased to say he enjoyed the reception—you did a marvelous job, Margo—and he seems delighted with our work."

"David's girlfriend seems pretty sharp herself."

"Who said she's his girlfriend?"

"They spent the weekend together."

"David loves to shock. He lives to get my goat. But I refuse to give him the satisfaction."

"Did he say he was coming home tonight?"

"One never knows."

In the morning Ralph was sipping fresh-squeezed orange juice and going over Calvino Bari's buy-out papers when David came into the breakfast nook. In the kitchen the Filipino cook was cracking eggs.

"Good morning, David."

"Morning, Ralph."

"Enjoy the reception?"

"It was fine."

"Glad you could make it."

"Rita wanted to meet you."

"Seems like a lovely girl."

"She's a woman."

"I noticed. Now what about this Nathan Silver?"

"What about him?"

"Where are the papers? The documents? What is his problem?"

"He doesn't have any. Just an old man who needs some sound business advice."

"You said it concerned a will."

"His will's in order. I looked it over."

"What's the nature of his business?"

"Music," said David, testing to see if his reply would make his father crazy.

Ralph swallowed hard. His heart seemed to skip beats. But he kept himself under control. "Tell me more about it," he said slowly.

"There's nothing more to tell. He has holdings in the music business."

"I want a detailed report—do you hear me? *detailed*—on the exact nature of those holdings. The music business is full of corruption."

"So is banking. So is law."

"That is not the point," insisted Ralph, his voice growing louder. "You don't know what you're doing."

"I'll know more when I get back from California."

"California?"

"Some time next week I may have to go to California."

"What for?"

"To see someone."

"Who?"

"An associate of Silver's."

"What's his name?"

"I forgot."

"*His name*. I must know the associate's name."

"Why are you so hysterical?"

"I'm not in the least hysterical. Merely thorough."

"I have the guy's name written down somewhere."

"Find it."

"What is this—the Spanish Inquisition?"

"I want to know what's going on. What's this Nathan Silver involved in?"

"I already told you. Music."

"That's not enough."

"Silver's already advanced me another ten thousand dollars in fees."

"Why should a reputable businessman advance those sorts of fees?"

"I insisted—just to satisfy your doubts."

"My doubts are far from satisfied."

"I'll know more when I get back from L.A."

"That trip is out of the question."

"Sorry, Ralph, but—"

"*I said it is out of the question.*" He slammed his fist on the table, knocking his pulpy orange juice on the freshly polished parquet floor.

DETROIT

1942

EVE SILK LET THE white slip fall to the floor. She stood there for a few seconds, allowing the Gent a long look.

Outside, the purple neon sign buzzed on and off, "Paradise Valley Hotel . . . Paradise Valley Hotel . . ." Down on the street a paperboy hawked the early edition: "Japs Sink Brit Ships!" A faraway jukebox was playing Artie Shaw's "Softly, As in a Morning Sunrise." The summer air was hot, sticky.

"That ain't what I came for," said Ruby Ginzburg.

"You don't like what you see?" asked Silk.

"You're a doll, Duchess. Anyone who'd say otherwise would be lying."

"I owe you and I don't mind paying."

"If it's like that, I don't wanna collect."

"I made some bad moves," said Silk, moving toward Ginzburg, talking as if she were singing—easily, slowly, a little behind the beat—"and then I saw you had a few moves of your own. At first I didn't know what to make of the Gent. Didn't know what kind of cat he was. Read him wrong. But then I saw the kind of job you got, and the way you do it, and I figured it ain't easy for you, baby. No, sir. And now you got me a record, and you got Lord singing, and I'm thinking to myself, this motherfucker ain't jive. He done fall in love with the music. He *hears* it, and he's smart about it, he's smart to get out the way and say, 'Hey, y'all go on and do it. Y'all tell *me* what you wanna do.' That's some of the hippest shit I ever heard. I see you're different, Gent, and I like what I see."

As he sat in a chair next to the bed, she bent down to kiss him. The touch of her lips on his mouth sent chills through him. He didn't argue, didn't say a word as she bent down further, sought him, reached for him, touched him, brought him out and licked him, sucking him softly, then hard, alternating from tender to tough, blowing a thin stream of air, biting, squeezing, cupping his balls, stroking his thighs, her fist, her mouth, her tongue slowly tracing up, slowly tracing down until the Gent, normally so composed, moaned and shivered and exploded and even then was amazed to see that she wasn't through, working him harder, coaxing him back up, back to the bed where she showed him things he'd never seen before.

That night he dreamt of Pino Feldman. The Gent was strapped into an electric chair. He was dressed in a tux. There was an audience of spectators, loud marching music, lightning and thunder. Cannons boomed. People cheered. The Gent looked straight ahead where, through a gleaming steel double door, Pino Feldman emerged as a cop or a king, the Gent couldn't tell which. He watched as Pino put his hand on the switch . . . and then, winking at the Gent . . . pulled it . . .

Ruby woke up with a muffled scream.

"Nightmare, baby?" asked the Duchess.

"Got a meeting this morning. Gotta get outta here."

"You got some explainin' to do?"

"To you?"

"No, in your meeting."

Ruby never failed to appreciate Silk's perceptions. She knew what was happening without being told. Her past, crowded with men—pimps, johns, bosses, abusers—gave her a sixth sense about survival. She was sexually in charge, just as she was musically in charge; she was able to lead men in her direction. Ginzburg felt led. Nothing like this had ever happened to him. It didn't matter that he was a married man with two little boys. Silk knew and Silk didn't care. She and Ginzburg lived in different worlds. They were business associates; and they were also friends. It was important that Duchess let the Gent know just how much she appreciated his loyalty. She thanked whomever she wanted to thank. She did as she pleased. She was a free woman.

Walking up the front stairs of Pino Feldman's Detroit home, Ruby Ginzburg was aware of his own lack of freedom. The Italian-styled mansion on Outer Drive in Palmer Park, just inside the city limits of Detroit, looked like a fortress—gray granite arches, stone lions, massive columns, marble foyer. The downstairs living room, with its gold-framed mirrors and gaudy chandeliers, was the size of a small bowling alley. In the center sat a long semicircular green velvet couch with gold piping and tassles. To the side was a white grand piano. Fingers Markowitz, standing by the doorway and eating a peach, looked like he'd gained weight. He had to weigh three hundred pounds. When he bit down, juice squirted on his wide yellow tie. He scowled and tried to remove the stain with a handkerchief. He ripped off the tie and stuffed it in his pocket just as Pino Feldman walked into the room.

Ginzburg noticed that his boss was wearing elevated shoes. Swaggering across the room, never once looking at Ruby, Pino sat down at the piano. "You know how to play this thing?" he asked Ginzburg.

"No idea," answered Ruby who, sitting on the couch, faced Pino's back.

Feldman hit a single note, then ran his hand up and down the keyboards, making only noise. "Why do you think niggers are so good at this shit, Gent?"

"You got me, boss."

"Come on now," said Pino, wheeling around and facing his underling. Feldman's face showed a crooked smile. A newly inserted gold tooth reflected the overhead light. His dark eyes were distracted—looking at Ruby, looking through Ruby. "You know niggers. You know what makes those monkeys tick."

"I don't know too much about nothin'," answered Ginzburg.

"To me, they're either fuckin' savages or they act like kids. I can't figure 'em out."

"Me neither."

"You play dumb, Rube, but that's why you're so smart. That's why you worry me—'cause maybe you're too smart. See, you asked me about making this record, this 'Southside Velvet.' So I say, 'why not?' You do me a favor, I do you a favor. But my favor to you don't turn out to be no favor. My favor turns out to be serious business,'cause this record you made ain't no silly little record. Your record is something every nigger in Detroit, Chicago and Cleveland is running out to buy. Now they tell me Diamond DeSanto wants it in L.A., which means maybe another twenty G's, and all I'm hearing about is this 'Southside Velvet,' and suddenly I got guys calling me from New York, big-time record guys, wanting to be my partner, wanting to know where they can find Lord Foreman and Duchess Silk and when's their next record coming out and can they distribute it and can they sell it down south and maybe even over in Europe? You see what I got here, Gent? I got a hit. Not a local Detroit hit like I had before where I could make good change, but something bigger than that. Something that lets me see that my Pino Records ain't just peanuts no more. Now they're telling me I'm a genius. But me, I know I ain't no genius,'cause I never made a record like 'Southside Velvet.' For my records I got some coon to play the blues with a guitar and maybe a drummer and that's it. But you, you got fancy, Gent. You got this song and you got the guy and the bitch singing to each other, and it's cute, it's real cute, except for one little problem. Can you tell me what the problem is?"

"The bitch."

"There you go. I said you was smart. You're right, Gent. The bitch is the problem 'cause the bitch didn't show me no respect, and I thought maybe she was dead or something, but then I see you used her on this here song and I figured she must have found you, or maybe you looked for her. I don't know your personal life or nothing, Rube—I don't know if you're fucking her, I don't know nothing. All I know is that the way you usually take care of things is very good—you're always clean, always sharp—look at that gorgeous blue suit you're wearing today—you ain't ever messy—but this here is a little messy because once I let someone go, that someone is gone for good. Am I making myself clear?"

"To tell you the truth, boss—"

"Before you say anything else, just think about what you just said. The 'truth.' That's the word you used, Gent, so I expect the truth. Without the truth here, you and me, we got a very big problem."

"I bumped into her in Buffalo . . ."

"When you went there to straighten out Marty Strazo?"

"Yeah, that trip. And I heard her and I thought, 'Gee, this broad ain't half bad.' Then I heard this horn player in Chicago and I knew he was a talent, and I mentioned it to you, I asked you—"

"You didn't say nothing about no Eve Silk . . ."

" 'Cause I wasn't even thinking about recording her or nothing except when the horn player, this Lord guy, he says she's around and maybe she'll sing 'cause if there's singing you usually make more money on a record than if you only got music and no singing. I didn't think too much about it. Naturally I remembered you got pissed at her, but I figured if this record don't make no money you'll be even more pissed at me, because I see you're a businessman—that comes first—and, like you always say, boss, making money is the main thing, and now we're making money with this song. And when people say to me, 'Where'd you find this Duchess?' I say, 'I didn't find her, Pino did,' even though the two of you didn't get along all that good. Maybe that had to do with Marty Strazo,'cause he told you about Silk and he turns out to be nothing but a fuckin' pain in your ass. I see everything you do has a reason, and I try to study those reasons as best as I can."

"You went against me."

"I don't see it that way," said Ruby, watching Fingers Markowitz out of the corner of his eye.

"When people go against me, I worry."

"You got nothing to worry about."

"In my position, if you don't worry you don't live. See, I got guys going against me all the time. If I don't worry about them, if I don't know where they are and if I don't watch their moves, I ain't worth shit. All day long, I gotta decide only one thing—is this guy for me or against me? Fingers over there, he's for me. I don't got no doubts. I got proof. With you, I thought I had proof. But maybe the proof wasn't all that good. Maybe I was wrong."

"We're just talking about this one song, this one singer . . ."

"It ain't the song, it's the principle."

"It's a business principle. I'm trying to do business."

"And I'm trying to figure out whether to believe you, Rube."

"What more can I say?" asked Ginzburg, watching Fingers move from one side of the living room to the other.

"It ain't what you can say, it's what you can do. I keep thinking that you're smart, maybe too smart. So maybe the smart thing is to see just how smart you are. I know you got this soft spot for the colored, and I know you like the nigger music, and I'm thinking maybe there's a future for these type songs, and I don't like the idea of someone else making money off this except me. This is how I'm thinking. I'm thinking Detroit ain't as big as Chicago, and I see a situation in Chicago, a record company run by a couple of brothers, the Raminskis. You heard of the Raminskis. They got a bigger operation, a better operation than anything around here, and I'm thinking—what if I set you up there? What if I introduce you to the Raminskis? Maybe they should be the ones, not Diamond DeSanto, to sell 'Southside Velvet' in California. Maybe they could teach you something. They been wanting some things in Detroit, they been begging to go in with me for years, so maybe we give and maybe we get. What about it, Rube? What if I said to you, 'Go to Chicago, Gent, and be nice to the Raminski boys'?"

"I'd be nice."

Pino smiled. "Sure you'd be nice. I want you to be nice. But I also want you to know that I'll be watching every step you take."

HOLLYWOOD

IRA CROSSMAN PRESSED A button on the remote control, ejecting the cassette from his digital audio tape deck.

"What do you think?" he asked his cousin David.

David didn't know what to think. The music sounded like hard cold rock 'n roll to him—not warm rhythm and blues. The guitars were screeching, the drums overbearing, the vocals hysterical.

"I'm not sure," David answered, thinking of what Nathan Silver might say in such a situation.

"Know how many calls I've gotten on this group?" asked Ira in his New York nasal. "Maybe a dozen, maybe two dozen. And do you know who called? Ahmet Ertegun, Joe Smith, Mo Ostin, Clive Davis, David Geffen, Dick Asher, Al Teller, Jheryl Busby, Louil Silas, Irving Azoff, Jerry Moss, Ed Eckstine. I don't know if these names mean anything to you, but these are the forces in our industry. These are the kingpins. These guys can make or break you in a minute. They run the show. They got the power. And they're calling me. Why? Because they're up in their glass and steel towers but I'm down in the streets where I got my ear to the ground and my nose wide open. I got a smeller for this stuff, and they know it."

David wondered whether Ira's smeller was filled with cocaine. He wondered what he was doing here, sitting in this stranger's penthouse office on Sunset. The room looked like the interior of a Titan missile. The spacey chairs were modular, the desk a slab of fire-engine red metal supported by two black projectiles. One whole wall held an assortment of audio and video tape machines. Three Sony TV screens were suspended over the desk. Four seven-foot speakers, built into angular corrugated containers, looked like high-tech sculpture. Dozens of gleaming platinum and gold records—presented to Ira—swept across another wall. And beyond the wide circular window, the famous HOLLYWOOD sign, huge white letters on the side of a parched mountain, seemed close enough to touch, as though it were the exclusive property of Crossman Communications, Independent Record Promoters.

As the wiry promoter, dressed in tight white silk shirt and leather bomber jacket, paced and fidgeted about his office, David couldn't deny the fact that he was finally facing his cousin. Ira wasn't as handsome as David—his nose was broader, his teeth uneven, his gums too prominent, his jaw a little too jutting—but the resemblance was strong. At six feet he had the Crossman stature, the pale blue eyes, the brown hair, and the overactive mind. In the center of his chin was a small mole, an exact replica of his grandfather's. Ira also had an impatience, a kind of ferocity, an unchecked need to be talking and doing that left David, not normally reticent, stunned and silent, and still reacting to the way the flight to the coast had begun, with ugly run-ins with Rita and Ralph.

"Walk out of this office," David's father had said, "and you'll walk out of a job."

"I'm sorry," David said. "I am. But I need to know more about the music business. It's a learning trip for me."

"Make this trip, and you'll learn you're out of a job."

"Is the trip really necessary?" asked Rita after she and David had made love in his fourth-floor bedroom in the East Side brownstone. "It feels like you're running away."

"I told you, it's business."

"Then why does it feel so personal? This Nathan Silver business."

"Who mentioned Silver?"

"Isn't this California trip a result of what happened in Miami? You said it has to do with music."

"I'm just exploring new avenues . . ."

"And what about my music? Is this Silver a contact for a record deal? Can I give you a tape to play for your man in California, whoever he is?"

Rita was aggressive about her career, sometimes worrying David that he was being used. But what had he really done for her? Taken her to dinner. Showed her a little of Miami Beach. He's promised her nothing and, aside from a few strong suggestions, she'd made no demands.

David very much wanted to tell Rita the truth. He wanted to tell someone. The secret information burned inside him. He tried to explain but it wouldn't come out. What was the truth anyway? And even if he were sure of the truth, did he know Rita well enough to trust her? True, she was different from any woman he had known—more insightful, understanding, certainly more beautiful—but the attraction, the desire to be with her, the need to confide in her, was also worrisome. For two weeks now his head had been filled with the most confusing and contradictory information of his life. His world had been turned upside down.

"Don't you think it's strange," asked Rita, "that you still live at home?" She was wearing one of his robes and sitting on the edge of his bed.

"It's free, and I have the privacy I need—my own entrance up the back staircase, my own record library up here and my own kitchen. Are you uncomfortable?"

"I guess I feel a little funny with daddy downstairs."

"He can't hear a thing. He doesn't even know we're here."

"I don't understand your relationship with him."

"We share a house—that's all."

"And an office."

"I guess I'm a creature of habit."

"You could afford a place of your own."

"Look, this *is* my place. If you don't like it—"

"I love it. I love . . ." She was about to say "you" but stopped herself, not sure what his reply would be. He came over and kissed her. She got up from the chair and hugged him, holding him for a long time. These past weeks had taught her that he was a man of enormous passion. Now, though, caught up in her arms, he felt like a little boy.

The next night he had gone to hear her at a yuppie bar on Columbus Avenue. The bleached wood walls and severe Danish furniture left him cold. Her voice, though, was caring and warm. She had a large inventory of standards—"Stairway to Paradise," "Anything Goes," "Spring Can Really Hang You Up the Most," "Guess I'll Hang My Tears Out to Dry." Singing, she seemed to be making love to her handsome Japanese piano player—and David was jealous. The bottom of her voice was deep thick satin, the top clear, light, her small sensuous vibrato, her eyes closed, her palms pressed together . . . she told a story, she wove a spell. She swung smartly. Intimacy was her forte. In her face, David saw a romantic concentration. He was lost in her music. Later that evening, in her tiny Greenwich Village apartment on Great Jones Street, with its lace curtains and lavender sachets, he was lost in her love . . .

But this was not the time to be lost, he thought the next day on his way to the airport. Non-stop to L.A., he reviewed everything Nathan Silver had showed him, everything Nathan Silver had said.

"You'll go to California," the old man had predicted. "You'll have to go. I can tell, you're too curious to stop yourself now. You've got a good head on your shoulders, David. That's why you can't call me crazy anymore. I'm making sense. Besides, there's a man out there called Ira Crossman, and just as I'm your grandfather, Ira is your cousin, the son of your Uncle Irving, may he rest in peace. Ira has a beautiful business out there. I'm happy that I helped him because now he has a very important job. I want to help him more, David, but I can only help him with your help. You'll go, he'll explain. The timing couldn't be better. Believe me, all this was meant to be. I don't want to talk for Ira because Ira is an adult, he's not a child anymore. He's five years older than you, he's your cousin, he's your brother. You'll be like two peas in a pod, the two of you. I know your father never told you about Ira. Your father never told you many things, but now you're learning, David. Your eyes are open and the future belongs to you and Ira, my wonderful grandsons. In my own small way, I can pitch in, but first go to California. No matter what your father says, go."

Nathan was right, David had to go. Besides, even before Miami, David's doubts about his work had been increasing. His duties at Crossman, Croft and Snowden were mundane, his cases bores. For a long while now he had thought about going off on his own—as a lawyer representing entertainers, perhaps as an agent. Music was his first love, and the music business, even if Ralph was right to call it shady, was glamorous. Besides, after Nathan's revelations, Ralph's haughty attitude was becoming more intolerable. He'd always been ambivalent about his father—identifying with his power, repelled by his pretentiousness—but now the repulsion was growing. David was infuriated that Ralph had been lying to him. Part of him wanted to blow the lid off Ralph's ridiculous posing; but another part of him was wary. No matter, it was music that kept David moving. Ever since he flew around the room to Sly and the Family Stone's "Dance to the Music" as a six-year-old boy, music had stirred him. Now an old Jewish man in Miami Beach was telling him that the music business was in his blood. David finally believed him. So how could he not go to meet his cousin? . . .

Yet here in his penthouse office, Ira was addressing David not as a cousin but a client. He was trying to impress, to sell him. At the start of the conversation, when David tried to talk music, mentioning his idols—Marvin Gaye, Jermaine and Michael Jackson, George Clinton, Gladys Knight, Al Green, Frankie Beverly, Luther Vandross—Ira hardly seemed to have heard him. They had no touchstones in common. In fact Ira appeared uninterested in black music. Could this be the grandson of Ruby Ginzburg, Bernie Crossman and Nathan Silver? Ira's passion was strictly for business. And he did everything he could to make David feel like a neophyte.

"You have any idea what independent promoters do?" he asked.

"No."

"Nathan didn't tell you?"

"Nathan said very little."

"He said enough to get you out here."

"It's all a big surprise," David said. "I told you that. It's another world I didn't know existed."

"Let me set you straight. If Grandpa Bernie sent you . . ."

"I thought Bernie's dead."

"You're right. He's Nathan. If Nathan sent you, that's good enough for me because Nathan doesn't do anything that's not good for me. He's my father and mother and grandfather and godfather and every other goddamn thing you can think of rolled into one. Nathan raised me. You and your people, I always figured you thought you were too good for me . . ."

"I didn't *know* about you."

"That's what Bernie—I mean, Nathan—that's what Nathan always said, and maybe he's right, but it doesn't matter anymore 'cause I've made it. I've made it on my own. Look at this," said Ira, handing David a recent issue of Billboard, the trade journal of the record business. "An article on Crossman Communications. Three whole pages. Tributes from everyone in the industry. They wanted to be quoted—all the labels, everyone that counts. No one wanted to be left out. Read what it says, 'At 32, Ira Crossman is the *wunderkind* of the industry, perhaps the youngest independent promoter in history to achieve national success.' '*In history*,' it says. I didn't write those words. Billboard did."

"You were going to tell me what an independent promoter does."

This was the moment Ira had been waiting for. He walked across the room to his desk, where he sank into his high-back black-leather chair, buzzed his secretary—"just stack up the calls, Sherry, I'm unavailable"—leaned back and let go.

"I have a staff of twenty-five people but the focal point is right here," he said, pointing to his brain. "Here's how it works. Every week the majors put out dozens of new releases. They're hungry for a hit, because hit records are what this industry is about. The big-tour money, the videos, the movie deals, the soundtracks, the T-shirt sales—nothing happens without a hit. You can't have a hit without getting your song played. That's where the indie promoter comes in. We work the record for the labels. We talk to the PD's—"

"Who are they?"

"You don't know nothing, do you? Okay, I'll do the Ding Dong School bit. PD's are the program directors at the radio stations. We make sure the PD's put the records on the air."

"How? Bribes?"

"What bribes? Contacts. I've developed the contacts. I sold advertising spots for radio stations back in New York and Chicago. I was even a jock for a while. Never went to college. Didn't need college. I was a program director when I was twenty-one, youngest ever. That was up in Fresno. Top forty radio wasn't as important then as it is now. Now the adds are everything—getting a record added to the play lists, the P-1 stations, the fat markets. If a label wants to break a single, they need us—it's that simple."

"How much do they pay?"

"Breaking a new single could cost them two hundred thousand dollars."

"Even if it's a known artist—a Whitney Houston or a Jody Watley?"

"Don't matter, Dave, if it's fuckin' Aerosmith," said Ira, calling his cousin by a name no one used. David didn't like the way "Dave" sounded. "The market's crowded, Dave, everyone's looking for that competitive edge. That's the edge I've been sharpening for years. The knife cuts both ways—I'm servicing the labels and I'm serving the stations."

"You're the buffer. The labels have to like you. It means they can't get caught—"

"What's to get caught? Some program director in Atlanta needs Super Bowl tickets? Big deal. I got 'em. That's not against the law. Maybe another PD is looking to vacation on Maui. My condo's available. It's a favor, that's all. Shit like this has been happening since Adam fucked Eve."

"How much does one of the major labels pay you in any given year?" asked David.

"Four, maybe five million," Ira answered through a sly smile.

"That's very big."

"Very fuckin' big, Dave. Now you know what I'm saying?"

"I don't understand how I can help."

"I'd have to teach you the business. I told that to Nathan. I told him that you don't know shit. You'd have to learn."

"But why do you need me?"

"Nathan thinks I do, but I'm not sure. He's got this idea about you. Maybe he's right, maybe he's not. But one thing's for sure—the business is changing. Things are getting cozier. The labels are calling me. They see how I can break a single, but they also see I got the best ears in the business. Like surgeons need good hands, record guys need good ears. You heard that thing I played you before—'Rock My Rocks'—that's a hit song. Maybe the lyrics gotta be cleaned up to get pop play, but the sound, the vibe, the goods are there. So I'm getting called up into different meetings. The labels are looking for me to help them out in new areas, not just promotion, but packaging and selling cut-outs—discounted product—things like that. The labels are getting bigger—they're owned by these international corporations—and they got money up their ass. These lame-brain bureaucrats don't know what they're doing, but they know I do. My phone's ringing off the hook—A&R guys, the artist and repertoire executives, looking for talent, PR guys looking for ideas. All of a sudden, though, I'm dealing with conglomerates, and from a legal point of view that can be tricky. My last lawyer fucked me good. The son-of-a-bitch was billing out his time at five hundred dollars an hour, and he *still* fucked me. When I mentioned that to Nathan, he mentioned you. He said my lawyer is the most important man in my life. He said you can't trust no one but family. I said there is no family but me and my Grandpa Bernie. He said I was wrong. He said you were family. I said I'd see. I'd talk to you. Understand?"

"I'm beginning to."

"And what do you think about all this, Dave?"

"I need to hear more about it."

"You'll be around?"

"For a couple of days."

"I'm busy as a cockroach. Deals popping left and right. I'll try to find more time for you, Dave, but it won't be easy. Maybe tomorrow for lunch. I'll squeeze you in. Meet me at the Palm at noon."

"Meet at the bar at seven," the message said. It was signed simply, "Carla Bari," and slipped under David's door at the Bel Age Hotel. Still reeling from his meeting with Ira, David held the note in his hand and laughed to himself. This was all he needed.

He took a beer from the minibar, cracked it open and threw it back. The cold liquid cooled his throat, tempered his brain. He downed the rest in a hurry and started a second. What about this Ira Crossman? What was he to think of his cousin? He was crude, no doubt. Even sleazy. And no, he didn't show any great love for the music. He was nothing but business, a used car salesman who'd sold his way to the top. But he was at the top—at least that much seemed clear. His contacts were tops. In a cutthroat field he had accumulated dazzling power. He went to parties with Bowie and Springsteen, U2 and Cher. In David's wildest imagination, though, he could not see himself working for this man. At the same time, Ira's situation was a thousand times more interesting than anything David had seen at Crossman, Croft and Snowden.

Perhaps the answer, thought David sipping beer, was to free himself of Ralph while at the same time setting himself up independently. It might not be any more complicated than opening an office and hanging out a shingle—in New York, maybe L.A. Why not float free for a while? Take off a little time to explore new possibilities. Perhaps even devote a few months to studying for the California bar. Without any commitment, without rushing himself, that would also enable him to see what

Nathan and Ira were really all about. Rita was right . . . it was ridiculous to be living at home at age twenty-seven. He was, to be honest, far too tied to Ralph. He badly needed change and, crude or not, the Nathans and the Iras of the world held tremendous fascination for him.

As did, face it, Carla.

She sat at the bar, her hair spiked in some newfangled funky arrangement, her legs crossed, her micro mini-skirt barely covering her crotch. Her eyes were focused on a man sitting next to her. He held a microphone and was conducting an interview.

"Other actresses, they act," said Carla with sincerity. "But when I make love in my love scenes, it's real. I come. I swear I do."

"How many takes does it take?"

"The more the better," she said, laughing.

Spotting David, Carla cut short the interview. "This is my lawyer," she told the reporter. "I've come all the way to California to see him. He's wonderful, you know. Very brilliant. This is the famous David Crossman. You should interview him."

"What other celebrities do you represent, Mr. Crossman?" asked the reporter.

"*Povero lui*, he's so timid," answered Carla. "He wants to embarrass no one."

"How'd you know I was here?" David asked after the reporter had left.

"Lawyers are easy to find. They have secretaries and schedules. They are not spontaneous."

"Well . . . it's good to see you."

"Are you spontaneous?"

"Try me." As he was trying himself.

"Are you willing to watch my orgasms?"

"Right here?" Very witty, David.

"At the premiere. It's a small art cinema in Brentwood. It'll be fun. Be my escort. Come."

At first the long limousine had David remembering the fights he had had with Ralph many years ago. The private grade school David had attended was over on the West Side, and his father had insisted he be taken and fetched by a chauffeur. This infuriated the boy, whose only friends were the black boys who attended the school on scholarship. He admired their energy, their daring, their sense of style. He hated being seen as a pampered rich kid and would beg the driver to let him out a block before the school. When Ralph found out, he fired the chauffeur, who was also black and chummy with David. For all his son's pleading and crying, Ralph would not give the man his job back.

"You are out in space," said Carla, putting her hand on David's thigh. "Are you back in New York?"

"I'm here." David blinked his eyes, looking at her.

"Good, because I want you to be with me. I'm converting you from a goody-goody lawyer to a bad boy, all in one night. This premiere is for us both."

The premiere was not in Brentwood but Westwood. The art theater wasn't small but quite large. The L.A. winter night was crystal-clear. The ultra-hip crowd—painters, poets, musicians and critics—were out in force. Paparazzi pursued the couple, Carla waving, mugging the cameras, David enjoying the crazy scene.

The movie was something else. The very woman sitting next to him, her hand in his lap, was also up there on the big screen, being loved simultaneously by a male and female. It was almost incidental that she was a spirited and accomplished actress. The texture of the film—its conflicts and themes—had overtones of Godard, shadows of Bergman. But the sex scenes left nothing to the imagination, and while actual penetration was not shown, the raw sensuousness of Carla Bari's body was explored in a fashion that had David rock hard from start to finish. Carla felt the effect of her performance.

Afterward, it started in the limo.

"Does this embarrass you?" she asked after smoking some hash and before going down on him as they sped east on the busy Santa Monica Freeway.

He moaned in appreciation. The muscle control of her mouth was as professional as her acting.

"You like to dance? Do I remember right?" she asked. "You like the new black music?"

"This is your night," he told her. "Lead the way."

He thought about Ira; he thought about Nathan; he thought how his life was changing. For a second he felt guilty—about cheating on his father, about double-timing his girlfriend. But who was he kidding? He was married to neither Ralph nor Rita. Besides, L.A. was a different world with a different vibe. Tonight he was doing L.A.

The limo pulled up to Catch One, a gay disco on Pico Boulevard just off Crenshaw, a world away from Beverly Hills.

"They say," said Rita, "that this is the hot spot. Madonna comes here to dance. I heard it from a friend in Paris. He was here. There's this new band."

The band rapped forward and backward: back to sixties soul, Motown and Memphis, Muscle Shoals and Stax/Volt; forward to the slam of heavy hip hop, with a skip, snap and killer groove that would not quit until every two-legged creature in the place was up and dancing like the city was burning down. For the first time all night, David was as unrestrained as Carla. The release came. The music pushed him over the edge. The band seemed to say it for him—don't think, just do. He did. He slid. He flipped and flew like a bird and a bullet. Carla cried, "*Forza*!" David outdanced her, shedding his coat, loosing his shirt. The tenor player was as tough as the vocalist, playing complex jazz riffs over the onrushing funk. Bathed in sweat, David rushed the stage when the song was over.

"What do you guys call yourselves?" he asked the black leader named Gemini Star who wore a Gumby hairdo and gold-framed sunglasses.

"Tomorrow's News," answered Gemini. "And we're looking for a record deal. Know anyone who can help?"

"Know anyone!" Carla broke in. "You're talking to a *pezzo grosso,* one of the very big-time music lawyers in L.A. You can get these brothers a deal tomorrow, can't you, David?"

David didn't answer right away, his mind flashing back to the meeting with Ira.

NEW YORK CITY

Margo wrote to the folks in Iowa two weeks before Christmas.

Dear Mom and Dad,
I wish you could see New York this time of year. The stores are all decorated with holly and wreaths, sidewalk Santa Clauses are ringing bells, and carols are in the air. I also wish I could be with you, but unfortunately it won't be possible this time. My friend Ralph—I've written you about Ralph before—is under a great deal of pressure and I don't want to leave him alone. He's having problems with his son. My own business has also been very demanding. Did you get the picture of my apartment in the magazine? I know it's not your style but I thought you'd like to see it anyway. My gifts will be arriving soon. And thank you, Mom, for the homemade candies and cakes. You're the best cook there is.

Henrietta Smith wrote back:

Dear Muriel,
I'm still not happy when I see your name in the magazine like that. You're *not* a "Margo" and you're not a "Cunningham" and I know you're a good girl and I'm proud you've made money in New York City selling fancy furniture but sometimes I think you're ashamed of where you came from and who you are. We've never met any of your friends so why don't you bring your Ralph here for New Year's or sometime soon. I finally got your father to go into Duluth for a new set of teeth so you have nothing to be ashamed of anymore.

Love, Mother.

Margo answered,

Dear Mom,
January is just impossible for us, and no, I'm not ashamed of anything. You must understand, though, that life is very different in New York. People are different. They take a long time to get used to, and I'm not sure that you or Daddy would

like it very much here or feel at home. In fact, I'm sure you wouldn't. I'll get home when I can.

While Margo wrote this last letter, her feelings for her parents chilled, remembering her sweaty father after a long day's work and her mother overweight in cheap dresses out of the Sears catalogue. No thanks. No more.

The bistro was bustling. This was the fourth time this year Rita Moses had appeared at the intimate Mondrian Club on Madison Avenue, but the first time she was being reviewed. She'd heard of Walter Gentry, a prominent writer in the field of jazz, but not until he introduced himself did Rita realize that the thirty-five-year-old Harvard-educated writer was black.

Captain of his college debate team and intercollegiate archery champ, Gentry was trained to hit the mark. He displayed the confidence of a man who knew how he affected the opposite sex. He was strikingly handsome. Walking down busy Manhattan streets, women would turn and stare, thinking they'd seen Billy Dee Williams. Unlike Williams, though, Walter had a faint English accent; after being a Rhodes Scholar at Oxford he'd lived in London for nearly a decade. At five feet nine his lean frame gave him the appearance of being taller.

"I think you're marvelous," said Gentry, standing at the end of a line of people congratulating Rita. "May I offer you a drink?"

She nodded and followed him to a corner table.

"I'm impressed by the purity of your approach," he told her. "I'm just sorry it's taken me so long to find my way here."

"I've been something of a secret on the New York music scene."

"I'd like to expose the secret. Start with an interview."

She knew he liked to knock street stuff. His broadsides against black pop culture—movies and music—had made his name. Like most writers, he couldn't see his name in print enough.

"I thought that classic jazz had died. You suggest otherwise."

"Thanks."

"About your background, Miss Moses . . . your influences."

Walter Gentry was smooth. Rita talked about her affinity for the past, singers of the thirties, forties and fifties. "I've always loved Sarah Vaughan."

"Her 1940's Musicraft recordings or after she signed with Columbia?"

"What's the difference?"

Which led him to cite the material and instrumentalists who accompanied Vaughan during her several distinct periods.

Before long Walter Gentry was doing more talking than Rita; a man who appreciated the sound of his own voice. Still, Rita felt he had something to say, like his thoughts about the Harlem Renaissance. She wasn't sure if his interest in her was personal or professional, but either way she had to admit she liked the attention. She also liked his opposition to current trends. He had no use for rap, hip hop and house music.

"I'm surprised you don't have a recording contract," he told her.

"It's not from lack of trying."

"Perhaps lack of publicity."

Sitting next to him in his aging Mercedes coupe as he drove her home to the Village, she thought *perhaps* he was genuinely interested in helping her career.

He glanced over at her with obvious desire. But what about David?

David was in California. He was also fascinating, passionate, energetic. She was intrigued by his wealth and style and apparent conflict with a father, who remained at the center of his crisis. David was different, and he was interested in her career . . .

"A career in jazz," Walter Gentry was saying as he drove around Washington Square Park, "takes real courage. The commercial prospects are pretty dismal."

"What about Anita Baker?"

"She's no jazz singer."

"I'm not so sure. Whatever she's doing, she's fabulous."

"Her songs are terrible."

"Which?"

"I don't waste time listening to Top Ten radio. I don't know the titles."

"Okay, then of the classic singers, who was the greatest?"

"The Duchess."

Rita smiled, thinking of dancing with David to Eve Silk in the penthouse of the Fontainebleau.

"Why don't we meet again tomorrow?" she suggested, putting him off while leading him on. "It's my last night at the Mondrian and I'll be singing a medley of Ivan Lins melodies. I'd like you to hear me."

"I'll be there," he said, and reached for her.

Now wasn't the time, she decided. If ever. "Goodnight," she said, slipping out of his sports car.

That night, her sleep was restless. In her dream she was skiing down white-powdered slopes—effortlessly, gracefully—while crowds applauded and cameras rolled. She was ice skating and bobsledding in Aspen and Gstaad, Sun Valley and St. Moritz. Walter Gentry snapped her picture and put it on the cover of Essence. David Crossman owned the ski lodge and reserved the honeymoon suite. Inside a French jazz trio waited for her to call the song. "Moonlight in Vermont," she said, and started to sing when suddenly she was at the Montreux Jazz Festival on the shores of shimmering Lake Geneva. People cheered, and now they were in shorts, it was summertime, and she wore a one-piece black bathing suit, stood on the edge of the diving board, looked down into the green-blue pool far below and dove, falling faster and faster as she realized the water was on fire. She felt the terrible heat, felt the scorching flames, but there was no turning back—

The phone rang. She woke up with a start.

"Rita? You okay?"

"David?" Happy to hear his voice, she realized how much she had missed him. "What time is it?"

"Ten A.M. Sorry I woke you but I just got back from L.A."

"What happened out there?"

"I learned a lot," he said, still reeling from the revelations about cousin Ira, still thinking, with some guilt, about Carla Bari. "Now I know I can do something for your music. I'm really ready to help, Rita. Can I see you tonight?"

She almost said "sure" when she remembered Walter Gentry. "Tomorrow night," she told him, "would be better."

CHICAGO
1943

EIGHT-YEAR-OLD MILTIE couldn't sleep. Ever since his family moved from Detroit into this small house close to Wrigley Field he felt unsettled. And tonight, with his mother in the hospital, the boy was especially anxious.

On the other side of the room, his younger brother Irving dreamt of fishing with his father in Lake Michigan. Meanwhile Miltie, wide awake, knew that Ruben Ginzburg was downstairs entertaining a woman who was not his wife.

If Miltie was quick to read reality, Irving didn't have a clue. Irving accepted the myth his parents presented—that Ruby had a regular job downtown at an office, that their life was normal middle class. But Miltie pierced the facade. He watched his father like a hawk, overhearing phone calls and eavesdropping on meetings.

He had the feeling that Ruben Ginzburg was living more than one life. Most children wouldn't even dream of such a notion, but Miltie was motivated to get to the truth. He studied the people who worked with Ruby—each business associate, each stranger who entered the house. Why all the whispering? Why the secluded conversations on the back porch?

Early on, the boy saw that one fearful little man from Detroit named Pino Feldman had some kind of power over Ruby. He also sensed that Feldman and his father really hated each other. It didn't matter that Pino gave Miltie and Irving white chocolate bunnies and five-dollar bills each time he came to visit. It didn't matter that he pinched the boys' cheeks and told them to call him "uncle." Miltie heard the way Pino talked to his father when the two men were alone.

"Already the Raminski brothers are unhappy with you," Pino had told Ruby in a gruff tone. Miltie, his ear pressed to the door of his father's den, took it all in.

"Why should they be unhappy? We're making money, ain't we?"

"They say you spoil the niggers. You pay 'em too much and give 'em too much say."

"To tell you the truth, boss, I don't know what they're talking about."

"Maybe you do and maybe you don't. Look Gent, I just wanna make sure we ain't missing the big picture here. The big picture is that I been taking care of you—I gave you a raise, I took you off the road. I said you didn't need to do no more dirty work 'cause I needed someone strong in Chicago. I wanted to set up a base and I figured you was the guy. The record business is nice, I'm glad you're happy with the music. Nothing wrong with that. But the big picture, Rube. You gotta keep your eye on the big picture. The opportunities are out there. Take the numbers racket. The Raminski boys own the South Side when it comes to numbers. Same with bookie joints. And saloons. This shit ain't glamorous but it pays good and it's a base. See what I'm saying? I'm giving the Raminskis some action in Detroit—nothing prime, but decent action—so I expect something in return here in Chicago. That's where you come in, Gent. What I'm saying is that you gotta work with these guys. They gotta like you, they gotta respect you, they gotta—"

"They're scum."

"Sure they're scum, but sometimes you need scum. Think about it. Chicago's bigger than Detroit, and you're still new in Chicago. You're still making your way around the city. That's why you can't afford to get so wrapped up in the music. You spend too much time with the music and too much time with the coons. My own guess is that you're fucking this Silk woman, and that ain't real smart either, but I'll leave you alone on that, Gent, because of how you always come through for me. Man to man, I'd have to say that you could do better than going around screwing some nigger. But that's personal—some guys like white meat, some like dark. That's your business, long as it don't mess with my business. Get it?"

"Got it."

"From now on, you treat the Raminskis the way you treat me."

"That ain't gonna be easy, boss."

"The big picture, Gent. Keep looking at the big picture. We got a toehold in Chicago, which can mean beautiful things for all of us. Now it's just a matter of patience. Am I making myself clear?"

"Very."

Quietly, Miltie hurried back to his room before the men left the den . . .

That had been two weeks ago. Tonight Miltie was even more restless—wanting to know, wanting to see what his father was up to.

He thought he heard something. Noise from outside. A strange noise downstairs. He wasn't sure what was happening. He wished his mother were home. He wanted to know what kind of operation she was having, but no one had explained a thing. "She'll be home in a couple of days," his father had said. "She'll be fine." Well, Miltie didn't feel fine. Feeling afraid, he got out of bed and looked out the window. Two Studebakers were slowly driving past the house. A few minutes later the same two Studebakers slowly drove by again. Stretching his neck, the boy saw the cars stop at the end of the block. Four men in long overcoats got out. They started walking toward the house. Now Miltie felt very afraid.

He began to sweat. He wanted to run or hide but didn't know where to go. If his mother had been home he'd call out to her. The men were getting closer. He'd have to get his father, even though he knew he didn't want to be disturbed. Hurrying downstairs to the den, he took another peak out the hallway window to see one of the men slipping into the shrubbery near the front door. Miltie panicked. He banged so hard on the den door that it opened before Ruby could respond. Inside, everything was fuzzy. Only a small lamp was lit in the corner. Shadows danced on the walls. Miltie couldn't quite comprehend what he saw. On the couch, on her back, a black woman held her legs high in the air, her knees bent, Miltie's father on top of her, his backside bare.

"What the fuck!" Ruby sputtered.

"Men!" Miltie yelled. "Men all around the house!"

"Down!" his father ordered, throwing Eve Silk to the floor with one hand and grabbing his son with the other just as a volley of bullets exploded through both windows of the den. Ruby fell on top of Miltie, shielding him with his body. Miltie could see the naked black woman only inches away. Another round was fired through the windows. Miltie screamed, held his ears, shook. Then the shooting stopped.

"It's okay," his father whispered, hearing the men running to their cars and driving away.

Minutes later, Ruben got up, put on his pants and carried the boy upstairs. Irving was still sleeping soundly.

"Nothing really happened," the father told the son. "It was all just a dream. *None of this happened.*"

Miltie shivered for the rest of the night. In the morning he picked up the phone to call his mother at the hospital—just to hear her voice, just to make sure she was okay. But his father was already on the line, and Miltie recognized the other voice as Pino Feldman.

"I told you," Pino was saying, "I talked to them. The Raminskis swear they had nothing to do with it."

"The fuck they didn't. Those scum—"

"Look, Rube, those scum got no reason to go after you. You ain't done shit to them. Besides, they think they're using me here in Detroit. They don't wanna piss me off. Now I don't gotta tell you that there's a bunch of people you've pissed off, so no telling who it could be. But don't worry. I got Jersey Brotman and Charlie the Flower Man coming out on the next train. Two of my best. They'll be with you all the time. You're valuable property, Rube, and I ain't about to lose you. Just sit tight and don't worry about nothing."

Which made the Gent even more nervous.

MIAMI BEACH

"IN THE COURSE OF a lifetime," Nathan Silver told his grandson David, "you learn many things. Now education is wonderful. I myself regret missing out on high school and college. Reading books is beautiful, but reading people, David, that's the most beautiful thing of all."

It was a quiet Saturday afternoon, and they were sitting on a bench in Lummus Park. Everywhere David looked he saw white-haired retirees reading newspapers, playing pinochle, chattering among themselves or snoozing alone, reclining in beach chairs or stretched out on blankets, soaking up the early March sun and enjoying the robust Atlantic breeze. It was a comforting sight. David knew that he had come here to be comforted, to make sense of his scrambled life. The old people, with their careers behind them and their struggles resolved, had time to relax and tell stories. Telling stories, in fact, had become their life's work. No more trains to catch, no more crowded subways, no more kids to raise. Now they could settle back and trade adventures, narrating events from the past that may or may not have happened.

Like novelists, they'd earned the right to reinvent their personal histories, mixing fact with fiction to create whatever myths their listeners would believe.

"What did your father say when you told him you were coming here again?" Nathan asked David.

"He doesn't know I'm here. When I fly back tomorrow he won't even know I've been out of town."

"Good," said Nathan, nodding his head, the long collar from his green polyester shirt flapping in the breeze. "Why bother him? Why tell him anything?"

"He already suspects a lot. He's no fool."

"You're telling me. Of my two sons I always said Irving had the heart, and Miltie, he had the brains. But tell me about your big cousin Ira. Tell me about your trip to California."

"Ira didn't tell you himself?" Said David, seeing that, as always, Nathan's eyes were shut tight behind his dark glasses.

"He called me just yesterday. He calls me three or four times a week."

"What did he say about me?"

"He wanted to know what I had to say about you. And what I said to him, David, I'll say to you. Both my grandsons are geniuses. They're different people with different styles, but both geniuses."

"I wish I could be so sure."

"About him or yourself?"

"He's not what I expected, Nathan."

"In what way?" the old man asked, leaning toward David to make certain he heard the answer clearly.

"His relationship to the music is . . . well, it's not—"

"Look, David, you have to understand—Ira's like his father. He ain't a thinker, he's a doer. He's a salesman."

"But you talked about him as someone really involved with music—"

"What are you talking about?" Nathan snapped impatiently, "lemme tell you something—this kid put his ass on the line. He went out to California and he did a job. All on his own. And, believe me, it hasn't been easy. This is one tough cookie, this Ira. This kid is involved with music up to his eyeballs. You should be so involved with music. Like me, he's risked everything for the music. It's his living, it's his life. Couldn't you see that?"

"We met only twice."

"Twice should have been enough. Are you telling me you don't want to work with him? Are you saying you don't want to help him? Are you worried what your father will say?"

"My father isn't the issue, my career is. I want to make a change, I'm considering going independent."

"What does that mean?"

"Opening an office in California. Going out on my own."

Nathan said nothing. For two, three minutes he sat motionless. The silence worked on David. The silence had him nervous, unsure. What was the old man thinking? Was he really angry? Did he disapprove? A few benches away an elderly couple started quarreling. Overhead, a flock of birds fluttered by. A car horn honked. Slumped against a tree trunk, a sleeping man snored.

Nathan finally broke the silence. "Do you know what I really think?"

David waited.

"I think I was right about you, David. I think you're a very smart boy."

"Well, I'm uneasy about working for Ira."

"I can understand that. But at the same time, you know you can't work for your father anymore."

"I should have left him long ago."

Nathan smiled for the first time all day.

"And you have projects, you have musicians you want to help. Am I right?"

"There are a couple of people I'm interested in."

"You want to be their agent? Their manager?"

"I'm not sure, that's what I'm trying to figure out."

"Well, your cousin can only help. I understand that you're different from Ira, just like Miltie was different from Irving. But blood is thicker than water, David. And the more time you spend in California the more you'll see how the two cousins need each other. To be independent is a wonderful thing. In my own life I paid and paid for my independence. How *I* could have used a brilliant cousin, someone to trust. You're lucky. You have Ira. It may take a while, but you'll learn to love him, just as I raised him and loved him. And you'll teach him, and he'll teach you, and in the not too distant future the two of you will be a team the likes of which the music business has never known. Mark my words. Remember, David, loyalty is everything, and everything I have is in your hands. I've trusted you with my life."

Gertrude came to fetch Nathan at three P.M., the hour when the old man grew tired and cranky. "I'll be with you in a second, Gert," said Nathan. "I'm almost through talking to David." Gert went off to wait on a nearby bench.

While Nathan caught his breath, David sat still, taking inventory. Had he been helped by coming here? Did Nathan ease his doubts about where to go and what to do next? He felt more excited than apprehensive but that had always been his way. In high school he welcomed fights. In college he never backed away from exchanges with his professors. He thought about Carla Bari, didn't really feel guilty about what had happened. He wasn't engaged to Rita, there'd been no commitment. She was a girlfriend . . . he'd watched Ralph behave the same way. Still, Rita Moses was different, he thought about her in a way he'd never thought about any other woman.

"She's a jazz singer," he told Nathan after mentioning the group Tomorrow's News. "But Rita's more than a jazz singer. When she's up there, well, you take it personally. I'm not sure what it is—but there's this powerful emotional experience that you have to feel to—"

"Tell me something, David," Nathan interrupted. "Is this a colored girl?"

"What?"

"It makes a difference. You sound like you're talking about a colored singer."

"African American."

"When I can't sleep at night I listen to the call-in shows on the radio and I hear all these names. First they want to be Negroes, then blacks. Now they're African Americans. That's fine, that's wonderful, and I'm sure your Miss Moses is wonderful because you have good ears and you know good from bad. I'm sure she has talent. But I want to ask you something else, David. Are you sleeping with this woman?"

"What does that have to do with anything?"

"You didn't ask me for advice, and I won't make any speeches because I know your father has made plenty speeches. Young people don't like speeches. So this isn't a speech, just something I learned through many years of hard experience. The colored woman is a beautiful creature. I know that better than most men will ever know. To help a colored woman, to manage her career, to promote her, to be her lawyer—all that is fine. But to marry a colored woman, David, this is a dangerous thing—"

"Who the hell—?"

"Don't get upset. It's just something I wanted to say . . ."

David wanted to tell the old man that he was a bigoted bastard, but he held back. He wanted to know more about Nathan's relationship with Eve Silk and saw this as an opening.

"Was there a point," he asked, "when you considered marrying the Duchess?"

"No, never. I already had a wife, a Jewish wife, may she rest in peace, who was devoted to me and her children until the day she died."

"But Eve Silk was your lover, wasn't she?"

"That's a long story, David, and it would take a whole weekend to tell it. Today I don't have the energy."

"One of the reasons I made this trip was to ask you some other questions. Your phony 1952 'execution' in Chicago, for instance . . ."

"I'm tired, David, but I'll tell you the main facts because I know you young people. You're curious. You're impatient. Me, I used to be the same. I understand. It got me in trouble and I learned. I learned to cover my tracks. That's what the execution was all about. I'd taken it too far with Pino. You see, while I was off doing my record business and making good money, Pino never let go. He was always watching me. He owned me, or thought he did. We never got that straight. He got bigger and bigger, more power in more cities. He got politicians, a mayor, a senator in California, he went all the way up. In this life, there are some people you never like even though you pretend to. Those people can be your friends. Sometimes even your son. Sometimes your business associates. That's the way it was with me and Pino. He had no respect for nothing. He hated the colored and he hated my acts. He hated Eve and Lord and he did everything he could to hurt them, even though they were making money for him. That's how jealous he was. But things were closing in around Pino. Kefauver, the Senator, knew about him. The Crime Commission was after him. He'd been going too far for too long. I knew it 'cause they also nailed me for certain things I'd done in Buffalo and Chicago. If I didn't nail Pino, they'd nail me. That was their deal. What choice did I have? I had a family, see. How could I take care of my family if I was rotting away in prison? Besides, I liked the idea of Pino rotting away in prison. It was a dream come true. So I did something I swore to myself I'd never do."

"What was that?"

"Don't interrupt, David. Don't ask. I'm telling this story. What I did was deal with the Feds—on *my* terms, not theirs. They said, 'Testify, say what you know about Pino, give us documents, then go into this Witness Protection Program.' I said I'd go, but only after I was dead. 'What does that mean?' they wanted to know. 'It means,' I said, 'that I'll fix it so it looks like I got rubbed out. That way Pino ain't looking for me. No one's looking for me. I can go down to Dallas with my Reba and my two boys and live a peaceful life.' 'How are you going to do it?' they asked. 'Just watch.' I wanted it public, so I did it in a synagogue on a Saturday. God is compassionate, God would understand. I found someone who looked like me, a Jewish fellow, and thank God he had no family and no one who would miss him. He was destitute. I gave him my shirt, my tie, my suit, my clothes. I invited him to synagogue—"

"And you killed him?"

"I *told* you, he had nothing to live for. He was a nothing."

"Like Nathan Silver. You killed Nathan Silver."

"Another nothing."

"And no guilt? No remorse? No—?"

"Look, David, I told you I'm tired. I told you more than I wanted to tell you today. You're used to nice colleges and law firms with your father *Ralph* where everything's clean and everyone's drinking martinis in clubs where people like me aren't allowed in. Well, the real world with real people ain't no private club. The world is run by people like Pino Feldman and it took a long time to find the guts to do what I did because if I didn't get him, he'd get me, and they put him away, and they kept him away, and I'm glad I did it, I'm glad I told what I told because this man, he has a black heart, he has no feelings and no soul, not for all the favors I done for him, not for nothing, and that's all I'm going to say to you today. Without my nap I'm no good to no one. You'll call me when you get back to New York."

Nathan touched his grandson on the cheek and nodded to the large black woman who came to lead him back to the old Cadillac. David watched them drive off—Gert behind the wheel and Nathan, slouched beside her, already nodding off.

Left alone, David was stunned. His grandfather was a *hitman*. His grandfather was a rat. His grandfather was a wildman. His grandfather was crazy. Could someone like this really be his grandfather? But at this point there could be no doubt—the facts were too many—and David's curiosity, coupled with a tingling fear, had him excited in spite of himself.

There were still so many things he wanted to ask. But now that Nathan was gone David had to ask himself why he was so easy on the old man? Why didn't he challenge him more? Why was he so . . . intimidated?

Take Ira, for instance. Nathan had called Ira a genius, but David saw him as a typical West Coast operator. Sure he was a supersalesman, and yes, he'd worked his way into the upper echelons of the music business, but there was no style, no knowledge . . . On the other hand, David was fed up with the Ralph Crossman style. He could choke to death on his father's conservatism, his style. In fact, if Nathan Silver hadn't risen from the dead when he did, David was certain he would have found another excuse to leave Ralph.

Driving the Hertz Buick Regal back to the Miami airport, David felt the old thrill of having information his father hadn't a clue about. It reminded him of those times when as a teenager he'd been high on grass and Ralph, sitting there in his study, buried in his books, didn't know what was happening. For all his power, Ralph didn't know what the hell was happening. This new knowledge—more powerful than drugs, headier than sex—now gave David a feeling of power as he thought of the horror that these revelations would bring to Ralph.

"I know your old man was a mobster," David practiced saying to the empty car. "And I like him. Hell, maybe I *love* him. He's rude and he's crude and he loves the right kind of music, he lived for his passion, he's a smart old fox who beat the odds and survived a fucked-up system and managed to fool the world. He's amazing, and he's still in charge, he can still embarrass your Wall Street ass and blow your cover sky high. He still has power over you, and because his secret is now my secret, so do I . . ."

When he pulled into the car return driveway at the Hertz depot, David felt sweat beading on the palms of his hands. In the minibus to the airport he remembered the time his father had been called to school when he was in tenth grade. David had been caught with a girl in the boys' locker room. He heard again Ralph's smooth defense that was an offense. His father reminded the headmaster of the hefty contribution the Crossmans made to the scholarship fund. At that moment, a scared David was grateful, even impressed. Maybe being a wealthy and powerful lawyer wasn't such a bad idea. Later he'd gone to court and watched Ralph's closing argument during a highly celebrated case in which Crossman had defended an insurance firm against the slickest personal injury lawyer in the land. Ralph blew him away. He'd also helped David get into his own alma maters, Princeton and Columbia Law. David had resisted, but, face it, he had gone anyway.

David was divided.

An hour later, as the 727 tore through scattered clouds, David reached into his briefcase and picked out a Down Beat magazine he had bought earlier that day at a Miami newsstand. He was tired of thinking, he just wanted to read and relax—until from out of nowhere, there was Rita's photograph. He looked again. It was Rita—the frame of her face, her mouth, her even teeth, her half-closed eyes. They had caught her in song.

"If the Pure Jazz Singer," wrote critic Walter Gentry, "is an endangered species, there is little danger that Rita Moses will ever sing anything but pure jazz. She is that sort of artist." The praise pleased David but also made him wonder: Who the hell was this Walter Gentry? And did his following description of Rita's physical beauty indicate he was interested in considerably more than her music? Besides, as the rest of the article indicated, his attitude of jazz-as-pure-art and Rita as pure-artist annoyed the hell out of David. Couldn't Rita sing dance songs, or pop songs, or any other goddamn thing she wanted? Okay, Rita was finally getting recognition, yet David couldn't help but read between the lines and hope that this Walter Gentry was seventy-five-years-old and walked with a gnarled cane.

SAN FRANCISCO
1944

METRONOME MAGAZINE, FEBRUARY 1944
THE DUCHESS SOUNDS OFF

With her name becoming known among jazz aficionados, Eve "Duchess" Silk has two people to thank.

"My manager Ruben Ginzburg and my friend Lord Lowell Foreman made all the difference in the world," she told Metronome in Chicago. "Ever since 'Southside Velvet,' I've been working pretty steady in nice clubs all over. Haven't been to the coast yet, but Ruben is looking at some possibilities out there."

The Raminski Records vocal artist has some new wax due out soon. "We did four songs in Chicago," she said. "Anotherduet with Lord and three pretty ballads. One of them is my tune, 'Morning After.' I've been singing it for years but no one recorded it until Mr. Ginzburg came around."

When asked whether the work was done in defiance of the present recording ban ordered by James Caesar Petrillo, president of the musicians' union, Ruben Ginzburg, sitting beside Miss Silk during the interview, interjected, "No. The songs were recorded way before the ban started."

What does the songbird think of the modern bop movement in jazz today?

"I know the young cats love Dizzy and Charlie Parker and all the others. I saw Charlie Parker once and he sounded like a man on fire. He was something to hear. Dizzy is wild too. He can blow. But my man is Lord Foreman, the way he plays the love songs, the sound he gets, his style for telling a story. I like the movies and I like romance."

Are the singer and saxist an item?

"Just friends. Best friends. He even signed up with my manager, so we're all trying to help each other. We're family."

SLIPPING INTO HIS CHARCOAL gray cashmere overcoat, the Gent handed Metronome magazine to Eve just as they walked outside the train station.

"Does it say nice things?" asked the singer.

"Very nice," Ruby assured her.

"I'll look at it later," said Silk, looking over the fog-covered city.

"How come there's no picture of me?" asked Lord Foreman, looking over Ginzburg's shoulder. He was wearing his thick glasses, a derby and a long gray topcoat.

"Because you're too fuckin' ugly," Gent told him.

"For your information, kind sir," Lowell replied in his best British brogue, "the ladies find me ravishing."

"You sure the rhythm section will be at the club tonight?" asked Ruby.

"You been asking me that same shit for a week now," said the saxist. "And for a week I been telling your sorry ass the same thing, 'Sure enough, the cats will be there!' "

"I'm beat." The Duchess yawned. "Chicago-Frisco ain't no easy haul."

For two days and two nights they had been riding the train in separate black-white sections.

"I wouldn't be coming here," Ruby said, cranky from the trip, "if it wasn't important. I'm telling you, California is the key."

"If you could only see it," said Lowell, intrigued by the thick winter fog. "Looks we done landed on the moon."

Ruby hailed a cab. The driver, startled by the mixed trio, put their suitcases in the trunk. In the backseat Silk sat between Ruby and Lowell.

"I'm going to the Palace Hotel," Ginzburg instructed the cabbie, "then you'll be taking my friends over the bridge to Oakland."

Better that way, Ruby thought to himself as he felt the Duchess' thigh squeezed against his own. Better to separate, better to have the colored in their own part of the train, better to send them to their own hotel—better to leave the Duchess alone.

It wasn't that he hadn't thought of her on the train. He had, especially late at night when the whistle blew and the countryside flew by, especially after he'd thrown back a couple of whiskeys and recalled those times in Detroit. But Detroit was Detroit and Chicago was Chicago. After the shooting at the house, Ginzburg knew he'd gone too far with Silk. Pino had been right. The Gent was losing perspective. And maybe Pino was also right when he said it wasn't the Raminskis who were after Ruby. Maybe it was friends of Marty Strazo from Buffalo or relatives of Nat Aronstein. After all, the Aronsteins were all over Chicago. Who the hell knew who it was? It didn't matter. Ruby saw he was getting sloppy. He was getting crazy. Fucking a colored girl in his own house was crazy. He was losing it. His dick was directing his brain. His dick was running his life. No more.

Time to put sentiment aside. In the past, he'd seen how the Raminskis treated their white artists one way and their blacks another. When their black artists weren't recording or working clubs, they were at the home of one of the Raminskis, washing windows, cleaning toilets or mowing the grass. At first Ruby had rebelled. He told the brothers they were treating their black artists like dogs. But after the shooting incident, he kept quiet. He no longer tried to explain to them or Pino that Eve and Lowell were special. "Look at them as merchandise," Feldman would say, "they're products. Sell 'em like salamis." "They're animals," Leo Raminski, the younger of the obese siblings, had told the Gent. "But they got this thing," added brother Harry. "They sing and dance. See, instead of brains, God gave them singing and dancing."

Ruby may have still considered the Raminskis scum, but he bit his tongue. His survival was on the table. From now on it would be all business. Silk and Foreman could sing—"Southside Velvet" proved their records could sell. "They sell to the darkies," said the Raminskis, "not to regular people." But the Gent knew that the same white people buying Louis Armstrong and Fats Waller would buy Eve and Lowell. The Gent wasn't about to give up. He slipped money to magazine and newspaper editors, guaranteeing his artists press coverage.

Things improved. The Raminskis saw how Ginzburg had changed his attitude. Now he was helpful and friendly. As a result, they cut a new deal with Pino Feldman and gave Ruby and his boys—Jersey Brotman and Charlie the Flower Man—a piece of South Side Chicago to work.

Gent learned everything the brothers knew about making and selling records. He saw there were two sets of books—one for the government and one for real. There were key radio stations, critical markets and certain retailers who could make or break you. And there were also cases of whiskey for disc jockeys, party broads for station owners, paid vacations in Havana for the guys who ran the network radio shows and the ad agency execs who found sponsors and produced programs. Sweet bands, rhumba bands, hot bands were all over the airwaves. A coast-to-coast spot on the "Camel Caravan" could send a record sailing through the roof. Gent knew the story of Benny Goodman's broadcasts on the National Biscuit Company's "Let's Dance," of how Benny arrived at the

Palomar Ballroom in Los Angeles to find a crowd of loyal radio listeners already wild for his music. How that led Goodman to a Hollywood movie and a first-ever jazz concert at Carnegie Hall. Radio was key, crucial. And radio was the main reason Ruby had decided to bring the Duchess and Lord to California while Jersey Brotman and Charlie the Flower Man were back in Chicago making collections and working the streets.

In his younger days Ginzburg had been proud of his street guts. Even as a teenager, if someone stood between him and something he wanted, Ruben Ginzburg didn't think twice about pulling a trigger or plunging a knife. His reputation, after all, had gained the attention of Pino Feldman, who gave him the first decent money he'd ever seen. That was way back ten years ago. He'd done the tough jobs. He'd proved himself. And over time, the idea of dancing to the tune of a Detroit wiseguy, no matter how powerful that wiseguy, was no longer what he wanted. Besides, deep down he hated Pino's attitude about music and musicians. Pino respected nothing. Pino was a prick. But as long as he could chase the music, Ruby decided to patiently play a waiting game. He believed in the music and the money it could make. He'd stay with the music.

During the train trip, Duchess had stayed with Lord. That was fine. That's the way it should be. But now, riding through San Francisco in the cab, Ruby silently returned to the question that had kept him up nights. Were Silk and Foreman fucking?

It was none of Ruby's business. It had nothing to do with business. Eve and Lowell were friends, they worked well together, and what difference did it make whether they were lovers? It was a silly thing to think about, but Ginzburg kept thinking. In his mind's eye he saw Eve's naked body. He remembered how she moaned and moved when they'd made love. Then after the shooting, when he told her how mixing business and pleasure was no good, she understood. She didn't put up a fight, didn't say a word. In fact, right after the shooting she was cooler about it than he was. "Sung in many a club," Silk had said, "Where fireworks went off. Once seen a bass player shot in the neck. Blood spurting every which way. I ducked behind the piano till the shit settled down. Then went on singing."

Truth to tell, it bothered Ruby that Eve took the end of their relationship so calmly. Had she let him do her just in return for a favor? Was it a business move on her part or did she really like it? Did she think white men knew how to make love, or was she only putting on a good show? Did she really prefer someone like Lowell? And what about that Italian, Marty Strazo? Did he have an oversized dick? The questions were making the Gent a little crazy, so he put them out of his mind.

The cab pulled up to the Palace on Market Street just as the fog lifted enough to give a glimpse of the baroque hotel.

"Swanky digs," observed Lord.

"See you at the club tonight," said Duchess, gently touching her manager on the hand.

"My friends will give you an address in Oakland," Ruby instructed the cabbie, handing him enough money for the trip. "Get some rest," he told Eve and Lowell.

In the hotel room, though, he himself couldn't rest. He tried looking out the window, but the fog had returned and there was nothing to see. He made a few business calls. In the evening, while shaving, he listened to the radio. "Your Hit Parade" featured the songs of Mark Gordon and Harry Warren. Songs they had written for a Glenn Miller movie, *Orchestra Waves*—"I've Got a Gal in Kalamazoo" "Serenade in Blue," — were smashes. As he listened, Ruby kept thinking that Lord and the Duchess had better material. Lord and Duchess belonged on "Your Hit Parade."

Lowell knocked on the door.

"Entrez," said Duchess.

Her bedroom was spacious. An evening gown hung in her closet. An open bottle of whiskey sat on the bureau. Also a razor blade. She always kept a blade for protection. There was a canopy bed and tassled curtains. The older woman who owned the big six-bedroom boarding house enjoyed hosting show folk. She loved good music.

While applying her makeup in front of an ornate mirror from the turn of the century, Eve wore only a bra and panties.

"Want a taste?" she asked, passing Lord the bottle. He passed her a joint. The room turned sweet.

"Up for the gig, Silky?"

"Feel good, baby. I like this place. Oakland's nice."

"And you still trust the Gent?"

"Ginzy? Ginzy's a funny kind of Jew. He seems to be about money, but then again, he ain't."

"He got attitude with me."

"How's that?"

"He thinks you and me is grinding, and it bugs him."

"I set him straight. Told him it wasn't like that between us."

"He'd sooner believe Franklin Roosevelt's Chinese."

"Don't matter."

"The hell it don't. It fucks with his brain. Ofays are strange. 'Specially ofay cats. For a long time they thought we had tails. That got them crazy. Then when they saw they was right—except for our tails being in front not in back, they got even crazier."

Duchess laughed. "Guilt, man."

"Guilt 'bout what?"

"Wife. Kids. Ginzy's a family man."

"He's a cold-blooded motherfucker who'd ice his own papa."

"I believe the cat's got heart," said Eve.

"Cat's got a hard-on for you, Silky, that's what he's got. And he ain't gonna put up with my ass for long."

"Ginzy's been doggin' you, Lord, only 'cause he's been staying away from me."

"On whose account?"

"His. I hipped him, Lord, I said it straight, I told him I can play bed games all night long 'cept I turn off my heart. That's how I am. Every time I give heart, I get kicked. So no more heart and no more kicking. I learned my lesson. I say, 'Look here, Ginzy, if you like bed games, I'll play. No big deal.' See, Ginzy's family."

"Think so?"

"Know so. The music's all up in his body. He can't stay away from the music. I ain't saying you're wrong. I know he's a killer. But right now, Jack, that motherfucker's killing for us."

The Gent walked into the Oakland club with two white men who had the power to put Lord and Duchess on the radio.

"You'll hear for yourself," said Ginzburg. "You'll see their talent and you'll make up your own mind."

He led the men to a table near the bandstand. The rhythm section was already cooking. A few minutes later Eve Silk and Lowell Foreman emerged from the tiny changing room, she in black evening gown and white pearls, he in cool blue suit and white derby. The Gent, no slouch himself in a green hamburg, felt proud of his artists. They looked like a million bucks.

Gent beckoned them to his table. "Miss Eve Silk and Mr. Lowell Foreman," he said, "this here is Edgar Stone of the Golden Delight Maple Syrup Company and Neil Browning of the Browning Advertising Agency of Los Angeles. They're thinking of putting you two on the air."

"I'm against putting on airs," said Lord, "but in this case I'll gladly make an exception."

"My pleasure, gents." Eve smiled. "Hope you enjoy the show."

The show was intimate. When Duchess sang and Foreman softly blew sax behind her, they seemed like twin halves of a single soul. When they sang together, the contrasts in their voices worked perfectly—his gravelly, hers smooth. Their material was witty, sometimes light-hearted, sometimes poignant, gently swinging, achingly slow or breakneck fast. Their subject matter was love, loneliness, infidelity, devotion and intoxicants. The all-black crowd went wild when they heard "Southside Velvet" and made them sing it twice. Lord and Duchess were delighted. The audience demanded three encores. Lowell played "Jitterbug Waltz," Eve did "Don't Get Around Much Anymore" and together they sang "Romance à la Mode."

"They husband and wife?" asked Edgar Stone.

"Nothing like that," answered Gent, his jealousy returning for a second. "But what do you think of the act? Ain't they something? Can't you hear them on the radio?"

"They're sensational," said Stone.

Lowering his voice, Browning said, "They have, uh, a rapport with their own kind, but frankly, Mr. Ginzburg, they'd be inappropriate on a national program. They're too ethnic for heartland America."

Ruben Ginzburg did not even try to answer. That night he escorted the men back across the Bay Bridge to San Francisco. And that summer, six months after their appearance in Oakland, the duo of Duchess and Lord appeared on the Golden Delight Maple Syrup Musical Hour radio program, live from Los Angeles. The Federal Bureau of Investigation and California State Police were never able to locate Mr. Neil Browning, the ad executive who mysteriously disappeared from his Wilshire Boulevard office a few days after returning from a San Francisco business trip.

NEW YORK CITY

WALTER GENTRY ENTERED RITA slowly. He was intoxicated by the smell of her skin, the softness of her thighs, her half-closed eyes, the small sounds rising from the bottom of her throat. He had long wanted this woman, from the first night he met her, and finally, with the arrival of spring, with trees budding green across from his apartment on Central Park, he had what he wanted. The sensation was unique, the triumph complete.

"There was no music," Rita said afterward, feeling uneasy.

"Are you complaining?"

"No. Just expecting a little jazz."

David always had music playing when they made love.

"You should have said something," said Walter.

Her silence frustrated Walter. He wanted to be told how good he'd been. Instead he sensed her mind drifting. Rita felt far away.

She tried to put David out of her thoughts, but couldn't. Since their relationship began, this was the only time she had slept with another man. Walter did have those beautiful eyes, his profile of her had brought her lucrative work. He was just wonderfully attractive, more intellectual than David, older, more mature. So?

So nothing, damn it, thought Rita, trying to decide whether to stay the night or go back to her apartment. Hey, David was the past; Walter was the present. David was moving to California, the last place in the world she wanted to live.

"But why?" David had asked Rita the day before in midtown Manhattan.

"Los Angeles is the pits."

"Have you ever been there?"

"No."

"Then how can you say that?"

"It's the wrong atmosphere for a jazz singer."

"I've been trying to tell you—you're more than a jazz singer."

"You don't understand me. Jazz is—"

"Just a name, a category. You can sing whatever you want to sing. Why be restricted?"

"What's the point of this?"

"I want to manage you."

"Boy, you sound possessive."

"I'm talking business, Rita. Pure business. I'm going to manage talent."

"This is really funny, David. For months when I suggested you might help me with my career you insisted the music business wasn't your thing. Now you're jumping into it and wanting me to help you with *your* career."

"I didn't say that."

"But that's it, isn't it?"

"We help each other, Rita, because—well—because we love each other."

"We do?"

"All right, *I* love *you*. Is that what you wanted to hear?"

She couldn't answer. She hadn't expected those words, and they touched her in spite of building resentments. Did she love him? Could she say it? And if she could, would that mean following him to L.A.? It was Walter Gentry and his article that had helped her career. The impact had been real strong. Booking agents were calling; record executives had inquired. She might actually get to make an album. Now David was confusing matters.

"Are you afraid to go out there alone?" she asked.

"I'm a lion," he said, trying to be light. "After all, I've never told a woman that I love her."

"I . . . I'll have to think—"

"Think about this. We both need a change. We've both been in New York too long. L.A. will give us the new attitude we need—"

"Need for what?"

"Change, growth . . ."

"You're talking Californian already."

"I'm excited; I'm breaking loose and I want you with me."

"Sounds like you're talking about your pet canary."

"You know I didn't mean it that way."

"I don't know what I know. I told you, I need time to think."

"I'm leaving in a couple of weeks."

"The man in Miami. He's responsible, isn't he?"

"In a way, I guess. Many years ago he was in the record business. He still has good contacts and he's helping me out."

"Why should he help? Is he a relative?"

"Just a guy who took a liking to me."

After lunch, when he kissed her goodbye, they were standing on Forty-ninth Street. Pedestrians streamed by, cabs honked and hard-hats whistled. It didn't matter. His kiss made her weak, and at that moment she wanted to tell him, "Yes, I think I love you, I'll go with you," but she held back. She did, though, invite him to dinner at her apartment that night.

Walking toward the subway, she made herself think about Los Angeles. Why was she prejudging? She liked palm trees. She liked nice weather. There was a jazz scene, there were record labels and opportunities for work. Her friends who lived there seemed fairly happy. David was talking about getting a place in Malibu, living by the ocean. Miles Davis lived in Malibu. Wasn't it worth a try?

When she arrived home the phone was ringing. It was her mother Rosy.

"Hate to break bad news to you, baby, but I just got back from the supermarket and I saw something I think you should know about. It was in the *National Enquirer.*"

"What are you talking about, Mama?"

"David Crossman. Want me to read the article to you?"

"Go ahead . . ."

Rosy described a picture. "There's this lady called Carla Bari with long legs and hardly any clothes on and she's jumping off the page with her arm around your friend David. It says right here, 'David Crossman.' Says Carla's a 'European jetsetting actress,' David's a 'rich eligible bachelor' and they were out in California at a premiere of her movie and they went dancing at a disco before riding back to a fancy hotel in a limo. Says all that right here. Want me to mail you this thing?"

"No thanks," said Rita, who quickly hung up and immediately called David, cancelling their date into his answering machine: "May you and Carla live happily ever after in La La Land," then slammed down the receiver. When Walter called a few minutes later, she accepted his dinner invitation . . .

That was last night. Twenty-four hours had passed and now Walter was asking her, "What are you thinking about?" He'd put on a robe and slipped in a disc of Wynton Marsalis playing ballads. Rita was still in bed.

"He has a sweet tone," she finally said, referring to the trumpet player.

"Beautiful, I agree. Can I get you a drink?"

"I'm fine, thanks . . ."

"You seem distracted."

"Sorry, I guess my mind's on music."

He sat in a teakwood-and-black-leather Eames chair near the bed. The room was dark except for the rays of a full moon penetrating the sheer curtains. The silence between them was severe.

Walter struck a match and lit his pipe, slowly drawing the tobacco before saying, "I want to produce you."

"What?"

"I've been thinking about it ever since I heard you at Mondrian's. I'd be your ideal producer. I've already picked out the songs. And I promise you, the rhythm section will be impeccable—"

"No orchestration? No strings?"

"Not for your debut. I want it pure. No compromising. Think of Cassandra Wilson's first album, recorded live to a digital two-track. That's what I have in mind. The sort of thing Norman Granz did with Billie Holiday."

"But Billie Holiday sang with strings before and after she worked with Granz."

"It was Granz who allowed her genius to shine in the sparsest settings. The career I see for you will parallel, say, Betty Carter's or Sarah Vaughan's, not concerned with short-lived fads or crass hits."

"Didn't Sarah have a hit?"

"'Broken Hearted Melody.' An aberration."

"And what about Duchess Silk?"

"A great singer whose career was ruined by her Jewish manager."

"What does Jewish have to do with it?"

"I'm merely stating a fact—"

"Wasn't your hero, Norman Granz, Jewish?"

"Why are you so defensive about Jews?"

"I think Silk sang like an angel her whole life."

"Her duos with Lowell Foreman were embarrassing."

"They were *funny,* like Fats Waller."

"A different category altogether. Fats had irony and wit. Silk and Foreman were simply looking to make money."

"And Fats wasn't?"

"He was exploited. Why are we arguing?"

"I'm not too sure," she answered honestly.

He walked to the bed and kissed her. "You're beautiful, you're a beautiful artist." He kissed her again, his tongue exploring her mouth.

She was moist, susceptible to his praise, stirred by his persistence, especially now.

But she was still distracted by thoughts of David Crossman. Damn you, David . . .

BEVERLY HILLS

IRA CROSSMAN SURPRISED THE little man, an employee who had displeased him, by grabbing him by the throat and throwing him across the den into the huge plate-glass window. The window gave way. Glass shattered, slashing the guy's head, back, arms and legs. He screamed as he fell to the ground, his skull smashing against concrete.

"Get him out of here!" Ira yelled to Larry Cutter, bodyguard and personal trainer.

"What do you want me to do with him, boss?" asked Cutter, a former Mr. Australia.

"Dump him. Take the jeep but cover the seats with towels. They're real leather."

Ira's attention quickly turned to the ringing phone.

"Who is it?"

"David Crossman," said his secretary Sherry, who officed in the cabana. She was a shapely woman in a small bikini.

"Grandpa Bernie's pipedream," Ira mumbled to himself before taking the call. "Grandpa Bernie's golden boy."

"Hi, Ira."

"You in town?" David's cousin asked.

"Still in New York but on my way. Should be there by the end of the month or the beginning of June."

Shaking his head, perplexed and annoyed that his grandfather was imposing this long-lost relative on him, Ira said, "We'll have to work out the details, Dave—office space, salary—"

"I won't need any of that," said David, not much liking the patronizing sound of 'Dave.' "

"You gonna work for free, Dave?"

"I'll be working for myself."

"Out here?"

"That's the plan."

"You licensed to practice law in California?"

"I won't be practicing law."

"So clue me in, Dave."

"Independent work in the music business—"

"Are you nuts? Independent promotion is *my* thing, Dave."

"I didn't say promotion."

"The music business ain't nothing *but* promotion."

"Of course, any help you can give me—"

"If you'd been here five minutes ago you'd see the kind of help I give people who screw me, Dave."

"You got it wrong."

"No, buddy, *you* got it wrong. And when I talk to Grandpa Bernie I'm telling him the same thing—*he's* got it wrong. You're either with me or against me. Out here is fuckin' war with live ammunition. And to tell you the truth, I don't need no candyass cousin with his finger up his ass riding around town like a yokel from Kansas with a map-of-the-stars'-home asking me the way to Beverly Hills. See, I live in Beverly Hills. And I got here the old-fashioned way—I earned it, with no help from any rich father—"

"Grandpa Bernie didn't help?"

"Leave Bernie the fuck out of this. Bernie don't exist."

"I'm moving to California to—"

"To do what, Dave?"

"I told you, to get in the record business."

"You got your head up your ass!" he exploded. "The record business will chew you up and spit you out before lunch. What are you going to do—find some singer? Look for an act to manage? Who do you know? How you gonna get your contacts? Me, my contacts are my fuckin' livelihood. My contacts are worth a fortune."

"I may have backers."

"Your father?"

"My father doesn't know anything about it."

"Who's backing you to do what? Nathan Silver? 'Cause if it's Nathan Silver, with one phone call I'll put an end to that shit."

"It's not Nathan."

"Someone Nathan set you up with?"

"Nathan doesn't know anything about it."

"You working behind Nathan's back?"

"Enough. Let *me* tell *you* something, Ira, baby—I'm moving out to L.A. As a courtesy to Nathan I'll call you when I settle in. If you want to talk to me, you will. If you don't you won't. That's it." David slammed down the phone.

Ten minutes later Ira had relayed the whole story to Nathan Silver in Miami Beach.

"David said he wanted to be on his own," said Nathan. "He told me that when he came to see me in March."

"And that don't bother you?"

"David's like his father. He's cautious, but in time, he'll be of help. In time you'll be working together. Believe me. Meanwhile, tell me, what'd you do about the man who was working for you, the one you caught skimming off the top?"

"I eliminated the problem."

"Sometimes that's the only solution. I can tell you that from experience."

"Eliminate cousin Dave."

"You're talking about your own blood."

"He doesn't talk like us. He doesn't think like us. Now he says he has his own backing."

"What backing?"

"He wouldn't say. But I'm saying that he's making a left turn on you, Nathan."

"It's nothing for you to worry about. I'll talk to him."

"You better."

"Give David a chance, Ira. The bigger you get, the more help you need. Things are changing out there. I can smell the changes. This employee, he smelled them too. He thought you were weak."

"Now he knows better. Have I told you about this new label starting up? It's why everyone's crazy. There's Japanese money behind it, and the sky's the limit. They're buying up talent left and right, looking for acts, getting ready to hit the market. Like this guy I had to deal with today, the pigs are lining up at the trough, waiting for the slop. Word is, the first year alone they got a ten million dollar promotion budget."

"So you'll meet with them."

"I already did."

"That's my boy."

"Now listen to this. You'll get a kick out of this. Guess who's their top man?"

"I'm too old for guessing games."

"Jay Feldman."

"Pino's grandson?" asked Nathan, feeling his heartbeat quicken. "I thought you said he was out of the business."

"He was. He's back."

"How did that happen?"

"He's good—that's how it happened. He sells records."

"His grandfather never had a clue. Pino never learned the record business."

"They made Jay the commissioner of a new basketball league. He was pulling down a five hundred thousand dollar salary but he got bored. Now they say the Japs are giving him two mill a year to run Sonsu Records, *plus* a piece of the action."

"What did he say to you?"

"He's no schmuck. He'll deal. I told you, he knows how to sell records."

"I don't like it. He comes from filth."

"Nothing I can't handle."

"That's why it's so important that David—"

"Fuck David! What the hell does that asshole bring to the table?"

"He's a lawyer, he's been to school, he's—"

"You calling me dumb? You saying I can't—"

"I'm saying, Ira, family's family. My whole life it took me to learn that. Now I have a new life, and I'm not making the same mistake twice. Remember, Ira—I got you started. I helped you with your people in Chicago and New York, didn't I? Were my connections good or weren't they? Are those people still helping you today or aren't they? Tell me."

"They're good connections."

"They're the best good connections," said Nathan. "You work in this business for a lifetime and you learn something."

"But the business is changing."

"Of *course* it's changing." The old man's voice was suddenly fierce.

"Didn't I see changes year after year for over fifty years? Why would it be any different now? Listen to me, Ira. Changes, you have to be ready for changes. Do what I say and the changes will work for you. Ignore me, Ira, and the changes will kill you, just like that."

NEW YORK CITY

"IF YOU'RE MOVING OUT of the city in a couple of weeks, I don't understand the point of this session," said Dr. Hector Carlos, psychotherapist.

"A friend of mine recommended you," David Crossman said.

"I appreciate that, but a single meeting usually isn't very conclusive."

"I have a lot on my mind. I've decisions to make."

"It sounds as though you've already decided," said Dr. Carlos, a broad-faced man in his fifties who wore thick glasses and a thin gray cardigan sweater. His Columbus Avenue office was cheerfully decorated with plants and paintings of New Mexican landscapes. His voice had a soft Latin lilt. "Have you been in therapy before?" he asked David, seated on a sofa across from Carlos' straight-back chair.

"In high school, but only for a little while. I had some, uh, discipline problems and my father thought I needed help."

"Did you?"

David laughed. "Probably. I was kind of wild. And sitting in someone's office and discussing my feelings didn't exactly come easy."

"Is it easier for you now?"

"Not much. It's just that the pressure is greater."

"The extraordinary revelations on the part of your grandfather must certainly raise some basic questions of identity. You've lived with those revelations for how long now?"

"Six, seven months."

"And told nobody until today?"

"Who was there to tell?"

"You mentioned a woman, a close friend."

"She and I had a misunderstanding."

"And your male friends?"

"It's easier for me to talk to women than men."

"Including your father?"

"My father and I have always had a way of avoiding each other on important things."

"But if you leave your job and move to California, isn't a confrontation with your father over the issue of your grandfather inevitable?"

"I'm not sure."

"You're not sure who's real and who's a fraud?"

"Look, Doctor Carlos, I'm not sure that psychotherapists aren't frauds."

"It sounds as though you're practicing on me. Is this a dress rehearsal for your confrontation with Father?"

"The man has based his whole existence on lies—"

"Which you bought into."

"Not all the way. I told you—in high school I was already breaking away from his bullshit."

"But you went back. You told me you work for him."

"What are you trying to do, nail me?"

"I'm trying to give you your money's worth. If you're coming here only once, we should at least try to define the issues. And isn't the main issue breaking away? You're reluctant to stay with your father, and apprehensive about going." He nearly smiled to himself, recalling the old Jimmy Durante song on the same theme. But back to business. "Going means abandoning one father while embracing another. Emotionally it boils down to leaving Father for Grandfather. But since your qualms about Grandfather are so great and your ambivalence about Father so deep, you're pretty well caught in between."

"I said I'm moving to L.A."

"You've said it to me. Have you said it to Father?"

"I will."

"And reveal what you know about his past? Will you tell him about your new relationship with *his* father?"

"My grandfather has warned me not to."

"Family secrets are often used to bond one member to another."

"You're saying my grandfather is using me?"

"I'm saying, Mr. Crossman, that I don't know. I do see you struggling with two powerful men who themselves—consciously or not—are battling one another. Issues are unresolved. Like it or not, like I said, you're smack in the middle of their relationship. In fact, yours is a three-tiered generational struggle."

"You suggesting I move to Iowa and be a farmer?"

"I suggest another session because our time is up for today."

David wrote a check for one hundred fifty dollars and left the office just as a black cloud cracked open, dumping rain on the city. With no vacant cabs in sight, he ran to the subway station. He was pissed. Hector Carlos seemed like a nice enough guy, but what the hell did Hector Carlos know? He wanted another patient, more income; of course he'd recommend additional sessions; naturally he'd put a damper on David's plans to move. Didn't David have friends who'd been in therapy for years and were even more confused than when they had started? Therapy wasn't a science or an art form. Therapy was elevated bullshit, that's what it was. But Dr. Carlos was right. David had needed to tell someone—that's all it was. He'd been holding it all in for too long.

Riding to Wall Street on a screeching express train, David's mind raced over the arguments of the past week. The conversation with Ira had only deepened his reservations about doing business with Nathan. Actually, he wouldn't be doing business with Nathan or Ira. Ralph should be able to see that. If only Ralph could be told. David no longer needed protection—not from anyone. David was finally getting the hell *out*, on his own. And Rita, goddamn Rita, what the hell was Rita so steamed about?

"That thing in the *National Enquirer*," he'd told her on the phone, "that's old news. That happened back in December."

"*What* happened?" Rita wanted to know.

"It was business. Daughter of a client."

"Son of a bitch, you're lying. I met the vampire, remember?"

"And what about this Walter?"

"What about him?"

"Am I supposed to believe his interest in you is strictly professional?"

"Believe any damn thing you like."

"And what about California?"

"Send me a postcard."

"So you definitely aren't going . . ."

"Look, David, I'm trying to get *my* career together. You're a sweet guy, you're a smart guy, you're even an interesting guy, you're a lot of things, but right now I don't need a lot of things, I need only one thing—a career."

"And Walter Gentry's going to make your career?"

"I didn't say that."

"You're thinking it."

"I'm trying to do my own thinking—"

"And I'm thinking we belong together."

"Then think again."

The subway came to a screeching stop. David's mind returned to the present. The idea of Rita living with him in a Malibu beachhouse was dead and gone. The idea of helping Rita's career was kaput. Okay, bite the bullet. He'd been talking to the band he'd heard with Carla in the L.A. disco, Tomorrow's News. The tapes they sent were raw but promising, the sort of slam-jam hip hop that was burning up the music charts. Tomorrow's News was headed up. He trusted his musical instincts. His musical instincts were strong enough to get him out of this rut, out of Ralph's law firm. His musical instincts were about to change his life. Let Rita make her safe jazz record. Let her eat crumbs off the plate of that horny phony critic.

By the time he arrived at the office of Crossman, Croft and Snowden, David had worked up a head of steam. Maybe the shrink had helped after all. At least now he knew he could get the words out of his mouth. He could say it.

"*I'm leaving.*"

Two words, three syllables. No big deal.

The deals on his desk in his windowless office were all perfunctory, the same sort of legal busywork he'd been given for the past two years—plain vanilla corporate agreements, backup assignments for a few of the partners. Because the firm was so painstakingly cautious, he was still in an apprentice position and trusted with only the most routine matters. The routine had gotten to him. There was no reason to stay. His mind was made up.

At five P.M. he walked down the long corridor to his father's corner office.

"Is he in?" David asked Ralph's secretary.

"Miss Cunningham is with him. Let me just buzz him."

Seconds later the door opened and Margo Cunningham came out. She smelled fresh and expensive, Van Cleef and Arpels, an asymmetrically cut gray-and-white Karl Lagerfeld suit, diamonds in each ear, blond hair recently dyed and bobbed in a sculpted sweep, eyes clear and purposeful.

"David," she said, brushing his cheek with her lips. "It's been far too long. Let's all get together for an evening. A concert. Isn't Bobby Short doing a Cole Porter extravaganza at Carnegie Hall? Wouldn't that be fun?"

At least she tried, thought David. Always looking for some common ground between him and Ralph.

"Go in and see your father," she urged. "He's in a wonderful mood. Something about an award. I'll let him tell you."

David entered the oversized office, shutting the door behind him. Ralph was at his desk. When he saw his son he didn't smile but stood up and handed him a magazine article. His dark tan Oxxford suit perfectly fit his tall frame. Recent facial treatments had his skin looking vibrant.

"Ralph Crossman Named Attorney of the Year," said the headline. The New York *Law Journal* had cited David's father for exemplary work in the field of business and financial law, commenting on his reputation for "uncompromising degrees of ethical degrees."

"This," said Ralph, "means more to me than a five million dollar settlement. *This* is what we're all working for."

"Congratulations."

"Thank you. Shall we celebrate over dinner?"

It had been months since his father had made such an offer. David couldn't refuse. His own news would have to wait.

The Droman Club was housed in a mansion on Fifth Avenue near the Metropolitan Museum of Art. The main dining room was nineteenth century in flavor—marble entryway, frescoed ceilings, crystal chandeliers, attentive male servants in their seventies who'd been there for decades. No one, claimed Ralph, mixed a drier martini than Eddie, the loyal bartender. Ralph had already downed two.

David was cold sober. He picked at his food while his father discussed plans to sail to Singapore at the end of the summer. Both had avoided the subject of David's unauthorized trips. It was only during the dessert of fresh raspberries that the issue was broached.

"I've decided that we should work together on the Jenkins Realty business," Ralph announced. "Bob Jenkins is contemplating a major purchase in Montreal—a parcel of skyscrapers and parking lots—and I want you to go up there with me next week."

David chewed a raspberry for a couple of seconds longer than necessary. He finally swallowed. "I can't."

"Why?"

"I'm leaving the firm."

"Oh, I see," commented Ralph. With the tip of his linen napkin he carefully removed a spot of cream from the corner of his mouth. "And where exactly are you going?"

"Los Angeles."

"I see." Ralph reached for his glass of claret and took a small sip. "Los Angeles. I presume this concerns the entertainment business."

"It *concerns* a new life for me."

"Which is to say, your present life is unsatisfactory."

"Right."

"I presume you'll be taking the California bar."

"No. I've decided not to practice law."

"Then what in God's name *will* you be doing?"

"Learning the music business. Maybe becoming a personal manager or agent."

"Absurd," Ralph mumbled.

"Why?"

"You're a babe in the woods. And the woods out there are infested with wolves. You don't stand a chance. The business itself is historically, intrinsically *corrupt*—as well as corrupting."

"How do you know so much about the music business?"

"These are just well-known facts. Read the business journals."

"It's what I want. And it's my heritage."

"What is *that* supposed to mean?"

David wanted to tell Ralph everything—that he knew about his grandfather, that his grandfather was alive, that he was in touch with his cousin, that the cat was way out of the bag. But something—perhaps the trust of Nathan Silver—stopped him from going all the way. Instead he found himself teasing his father with snippets of information. His father, the distinguished lawyer, began to squirm.

"This man in Miami," said David. "He said he knew your father. He said your father was in the record business."

"I'm not sure what my father did," Ralph said coolly. "His business life was always a mystery to me. Perhaps he once worked for a record distributor, I'm not certain. What else did this man, this Nathan Silver, have to say?"

"Was your father successful?"

"He was a failure. But you haven't answered my question. How did this man know my father?"

"He was a business associate."

"What was his business?"

"He didn't say."

"He sounds questionable . . . was he the one who gave you your contact in Los Angeles?"

"He put me in touch with my cousin."

"What *cousin*?"

"Ira Crossman."

"Dear God. I thought he had disappeared years ago."

"You never told me he existed."

"I never knew where he was."

"And what about his father Steven?" asked David.

"I never mentioned him to you because he died before you were born."

"And you were never interested enough in your nephew to see what became of him?"

"My family were all strangers to me. I've told you that before. You must have realized it yourself when you met Ira in Los Angeles. What does he do?"

"Promotion."

"Stay away from him."

"Why?"

"If he's anything like his father he's no good."

"But what did his father do? What did *your* father do?"

"I've already told you, they never accomplished anything. They were small-time promoters."

"Ira is not small-time."

"I wouldn't know. But you met him. Would you consider him a man of character?"

"He's rough. His contacts are strong."

"Criminal, no doubt."

"What makes you think so?"

"It's in the blood."

"In *our* blood? In *my* blood?"

"In *their* blood."

"Never mind. I'm going out on my own—"

"On whose money?"

"My trust fund—"

"That means my money."

"I didn't ask you to give it to me. You did it to avoid taxes."

"I didn't expect you to use it foolishly."

"I won't. I'm opening an office. I intend to do business."

"With what prospects, other than a cousin who operates outside the margins of legitimate business?"

"I have no proof of that. The truth is that he does business with every major record label—"

"Which themselves may be suspect. The record business is full of shady operators."

"Calvino Bari is interested in the American record business. He considers it one of the most lucrative investment areas in America."

Ralph didn't raise an eyebrow. Inside he was going crazy, but outside he continued to play it cool, calling over the wine steward and requesting another claret. "I'm afraid this tastes a bit acid," he said. "If you check my private stock you'll find a bottle marked 'Château Dufour.' That should do nicely."

Returning his attention to David, Ralph said, "You mentioned Calvino Bari. What makes you think he has any interest in the record business?"

"Carla told me."

"You use a woman, a romantic liaison, in order to further—"

"It was her suggestion, not mine. She loves American music, she's trying to convince her father that an independent record label headed by the right person might do well."

"Headed by someone with absolutely no experience—"

"I have a lot to learn but you've always said I'm a quick study."

"This severely complicates my relationship with Calvino Bari," Ralph said as his private-stock claret arrived. Struggling to maintain composure, he sniffed the bouquet and sampled the wine before nodding his approval.

"Why didn't you mention any of this before?"

"For the same reason you never mentioned Ira Crossman," David said.

* * *

Ralph Crossman did not sleep well that night. He wondered about this Nathan Silver. Who was he? Ralph considered the worst but had no proof and was not about to probe. He didn't want to know. It wasn't possible; Bernard Crossman was dead. Ruben Ginzburg was dead. The *past* was dead. The Witness Protection Program was impenetrable. Files had been burned. Nobody knew. Nobody would ever know, not his proper law firm, not the legal community, no one. He had made it this far and he would make it all the way. One day he'd probably be appointed to the Federal bench—if he wanted it. He was in control of his life.

But his father—the *Gent*—always had a way of extending his life. The Gent had always got away. Switching identities was his specialty. So why couldn't he have done it again? He had tortured his little Miltie as a child, and now he was torturing him as an adult, and using David to do his dirty work. Fathers against sons, generations against generations. It made no sense, it made perfect sense. If Ruby was alive, so was the shame of his son Miltie's past. If Ruby was alive, no telling what he would do, especially with Irving's son Ira on the scene in L.A. What was David getting into? He had to protect his own son. But just as Ruby had no control over Miltie, Ralph had no control over David—at least not now. On the other hand, thought Ralph, all this could be a seizure of paranoia on his part. Why, after all these years, would his life be thrown into such disruption? His father was dead and buried. Wasn't he? Was he? . . .

"What's wrong?" asked Margo, who had been thrown into something of a crisis herself earlier that day. "You're still up."

"Just thinking . . ."

"What about?"

"Nothing, really."

Margo began thinking about that morning's letter from her mother . . .

> Dear Muriel,
> I have some big news for you. Daddy and I have decided to retire and sell the farm. We have a buyer and we'll be moving to Duluth. With this extra money we want to do some traveling. We've never traveled before and being that there are so many places we want to see, I'm looking forward to seeing as much as I can. We want to go to the Holy Land, of course, but first we want to come to New York to visit *you*.

Her stomach churning, her throat dry, Margo called home. "I want to see you, too," she told her mother, "but I'm afraid this is my busy season, I'll be frantically busy for at least a month . . ."

"Seems like you're always busy."

"The work I do is very demanding, please try to understand . . ."

"I do. We'll just wait till you're not so busy."

Margo figured it was possible to slip her parents in and out of town without introducing them to Ralph or any of her friends. A matter of logistics. So for both Margo and Ralph, on opposite sides of the bed, it was a night to remember.

The next day, a Saturday, after strong espresso and cheese croissants, they went to an auction at Sotheby's, where their nervous attention was torn between people from their past and an especially enchanting miniature landscape painted in 1837, a view of Florence at sunset from the hillside of San Miniato.

From his front-row seat Ralph couldn't stop thinking—what was his son getting into and how could he stop him? Ira Crossman had to be tied to one mob or another. Ira had to be as bad as his father. David had to see that. For years Ralph had feared his son would never adjust to the law firm, while hoping that somehow he would.

Pushing back her own conflicts, Margo whispered to Ralph, "Isn't it beautiful?"

The scene was infused with a coloration of misty purplish gold. Giotto's companile, Brunelleschi's dome, the Ponte Vecchio—all caught in a moment of precious quietude. You could smell the pine trees, hear the flutter of sparrows' wings, see the flow of the River Arno.

"Do I hear one hundred twenty-five thousand dollars?" declared the auctioneer.

"Go ahead," Margo urged, squeezing Ralph's hand. "It's fabulous."

Ralph raised his hand.

"Sold!"

She kissed his cheek. "What a wonderful painting! Aren't you delighted?"

He thought he was—the thrill of purchase almost annihilated his and Margo's fears—until he suddenly remembered last night's dream. The details were vague, but the figure of his father had been clear. Ruben Ginzburg/Bernard Crossman had appeared in his dream, walking and talking and carrying on as though he were still alive.

He was coming to Manhattan to visit him.

MALIBU

SUNDAY IN JULY AND Pacific Coast Highway was a mess. Murderous traffic, sweltering sun and this used black BMW convertible overheating. The dealer was down in Venice. How could he bring in the car tomorrow and still look for a place to live? Today the great urban sprawl known as Los Angeles seemed anything but angelic; it was downright demonic, unmanageable, insidious. The car was boiling, the gridlock getting worse, leggy blonds running across the road, hordes of surfers, jeeps, pick-ups, Hyundais and Subarus and fat guys with tattoos straddling smoke-belching Harleys.

The past week had been hell, the city choking under the worst smog attack in a decade. David felt unstrung, unattached, on the edge of nothing and in the middle of nowhere. He thought of going back . . . to what? To his father, who expected him back? Who clearly implied he wouldn't make it?

Last Monday his first stop had been Inglewood, a predominantly black community, home of the airport and the Lakers basketball team. Driving across Imperial Highway between Crenshaw and Prairie, he saw half-clad women giving him the high sign—so-called "strawberries," women selling themselves for dope. Turning on Cherry Avenue, heading down 118th Street, he watched men stumbling out of crack houses, some smoking the pipe on the porch, others strung out on the street. Though it was light out, it felt like midnight. What the hell was he doing here?

It was the music. He felt *close* to the music. And walking toward the rundown apartment complex, he heard music in the distance. It was music that led him on.

Inside the tiny one-bedroom flat the music was ferocious, sounds that seemed to fight off fear. Gemini Star, the Gumby-haired leader of Tomorrow's News, was rapping about everything David had just seen.

Stink of death from down the block
Cats sucking up the nasty rock
Babes crying for mama's milk
Mama rolling 'round in filth
What you see is what you get
Only hope's in self-respect

Rhythm on the street is from on high
Hope's the message across the sky.

Gemini, a slender twenty-year-old in gold-framed sunglasses and blue Dodgers baseball cap, spoke/sang in a rich, husky voice. At five feet five, one hundred forty pounds, he sounded like someone twice his size. He could growl in a baritone bag, but also soar into a Smokey Robinson falsetto. His range was vast. His cuteness was wed to a sensuality David felt would appeal to young girls.

Plucky P, the chubby bass player, popped and slapped his instrument with fiery spunk. His hair was cut in a new-style "fade"—sky-high on the top, cropped close to the skin on the side and back. Saxman Isaiah Z was taller than David and improvised in several styles at the same time—post-Coltrane jazz, soul-based R&B, nervous New Jack Swing. Dale Summi, Japanese-American, was the serious-minded keyboardist who cooked on synthesizer while scratching LP's on the turntable. Greg Casey, a big ol' West Texas white boy with a shit-eating grin, kicked everyone's ass from his sparkling Panther-black Yamaha drum set.

Together, they played like a single body with five heads. Isaiah had a tiny nose ring, Plucky P a huge cross dangling from his left ear, Summi purple-and-yellow hightop Nikes, Casey a white ten-gallon Stetson. David surveyed the scene, expecting to find booze or drugs. There was none. The guys looked wild, played wild, but were straight as a board.

"This is serious funk," Gemini told David during a break. "We're serious. We can bust."

Some songs had an angry political surface, others a soft romantic heart. Titles like "People Pushing Back," "Hurting Heart," "Get It While It's Hot," "Malcolm in America" featured original lyrics—ironic, sweet, mellow, manic. All at once, the music sounded new and old.

Later David was able to talk to the band about the musicians he loved best—Curtis Mayfield, James Brown, Barry White, Sly Stone, George Clinton, Bootsy Collins, Gil Scott-Heron. The guys knew their history. Their dialogue was hot. David thought about his old law clients—boring men twice his age—and how much more exciting it was to be hanging with Tomorrow's News.

"Our music's positive as all hell," said Gemini. "It's the music business that's so negative. But what about it, David? Can you get us a record deal?"

"You guys deserve to be heard. As soon as I get settled you're my first priority."

The problem, though, was getting settled.

Carla would help. She'd telegrammed that she'd be arriving from Paris that very day he was with Tomorrow's News in Inglewood. It'd be good seeing her—at least she was connected in this Hollywood community.

David got to the airport early, remembering the heat of their last encounter. He was ready for more. With Rita apparently gone, he was especially ready. Bring on Carla. Bring on this crazy woman to this crazy city. Still buzzed by the beat of Tomorrow's News, David considered Carla's arrival a blessing. Waiting for the Air France jet to taxi to the gate, he watched as the passengers filed out—Americans, Frenchmen, a statuesque model, a few Africans in native garb. Where was Carla? Thinking he'd missed her, he ran down to the luggage area. No Carla. He looked around for thirty minutes before deciding to call Rome. No one home in Rome. *Forget it,* he finally told himself. Carla was too wacky anyway. Who needed her?

He had one or two marginal contacts from New York—friends of friends, guys he knew in college or law school, entertainment attorneys in Century City. They were all busy.

One record executive told him, "If you don't know somebody, this town is a closed shop." Others, recognizing the last name, asked whether he was related to Ira Crossman. When he said yes, they nodded noncommittally or asked whether he'd be working with Ira. He said he was on his own. More nods and fast exits.

He considered calling his cousin but didn't. Better to concentrate on finding a place to live. He was in a hurry to get out of his expensive Beverly Hills hotel room, but the real estate market was crazy. Buying or renting on the west side of the city was pricier than Manhattan. Three-bedroom dumps could cost a million. And Malibu, where he wanted to live, was even worse.

Now sitting in Sunday traffic, making his third trip up the coast in seven days, still searching for a house, he went back to wondering whether it was all worth it. The bodybuilders on the beach made him feel skinny and weak. The women had him horny. Where was Carla? Where was Rita? Rita was singing jazz in some Manhattan bistro. In Manhattan he had friends, any number of ladies who were always happy to see him. Here he knew no one, he was an outsider.

Arriving at Alice's Restaurant on the Malibu Pier—the gridlocked twelve-mile drive from Santa Monica had taken him two hours—David was about to meet his fifth or sixth real estate agent of the trip. They were all the same. She'd take him around in a big fancy car, showing him rundown cottages or tiny condos far from the ocean for eight hundred thousand dollars. Hell, his trust fund was worth half that. He couldn't afford anything like those prices. "Then forget Malibu," all the other agents had told him. This one, though, was different. She said she'd found something.

"Let's take my car," said Jeanine Bloom, whose face had been lifted and nose clipped. Driving along, she spoke with the nasal cadences of a grown-up Valley Girl. "You're from New York and I know New Yorkers love Malibu. I know Malibu like the back of my hand. Do you know how many New Yorkers live in Malibu now? I swear, it's a suburb of New York. Barbra Streisand lives right up there, and Berry Gordy, his house is right over there. Berry is just fabulous. Are you in the entertainment business, David? Do you know Berry Gordy? That's Barry Diller's house—he threw a marvelous party for my sister-in-law just last week—and his neighbors Dick Clark and Jerry Weintraub . . ."

With the traffic thinned out it didn't take long to drive a few miles north of the Malibu Colony, the trendy strip of beach where the stars lived. Jeanine kept dropping names like a B-52 dropping bombs. Finally they pulled into a driveway off the main road. The garage door opened automatically. From the rear, the place appeared unimpressive. They went through the back, through the garage, into a Spanish-tiled kitchen of gleaming azure. The floors were terra-cotta, the walls stark white. The ceilings were crisscrossed with massive wood beams. There were two bedrooms, dining room and open living area, each room looking out onto an immaculate private beach, and fifty yards beyond, the blue Pacific. The sound of crashing waves filled the house while David just stood there, taking it all in, the sliding doors wide open, the smell fresh and salty, the breeze clean, burnished gold sunlight splashing everywhere.

"This is crazy," he told Jeanine. "What are we talking here—two million? Three? More?"

"Didn't I tell you on the phone? It was bought last week. It's already in escrow."

"Then why the hell are you showing it to me?"

"The buyer told me to bring you. He said you were the tenant."

"Who's *he?*"

"The man who bought the house over the phone. Mr. Silver. Mr. Nathan Silver from Miami Beach."

CHICAGO

1945

DRESSED IN A WIDE-SHOULDERED new blue serge suit, the Gent was backstage and more than a little nervous. He had never done anything like this before—not on this scale, not with so much at stake. This was the North African-styled Regal Theater on South Parkway, with its Moorish lobby of white marble and its red velvet auditorium of thirty-five hundred plush seats; this was "All-Star Jazz . . . presented by Ruben Ginzburg." His name was actually on the program and his—or at least Pino's—money was behind the concert.

The lineup was strong. Two former Benny Goodman sidemen, pianist Teddy Wilson and drummer Gene Krupa, were being featured with small groups of their own. Coleman Hawkins, a towering figure on sax, was scheduled. So was Tiny Bradshaw's big band, with Sonny Stitt on tenor and Charlie Fowlkes on baritone. The highlight, though, the real reason the Gent was putting on the show, was the debut appearance in Chicago—live and in person—of Duchess and Lord.

Against conventional wisdom, the Gent had packaged a jazz duo—singer and saxist—and actually made a real dent on the charts. The radio broadcasts from California had made the difference. Following "Southside Velvet" and Silk's solo "Morning After," "Twice as Good" was an even bigger hit, another Eve and Lowell vocal dialogue. The critics in Metronome and Down Beat, though, had been harsh—another reason Ruby was worried about this concert tonight—calling the song "trivial" and claiming it "pandered to the public." Ginzburg had been enraged by the attacks. He understood the tune had caught Silk and Foreman's playful personalities in a moment of honesty. "And why are these writer schmucks against us making some money?" he said. "Forget 'em," said Silk. "They don't buy tickets," said Lord, "and they get the records for free."

The Raminski brothers represented a more serious problem. As soon as "Twice As Good" started selling they demanded a change in their deal with Ginzburg, a bigger cut. Ruby flatly refused. Pino Feldman intervened. "We got deals with them now all over Detroit and Chicago," he told Gent. "We're married to these guys. They're our partners. They make us money. I told you, don't fuck it up. I know how you are with your niggers, but enough's enough."

"The fucks are robbing us blind, Pino."

"On my interests in Chicago, they pay like clockwork. I got no gripes."

"We can keep everything else in place. Just let me break off on my own with the music—"

"You're getting too pushy for your own good, Gent."

"I'm bringing you in on everything, boss. I'm telling you just what's going on."

"The Raminskis feel like they're entitled. When it comes to music, they ain't backing off. They got a lock on all the music in Chicago—"

"So give 'em something else, something that looks better now but in a year, I guarantee you, Pino, in *less* than a year my records will be making twice what they're making today."

"So you say."

"Have I ever let you down, boss? Listen to me, I know what I'm doing. I'm helping you plan for the future. I'm protecting you. You trust the Raminskis. I don't. I'm going a different route. I'm taking us into concerts. Last month Norman Granz had this Jazz at the Philharmonic at the fuckin' Civic Opera House here and *sold out*. He had Lester Young and Meade Lux Lewis and I don't know how many others. Grossed ten K. That's nearly three bucks a ticket. That's what I'm looking at. I'm telling you, people will pay for good music. But this is something I gotta do on my own, without the Raminskis hogging in."

"You're too caught up in this shit—"

"Believe me, if we can keep the Raminskis out of the cookie jar we'll make some real money."

"I ain't sure. The Raminskis . . ."

"If you think they're too strong for us . . ."

Finally he had pushed the right button. "There ain't no one too strong for us."

A few minutes later Pino agreed that the Regal Theater concert would be a test. He told the Raminskis hands off. The Raminskis didn't like it, but the booking was already made—posters printed, musicians hired, hall rented. It was a Ruben Ginzburg production.

The place was practically sold out. By the time Gene Krupa and tenorman Charlie Ventura kicked off "Stomping at the Savoy"—the name of the ballroom next door at Forty-seventh Street—only a hundred seats were still empty. Looking out from the wings, Ruby could feel electricity in the air. A few fans were already up dancing. He went backstage to check on the other stars. Teddy Wilson, Coleman Hawkins—the cats called him "Bean"—were milling around the dressing room. Members of Tiny Bradshaw's band were warming up.

"Where's Lord?" a good-natured Bean asked Gent. "Told him not to mess with me. Said I'd blow his ass away tonight."

"Him and Silk ain't here yet?"

"Not a sign of either one."

Ruby wasn't too worried. They were often late to a gig. Krupa was just winding up "Limehouse Blues." Things were fine.

Lowell had been living in a boarding house on South Garfield and Silk had a place on East Michigan. The Gent had been relieved to learn the two weren't lovers. That made things easier. Over time his own resistance had broken down. Never again, though, would he bring Eve into his home, especially since he'd moved his family to a swankier part of town. He got her an apartment instead and furnished it with plush couches and love seats and a big four-poster bed. At least once a week he'd visit Duchess for an evening. "I ain't putting no pressure on you or nothing like that," he'd tell her. "You don't gotta say a word," she'd reply before giving him what he came for. "Ginzy's like a junkie," she'd tell Lowell. "And, Jack, I'm his jones."

"I'm Through with Love," Hawkins was singing through his sax. His set was winding down. Teddy Wilson had already performed and it was nearly intermission. Still no Duchess and Lord. Their backup band had been there for over an hour but hadn't a clue about where their leaders were. Gent started pacing, making calls. His throat was turning dry, his stomach tightening. It was getting serious. Tiny's band was taking the stage. A few minutes later they were into "Bradshaw Bounce." The crowd loved it, cheering long and loud for drummer Earl Walker's breakneck solo. Ruby ran out back, looking up and down the alley. Where the fuck were they? He thought of calling an ambulance, calling the cops—he'd never called the cops for anything in his life—calling somebody, anybody, to find them, but who? Tiny was through. The emcee, a local deejay, sought out the Gent. "Where are your stars?"

"Can you stall?"

"For a minute. I'll tell a couple of jokes but that's it."

Frantically, Ginzburg ran from the wings to the alley to the front of the theater, hoping they'd pull up any minute. They didn't. He talked to Hawkins and Krupa, said something to Tiny and then clued the emcee.

"Due to circumstances beyond our control," the emcee told the crowd, "Duchess Silk and Lord Foreman will not be appearing tonight, so instead we have a surprise treat for you, a jam session featuring all the great talents—"

Boos drowned out the rest of his sentence. "Gimme my money back!" someone yelled. "You better do something," the theater owner told Ruben. "What can I do?" "You're the promoter!" the proprietor yelled. "Any damages come out of your hide." "I ain't giving no money back," Gent insisted. "The Raminskis said there'd be trouble!" the owner screamed even louder as an angry patron threw a whiskey bottle that smashed against the piano on stage. The musicians fled.

When the cops came, the theater was a mess. The next day the papers called it a riot. That same night of the concert, after forking over the total receipts—nearly eight thousand dollars—as partial payment on damage done, Ruby drove all over South Garfield and East Michigan to look for Duchess and Lord. He was ready to kill them. In both places, though, eye witnesses told him the same story. A black guy had come by in a yellow Cadillac to pick them up and take them to the Regal. It sounded crazy, but Gent realized what had happened: they had been *kidnapped*. The Raminskis were playing hardball. Real hard.

ROME

"WHAT'S THE POINT OF being mad?" Carla Bari told David over the phone. "Things change in this world. Without change, life is very boring, wouldn't you say?"

She stood naked on her sixth floor veranda overlooking the Pantheon in the ancient center of the city. The Roman summer sun was beastly. The plastic from the remote phone was burning her ear. On the narrow streets below, the high-pitched roar of motor scooters collided with shouts of men peddling fruits, chickens and calamari from an open market. Japanese tourists congregated outside an espresso bar. Little boys kicked soccer balls around Piazza Rotonda.

"The point is, now I know I can't count on you," said David from his hotel in Beverly Hills.

"You are very wrong, my dear. My friends—and I have friends all over the world—will tell you that they count on Carla—"

"Then where the hell were you?"

"There was a party for me in Venice. I thought it would last a few hours. It went on for days. How could you ask me to leave? It was my thirtieth birthday. The start of something new and exciting. More time in America. I told everyone there, I told Rod Stewart, I said I will be spending more time in America and more time in California and more time with my wonderful new friend David Crossman because I have changed his life. Italian men, French men, the Spanish and the Greeks, they never change. They are the inventors of machismo. Women will never change their lives. But in America, especially among the Jewish men, there is a difference. You left the city of your birth for me. You left your father for me. Carla will never forget."

David began to argue. He was ready to tell her that her thinking was off the wall. Coming to California had little if anything to do with her. But why bother? Better to let her talk. "I'll see you when you get here," he said, already over his anger. "When I get my phone in Malibu I'll let you know."

"*Che meraviglia!*" she said, spreading tanning cream over her thighs while noticing the binoculars of a nearby neighbor aimed directly at her. The attention made her moist. "Malibu is a dream," she told David. "We will be so happy in Malibu. I'm tired of the Bel Air Hotel—same old boring crowd. Malibu is a fresh breeze. Thank you for thinking of Malibu. What is today?"

"Monday."

"In a few days—I don't know how many—I will be there. I will call you. I will see you. I will change your life and you will change mine. Who cares about being an actress? Music is the most beautiful thing in the world—no silly studios or directors in love with themselves. *Ti voglio bene.* I love you, David."

She went back inside her spacious apartment filled with erotic images of men photographed by Herb Ritts and Bruce Weber. There were also snapshots of her with celebrities from Paul McCartney to Marcello Mastroianni. Two "Best Actress at Cannes" awards stood on her seventeenth-century mantle. Ancient Persian carpets were thrown about the marble floors. An elaborate stereo/video system and a huge white free-form neon sculpture dominated the living room. In the darkened bedroom Fausto Pane, the thirty-five-year-old Florentine who had recently been named head of Calvino Bari's extensive European operations, was in his bathrobe. Pane was the economist-executive who spearheaded daddy's multifaceted banking network in Italy, Germany, Switzerland, Spain and France.

"You must vacate," she urged the graduate of the University of Bologna and the Wharton School of Business. "My schedule . . . I'm leaving for America and I haven't even started to pack."

"What am I?" asked the green-eyed Fausto. "Some whore to be thrown out with the morning garbage?"

"You are not garbage," she assured him. "You are most delicious. But Calvino will be looking for you and I am looking for my passport. America is calling."

"And what's in America, a man?"

"A hundred million men."

"How many does it take to satisfy you?"

"You are brilliant," she assured him. "That's what Papa says, and that's what I have learned. I adore you. I sing your praises. Now get out, please. And hurry, goddamn it."

Two hours later Carla was leafing through a magazine and sipping *acqua minerale* at an outdoor cafe on the sun-splashed Piazza del Popolo. "Sex addiction," said an article in L'Espresso, the leftwing periodical, "is a major myth of the day. It is a myth created by the perpetrators of a puritanical culture who view any form of guilt-free commitment-free sex as a sin." The author was a therapist named Victor Susman. Ordering a small slice of cake, Carla read on with increasing enthusiasm. When she was through she looked at her watch. Three o'clock. She was due at a producer's house at three-thirty. She also needed to see her travel agent about booking a flight to Los Angeles. She wanted to leave tomorrow, or maybe the day after. Instead, though, she went to a phone and called her father's secretary. "I need the home number of a Victor Susman. He writes for L'Espresso."

A short while later she had Susman on the phone.

"I'm Carla Bari and I'm one of your admirers. Your article was fabulous, I want to meet you. We have things to discuss. I would like to meet you as soon as possible. I am an actress and this is very important for my work."

"I know your work," he said, unable to hide the excitement in his voice. "The problem is that I'm leaving for Montreux in just a few hours—"

"What a delicious coincidence! I'll be there myself this week!"

Le Montreux Palace was Switzerland at its most opulent. The view from Carla's room was of Lake Geneva, the majestic peaks of the Alps reflected in its mirror-sleek surface. Swallows soared through a cloud-scattered sky of dewy gray-blue. Down the coast, on the edge of the still water, stood Château du Chillon, the castle where Byron set his "Prisoner" poem and carved his name on a pillar in the medieval dungeon.

"Did you have a good night's sleep?" Carla asked Victor Susman over the phone.

"Are you actually in Montreux?"

"I said I was coming, didn't I? Well, I'm here."

"You're serious?"

"Yes, and quite hungry. Will you meet me at the Palace for lunch? We have much to discuss."

The dining room afforded a sweeping panorama of the city, the pearl of the Swiss Riviera and a playground for the European rich. Elegant summer homes and stately mansions dotted the green hillside. Flowers and fruit trees bloomed everywhere. The clouds had darkened over the lake and a misty afternoon rain had begun to fall. In the distance one could hear the gentle sound of ancient church bells.

"You're here for business?" Carla asked Victor, an Austrian who had lived in Rome for a decade but preferred speaking English. He was fortyish, bald and bearded. Carla liked the look. He appeared to have a hard stomach and strong legs. She liked his dark brown eyes and bushy eyebrows. She especially liked the prospect of playing with his mind. He was, after all, a sex therapist.

"I'm here for a meeting," he said. "And you?"

She glanced over at the morning paper, opened to the entertainment page, and spotted an ad for the Montreux Festival du Jazz. "I'm here for the music," she said. "I follow music all 'round the world."

"You're not working on a film?"

"I'm working on myself. The films must wait. I'm thinking, I'm reading, I'm searching. That's why your article fascinated me so. Only last week a friend called me a sex addict. Now you say there is no such thing. Bravo, Professor Susman!"

"I've just returned from America where I saw that the anonymous groups—Alcoholics Anonymous, Cocaine Anonymous, Overeaters Anonymous—are growing like weed. It's phenomenal. To lump sex in that category, though, is to misunderstand the very nature of the carnal impulse, don't you agree?"

"Yes, *yes*!"

"Most of these so-called sex addicts are former drunks or drug addicts who lack the strength to leave their support groups. They've become addicted to those groups. And they view one-on-one therapy as a distinct threat."

"Poor thing," she said, placing her hand on his knee. "Your business has fallen off."

"They're given a book, a twelve-step program, which is nothing more than a New Age bible. They're instructed to believe in a higher power. They're told there's nothing to feel guilty about when, in fact, guilt must be looked at and worked through before any real progress is made."

"Without guilt, dear professor, there is no fun. Is that your point?"

"Not exactly," he said, finishing his first glass of champagne. "Therapy should not be placed in the hands of amateurs—that is the point."

"And when it comes to sex," Carla added, her hand crawling into his lap, "you are the ultimate professional . . ."

"I'm writing a book."

"I want to read it. Will you read it to me? Do you have the manuscript with you? Shall we have dessert in my room?"

"I have a meeting."

"Come with me. It will be quick."

And it was, quicker than he had ever imagined possible.

"It's never happened like this before," he said afterward. "This has never been a problem."

"I'm new for you," said Carla. "I am different. You wanted to get to your meeting. You were in a hurry. You are a compulsive about being on time. Am I right? I think you have a marvelous mind, a marvelous theory. You have cured Carla's addiction by declaring that it never existed. I thank you, professor, and I say, forget my orgasm. I can live without it for now. Forget your meeting. You can live without it. Skip the meeting and let us sleep the afternoon away. Let us listen to the thunderstorm, dream and wake up and try all over again."

"I *can't* miss the meeting, the meeting is my whole purpose for being here—"

"Purposes change. Are we looking for purpose or adventure?"

"If I have time after the meeting . . . I've got to get to the meeting," he said, pulling on his pants and heading for the door. In his rush, the therapist left his undershorts in a lump on the floor.

That night Carla went alone to the Casino, scene of the jazz concert. Victor Susman had not called. No loss. It was an interesting lull between Rome and Los Angeles, a diversion. Besides, an evening of music and being alone for a while would be a welcome change of pace. Looking over the program, she noted that pianist Alan Broadbent and bassist Charlie Haden were scheduled along with master saxist Branford Marsalis, whom she recognized from Spike Lee's movies. Toots Thielemans, the Belgian harmonica virtuoso, would also be playing—suddenly something on the page popped out at her.

It was a name. At first she couldn't place it, until, in a flash she saw the singer's face—Rita Moses. "Rita Moses," said the program, "young American jazz vocalist from New York City, who is working on her debut album, will be performing with a trio."

Was it possible that David was here? Could he have traveled with her? Of course not, she'd just spoken to David, he was in Los Angeles. If he had plans to be in Europe he would have said so. No doubt his move to California had ended his fling with Miss Moses . . . Or had it?

Rita Moses could sing, Carla decided after Rita's first song. She had the sculpted look of a model—the high forehead, the angled cheek bones, the tailored, understated clothing. Her voice had the classic intonation of timeless jazz. Interpreting Billy Strayhorn's haunting "Blood Count" and Matt Dennis' "The Night We Called It a Day," she phrased with subtlety, reading the lyrics with a sense of drama that won over this audience. Carla fought back a rush of jealousy. So the stunning black woman was talented. So what?

The concert was over, and back in the musicians' bar the performers were relaxing over cognac and light conversations. It was one in the morning. Carla was chatting with festival director Claude Nobs, an old acquaintance, when she spotted Rita Moses on the arm of a man whose penetrating eyes sent messages straight to her erogenous zone.

"Rita!" she declared, breaking away from Nobs. "What a delicious coincidence! We haven't seen each other since Ralph Crossman's party in New York. You truly are quite a singer, aren't you?"

"Carla?" Rita was obviously surprised to see the Italian actress.

"Carla Bari, yes."

"And this is Walter Gentry."

"Are you an actor? A model? A gigolo? Tell me everything, Walter Gentry."

"A jazz critic," said Rita, aware of Carla's designs.

"And producer," added Walter, his eyes drawn to Carla's short black skirt.

"I just spoke to David in California," Carla told Rita. "Do you know David Crossman, Mr. Gentry?"

"I know who he is."

"I'm on my way to see him. Where are you two headed?"

"I'm due in Nice tomorrow," said Rita. "Walter's going to Paris."

"Another delicious coincidence," Carla announced. "I'm stopping over in Paris on my way to the States." She turned from Rita to face the new prospect. "I wonder, Walter, if we'll be flying together?"

LAS VEGAS

IRA CROSSMAN TOOK THE tall, frail blind man by the arm and led him down the hallway of the raucous Circus Circus Hotel.

"I don't know what we're doing in a joint like this," said Ira. "We should be staying at Caesar's or the Mirage. They put seven hundred million dollars into the Mirage. You gotta see it."

"Too flashy," said Nathan. "Who needs to be conspicuous? Here I'm just another grandfather taking his grandson to the circus."

"Ain't I a little old for that?"

"No one's ever too old for the circus. I remember taking your father. Irving loved it. Miltie, he'd never come. Even when he was a little boy, Miltie acted way above it all. 'I don't like the smells,' he'd say. 'I don't like all those people.' I could never understand Miltie. To me, the circus was exciting. My father never had time to take me anywhere. He didn't care. I would have given anything for him to take me to the circus. So tell me what you're seeing, Ira. Where are we now?"

"The wedding chapel. A couple's about to get hitched. She's got big tits and doesn't look more than fifteen. He's wearing a red tux jacket and this baseball cap that says John Deere Tractors."

"That's Vegas. Vegas hasn't changed. I haven't been here for fifteen, maybe twenty years. Who can remember that far back? I kept away on purpose. Discipline. I don't have to tell you, Ira, I'm a believer in discipline. But how much longer could I stay in Miami Beach cooped up like a prisoner? I had to get away. Even for a just a couple of days. Just to smell the action. Where are we now?"

"The middle of the place, center ring."

"What's it like?"

"It's a zoo. Little kids and townies and tourists from Hicksville. Low-rent shit. You should see this trapeze broad. She's a hag. There's a dog show with a bunch of yelping poodles. And a million carnival games."

"Which one do you want to play?"

"None of them."

"Here," said Nathan, reaching in his pocket and handing Ira a couple of hundred dollar bills. "I want you to play the games. Maybe you'll win something."

"This is nuts." The grandson tried giving the money back but Silver refused.

"Do me a favor, Ira. Make an old man happy. They have ring toss around here? Your father, he was good at ring toss. He was the best."

With his grandfather on his arm, Ira walked over to the ring-toss booth. Within a few minutes he had won a giant green-and-yellow stuffed parrot.

"Let me feel it," said Nathan. "It's huge. See, I told you you were a winner. Now what about ski ball? Do you like ski ball?"

"I like craps."

"You'll go to the casinos on your own time. Today I'm taking you to the circus. Where are the clowns? How about the acrobats? Let's find the goddamn acrobats."

That night they ate alone in their room in a nearby hotel. The smell of stale cigar and cigarette smoke hung over the place. The orange-and-green bedspread was threadbare. The window afforded an expansive view of the world's largest recreation vehicle park. The air conditioner huffed and puffed, barely working against the oppressive heat of the August night. Gertrude, Nathan's companion nurse, had gone out alone. As he finished off his grilled fish and second glass of sweet wine, Nathan was still excited from his afternoon at Circus Circus. And, as often happened after drinking, his thoughts tended to wander . . .

"I remember when I first came to this city. It was 1948, 1949. I remember the Flamingo. That started the whole thing. You should have seen it. Bugsy Siegel was a wonderful manager. Meyer Lansky, he was behind it. It was Meyer's money. Me, I had nothing to do with no one. Sure, I heard this and that and because I was already in the music business I had plenty of opportunities to operate here. And it wasn't that I didn't love the place. I did. Big sky. Warm weather. Open spaces. And the women, Ira, we won't even mention the women. It was a grand city for a young man with a future, and maybe it still is, but me, I stayed clear. Do you know why, Ira? The lights. The lights were too bright. I worried about the lights. I worried about the publicity. When I was young I wanted my name on everything. That was the first thing that got me in trouble. When I first came to Vegas I had already been in trouble and I didn't need no more aggravation."

"What kind of trouble?" Ira hoped to hear something new.

"Ancient history. Who needs to go over it? The past is gone. Now is all that matters. I live for now. You see, that's why I'm here. Since Bernard Crossman died—it was four years in January—Nathan Silver hasn't left Miami Beach. Not once. And even when Bernie was still alive, what did Bernie really have to do after you went out on your own, Ira? Once or twice a year I'd visit you wherever you were working—New York, Chicago, I even went to see you in Fresno. That was nice, but when my eyes got sick so did my heart. Nathan Silver wasn't a bad man. A little grumpy, maybe, but that's because he was lonely. What did the poor schmuck have to live for? Sure, his printing company made him a good living, but he had no relatives, no one to give anything to. Then I got my brainstorm. Remember when I called and told you, Ira? If Nathan goes—I said—who would know? Who would care? I'm better off as Nathan. Let me say goodbye to Bernie. Bernie was never a happy man. He hated being a prisoner in the Witness Protection Program. It was jail. He wanted those people off his back. He wanted to move around again like a normal-type person. See, I wanted to help you, Ira, without being watched every minute of my life. Without some action I knew I'd die. That's the God's truth. When I lost your father—may he rest in peace—when I lost my Irving, I almost died then."

"You always act like it was your fault . . ."

"Why did he have to go to Detroit? I told him not to. It was like there was something in Detroit I'd left behind that *he* had to find. I begged him. I said, 'Irving, stay in Dallas. We have a nice liquor business. It provides. It's enough.' But it wasn't enough, and I could understand because he was a young man, like you're a young man, like all young men want more. They got to prove themselves. 'But why in Detroit?' I asked him. 'Detroit belongs to Pino Feldman. Pino knows every cockroach crawling in every alley of Detroit. Go to St. Louis, go to Cleveland, go anywhere but Detroit. I can't help you there. I can't leave Dallas.' Irving had a hard head. All my damn stories made him mad at Pino. He said he wasn't afraid of Pino. Why should he be afraid of Pino? Pino was in jail. But Pino had a son, and being in jail didn't mean nothing. Even in jail Pino could do whatever he wanted. He might as well be on the streets. Irving, may be rest in peace, was proud. He said he couldn't hide his whole life. He said he had two good friends who'd gone to Detroit to open restaurants and they needed help, they wanted a partner, and by then he was married to this *shiksa,* this Baptist country girl, and you were just a little baby and that was it. He took you and his *shiksa* off to Detroit. I worried night and day because I didn't think he had business sense. I asked Miltie to help him, but Miltie was busy at his fancy pants law school. Then Irving proved me all wrong. The first restaurant made money and so did the second—he had good partners, they were smart boys—and now they were opening a nightclub. Feldman's son was still a big shot and a power in Detroit, but he didn't know that Steven was Irving and that Irving was Ruby's son. For a year my son was happy. Doing fine. Then, don't ask me why, but I think it was liquor . . . He must have been drinking. Irving was no drunk but he liked to drink and sometimes he drank too much because when he drank he bragged and then he fought—your father was a fighter, Ira, just like you. That night he bragged about me, and about who he really was. I was the greatest this and he was the greatest that, and that's all it took. He called me and told me what happened and I said, 'Hide, run, get out of there.' But he wouldn't listen. He said he wasn't afraid. A week later they dumped his body in the parking lot outside the big Chrysler plant. They did things to his body that they didn't have to do. But I understood Pino. This was his way of getting back. I couldn't even go up there to get my son. I couldn't take a chance because they thought I'd been murdered back in Chicago. I had my family to protect. This was 1959. By the next year old friends of mine in Chicago, friends I can count on to this day, took care of Pino's son. You know the story, Ira. You know all these stories. You've heard me tell them before.

"Your mother, she was a nothing. She was a tramp, and right after this she disappeared. I call that woman filth, and I'm glad she left you with me. It was a blessing. I told Irving when he brought your mother to the house for the first time, I said, 'Be careful. What do you know about her background? She's not Jewish. She'll never understand you.' My Reba was the only mother you ever knew or needed. For two years she was a perfect mother. When she was dying in the Parkland Hospital—this was, let's see, the winter of 1961, there was a terrible ice storm—she said, 'Take care of Ira, Ruby. Now you're his mother.' See, your father took care of you, not your mother, because your father had a good heart. Irving was my favorite. Not that I didn't love Miltie. I loved both my children. When you have children, Ira, you'll see—there's no greater love than the love between a father and a son. I don't have to tell you, I worked like a dog so my sons wouldn't want for nothing. And they didn't. My wife, my children, my family always came first. *Always.* So

I ask you—why did Miltie come to hate me? How did he turn his back on the man who gave him life? He broke his mother's heart. How can I forgive him for that? This boy, this smart man, this *Ralph* Crossman . . . you shouldn't know the aggravation he's given me, Ira. Together, as a family, we would have been happy, big and powerful, no one would dare touch us. I had it all planned. Irving had the guts and Miltie had the brains and there'd be no stopping the two of them. I'd teach them everything I learned. I'd show them how to avoid all my mistakes and believe me, Ira, Gent Ginzburg made plenty mistakes. But the beauty part of a family is that sons learn from a father's foolishness. Except Miltie didn't see it that way. When we moved to Dallas and we had to call Miltie *Ralph,* Miltie forgot who he was. That was the end. I should have seen it but I wasn't that smart. I was busy hiding, starting a new life and trying to save my family. Did Miltie ever appreciate that? Did he ever once say thank you? Would that be asking too much?"

By now Nathan had raised his voice while Ira stared at the ceiling. He'd heard this stuff about Miltie before. As Nathan reached for the bottle and carefully poured himself a third glass of wine, Ira thought of stopping him. The more Nathan drank, the more he rattled on. Ira was ready to leave. His secretary Sherry was waiting for him back at the Mirage. He wanted to get high and he wanted to get laid. But he also understood the old man needed to talk.

"Can you blame a man for trying to save his family?" Nathan was saying. "That's the decision I had to make back when I turned against Pino. I knew what it would mean—no more business, no more music, no more friends. The hardest part was Eve. And Lowell too. I had an obligation to them. But family—do you hear me, Ira?—my family was my life, my blood. Who could have known that one of my sons would destroy his own family? Because as sure as we're sitting here, that's just what Miltie did. Every step of the way—when I tried to reason with him, when I offered him plans, when I told him his brother Irving needed his help—he turned his back on us like we were dirt. He treated me worse than that piece of shit Pino Feldman. Never mind that I paid Miltie's tuition and living expenses through college—Princeton, Columbia Law School—never mind that it cost me an arm and a leg. He wasn't too good for my money. He never refused a dime. But I could never visit him, I could never come to the college and meet his fancy friends and his famous professors. He was ashamed of his own father. Alright, I thought, forgive and forget. Let him be. Enough that I provided him with the best education money could buy. Let him be Mr. Big Shot. But when his own mother died, I called and I said, 'Miltie, come home. Miltie, I need you to be here.' And do you know what he told me? 'There is no Miltie,' he said. 'I'm Ralph, and I'm busy. I don't expect you to understand but that's the way it is. I'm not coming.' And that was that. It was worse than a death. It was an insult to everything I've ever tried to do. And the pain stayed with me—for years and years I carried it in my heart—until the day I found out about that article about your cousin David. That's when I knew that my patience had paid off. When I read about David's records and how he loved music I realized my plan would work anyway—not with sons, but, even better, with my wonderful *grandsons*."

"David's a shit. He hasn't called me."

"He will. Give him time."

"Where's he living?"

"In Malibu. David's like me. He loves the water."

"His father buy him a house?"

"David's a little confused right now," said Nathan, ignoring the question. "For the first time, he sees his father for what he really is. Such a thing is not easy. God only knows the pressure Ralph put on the boy to stay in New York and keep working at that fancy law firm. Ralph Crossman is a powerful man. But not powerful enough to keep this family apart. He tried once, and he thought he succeeded. But then you and David came along. My grandsons give me life. And now, with Bernie dead and buried a good long while, Nathan can start moving around. I'm back in Las Vegas and it feels a little like the old days because I'm waking up in the middle of the night and I'm getting ideas. For example, I'm thinking about the Silver Printing Company."

"What about it?"

"Remember you were telling me about Jay Feldman. You said the Japanese were bringing in Pino's grandson to run a record company. What's it called?"

"Sonsu Records."

"Sonsu Shmonsu. We don't need Japanese money. We need the same thing I needed back in the forties—a couple of acts and a couple of hits. We record it ourselves, we print the record sleeves—"

"Records are history. Now it's cassettes and CD's."

"What difference does it make? CD's have labels, right? There's printing . . ."

"There's a shitload more than just printing."

"Who you telling? I don't know about distribution? I don't know about rack-jobbers? I don't know about the trade magazines and the program directors and the hype? You're forgetting, Ira. I taught *you*."

"You taught me to be independent. You showed me how to be a promoter. You said, 'Work both ends against the middle. Work for everyone and no one at the same time.'"

"I taught you to do for yourself. And you've done beautifully, Ira, but I'm saying now we're a family and a team and we can do even more. We'll start small, we'll find our own artists and we'll make our own records—"

"Maybe that's what David wants, but that don't mean jackshit to me. Artists are a pain in the butt. You can forget your crazy artists. I'm strictly a middleman."

"Making a fifth of what you'd make if you were turning out a product instead of just being in the service business."

"I ain't giving up my service business. I worked too hard to build it."

"I'd be the last to tell you to give it up, Ira," said Nathan, getting out of the chair, stretching his long arms and taking a deep yawn. "Your service business only makes the whole thing better. Your service business is why no one will be able to touch us. It's why our record label will succeed while most others fail after a few months. All of us will get what we want—you, me and David—if we think big, if we think like a family and follow my lead, because, believe me, Ira, your grandfather knows just where he's going."

PARIS

"YOU TAKE YOURSELF VERY seriously," Carla Bari told Walter Gentry. They had been dealing with each other at arm's length, sitting in a sidewalk cafe watching a smoggy summer sun set behind the Seine. Many Parisians had fled the heat for the mountains and seaside, abandoning the city to wide-eyed tourists and beleaguered workers.

"Things are serious in America," Walter told her. "Especially in the arts, and particularly for blacks—"

"I don't think you like to see people having fun."

"You're wrong. The reason I'm here with you is to have fun."

When Carla had called Walter's hotel and asked him out he was hesitant—but only because he wasn't certain of her motive. After all, he'd only met her two days before in Montreux. And besides, Rita's remarks about Carla had been decidedly negative, calling her "a sexual manipulator." Well, Walter figured, wasn't his commitment to Rita more professional than personal? Carla exuded sex—and who was he to deny such a woman?

"I don't think you take me seriously," she said.

"You don't take yourself seriously."

"You're playing with my mind."

"Look, I have to be at a reception in a half-hour. Can we meet later?"

"We can, or we can go to the reception together."

"Fine, you'll probably know more people there than I will."

She did.

The reception, in a handsome nineteenth-century home in Paris' tony sixteenth arrondissement, was in full bloom. Kiko Ohisto, host and chairman of a multi-billion dollar Japanese electronics firm, was entertaining prominent members of the European entertainment community. Through media connections Gentry had learned of Ohisto's plans to start a new music label—Sonsu Records—and had sent a tape of Rita Moses. The New York office liked what they heard, phoned Walter and after learning he was on his way to Europe, invited him and his artist to this party in Paris. Only Rita's booking at a festival in Nice kept her from attending.

"We have international meeting of all my executives," Ohisto told Walter. "You must meet Mr. Feldman. He is here from New York. Mr. Jay Feldman, Mr. Walter Gentry." Kiko Ohisto then moved on.

Jay Feldman, in thin-framed aviator glasses, had a manicured short-cropped beard, dark nervous eyes and widow-peaked black hair pomaded and combed straight back. He had practically no eyebrows. His elevated shoes boosted him to only five feet five. His hands seemed too big for his arms, his ears too large for his head. His gray suit and blue Sulka tie seemed more conservative than his edgy disposition, as though he were using his clothes to legitimize his identity.

"I'm producing Rita Moses," said Walter.

"Who's that, pal?" asked Jay. He spoke with a slight lisp as he stood in a solid Napoleonic stance.

"Your jazz division in New York expressed interest."

"Jazz. Yeah, Kiko likes jazz. He's a fan, I'm not. He thinks there's money in it, I don't. But Kiko's the boss so I hired a jazz guy. He'll sign a couple of artists, put out a few releases. No big deal. Get in touch with—"

"I've already been in touch," said Gentry. "He was kind enough to invite me to this party. He wanted us to meet."

"Nice meeting you, pal," said Jay, looking around for an escape, "but I've been running a basketball league the past couple of years and I've mainly been reading the sports page. Now Kiko's got me back in records and I'm personally concentrating on heavy metal and pop acts. If you've got a Motley Crue or a New Kids on the Block, I'm all ears."

"I don't think even Mr. Walter Gentry knows quite what he has," Carla broke in, looking Jay over from head to foot.

"Are you an act?" Jay Feldman wanted to know.

"Actress," Gentry said. "Carla Bari, this is Jay Feldman, head of the Sonsu record label."

"Miss Rita Moses," Carla went on, "was the sensation of Montreux. I saw her myself. Extraordinary. All she requires is the right promotion and production."

"The production," Gentry snapped, "is my domain. We're dealing with a pure jazz artist—"

"Nothing in this world is pure," Carla said.

"I like the way you think," said Feldman, taking in the actress' long legs. "You live in Paris, babe?"

"Rome, but headed for L.A."

"Me too. Kiko wanted Sonsu headquartered in New York but I like L.A. I like the beach and I like the weather. I'll be looking for a building to buy but you can reach me at the Beverly Hills Hotel. Call me. You can tell me more about . . . what's her name?"

"Rita," said Carla.

"Carla has nothing to do with Rita," put in Walter.

But by then Jay Feldman had moved on.

* * *

"You shouldn't have stuck your nose in my business," Gentry told Carla in the cab speeding across Paris.

"Why? Because I helped hype you and your Miss Rita Moses? Because I talked business with a businessman? You may be an intellectual but business in fascinating to me . . . my father is a businessman and I've grown up around the species. The record business is especially intriguing, don't you think? and men like Mr. Jay Feldman are not selected by men like Mr. Kiko Ohisto because they are intellectuals like you but because they understand what Americans call the 'street.' I am fascinated by the street. Look out the window." Walter turned his head and saw a hooker give the high sign. "The street," Carla continued, "is the guts of the music that makes the money."

"We see things differently."

"Do we?" she said, and kissed Walter full on the mouth, her tongue speaking its own language.

When they arrived at the Plaza Athénée no words were spoken, none needed as Walter led her to her suite, where her passion and technique tested his endurance.

He passed the test, though in the morning ached from the effort.

"Come back to bed," she said then, her eyes only half-open. He pretended not to hear and slipped out of the room.

"The woman is mad," he muttered to himself as he took a long walk back to his hotel, where he drank strong coffee and read French music journals all morning long.

CHICAGO

1945

LEO AND HARRY RAMINSKI, sitting in the small back room kitchen of a South Side butcher shop, were about to eat dinner. Their mood was upbeat. The butcher, who knew they liked their steaks blood rare, always saved them the best cuts. The brothers were serious meat eaters. At thirty, Leo was five years younger than Harry although he weighed slightly more. Together, they represented a good seven hundred pounds. Their food capacity was legendary. Only last year in a Miami all-you-can-eat seafood restaurant the cook came out personally to shake the hands of the two men who singlehandedly had wiped out his entire supply of flounders, shrimps, scallops, oysters and clams. One look at the Brothers Raminski and the cook understood. Beyond their obesity, though, they were also oddly handsome, with thin noses, sandy blond hair and clear gray-blue eyes.

Except for an occasional grunt of satisfaction, they ate in silence. Tonight they were especially ravenous. Perhaps it was the freezing January winter, or the fact that it was an hour past their accustomed dinner time. They wolfed down their greens—each was given a salad bowl large enough to feed five—in minutes. Their T-bone steaks, nearly three pounds apiece, were served with mountains of creamy mashed potatoes and buttery lima beans. With their heads down and jaws snapping, the brothers took enormous bites, furiously shoveling in the food. When the butcher brought out dessert—a small but whole deep-dish apple pie per man—the Raminskis were still too focused on eating to notice his nervousness.

Harry stuck his fork in the pie and brought a combination of sugary crust and dough to his mouth. It tasted foul. Just when he was about to say something, Leo let out a high-pitched scream. Harry turned to see a fat white rat, its head partially severed from its blood-streaked body, dangling from the end of his younger brother's fork. Half of a rubbery tail was sticking out of Leo's mouth. Leo had swallowed the other half. Harry dug into his own plate of pie and found another rat, somewhat larger than Leo's, dissected into three sections—head, body and tail—floating among the gelatinous filling. Leo spit out the tail and gagged. Moments later he tossed up the contents of his hastily digested dinner onto his brother.

By now Ruben Ginzburg had made his entrance into the room. In his hand was a long butcher's knife, still dripping with the blood of rats.

"You fucks tell me what you've done with my people," he said, "or I'll shove this thing so far up your blowhole it'll come out your mouth."

Driving south through the frozen countryside toward Indiana, Ruby was feeling desperate. How in hell would he ever find his people?

An hour before, the Raminskis had called over their employee, the black man in the yellow Caddie, while Gent waited with them in the butcher shop. Leo was seriously sick. His nausea had turned to diarrhea when the driver arrived.

"Tell him where you took 'em," said Harry, himself on the verge of throwing up. "Tell 'em the truth. This guy is nuts."

"I dropped him off on the road to Hammond. Just on the other side of the state line."

That could be anywhere, Ginzburg was now thinking to himself as he slowly drove down the lonely two-lane highway. The wind was howling across the moonless night. A wet snow started falling and visibility was poor. *How in hell am I supposed to find anybody?* Gent wondered, worried that Duchess and Lord were freezing to death somewhere out there.

For long stretches the landscape was deserted. Finally Ruby saw a few shacks. He stopped and asked the occupants if they'd seen his artists. When they looked at him like he was crazy the Gent got back in the car and kept fighting the elements, driving into Indiana as the wind kicked up and the snow turned to sleet.

It was nearly midnight when he pulled over halfway between Hammond and Gary and spotted a building that looked like a renovated old barn. Black people were milling around the entrance. Gent got out of his car. Music was in the air. Inside the barn was sawdust, beer and the heavy perfume of reefer.

"You hung up on your looks," sang Duchess Silk from the makeshift bandstand, fans crowded all around, waving their hands, shouting encouragement. "You think you got it made . . . but when it comes to lovin' . . . listen here, Southside Velvet, you haven't made the grade . . ."

Next to her, Lord Foreman angled his gold tenor toward the ceiling, his derby cocked to one side, his eyes closed, his sound airy, smooth and soft as spring.

"What the hell happened?" Ruby asked them during the break.

"Good of you to drop by the gig, Ginzy," said a smiling Eve as she lit a Chesterfield. "We were worried about you."

"Worried about *me*? What about you two?"

"Cat gave me a ride home," said Lowell. "Most affable gent."

Duchess laughed. "Lord said, 'Head north, man, go north. Take us up to Evanston, take us to Winnetka, I got my people up in North Chicago,' So naturally the hood drives us in the opposite direction and throws us out of the car . . ."

". . . a mile from where I was born," Foreman told Ruby. "They should put up an historical marker for me."

"First thing Lord's people do," said Eve, "is ask us to play. Don't wanna hurt your feelings, Ginzy, but we got ourselves booked for a whole week."

"Ain't gonna cheat you out of your cut, though, Mr. Manager," promised Lord. "I know you got burnt bad at the Regal. It hurt my heart 'cause I wanted to play with Bean. How'd it turn out?"

"Don't matter," said Ruben, "long as you two are okay. Believe me, folks, nothing like that will ever happen again. Bet on it."

The war raged in the neighborhoods—first in Chicago, then Detroit—for over a month. Ginzburg was relieved. The alliance between Feldman and the Raminskis, which Ruby had long resented, had finally ruptured. At first, Pino was furious. He blamed it all on Ruben's obsession with music. But when he himself ducked a hail of bullets from a passing car as he drove in from Windsor, Canada, he realized anger was beside the point. He had to act. Within a week a half-dozen of the Raminskis' best Michigan men were murdered in a Dearborn used-car lot. Two days later Ruby's allies, Jersey Brotman and Charlie the Flower Man, were fitted with concrete shoes and dumped into the Chicago River. Back in Detroit, Fingers Markowitz, Pino's main man, was wounded by machine-gun fire seconds after leaving his mistress' apartment on Livernois Avenue.

While the skirmishes flared, the Gent moved his family—ten-year-old Miltie, nine-year-old Irving, and his wife Reba—out of their house into an anonymous motel in Joliet, forty miles from Chicago. Irving loved the adventure, but Miltie and Reba were badly shaken.

Ruben was patient. He did his homework. He waited until March when the Raminski brothers went to the cemetery to place a stone on the grave of their father, commemorating the first anniversary of his death. It was there, crouched behind a nearby headstone, where the Gent blew their heads off with a bazooka, inadvertently killing their sixty-five-year-old mother as well.

SANTA MONICA

DAVID CROSSMAN LOOKED OUT the window onto Ocean Avenue. This was the edge of America, the palm tree-lined promenade at the end of the line, the western extreme where the weather was mild and the living supposedly easy.

Not for David. David was struggling.

His new office represented a compromise. Operating out of his new home would be too confining. He needed to get out every morning and go where he'd feel part of the action. Driving ten or fifteen miles down the coast, even in traffic, was usually bearable. But traveling to Westwood, Beverly Hills or Hollywood was too much of a hassle, too similar to Manhattan. Why move across the country for an even swap? David wanted to upgrade. He wanted an ocean view even during working hours.

His small office—one room and tiny reception area—did face the Pacific, while David tried to face reality. He had too few calls to justify a secretary. A long way from the paneled offices of Ralph's firm. His calls to high-level industry leaders were rarely returned. His efforts on behalf of Tomorrow's News had reached dead end. He tried contacting Jay Feldman, whose new Sonsu Records was aggressively signing new acts, but couldn't get through Feldman's bitch of a secretary.

The city was filled with talent, in local clubs and even churches, but the singers and groups needed polishing, and to produce quality demonstration tapes or showcase performances they needed money. He had no income.

His one investment prospect, Carla Bari, had copped out. She'd called from New York weeks back cancelling her L.A. visit. Something about staying with her father who had just joined her at the Carlyle Hotel. "He insists I spend time with him," she told David on the phone. "But I'll be there, and this music, I just love how everyone is rapping and dancing and making money on this American music. I have ideas, I know we'll be working together and making musicians famous. You'll become famous, too. Just wait."

It was just more Carla Bari bullshit. He also figured his father had gotten to Calvino and nixed the idea of the Italian investing in a record company. David's contacts with Nathan had been minimal, mainly because he knew what the old man had in mind—collaboration between him and Ira. But Nathan knew what his grandson was going through; he understood David's resistance to Ira and had the wisdom to leave David alone. For now.

"You'll call me when you need to talk, and if you want to visit me, you're always invited," said the old man, not mentioning that he'd just returned from Vegas. "I know everything is changing for you, David, and, believe me, what you're doing isn't easy. It takes courage. I'm proud of you, taking a chance like this, going off on your own. Didn't I do the same thing at your age? Don't I remember how scary it is?"

The old man was his only real supporter, but he also remembered Nathan's blind spot when it came to Ira . . .

At ten-thirty the phone rang, his first call of the day.

"I'm just taking a chance," said the female voice, "that you're free for lunch."

"Margo? Margo Cunningham?"

"Will you meet me at the Bistro Gardens? It's been years since I've been there."

"When did you get in?"

"Last night. It was a last-minute thing. Can you believe that I'm in demand in Beverly Hills? A client in East Hampton recommended me to her sister who's redoing her house. She insisted I fly out, first class, all expenses paid, no questions asked. We meet at three and I was hoping I could see you before that. The Bistro Gardens at one."

The Bistro Gardens gave off a soft buzz—energy, status, money.

"It's a little hard to concentrate," David said to Margo after their first glass of Chablis. "One gets stars in one's eyes."

"I guess I find Beverly Hills vulgar," she said. "I hear my client favors Chinese modern. The prevailing style here is gaudy."

Margo was not gaudy. Her conservative slate-gray dress matched her eyes. Her Elsa Peretti brooch was a free form in silver. The shape of her face, the angle of her chin, the size of her nose, all said patrician.

"But tell me about you," she urged. "Are things progressing?"

"I'm not sure," he answered honestly.

"Your father . . . is concerned. He hopes you'll reconsider."

"Reconsider what?"

"California. You're throwing away all your advantages, and for what? You'll excuse my candor, David, but if you realized how much your father respects your ability you'd see why I so wish you two could find common ground. In his own way, Ralph needs you."

"I don't know anyone who appears more self-sufficient than my father."

"*Appears* is the right word. Beneath the appearance is a different Ralph, one who cares, above all about reestablishing a relationship with his son. Why else do you think he worked so hard to create the most respected legal firm on the east coast? It's his legacy, after all, and you're his sole heir."

David's head was filled with conflicting thoughts. He was tempted to tell Margo the truth. What would she think about Ruby Gent Ginzburg? After all, she was living with the same lie David himself had lived with for so long. And Ralph went right on perpetuating the lie. On the other hand, Margo wasn't a mean-spirited person, just a harmless and ambitious snob with decent intentions. And the fact that Ralph was saying some nice things about his son, even if he couldn't do it to his face, wasn't so bad to hear. In a way he supposed he even missed his father.

"Thanks, Margo, I appreciate what you're trying to do, but I'm trying to hang in here."

She was smart enough to leave it at that. She kissed his cheek on her way out, leaving before him and promising to give best regards to his father. David's afternoon was empty. Just as he got up to leave, he heard his name called. A few tables away he saw Ira Crossman signaling to him and went over to his cousin.

Ira was with a man who had a dark beard, swept-back black hair and jumpy eyes.

"Jay Feldman," said Ira, "meet my cousin David Crossman. He wants to get into the record business."

Even though David had tried reaching Feldman many times, Feldman obviously didn't recognize the name. He nodded, looking right past him.

"Call when you have a chance," said Ira. "I might have a little time next week."

"Been busy myself," said David, waiting to be asked to join them. Nobody asked.

"Was he at all receptive?" Ralph Crossman asked Margo as soon as she came back from lunch to their suite in the Bel Air Hotel. The night before had been rough for him. The recurrent dream about his father—alive and well in Miami Beach—haunted his sleep. In the dream, father wanted to reach son; Ruby wanted to reach Miltie, Bernie wanted to reach Ralph. And in real life, Ralph wanted to reach David, but didn't know how to show his feelings. Or risk the exposure . . .

"I think you should talk to him yourself, I really do. I had little effect."

"Did you tell him I . . . cared?"

"Of course I told him, but I also felt foolish and somewhat dishonest, knowing all the while that you were only a few miles away. Talk to him yourself, Ralph."

"If he's beyond reason what's the point?"

"To show him reason—that's the point. After all, you are his father. Why don't you call him while I go out for a while?"

"Where are you going?"

"I told you, my client's waiting for me at the decorator center. We're picking out fabrics. Call David."

Ralph did not call, and an hour later Margo was meeting her own parents at the Farmers' Market, an open-air old-fashioned tourist mart on Fairfax Avenue.

Her father's teeth were fixed but his white polyester sport shirt was stained. Mother's flowered dress looked like a housecoat. She had gained weight and looked bigger than ever. Margo may have loved these people with her child's heart, but the social climber in her was put off by their appearance.

"I knew you'd like Los Angeles more than New York," she said, kissing them both. "It's a calmer place. The weather's better and there's more to see. Come on, let's have a cup of coffee. I've gotten you VIP tickets for the Universal Studio Tour tomorrow. If things work out I should be able to meet you afterward for an early dinner. I won't be able to stay long, but whatever time we have together we'll have fun . . ."

Listening to herself, she felt like a shit, but she long ago had learned to handle it.

"You in the mood for a visitor?" asked Nathan. The call came at four P.M. after David's lunch with Margo.

"Sure," said his grandson, "but are you up for a trip?"

"I can manage. I just don't want you to feel like I'm imposing."

"It's your house," said David, "I'll pick you up at the airport. Tell me when."

He found he was looking forward to it.

NEW YORK CITY

RITA MOSES WAS ALSO on her way to a family meeting—a Friday night dinner. She looked much better than she felt. As she walked across the Village from her Great Jones Street flat to her parents' apartment, where she had been raised, on St. Luke's Place, she took her time. At summer's end the city air was humid and still. Children played on stoops, NYU students strolled down Bleecker Street, artists and tourists, poets and dope dealers, short-sleeved cops and white-bearded gurus all went their own way, sipping espresso in corner bars, buying beads, frozen yogurt and bootleg rock concert cassettes.

Rita knew it wasn't going to be an easy night, which was why it took her so long to make the short walk. She had not seen her parents for nearly two months, not since she had returned from Europe, not since she had been associating with Walter Gentry. She had kept them only peripherally informed, mostly with good news. Now that the news had changed, she was reluctant to give an accounting.

She stopped in front of the rent-controlled building just off Seventh Avenue. The small park across the street held happy memories. Papa brought her there every single Saturday, Sunday and holiday of her childhood. As a postal worker he never worked late or made out-of-town trips. He was the one man she could always depend on. But like Mama he was also conservative, uptight.

"You look awfully skinny," said Rosy Moses, a tall dark-skinned black woman who had once been thin herself. Now fifty, Rosy's girth had grown though she still bristled with energy. She hugged her daughter and looked her over again. She approved of the finely knit tangerine tankdress but worried about the weight. "Sure you been eating, sugar?"

"Sure I'm sure."

"I don't think you've been eating right. But, child, you sure gonna eat right tonight. Come set the table. Your daddy's downstairs helping the super fix a busted pipe. You know your daddy, helping everyone but himself. He'll be up in a minute."

The kitchen was filled with the aroma of Rita's youth, traditional sabbath dinner—matzo ball soup, roast chicken, crispy potato kugel. As the best-earning waitress and a twenty-year veteran of the Second Avenue Deli, Rosy had learned to cook for her Jewish husband in the style to which he was accustomed. At the same time neither she nor Rita participated in the lighting of the candles or reading of the Hebrew prayers. Hy Moses did that alone. Long ago he had agreed that Rosy would raise their child in Rosy's faith. Which meant each Sunday for many years mother and daughter took the subway to the Bedford Stuyvesant section of Brooklyn to hear the learned sermons of Reverend Gardner Taylor at Concord Baptist Church. When she was twelve Rita joined the choir. But by the time she was eighteen—eight years ago—she moved out of her parents' apartment and, much to Mama's chagrin, stopped attending church.

"Been to church lately?" asked Rosy as Rita reached for the white tablecloth in the hall closet. She peeked into her old bedroom and saw nothing had been changed—the Georgia O'Keeffe desert-flower poster, the quilt Rosy had sewn when Rita was twelve, the small framed photograph of her father he had given her when she was thirteen.

"Isn't it about time you did something with that room?" she asked, avoiding her mother's question.

"Your father would kill me. He says that's your room for life. If I'm good, he lets me go in there and sew. What about going to church with me this Sunday? I'll come fetch you."

"I'm singing Saturday night."

"Where?"

"Club out in Jersey."

"The one in Montclair? You played that years back. I thought you were doing better . . ."

Hy Moses walked through the door. "Rita! Hasn't anyone been feeding you? You better start coming round here more often so your mother can feed you."

Her father hugged her tight. He, too, felt thinner. "Doctor's orders," he told her. "Said I had to lose weight. But let me look at you. Pretty as a picture, that never changes."

Hy Moses, an unassuming man, stood several inches shorter than his wife, who was nearly six feet. His dark hair was thinning and he now walked with a stoop, making him appear older than his fifty-three years. Age had wrinkled his face and neck. His hands were delicate and he spoke quietly. Rosy was the extrovert, not Hy. Five years ago he was named manager of the Chinatown post office, where he'd been working for the past two-and-a-half decades. He quit high school in the seventh grade and considered himself lucky to have such a secure job. His one and only gesture of unpredictability had been marrying Rosy, an act that permanently estranged him from his family in Baltimore. Rosy's family—most of her people still lived in Mississippi—were more accepting, though only after the birth of Rita. It didn't matter to Hy and Rosy. They'd made a good life for their only child. They had savings. Each year they took a three-week vacation—to the Grand Canyon, Santa Fe or Lake Louise. They loved nature. They loved one another and just as importantly, they knew when to leave each other alone.

As Hy observed his sabbath ritual of candles and prayers, mother and daughter stayed in the kitchen, waiting for him to say "amen" before bringing in the food.

"Rita was saying she's singing in Montclair again," Rosy told Hy.

"I thought you were making a record," he said. "Didn't you say something about a record?"

"We're trying to get a deal, Daddy."

"Who's 'we'?" Mama wanted to know.

"Walter Gentry and myself."

"Is he the one who wrote that article?" asked Hy.

"The same," said Rosy. "He got her the work in Europe. He's managing her. Isn't that it, baby?"

"Not exactly."

"Has he gotten you a record contract?" Daddy pressed.

"You should have had one long ago," her mama put in.

"It's not that easy . . ."

"Now what about this David, the one whose picture was in the *National Enquirer?*" asked Rosy. "What's become of him?"

"Moved to California."

"How come?"

"He says he wants to manage talent."

"Can't *he* get you a record contact?"

"That wasn't a business arrangement," said Hy. "He was dating Rita."

"What difference does that make?" said Rosy. "These days it's all the same—"

"Wait just a damn minute!" Rita had to let it out. "You're already in my business and we're not even on the main course. What's wrong with you people?"

"*We* care, honey" said her father. "That's all."

"Can't talk to this girl," said Mama. "Can't say nothing. See, she's superior to all of us. Wants to be on her own. Thinks she knows what she's doing. No college, no nothing. Who needs college?"

"For Christ's sake, Mama . . ."

"Now she takes the name of her savior in vain. Lord have mercy . . ."

"You act like I'm falling on my face."

"You been singing in nightclubs for—what?—eight, nine years now. I'd like to see just one record. I'd like to hear you on the radio—just once. You still living in that nasty little apartment, still scuffling like—"

Rita was up from the table, threw down her napkin. "You're impossible!"

"Your mother means no harm, it's just—"

"It's just that no one understands me in this house—no one ever has and no one ever will!"

There were tears in her eyes as she ran out. Hurrying back to her place, she was upset by much more than her mother's attitude. After the initial excitement of being booked at two jazz festivals, things had cooled off. Walter was finding the transition from critic to producer not all that easy. Under his so-called tutelage Rita had been rejected by a half-dozen labels. Beyond that, she found herself thinking more and more about David. Was it because she wondered if he had better connections than Walter, or because she missed him? Either way, her mama's remarks about her career had hit home.

"Half-smiling through some tears, she was also annoyed that she'd lost her temper before eating Rosy's delicious baked chicken. Dumb. Rita looked at her answering machine for messages. There were three.

"I didn't raise no daughter of mine to be ill-tempered and ill-mannered!" It was Mama, of course. "I don't care how you treat your friends, but you will never stomp out of my house like that again. You owe me and your father an apology." Click. Rita sighed and decided she'd call Rosy in the morning.

"Rita," said the second message, "this is David." Her palms began to sweat. "Nothing much to report. It's just that we haven't talked in a while . . . How you doing? I hope you're making a record—I mean that, you deserve it. I hope that whatever happens we'll stay in touch because . . . well . . . I just don't want to lose touch, that's all . . ." Click. Rita started to call him back when the third message beeped on.

"Wonderful news, darling." Walter Gentry. "Marlon Tidewater, the head of jazz at Sonsu, finally got back to me. He offered us a deal. The production money is limited but I think I can push for a little more.

He's very enthusiastic about your voice and agrees with my concept of a pure jazz album—no pandering, no compromising. Isn't that great? I'm not sure whether it was that party in Paris—whether Kiko Ohisto received the tape I sent him or whether Jay Feldman didn't dislike me as much as I thought. Either way, we're in business. The artist advance is modest but that doesn't surprise me. After all, this is jazz. Marlon had some ideas about a rhythm section, but I assured him that I'd already selected the musicians. I told him I appreciated his input but I'd have to take primary responsibility for all production. He accepted that—he likes my writing—and only asked that we submit a list of songs as soon as possible. I agreed. So call as soon as you get in, honey, and congratulations. Patience, like they say, is its own reward."

Rita turned off the machine. The man sure had a way with words. Come off it, she told herself, the man has good news. Then why wasn't she feeling better? Why wasn't she at least calling her parents? This was her chance to show them that she was making it, after all. Why wasn't she phoning Walter back? Why was she just sitting there, in the darkness of her bedroom, staring in space and thinking of David Crossman?

CHARLESTON, SOUTH CAROLINA

1946

WITH ONE SUDDEN MOTION, Eve Silk took the long razor blade from under her pillow and cut the shaft of the man's engorged penis. Blood shot everywhere as his scream filled the room. He grabbed for her but not before she made another jab, this one at his neck. She missed, cutting his left eye instead. But he kept coming at her, kept reaching for her as she kept slashing, slitting his lips and tongue. They were both covered with his blood. It was only when she found her mark and finally caught his throat that he stopped his attempts to grab her, fell back onto the floor and rolled over, blood pouring from him.

Duchess threw on a robe and ran from the room. She wasn't thinking, only moving. It was drizzling outside, the March winds howling through a moonless night in a city she had never seen before. She wore no shoes, felt nothing except the need to get away, the urgency to keep moving, to where she had no idea. All she knew was that she'd cut a white man in the deep South and nothing mattered except getting away. She was running now—down cobblestoned alleys and up tiny pathways from another era . . . the Civil War, slave markets. Flashing in her mind was the black club she'd played that night and the taunting white men who had come to watch and the one who had followed her back to the rooming house and the sass she'd given him . . . "Get your ugly motherfuckin' ass out my way," she'd told him as she slammed the front door in his face. He went after her, kicked down the door and broke into her room, Silk realizing he was drunker and younger and stronger than she'd thought. And when he hit her across the face, when he grabbed her breast and ripped her dress and squeezed her crotch and threw her on the bed and yanked down his pants, she knew she had better cut this bastard and cut him good . . .

The light rain had stopped, the winds had picked up and she could smell the ocean somewhere near, she could smell magnolias and cat piss and lilacs and rotting garbage in the alleys. If only Lord Foreman had made the gig, she thought, this wouldn't have happened. But Lord was laid up in Chicago with a fever and chills . . . it was getting chilly here as she kept running, her feet torn by pebbles and stones. Ginzy had said he would come but she said no, Pino Feldman was celebrating his son's bar mitzvah in Detroit and Ruby had better go, Silk didn't want any trouble between Ruby and Pino, Silk could handle a mini-tour of Virginia and the Carolinas by herself, no big deal, picking up rhythm sections as she went along, making decent change, keeping it together until May when she and Lord and Ginzy were due to meet in New York and record, along with a big string section, a bunch of beautiful songs from *Porgy and Bess,* which was why she now felt like she was in some opera or dream, like it was all make-believe and none of this had really happened. Just pinch yourself and you won't have dried blood on your hands and fresh blood on your feet and the man with the crazed blue eyes wouldn't be bleeding and you wouldn't be running except she was running even faster on the outskirts of the city, over an old rickety bridge where she could hear the steady rhythm of waves breaking on a beach, breaking her own frantic rhythm, slowing her down. She fought for breath, walking through a swampy marsh, the wet soothing the battered bottoms of her feet, cool sand and an ocean beyond, moon breaking through racing clouds and the squawk of birds and reeds blowing in the Atlantic wind, a tanker on the horizon, sandcrabs scurrying by. She stepped into the water, thinking of going further, going under, ending the dream, the nightmare, starting over and washing the night out of her brain, the man and his mangled face and his putrid breath and his swollen cock and his bleeding blue eye and his bleeding mouth and the vein in his neck, water washing everything away, salty water so cold and clean against her skin . . .

An hour later, when she felt a strong tap on her shoulder, she wasn't sure where she was, what was dreaming and what was real. She had fallen asleep on the beach. Clouds had returned. The dawning sky was gray. The man standing over her was a cop pointing a gun at her nose. His badge said County Sheriff and his face seemed an older, fatter, weather-worn version of the face of the man who had tried to rape her. The crazed blue eyes were the same.

"Nigger," he said, tears in his eyes, "I wanna kick your brains in right now. I wanna kill you so bad I can taste it. But I want you to suffer. I want the sufferin' to last a long time. For what you did to my nephew I'm gonna make you suffer like no one's ever suffered before."

DALLAS

"THE ARCHITECTURE IS TOO trendy, *non é vero?*" Carla Bari asked her father.

They were alone in a wood-panelled office on top of the tallest skyscraper in the city. The flat urban landscape—patches of green, rings of freeways—sprawled in every direction. The Texas sky, cloudless and deep blue, stretched over the land. Nearby downtown office buildings looked like pieces of sculpture—glass cubes, green pyramids, sleek cylinders, post-modern arches and pillars, avant-garde angles of asymmetrical marble and gleaming steel.

"E *una citta richissima,* an extremely wealthy city," Calvino told his daughter, "filled with undervalued real estate. That's why I'm here." He was his usual immaculate self in double-breasted black wool suit and hand-painted silk tie of tiny white-and-silver dots. His bald head reflected the light from the circular walls of windows as he impatiently glanced at his watch.

"Look over there, *babbo,*" said Carla, pointing out the window. "That's the symphony hall. I.M. Pei's design. What do you think? I think it is too pristine, too cool. This city has imported all its good taste. They have bought their culture. Look at the streets. The streets are deserted. This place makes me nervous. It is too clean, too white. I must get out of here."

"You've just arrived."

"I want to leave. I want you to come to California with me."

"Ralph Crossman will be here any minute—"

"He is boring. I want you to meet his son David."

"I met David in New York. He seemed uncertain of himself."

"He has changed."

"His father is very smart."

"*Appunto*! So is the son."

"Carlina, try to understand. You are my daughter, my only child. I adore you and I'm delighted you came to see me. I'm truly sorry it has been so hard for us to spend time together, *tesoro,* but you know better than anyone that the demands on me are overwhelming. I am here, I am there, everywhere. As soon as Ralph Crossman arrives we close on this building. An hour later we open negotiations for a huge shopping center between here and Fort Worth, the biggest in the state of Texas. Many many millions are involved. We will be here for at least two more days."

"Then you'll meet me in California?"

"Then I am due in Milan."

"Fuck Milan."

"Why must you talk that way?"

"How else am I to get your attention? You're short-sighted. You see American business only as buildings to buy, parcels of land, savings and loans and these godawful shopping strips. I am trying to say that the entertainment—"

"The movie you convinced me to finance cost us nearly five million francs."

"The French. The French are ridiculous. I will never work with the French again. The director had a serious psychological problem. I admit I misjudged him. But the script was so good, the story was marvelous—"

"And the movie was never released."

"*Per fortuna.* I've never performed so poorly."

"You are a good actress, Carlina, and you came right back. Stay with your art. Leave business alone. Indulging you only costs me money."

"But I love business. I want to work with you. We need to work together. We're a great team, you and I. Acting comes too easily to me. I need the challenge of business—the business of the arts."

"Popular music is not the arts."

"Of course, it is. Music is exciting. It's the one area where I have personal knowledge. I'm an expert at this popular music. I travel everywhere. I dance at parties and clubs all over the world. I see trends before anyone. Carla has, as they say, a sixth sense for the sounds that make people dance. And this David, he is much the same."

"His father has advised me against getting involved in any record scheme."

"Why do you say scheme? Already you prejudice my proposal."

"What proposal? I've only heard talk. I've seen nothing on paper—"

"Then I shall produce paper—reams of paper, volumes, books. I'll produce so many proposals you'll be dizzy from the numbers."

"Good. Do that. Make me dizzy. But let me go over these figures," he said, pointing to the papers on his desk, "before my lawyer arrives."

"Mr. Crossman has arrived," a female voice announced over the intercom.

Calvino sighed. "Send him in."

Ralph entered with Margo Cunningham.

The lawyer was visibly tense. He had not been in Dallas, scene of his secret, humiliating teen years, for a very long time. He hated the place. This city held feelings of shame, memories of his own inadequacy. If he had to return, though, at least he was representing one of the world's leading landlords. He was coming back to buy the biggest building in town. He was also pleased that Margo had come along. Even in his late middle age, it was important to Ralph to mitigate his past as a high school nerd. At the same time he was still uneasy about his inability to confront his son David in California. Now, as a complete surprise, here was Carla Bari asking him, "Have you spoken to David?"

He coughed. "Not recently."

"I'm going to see him in Malibu. I'm going quite soon. I may even leave today. Do you know how he is doing?"

"I'm sure your information is more current than mine," said Ralph, not mentioning that he and Margo had just left Los Angeles that very morning. He quickly turned his attention to Calvino.

Margo and Carla were surprised to see one another. Still tense and exhausted from having squeezed in her parents' visit, Margo had little patience with Carla. She thought her pixie hairdo and flowered tights-under-denim-shorts outfit looked rather ridiculous. For her part, Carla considered Margo a blond Jackie-O clone, her Chanel canary-yellow dress a major bore.

"Perhaps you ladies can do a little sightseeing together while we conduct our business," Calvino suggested as he and Ralph, opening his Hermes attaché case and pulling out a set of legal documents, readied themselves for business.

"*Porca miseria!*" Carla said. "This is chauvinism in pure Italian form. Listen to *babbo*: 'There is important work to be done. The women must wait in the kitchen . . .'"

"Carlina, I said nothing of the sort—"

"We have a car and driver downstairs," said Margo. "And there's a section of the city I'm anxious to see. Come with me, Carla. It will be an opportunity to get to know each other better."

Carla resented Margo's interference, but she also was curious about New York so-called society women. Actually she viewed Margo as a high-priced hooker. Carla accepted the invitation.

A quarter-hour later the ladies were seated in the back of a cream-colored Mercedes limousine listening to strains of Debussy as they surveyed neighborhoods of spacious lawns and baronial mansions.

"I find this area quite elegant," said Margo. "Greer Garson told me that she lives here. Do you know her?"

"No. Hollywood is phony—"

"Greer is genuine. We should all look so good at her age. Aren't those flowers magnificent? Shall we take a stroll?"

The driver parked along a meticulously groomed park bordering a gently winding creek. Azaleas in pure white and various shades of pink were in bloom. Yellow daffodils encircled live oaks and lush ferns. Lily ponds floated on the still creek. Nursemaids in starched white uniforms pushed infants in navy-blue Aprica strollers while well-dressed couples strolled along the water's edge in a setting that seemed more English than Texan. The air smelled sweet.

Margo and Carla walked over an arched stone bridge, stopping on the other side to sit on a small wooden bench.

"Do you go everywhere with your Ralph?" asked Carla.

"What? Oh, no . . . my business keeps me in New York—"

"I didn't know you had a *business*."

Margo, with straight face, told about her career as an interior decorator for clients in Manhattan, Fire Island, the Hamptons, Newport and Palm Beach.

Carla yawned. "Why don't you marry Ralph?"

"You *are* direct, aren't you?"

"I'm curious about the Crossman men."

"They're different. But in some ways, alike. They're confirmed bachelors. And very ambitious."

"I think that's exciting."

Margo looked at the Italian. "I know you do. And to be direct myself, I'm not sure you wish them well."

"You're fucking one, I'm fucking the other. Maybe you'd like to switch?"

"How dare you—"

"If women aren't daring they wind up like you. Boring."

"I find bad manners boring," said Margo, turning from Carla and lighting a Virginia Slim.

Carla didn't pursue the verbal cat fight. She wanted a different sort of stimulation. She reached behind her ear and produced a neatly rolled joint, struck a wooden match on the sole of her shoe and took several long tokes to slowly light the thing. The tell-tale odor floated over the cool afternoon air.

"Have a hit, honey," said Carla. "You need it."

Margo got up and walked back to the limousine.

"Are you coming?" she finally called out to Carla after waiting a few seconds.

"Don't worry about me. Hurry home to Ralph. I'll hitchhike back."

As a child Carla had fantasized about being in movies, but since those fantasies had been realized they no longer much interested her. Staring into the motionless creek, Carla's restless mind moved to other fantasies—about the music business, about David Crossman, about living in Malibu; she had never lived in Malibu.

MALIBU

DAVID SAT ON THE floor close to the roaring fireplace, his grandfather in a nearby bentwood rocker. Outside a storm was brewing over the coast. The old man with his dark glasses, green polyester trousers and yellow cardigan sweater rocked back and forth to the motion of the crashing sea and swing music on the stereo. He had brought his own records from Miami—Jay McShann, Lucky Millinder and a song written and recorded by Eve Silk called "Defend My Heart."

"I want to tell you the story behind Silky's tune," said Nathan as he sipped from a mug of raspberry tea that Gertrude had made him before retiring for the night. It was one of the coldest Novembers in Los Angeles history, and even though David was glad to have his grandfather here telling him stories, his newly acknowledged emotional attachment to Nathan tended to embarrass him, make him uneasy. But since no one knew about Nathan Silver except Ira, his feelings were a safe secret, he told himself. The truth was that since he'd met Nathan and Gertrude at the airport earlier that morning David had been on a high. It was a relief to have company, a welcome interlude from his daily struggles with the closed doors of the music industry.

"You have no idea," said Nathan, his voice calmly riding over sounds of the driving storm and syncopated music of another era, "you don't know what went into the making of this song. It took a year, David—no, it took eighteen months if you count from the time the police called me from Charleston. I tell you the story because I want you to hear it the way it really happened, not the way the newspaper wrote it up. Never trust the newspapers, David. They're in business to sell newspapers not to tell the truth. If you're in the music business it's never easy—not now, not then, not ever. I suffered. My wife, my children, they suffered. Eve Silk, poor thing, she suffered. Look, David, I know it's been hard for you. You haven't complained, you haven't said a word, but I can feel what you're feeling because I've been there."

"All right . . . this was 1946. The war was over. The Japs, the Germans, they were beaten. Me, I missed the action because of my family and my work, I couldn't get away, but I followed the news and the news from Nuremberg said that they were going to hang Goering, the bastard, and the rest of Hitler's mob. I remember because I was in Detroit for Pino's son's bar mitzvah and I'd just left *shul.* It was a Saturday, and I was back in the hotel reading the newspaper when the call came."

"'Eve Silk is booked on murder,' the cop said.

"I didn't start yelling. I didn't go crazy. I knew I needed to be calm. 'Let me talk to her,' I said. Her voice sounded tired. 'What is this?' I asked her. 'They set you up?' There was a long silence and then she said, like it was nothing, 'Ginzy' she said, 'I killed this guy.' Now I knew Duchess better than anyone, and I knew she never lied or exaggerated. She was kind of the dame that if her ass itched, she scratched. No airs, no coverups, just take-it-or-leave-it. Real as rain. I loved that about her, David, but it also scared me to hear her admit to this thing because I knew she was telling the truth."

"'Look,' I said, 'just don't say nothing to nobody. Soon as I get off the phone I'm seeing about coming down there right away—today, to-night, I'll be there quick as I can. Sit tight and for God's sake, keep your mouth *shut*. Remember where you are.' First thing I do is call Pino. I didn't even wanna tell him what happened 'cause I know he's gonna say, 'I told you so,' but the thing is, Pino is still Mr. Big in Detroit and since I helped the Raminskis retire he's also got a nice chunk of Chicago and he's feeling good about me, so he laughs. He says he's seen this coming ever since he laid eyes on the bitch. 'Let her rot in jail,' he says, but I say, 'Look, Eve Silk's an investment, a damn good investment that's starting to pay off,' and he knows I'm right and he says why don't I call Nushky Gold, the lawyer in downtown Detroit we use all the time and I say, 'Nushky's alright, but I gotta have someone better, boss, I gotta have the best' and he laughs again and calls me a fuckin' pain in the ass, but okay, he says, call Mr. Flower Lee at a certain number and I say I don't need no shirts laundered and I don't want no wonton soup and Pino says, 'Schmuck, Mr. Flower Lee is the most brilliant fuckin' criminal attorney in the country. He's in New York City and you better be prepared to pay through the nose and even then he might not take your case except if you mention me 'cause he's gotten big business out of Detroit and he knows who I am.' "

"So I call Mr. Flower Lee and he talks like a real American, no Charlie Chan accent or nothing, and I can tell he's very sharp by the way he's asking questions, and he says he needs a certain advance and I say okay whatever you need 'cause it's a matter of life and death. 'Wire this advance to New York,' he says, 'and meet me in Charleston.' "

"Now Charleston's a cracker town. I remember it was hot and humid, and there was pretty trees and flowers and old hotels and big houses, but believe me, it was a cracker town. And when I see Silky, and when she starts telling me how this guy was gonna rape her and how she cut him and how he turns out to be the nephew of the sheriff, I start thinking it's all over, they'll be hanging Duchess from the tallest tree before spring turns to summer. And I'm not saying Silky's going crazy 'cause she's not. Silky's one strong woman. But she knows she's killed a guy, and she's very fuckin' worried and you'd think she wouldn't be writing a song, but that's just what she's doing. 'Got this melody in my head, Ginzy,' she says. 'I can't get rid of it.' And she starts humming and asking what I think of it and I think it's fine, it's beautiful, 'but, baby,' I say, 'this isn't the time to be writing songs because we got this here problem.' 'Wanna get this song out,' says Silky, 'before the problem eats me up. I ain't sure I'm gonna get past this problem.' 'I am,' I told her, 'I got this lawyer.' "

"In walks Mr. Flower Lee. I wish you could've seen this guy, David," said Nathan, taking another sip of raspberry tea as the storm grew more violent, lightning flashing over the ocean, thunder crashing down the coast on Santa Monica Bay. "Mr. Flower Lee was a midget. Well, maybe not exactly a midget, but I'm telling you, David, he was a very small man, but nicely dressed—sharp suit, gorgeous fabric. I could see he had taste and a way with words. They flowed out of him like he was reciting Shakespeare or something. If you closed your eyes you'd think he was an Englishman, that's how beautiful he talked, taking notes with a gold pen, crossing his t's and dotting his i's and talking like he's got a case, a solid self-defense case while I'm thinking—how in the hell is a jury in South Carolina gonna take to a fuckin' Chinaman in a Brooks Brothers suit? Meanwhile, Silky's whispering to me, 'Get Lord down here, you gotta find a studio for me and Lord, we gotta cut this record,' and I'm looking at her like she's nuts 'cause her neck is in the noose and she's talking about some cockamamy song."

"Was there a trial?" asked David, mesmerized by the old man's story.

"Was there a trial! I brought you newspaper clippings from South Carolina, California, Chicago and even over in Europe. The case made headlines all over the world."

"Tell me about—"

A buzzer interrupted David, who reluctantly got up and went for the front door. Standing there was Ira Crossman.

"Grandpa called. He said you wanted to see me tonight."

"I did?" said David, angry that Ira had arrived just before the climax of the story and, even worse, that he was barging in on Nathan's private visit.

"Of course David wants to see you, Ira," said Nathan from the rocker. "Invite your cousin in, David. Make him feel at home. Make him a cup of coffee. He likes his coffee black and strong."

CHARLESTON, SOUTH CAROLINA

1946

MR. FLOWER LEE HAD just addressed the jury, and the Gent was impressed. The Chinese-American, immaculately turned out in a black serge suit, could not have been more eloquent. He had even quoted Jefferson Davis on justice, a brilliant tactic down here in the Deep South.

From where she was seated, though, Eve Silk didn't exactly share her manager's confidence. In spite of his reassurances, she expected the worst. Her mother's brother had been lynched in Georgia. She'd been told that the Klan had stolen her father's family's land in Kentucky. This all-white jury had little sympathy for a dark-skinned torch singer, especially someone who spoke with confidence about her place in the entertainment world.

Besides, she had killed the son-of-a-bitch, and said so. The prosecuting attorney had to do no coaxing. "I knifed him," she announced in the courtroom, "and I'd do it again. It was his life or mine."

"I didn't ask for your interpretation, Miss Silk," said the Clemson graduate, blond-hair blue-eyed lawyer, former marine and potential candidate for governor of the state. "I just asked you if you did it."

"I said I did it. Said I had to."

"You're interpreting again."

"Please restrict yourself to answering the questions," the judge instructed Eve.

"What indications did you have that the deceased intended you harm?"

"Kicked in the door, threw me down, slapped me—"

"Before or after you cut his genitals and—"

"Can't remember. It all happened real fast."

"You cut him before he had time to act."

"Damn straight."

"Yet eye-witnesses have testified that your show, only minutes before, had been itself an act of provocation, that you singled out the subject and sang directly to him, dancing in front of him, gyrating your hips, thrusting your pelvis, virtually promising sexual favors—"

"Bullshit!"

"Miss Silk," said the judge, "you will restrain yourself . . ."

"Can't listen to lies. Won't let him . . ."

And so her testimony went, a bad day on the stand for the Duchess.

That evening Mr. Flower Lee had been candid with Ruben. "It's not going well," he said. "She's arrogant. She's too sure of herself. I've tried to tell her that being at least a little contrite might soften the jury."

"You can't tell Silk nothing."

"She has to realize that the forces in this city have gathered against us to such a degree that—"

"I want more press here," Ruby interrupted. "Life magazine sent someone, but where's the Saturday Evening Post? And the New York papers? Is there a reporter from the *Times*?"

"There are more reporters than spectators. That's the least of our concerns, Mr. Ginzburg."

"You're a lawyer, Mr. Lee. You keep lawyering. Leave the promotion to me."

The summation against the Duchess had been devastating. The prosecutor kept reminding the jury of the dead boy's long line of character witnesses who had testified to his sterling reputation—his eighteen-year-old wife, teachers, friends, deacons, ministers and, of course, his uncle the county sheriff.

"This category of lewd music," said the clear-eyed prosecutor, "this category of singer, is seduction personified." He then quoted from the song Duchess herself had written, "Silky Web":

"'Silky web,' say the lyrics, 'I want to pull you into my silky web.' Could the message be any clearer? Could the intent of this so-called artist, this striptease dancer, be mistaken by anyone? Her act is an open invitation for men to follow her into that web. One such man—more vulnerable than most, perhaps weak of the flesh—heeded her savage siren's call. Then, so she says, she had a change of heart. And so, right then and there, without so much as a mark on her own body, without any indication that she herself had been touched, she murdered the unsuspecting boy, snuffing out a life of only nineteen years, a life of promise and hope."

She's dead, Mr. Flower Lee thought to himself, certain that this time his powers of persuasion were useless.

In the very back row, where blacks were forced to sit, Lord Foreman, down from Chicago, thought the same thing.

She's dead, the sheriff thought confidently.

The judge's instructions to the jury left little doubt about his sentiments. He, along with the rest of the city—indeed the whole white South—seemed especially infuriated by the killing. As the jury retired for deliberation, the courtroom emptied out into the street.

The crowd outside the Charleston County Courthouse was buzzing. Foreman wore a wide-brim straw hat to protect his head from the summer's heat. He went over to Ruby, busy writing in a small notepad. "Not looking good," said Lord.

"You kidding?" asked the Gent. "Look around you. I've counted over twenty-four reporters. This weekend we drive to Pittsburgh. They wouldn't let her out on bond, we couldn't record that song, that 'Defend My Heart,' but we'll cut it this weekend, I swear on my mother's life we will. It was Silk's idea, and Silk was right. We need to record."

"You're crazy, Ginzy. You done lost all your sense."

"You're a wonderful singer, Lord, better than even you think you are. I think you should sing more. The people love it when you sing."

Foreman walked away, shaking his head.

No decision came that afternoon. That night, in a boarding house on the other side of the Ashley River, Lowell Foreman drank and prayed. He asked God to save Silk's life—because she was an honest woman, a good woman who didn't mean anyone harm. If she had killed, it was because she had to. Finally the whiskey put him to sleep, but when he dreamed he saw Silk sitting in an electric chair, the currents shooting through her, her body twitching from the charge, collapsing, slumped over. He woke up with a start.

He went to the courtroom around nine A.M. and waited with the others. It was a humid, puffy-clouded morning. The Gent, dressed in big-padded sky-blue suit and hot pink tie, was talking to a newspaper man from Baltimore, making sure the reporter knew the names of all Eve's records. Ruby called Lord over. "This is Lowell Foreman, the great horn player," he said. "Wrote and sang 'Southside Velvet' with Silk. Big hit from coast to coast—"

"Jury's back in!" someone yelled.

Still singing Eve's praises to the reporter as the crowd filed inside the courtroom, Ginzburg took his seat on the front row. Lord went to the back, remembering his dream, his throat dry, his empty stomach contracting.

Eve was called in. In spite of the prisoner gray, she carried herself with dignity. She may have expected the worst, but she would never break down in public, not the Duchess.

"Have you reached a verdict?" asked the judge as he turned to the jury.

The foreman of the jury, a heavyset man with thick glasses and strong southern accent, stood up and cleared his throat. "We have, Your Honor."

"How do you find the defendant, sir?"

"We find her not guilty, Your Honor, by reason of self-defense."

The courtroom gasped. The judge, the sheriff, the blood-thirsty spectators turned apoplectic. Lord Foreman let out a cry of relief. Silk hugged a stunned Mr. Flower Lee. She turned to find the Gent, but Ruby was in the middle of the reporters giving out statements.

"Your wife and daughter should be home by the time you get there," Ginzburg whispered to the apprehensive jury foreman a few minutes later. "Their little boat ride is over."

A minute later, having anticipated that the mood might turn ugly, Gent whisked Eve and Lowell into a big Buick driven by his associates from Detroit. They were on the highway, speeding north, before anyone knew it.

By the time the recording session was finished in Pittsburgh, photos of a smiling Duchess appeared in newspapers from California to Connecticut. "Defend My Heart" was shipped to record stores two weeks later, an immediate hit. Reporters who wrote about the trial also wrote about the song. Record stores couldn't keep it in stock. For the first time, Eve was selling to curious whites as well as devoted black fans. By the time the Marshall Plan to rebuild Europe went into effect, Eve Silk was a bonafide nationwide star in a country clamoring for popular music, music reflecting the hard-won peace, free-flowing music offering relief from years of nightmares, images of a psychotic Hitler. Mellow funny sweet-drinking dance-and-romance music was all the rage. The short supply of shellac during the war had left the public starved for records. Everyone wanted records. The boys were back home; money was back in circulation. The music business was exploding. This was the moment the Gent had been waiting for.

HOLLYWOOD

DAVID WAS SEATED IN the posh reception area of Sonsu Records, the walls lined with gold records, the sleek side chairs and low-slung couches forged from chrome and olive-green suede, the smoked-glass coffee tables covered with magazines—Billboard, Cashbox, Black Radio Exclusive. The wait to see Jay Feldman seemed interminable. David had more time than he wanted to think about the circumstances that had brought him here.

The night of the storm, the night Ira arrived, had given David new insights. For the first time, he saw his cousin and grandfather side-by-side. The interplay was tricky. The old man's motives had been clear from the start—he wanted to bring Ira and David together. He had come to California now to force the issue. But it was obvious to David that Nathan hadn't told Ira that he had bought the Malibu house. On the other hand, Ira was quick to mention the trip he and Nathan had recently made to Vegas. Nathan was not pleased with Ira's revelation; he wanted neither cousin to feel like the favored grandson.

Ralph had indoctrinated his son with the notion that good lawyers are first of all good listeners. "Evaluating a situation in silence," Ralph would say, "always strengthens your position." Well, between Ira and Nathan, there was a lot to evaluate.

On one level, they merged . . . Ira was Nathan as a young man, aggressive and shrewd. But on another level Ira was far more conservative than Ruben Gent Ginzburg. As an independent promoter Ira had a niche he wanted to protect. He also lacked any passion for music, which was why David was so important to Nathan. Nathan needed both his grandsons . . .

"This Jay Feldman connection is solid," Ira had said as the storm subsided. He ignored David, talked directly to Nathan.

"Watch your back," warned Nathan.

"I'm watching everything," said Ira, "and I'm seeing this guy's got Jap cash up the ass. They understand promotion is muscle and muscle is money. He's given me over a million to break his first four singles. I'm charging him twice what I charge everyone else, and he doesn't give a shit. He likes it 'cause he wants me to personally service his acts."

"Has he mentioned Rita Moses?" asked David.

"Who's she?"

"A jazz singer signed to Sonsu."

"Fuck jazz. Jazz ain't no money. This is heavy metal, rough rap, dance."

"David's been telling me," said Nathan, "about some talent he's found."

"Oh yeah?" asked Ira indifferently. "Who?"

David described Tomorrow's News.

"You got a tape?"

"I'm working on one."

"When it's done maybe I'll send it around."

"Why not have David take it around himself?" said Nathan. "Maybe Jay Feldman would like it."

"I thought you were against me working with Jay Feldman," Ira reminded his grandfather.

"Why not sell him the idea of a subsidiary label?" Nathan said. "We don't need his money for recording costs. We got money of our own. All we need is distribution. Didn't I do the same thing with his grandfather?"

"One fuckin' act," said Ira. "David's only talking about one act."

"One act is all we need."

Nathan was obviously excited by the idea of history repeating itself.

"Why should Jay fund an indie when he could finance it himself?" asked Ira.

"Because that's the only way David's act is being offered. We're starting our own label."

"Feldman's no fool."

"Neither was his grandfather. Pino had smarts, I'll grant him that, except for one thing—he never understood that whoever controls the talent controls the profits. When it came to dealing with the artists, Pino was never home. I was the one who dealt with the artists. And that's just what David's going to do."

"Look, I get paid to get records played. Period. It's a simple business. It's made me a lot of money. It's built me a big company. I know what I gotta do and I do it. Why screw up a good thing?"

"To build a better thing, Ira. Can't you see it? David's coming in with a new angle—"

"Dave or you?"

"All of us. I keep telling you—we're all working together."

Bullshit, was what Ira thought and didn't say.

"Never mind costs," Nathan told David, "just make sure it sounds good." So while Gertrude took Nathan for walks on the beach in the afternoon, David was down in Inglewood helping the band select the tunes to record.

"Everything we got is kickin'," said Gemini Star.

"Let's go with the dance stuff," David said. "Things like 'Malcolm in America' will go on the album for sure. But first I want these suits to see we can sell records."

"Was it different in the old days?" David asked Nathan when he reported in that night.

"Old days, new days, it's all the same. It's dance music. Benny Goodman said 'Let's Dance' and made a killing."

"The killer is 'Get It While It's Hot,'" said Gemini Star the next day at Westlake audio on Beverly Boulevard where Michael Jackson and Quincy Jones had recorded *Thriller* and *Bad.*

Your love invites me
Your sexy dance excites me
You cause stimulation
Raise my anticipation
The way you tease is shocking
Now's the time to start rocking
Get it while it's hot, baby
Get it while it's hot

David rented a forty-eight-track board at the studio for a week. He brought in an engineer who'd been recording Janet Jackson and Babyface and together they worked fourteen-hour days—Gemini Star, Plucky P, Isaiah Z, Dale Summi, Greg Casey—devouring gallons of apple juice, cartons of Chinese food, tins of pretzels, stacks of tortillas, tracks of smokin' house music, the nervous hip hop hype hard as it could get.

"Make your artists comfortable," Nathan advised David as Gertrude, before going off to knit, served the two men a clear-morning breakfast on the patio overlooking the ocean. "If they have talent like you say they do, they know their music better than anyone. That's the way it was with my Silky and Foreman. Other people told them this and that. Me, I said nothing. I sat there. I asked them whether they wanted cream and sugar in their coffee. Maybe after hearing one version of the song I'd say, 'You know, as great as that was, I'm wondering if it could be even better? But you decide. You do what you want.' And you know what, David? They'd usually do it over and it'd usually be better."

David took the old man's lead. He let Gemini lead. He took a backseat. But when he did say something—a suggestion about background vocals or guitar fills—he was usually paid attention to. He was happier than he'd ever been. It wasn't work, it was joy. As he watched the process unfold, as he saw the layers of music build—the flavors and rhythms and sounds—he felt privileged to have anything to do with the magical process. More than ever, he knew the band was sensational.

He also knew he was being manipulated. Nathan had put him in Malibu and now, through Ira, he was putting him in touch with the very record executive David had never been able to get to. But unlike Carla—whose California trip had been cancelled again, this time because of a director auditioning her in Denmark—at least Nathan was constant support, and he cared. He was, after all, helping his grandson get what he wanted, a chance to boost his band. Nathan understood the obsession of music.

Months back when David had first heard of Jay Feldman he'd asked Nathan whether it was the same Feldman family from Ruby's Detroit days.

"Ira says he's the grandson or something, but who really knows? And who cares? Pino Feldman and his son are long gone. Scum. Rotten to the core. Best thing I ever did was put those bastards away. You see, David, I'm still here, and so are my grandsons. We're not just surviving, we're conquering. With Ira's promotion and now your production, we're just getting started."

David worked his way through the most creative week of his life. The end result was an audio cassette with two songs, the tape David now carried in his pocket as he was called into Jay Feldman's office.

Feldman looked Mephistophelian—widow's peak, black razor-thin beard, unsettling eyes—Now he sat behind a shiny lacquer desk that rested on a riser, elevating the diminutive Jay above his much taller guest. The office had a commanding view of the buzzing Hollywood Freeway below. On a long credenza behind Feldman's desk David noticed a cassette marked "Rita Moses."

"Rita Moses is a friend of mine," he told Jay after the man shook hands. "How's her record?"

"Just came from New York. Haven't heard it. Probably won't. She's gorgeous, but she's jazz. The Japanese like jazz. Maybe it'll sell over there. So Ira says you've got something. What is it, pal?"

"Tomorrow's News," and David handed him the tape.

"Got a picture?"

"Not yet. Just the music."

"They white, black, what?"

"Mixed."

"Mixed is no good. Mixed doesn't sell. It's easier, one or the other."

"Just listen," said David, adopting Jay's clipped business tone.

Feldman slipped in the tape. "Get It While It's Hot" exploded like a Mike Tyson uppercut.

"This shit will sell," said Feldman before twenty seconds went by. "I want it. But it's a black sound, pal. Make it an all-black band. That way we'll break 'em on the black chart and cross over to pop. No problem. I'll be generous. I'll give you a couple a hundred thousand. You'll be a hero, Crossman."

"It's not that easy. They don't want to change personnel and I don't need a record deal for them. They're the first act on the David Crossman label. I'm not looking for financing, Jay. Just distribution."

"Ira didn't say nothing about that."

"It's not Ira's deal, it's mine."

"Your cousin got you in here. Now you're saying that you two ain't together."

"I want you to hear the rest of the tape. And then I'd like you to hear the band. We'll be showcasing at the Roxy in three weeks."

"Wait a minute, I thought this was an exclusive. Now I see all you're doing is inviting me to a fuckin' auction."

"An exclusive would require an option."

"You sound like a damn lawyer."

"I am."

"Alright, look, Crossman, I like this band, and we'll work something out. I understand Ira and I understand you, and we got money and we ain't afraid to spend it."

"I also think I can do something with Rita Moses."

"What does she have to do with anything?"

"She's being produced wrong. She's more than pure jazz. She could have hits like Regina Belle. She could sell like Anita Baker. She's as good as Diane Reeves."

"Now you're a producer?"

"I know you're busy, Jay, and I'll get out of your way. I just wanted to make you aware of what I'm doing—"

"I'm aware, I'm *aware*. I'll be in touch with you and Ira before the end of the week."

David left feeling like clicking his heels. Beat the hell out of torts.

ALBUQUERQUE

IT WAS THE NICEST trailer park in the city. A brilliant sunshine was melting the previous night's snowfall, the first of the season. The air was crisp and the white-capped mountains, far in the distance, rose high into a sparkling blue sky. Looking out his tiny window, the diminutive old man, stooped over but still clear-eyed, sipped his coffee and surveyed the broad New Mexican mesa. He liked what he saw. Only the ringing of the phone interrupted his pleasant reverie.

"Hello," he said impatiently.

"It's me. Jay. You'll never guess who walked into my office."

"I don't like guessing games, Jay. Just tell me."

"Another Crossman."

"Must be Miltie's son."

"I don't know, but his name's David, and he's working with Ira."

"You call them Crossmans. I call them Ginzburgs. I know them for who they are. So now you got two of them working for you."

"Or against me—you tell me."

"I'll tell you that it's awfully goddamn interesting. Remember, I promised you the basketball league would be interesting. Well, it was. In no time it made for you what it takes others a lifetime to make. We took care of all our friends and they took care of us—concessions, a cut of the gate, a fix on the players, the whole thing. We got in right and we got out right. I can smell the same situation at this Sonsu."

"So can the Crossmans. They want in."

"Let 'em in. Use 'em. But keep the fuckers on a short leash."

"I don't trust them."

"Why should you? They're a family of traitors. They destroyed your father. They tried to destroy me. And then, like rats, they hid. But now they smell the cheese and they're coming out. All we gotta do is be patient, lead 'em to the trap and watch their fuckin' heads snap off. Meanwhile, you got the key to one of the biggest Jap banks, and you can take whatever you want. Just remember, we have friends to help, people we have to let in."

"I'd never forget."

"I know you wouldn't, Jay. You're all I got."

"You feeling okay?"

"My days are alright. I sit. I have a nurse, I have a therapist. I'm lucky to be living. I'm ninety and I can still make my own breakfast. But my legs are weak. My back is no good. And my nights . . . I'm up running to the bathroom every half hour. Sometimes I don't make it. Sometimes I don't sleep. He's supposed to be dead and buried but I never believed it. I keep dreaming he's alive. I keep feeling like I gotta get him."

"Get who?"

"The Gent."

"That's crazy."

"I know it is," said Pino Feldman, who, just the year before, after nearly four decades in prison, had finally bought his freedom from a cooperative parole board. It had cost him over two million. "But this dream," he told his grandson, "it doesn't go away. Every night I see him. Every night I hear him. I don't care what you say, I feel like the son-of-a-bitch is still plotting against me."

PART TWO

LOS ANGELES

DAVID CROSSMAN, CARLA BARI, Walter Gentry, Rita Moses, Ira Crossman, Jay Feldman, each tried to play it cool. Of course, it was an act, since they were all enormously nervous and excited to be at the Shrine Auditorium for the Grammy Awards and in the presence of Miles Davis and Madonna, Barbra Streisand and Bobby Brown, Bob Dylan and Linda Ronstadt, Prince and Paul McCartney, Jimmy Jam and Terry Lewis and George Michael and Kool Moe Dee and John Cougar Mellencamp.

David was most apprehensive. After eighteen months of living in Los Angeles he felt the battle lines drawn around him. Carla was by his side—after all, she had encouraged him to record Tomorrow's News' first album, she had invested in him—but she herself was too crazy to offset his nerves. In fact, she had brought a boom box—a gigantic Sony ghetto-blaster—and switched it on, broadcasting Tomorrow's News smash song, "Get It While It's Hot," right in the middle of the ceremonies. Security men managed to pry the bulky machine away from her, but only after she slapped one and kicked out at another. Paparazzi recorded the event. "Win or lose," she whispered to David, "we've won the publicity war." She smiled happily at her cleverness. David tried to wear a straight face.

But who would win the Grammys? Although Rita's album wasn't a huge seller, the critics had applauded her and her debut album, *Lullaby of Birdland*, which resulted in her nomination for Best Female Jazz Singer. David had seen her only a few times in the past two years, and both times had been strained. Their attraction for each other hadn't diminished. If anything, separation had fueled the old fire. It was "circumstances," they both suggested, that kept them from renewing what they had had, although neither could be sure what exactly that was. Besides, in matters personal and professional, they were, in their fashion, involved with other people—David with the unpredictable Carla Bari, Rita with Walter Gentry. Their lives seemed to be moving in opposite directions.

But not tonight. Tonight they were separated by only a few aisles, and when the announcement for Best Female Jazz Singer was made, and when Rita was mentioned as a nominee, and when the presenter, Harry Connick, Jr., paused and teased and paused again before announcing the winner, David felt a knot in the pit of his stomach. He was rooting for Rita, and deeply disappointed when she lost.

The next Grammy was for "Best Rhythm-and-Blues Duo or Group." Rita liked Tomorrow's News—she liked their energy, she felt David in their work—and was delighted when they were nominated. Now she wanted them to win. Stevie Wonder played a waiting game at the podium before finally announcing after a good thirty seconds that an older, more established group won. Rita turned and gave David a look of sympathy. David acknowledged it. Walter didn't notice. He was still full of himself after his essay on the art of jazz singing, reproduced on the cassette and compact disc for *Lullaby of Birdland,* had been selected as "Best Liner Notes." *He* had won a Grammy.

The big winner, though, was Pino Feldman's grandson Jay. His Sonsu label had swept six big awards for Heavy Metal and Pop. Nightmare, the raucous white group Feldman had discovered, dominated the evening along with Sashee, a sexy new female dance sensation. In each case, Sonsu had used Ira Crossman's independent promotion firm to guarantee airplay for the winning artists. It was a clear victory for Jay and Ira, proof that the synergism between them was powerful and real. Both considered David Crossman an upstart, a one-hit wonder. He refused to do business with them, used independent distributors and word-of-mouth promotion. They were glad his group lost, and in tomorrow morning's newspapers Tomorrow's News would be no news at all. Record executives would pay court to Jay Feldman. Industry insiders knew that without Ira Crossman, the behind-the-scene promoter, Sashee and Nightmare would be nowhere. David's group meant nothing.

"Flash in the fuckin' pan," was how Ira, with his customary way with words, described Tomorrow's News to his grandfather, who for the last several months had been recovering from a heart attack. Nathan Silver's inability to bring his grandsons together had undoubtedly contributed to his stress. At the same time he maintained his own relationships with both Ira and David, believing that with patience his undying plan of family unity would eventually work.

* * *

"It's working out beautifully," Pino Feldman told his grandson Jay the day after the Grammys, calling from his trailer in New Mexico. "When it comes to the record business you're almost as smart as me."

HONOLULU

KATE MATSON SAT OUTSIDE her father's house and thought about burning it down, she was so pissed. She'd begin here in the backyard by the pool, and pour kerosene everywhere, then strike a match and watch it go up in flames. The next day the papers would tell about the destruction of the mansion of Mitchell Matson, super-rich music mogul, owner of MM Records, a man whose heavy-metal bands and ultra-violent action-adventure movies scored with raucous rock had made him fortunes on five continents.

The fire, of course, was a fantasy, a way of indulging her feeling about her father, whom she had not seen in nearly a year. "If you want to see me, come to Hawaii," he had told her. "That's where I'm most relaxed. Come soon." They had even arranged a date, but yesterday, when Kate had arrived, all she had found was a familiar note: "Called away at last minute. Had to fly to New York. Important music business. Couldn't wait. Tried to locate you, honey, but you had already left the city. Be back in a week or so. Try and wait."

She tried not to cry; the last thing she wanted to feel like was a teenager. She'd been *through* all that. She was *over* all that, right? Even when her father left her mother and her mother flipped out, even when she moved in with an aunt she barely knew in Connecticut, even when her father had made it clear he was living another life in Los Angeles with another woman who had no love for Kate, Kate had survived. Damn right. At fourteen she had managed without either parent. Whatever memories she had of her father—some happy, others frightening—she had pushed down and away, locked in the dark recesses of her memory bank.

When she was eighteen, the year her mother committed suicide and her father came to the funeral, she asked him for nothing, not even college tuition. She was on her way to Barnard on scholarship. She was a brown-haired, brown-eyed beauty, a Phi Beta Kappa some of the guys called "the Ice Queen." True, she could be aloof, and her boyfriends tended to be put off by her fierce independence. A relentless competitor, she seemed to put achievement ahead of everything. At Columbia, where she earned a graduate degree in broadcast journalism, she was first in her class. She was also first to get an on-the-air job. She reported for the local CBS station in New York, then was transferred to Los Angeles before being sent back to New York, where she worked for the network itself. The big break had come two years ago when at twenty-six she was hired as anchor woman for "Show Business Today," a gossipy high-rated prime-time program focused on entertainment personalities.

At first she had turned down the job. The content was lightweight, superficial, news manufactured by public relations agents with little real reporting. Kate was by now a hard-nosed journalist who'd paid her dues covering fires and riots, oil spills and gangland murders. Finally, though, the national exposure and, admit it, a three hundred fifty thousand dollar yearly salary won the day. She also liked it that her father saw her on the tube every night. For the first time in her life her handsome father, celebrated for his record and film production companies, actually paid attention to her, even was heard to brag about her to his friends. In fact, to the public *Kate* Matson was better known than Mitchell Matson. He even asked her to feature one of his trashy action films or hard-rock recording artists. She liked it that he seemed to need her.

Given her less than ennobling background, Kate wasn't sure where her principles came from, but they were there. Maybe it was her aunt, director of Amnesty International. Her early career included exposing a drug-addicted police chief, scooping a story on a city-council payback scandal, blowing the lid on a corrupt baby-adoption service. Repulsed by her own father, whom she considered a smooth liar and manipulator, she felt drawn to the truth.

Ironic that her biggest success should come in the field in which he was so dominant—show business. Last week's Grammys in Los Angeles, however, where Kate interviewed the latest rock-group rage, Nightmare, played out like a bad dream. She'd fought against the idea with her producer; she considered the group degrading to women. Only when the network president called did she reluctantly agree. During the course of the taped interview, Nightmare's shirtless lead singer, complete with dragon tattoos and stringy shoulder-length bleached hair, leaned over, put his hand on Kate's knee and said, "Horny women made us rich." Kate pushed his hand away and walked off the set.

"You can't do that!" the producer called after her.

But she did . . .

Now seven days later, sitting in the beachfront backyard of her father's home on Mamala Bay in the exclusive Kahala suburb on the island of Oahu, the surf high, the sun warm on her skin, Kate's eyes suddenly filled, and for the first time in years she let go, allowed herself to *cry* . . . for a mother who'd gone crazy, a father who'd gone away and never come back, for a career that had taken off in a direction that seemed foolish and self-serving in which she'd become a mouthpiece, a talking head. She cried for the spectre of the daughter *still* chasing after the father, still looking for his approval, still caring, to be honest, what he thought and did, still putting herself in a position where he could humiliate her, hurt her worse than anybody or anything else. Twenty-eight, everyone thought she had it made. And the damn tears flowed. Self-pity, she hated it. And yet . . . She put her head in her hands, her body actually shaking. Goddamn it, what was she *doing* here? What did she expect her father to do? Advise her? Comfort her? After all these years, how could she even begin to think that he could be sensitive to how she felt? Or even care? What the hell was she thinking of when she called him and made the plane reservation?

Well, there *had* been a solid reason behind the trip, contacting him hadn't been altogether self-deluding. Only a month ago she had dined at an out-of-the-way Oriental bistro with Paul Abel, executive producer of "One Hour," the most popular documentary news program in the history of television. It was Abel who had her thinking in a new direction.

"You're ruining your reputation," said the plain-spoken Brooklyn-born producer, a hyper sixty-year-old who had made it to the top on guts and common sense. 'Show Business Today' is shit. You're too savvy to be throwing away your talent."

"They're promising me more editorial input—"

"Perfumed shit. Look, Kate. I watched what you did out in L.A. with that social-security swindler bilking old folks. You nailed the bastard. I saw when they sent you to Central America for a week, you didn't flinch. You went, you ducked real bullets. I respected that. Then all of a sudden I see you batting your eyes, smiling like a Barbie doll, for Christ sakes, and reading news about boob jobs and tummy tucks in Hollywood and I think to myself, What the hell happened to this reporter?"

"If you're trying to make me feel bad, Paul—"

"I don't want you to feel bad," Abel said, biting into a spicy pork dim sum. "In fact I'm here to say that you've done me a favor. I like watching you, Kate. Even if you're reading dumb news you read it good. You have style and presence. I don't like the show, but the more I watch this horseshit, the more I'm thinking to myself America is fixated with show biz, no doubt. These shows are spreading, like cancer. It's gossip but it's selling big. At the same time I keep thinking there's gotta be lots of people like me who know that underneath all the gloss and glitz must be filth and corruption. I get angry, and when I get angry I get excited, and when I get excited ideas start coming, and all of a sudden I see you again, Kate, only this time you're not on 'Show Business Today' you're on *my* show you're on 'One Hour,' and you have your own quarter-hour segment—let's say once a month—and it's dedicated to show business, only not the press-agent crap but its opposite number. I give you the time, the budget, I give you researchers, and you give me and the public a look inside the *real* show business, inside the movie business, the record business, concerts, videos, the whole *schmear*. You go after, for instance, how they really make a record into a hit—the maneuvering, the sandbagging, the under-the-table money.

"Hey, to be frank, the reason I think Kate Matson will have a better chance than most anyone of getting these stories is because right now Kate Matson's image is soft. You're no threat to these people. They probably think you're on their side. In a way, with the softballs of 'Show Business Today' you've set them up. Okay, now knock 'em down. Be a reporter again. Get those greedy sons of bitches who buy the system and bend it. Get the cheaters . . ."

Paul Abel had got to her. She didn't sleep well that night or the night after. Paul's show was known for muckraking. His show was good—maybe extreme in going after targets but mostly fair and revealing. And his show was popular and could easily match her present salary. So what was there to lose? Why was she hesitant? Why did she suddenly feel the need to do something she'd never done before—consult with her father?

Well, it made sense, she'd decided during the following days going back and forth from her West Side apartment to the studios on Tenth Avenue. It made sense to contact her father, who after all knew show business as well as anyone. He could answer the basic question: Is there really enough corruption to justify a monthly segment on a national news program? Except why should she trust his opinion? Because, after all, damn it, he was her father. Even if also a stranger. Well, what *harm* could come of asking him? All right, she wanted to see him, what was wrong with that? So maybe she was using this as a way to try to form a relationship. Well, hadn't she taken the job on "Show Business Today" to get his attention, force herself into his world?

A week after dinner with Paul Abel she decided to telephone her father. Mitch Matson was delighted, charming, quick to set up a date. "I'll give you a decision," Kate had told Paul, "when I get back from Hawaii."

Now that she was in Hawaii, now that she was forced to face her father's disregard for her, she realized that the bastard, not knowing it, had helped her reach a decision after all.

"I'll do it," she told Paul on the long-distance phone as she sat at her father's desk looking over the collection of photographs of him with his twinky starlet girlfriends. "I'll take the job."

"Good," Paul said. "Before you go on the air, though, I want you to do at least a couple of months of interviews and investigations. You need to get back into real reporting. I've set you up with a man in the Los Angeles D.A.'s office who's been sniffing around the record industry. I want you to start with the record industry. You may be able to help each other. This guy's good, Kate. His name's Mario Washington."

LOS ANGELES

UP AGAINST THE ROPES, Mario Washington saw a small opening and let loose an uppercut to the chin of his opponent, sending the man, twenty pounds heavier than Mario, to the canvas.

"He's really hurt," said an observer. "What the hell did you hit him with?"

Mario took off his headgear and saw that he'd actually injured a guy who, like himself, was supposed to be just sparring, for the exercise.

It was like Mario had been out of himself, in a sort of trance. It was really the reason he kept coming to the gym. He liked losing himself in these furies; he needed the outlet, the release. Working in the D.A.'s office was frustration, especially given his doubts about his boss, Lawrence Kalb. At twenty-eight, only three years out of law school, Mario Washington was a fighter without a fight, his cases boring and prosaic. He'd spent nine months developing leads into corruption in the record business, only to be discouraged by his boss Kalb, the man whose face he'd envisioned just moments ago when he'd flattened his opponent.

"You all right?" Mario asked the guy who was just coming to.

"You're crazy. You're some goddamn killer . . ."

"*Some goddamn killer*"—the very three words that had changed Mario's life, words heard fifteen years ago when barely a teenager he'd come home from school to his parents' small house in South Central L.A. and found the place filled with cops and strangers, his mother crying, his baby brother screaming. "*Some goddamn killer,*" was what young Mario heard someone saying on the phone. "Ben was nabbed by some goddamn killer."

Ben was Mario's father. Ben was a cop. Only a few months before, he'd been promoted to detective and was assigned a detail investigating organized crime in Watts. A black man with a Chilean wife whose leftist-leaning family had barely escaped General Pinochet, Ben was devoted to his sons, taught them soccer not football. Soccer, he said, was a sport played all over the world, not just in North America. Every night he read to his sons stories and fables in which heroes won out. "No matter how complicated things get," he told them, "it always comes down to good over bad." He put away money from his and his wife's paychecks—she worked as a nurse—into a college fund for his kids.

The trauma of his father's death—the grief, the confusion—turned Mario dead serious. He was at the top of his class at Crenshaw High, Cal State and the Boalt Hall law school in Berkeley. Sinewy and quick, he excelled at soccer, but it was boxing that allowed him to release the anger inside, boxing that had him slamming at "some goddamn killer" who'd taken away his father.

Mario's relationship with his mother, who had remarried, was strained. He couldn't handle seeing her with another man. His younger brother had moved to Chile. Mario was alone. His reputation as a loner had followed him from law school to his job in the district attorney's office, where some women made a play for him, turned on by this remote man with high cheekbones and intense brown eyes who exuded a toughness, a strength women found exciting. Quiet and polite, he resisted flirtations, making him for some that much more desirable. His only noticeable passion was for work.

Now his workout was over—it was six P.M. He drove to his mid-Wilshire apartment to change for his dinner appointment with a woman he'd never met before.

By seven-thirty he was dressed and back in his second-hand Pontiac, driving into West Hollywood, where he was meeting Kate Matson at the St. James's Club high on Sunset Boulevard.

He looked around the opulent art-deco dining room.

"How will I know you?" he had asked her on the phone.

That one startled her a little. She was pretty well-known on television. She smiled to herself. "I'll be wearing a blue suit . . ."

A woman in a blue suit sat alone at a table by a window. Beyond and below, the lights of Los Angeles flickered. The woman had serious brown eyes and soft brown hair that fell to her shoulders. Her suit was tailored, her smile was professional, her handshake firm. Her hands, he noted, were small. She was a knockout.

He was uneasy here—that much was clear to Kate. His suit came off the rack from J.C. Penney, his shirt was too tight for his muscular neck, his plain gray tie an afterthought. He was straightforward, and, remarkably, even before he said a word she felt herself responding to his physical presence. Stop it . . . for both of them, tonight was strictly business.

"Miss Matson?"

"Mr. Washington, thanks for joining me."

Neither of them drank. Neither of them ordered appetizers. Strip steak for him, swordfish for her. No small talk.

"Paul Abel said you could use my help," he said. "I'm not sure how."

"I'm just starting out in a new job. How do you know Paul?"

"He called me, said he produced 'One Hour' and had heard I knew something about the entertainment business."

"Do you?"

"Some."

"Have you ever watched 'Show Business Today?'"

"I'm afraid not. Abel said that's the show you're leaving."

"Yes, I'm sort of changing directions, moving from soft features to hard news, as they say. We're starting out by looking at the record business. We plan to do it head on."

He liked the way she talked. She liked the way he looked.

"Are you anywhere near indictments?" she asked after he told a little about his work.

"No. While you were stuck in a soft-news format I've been in a soft D.A.'s office."

"You've got the goods?"

"I think so. At least the basis of a solid case."

"Names?"

"Major players, with tie-ins to outside forces. There are still connections I have to make, but pieces are starting to fall into place—"

"And you can't move on it."

No answer.

"What will you do?"

"Maybe quit," Mario said, surprising himself. He hadn't said this to anyone, and here he was telling a stranger.

"And after you quit?"

"I'm not sure."

Between bits of business talk they sat silent, feeling the attraction, and the need to talk about more than business.

Kate began. She mentioned Hawaii. Mario asked her why she had been there. She told him, mentioning her father.

Silence. Then Mario said uneasily: "I didn't realize that Mitch Matson was your father . . . His name has come up in my investigation—"

"How?"

"His friends, influence."

"Are you talking influence-peddling or something worse" she asked, heart beating too loud.

"I haven't gotten a handle on him yet. I'm still talking to people. Mitchell Matson is close to my boss, Lawrence Kalb. They grew up together—"

"My father . . ." Karen sighed to herself.

"Tell me about him."

"Truth to tell, I hardly know him."

He waited. And she proceeded to tell her family story, straight and unvarnished, which attracted him even more closely to her.

She wanted him to talk about himself, and reluctantly at first, he did in a way totally uncharacteristic for him. When he was through Kate reached out across the table and touched his hand, and he welcomed it, *wanted* it. This wasn't like him; this wasn't like her. Business was receding. Something else was building.

"You . . . must have a busy life. Personally . . ."

She laughed. "If you mean men, I'm afraid not. Maybe it's my fault. I don't have the time. What about you?"

"Pretty much the same." God, this was no good. He hated small talk. Suspected she did too. Anyway, he ached for this woman.

And it was mutual. When was the last time *this* had happened? She couldn't remember. Who cared? She tried getting back to the purpose of the dinner—work, investigation, her new job. And here was a man who like herself, in his fashion, was pursuing her father. A man capable of getting him . . .

Mario tried ignoring her sensuous mouth, the drops of moisture on her lipstick. She told herself this was crazy, she was about to do something crazy. She didn't know him, she was on assignment. It would be a mistake, irresponsible.

They drank cup after cup of rich Kona coffee, until he finally asked, "Where are you staying?"

"Here."

"I didn't know it was a hotel. I thought it was an apartment building."

"It used to be. They converted it."

It went on for hours, their exchange of passion, of release. It went on that night and it went on the next morning. She cancelled her flight to

New York and he called in sick, for the first time in his entire life. He could not leave her, could not stay away from her.

What was happening? he asked himself. "What are we going to do?" he said to her.

"Be together," she told him, tracing his neck with her mouth.

The music business, and its eddying waters, were out of the picture.

NEW YORK CITY 1947

AT THE SAME TIME delegates at the United Nations were arguing over the partitioning of Palestine, Gent Ginzburg and Pino Feldman were arguing over singers. It was wintertime, and they were downtown on Second Avenue at a dairy restaurant eating bowls of borscht and sour cream. The place was crowded with men smoking cigarettes, sipping tea, eating soup and talking Yiddish.

"Tell the truth. You ever seen a doll that looked so good and sang so pretty?" asked Pino, referring to the audition they had just attended at an agent's office off Times Square.

Gent shrugged. He had hated the way this woman had sung.

Pino got mad. "What the fuck's wrong with you? You jealous or something?"

"Jealous of what?"

"That she sings better than your Silky bitch."

"Boss, let's not get crazy here. What's her name—?"

"Dolores. Dolores Delite."

"Your Dolores got a disadvantage. She's white. Whites don't sing as good as the colored."

"What about Crosby? And this new kid, Sinatra? You telling me they can't sing?"

"Whatever they got, they got from the colored."

"Know something, Gent, your brain's fucked up. And that's probably 'cause you're still fucking the Duchess. Well, my brain's not fucked up. My brain's working good, it's working perfect, and it's telling me to tell you that a white woman who sings good is going to outsell a nigger singing good because for every nigger in this country there's a dozen regular people and us regulars would rather hear someone regular singing without all the jazzy shit, just singing regular where we can understand it. You understand me?"

Ruby spooned his borscht without replying.

"I'm glad you understand," Feldman went on, "because I got a plan where we can sell more records than you or me ever dreamed."

"You wanna *record* this Dolores Delite?"

"It's better than that, Gent. I want her to sing that song you played me when I first got here."

"What song . . . ?"

"The one Duchess recorded."

"'Mellow Love?'"

"That's the one. Can't you hear Dolores singing it?"

"But Silky's already recorded it. We're about to press it. 'Defend My Heart' sold a half-million. This one's gonna be even bigger—"

"You had publicity with 'Defend My Heart.' The trial and all that shit. Now it's old news. Maybe you'll sell a couple hundred thousand copies—*if* you're lucky. With Dolores you'll sell a million."

"She's unknown—"

"Now she is. That why I'm turning her over to you. You'll train her, you'll record her, you'll make a mint for us."

Ginzburg wanted to ask whether Pino was laying this woman, but he already knew the answer. Besides, he understood his boss, he knew what was happening. Feldman had never forgiven Silk for standing up to him seven years ago. He resented her success. Seeing that she'd gained national prominence, Pino had devised a scheme to replace his underling's woman with a woman of his own. This was tricky business. The Gent eyed Feldman's man, fat Fingers Markowitz, a hard man to kill, sitting at a nearby table where he was putting away a small mountain of blintzes. The boss never went anywhere without Fingers.

Ruby reasoned that restraint was the order of the day. Why look for trouble? Pino, not Ruby, owned Pino Records, the label that recorded Eve and Lowell after the demise of the Raminskis. Pino, not Ruby, had the financial resources. Pino, not Ruby, was more and more suspicious of his partners and subordinates. Pino needed only the smallest excuse to eliminate a conspirator or competitor. Ruby would not give him excuses.

"I can work with the broad," he told his boss.

"Good. Bring your sax player. Hire all the fiddlers you want. I don't care what it costs."

"I'll start next month—"

"Next month? What about tonight? You said you got a session tonight."

"It's for Duchess. We're starting on the songs from *Porgy and Bess*. I've been planning it for a year—"

"Scrap it. It's nothing but high-class horseshit and it ain't gonna sell. I'll bring Dolores by tonight. You and Silk'll show her that 'Mellow Love' number. You got the arrangements, you got everything. Have everyone ready by eight."

The first sound out of Dolores Delite's mouth when she came to the microphone to sing the opening line of "Mellow Love" was a burp, small but distinct.

"Don't worry," said Pino, sitting next to Gent and the engineer in the control room. "She just ate. She'll be fine."

"She'll be singing over my dead body," Silk had told Ruby when she learned of Pino's plan. Eve was staying up in Harlem.

"If it wasn't a matter of life and death," said Gent over the phone, "I wouldn't argue. But we got no choice."

"Maybe you got no choice, Ginzy, but I ain't showing up and I ain't showing the bitch shit. If she's gonna sing my song, let her figure it out by herself."

Ruby wasn't surprised, then, that neither Duchess nor Lord had come to the session. Fortunately their boycott wasn't even noticed by Feldman, who was busy demonstrating to Dolores his power as a producer.

The truth was that after digesting her dinner, Dolores proved to have something of a voice. Gent did not like it, but he had to admit that her sort of sound was selling these days. She was a warbler, and warblers were popular. Her little-girl tone was white and light and she certainly sounded better now than she had that morning. More to the point, she had flaming-red Rita Hayworth hair, a prominent beauty mark just below her long thin lips and a full-bodied figure poured into a black-and-white polka-dot dress. Even in his elevator shoes Pino stood a good foot shorter than Dolores. When she sang she insisted on wearing a turban with a silk rose angled to one side. The long ermine coat Feldman had just bought her was draped across a chair. The way she arched her eyebrows reminded Ruby of Veronica Lake. She was a pushy girl with a thick Brooklyn accent—her real name was Ethel O'Malley—who, at nineteen, tried to appear older but still looked young enough to be Pino's daughter.

Eve's original line read, "Mellow love ain't mellow if you push it too hard."

"Don't say 'ain't,'" Feldman advised Dolores. "This here's a classy song, Say 'isn't.'"

Before Dolores started singing again, Pino told Ruby to play Eve's version. Dolores listened to Silk at least a half-dozen times before she tried copying the feel. The melody was so beautiful, thought Ruby, practically anyone could sing this song. And even though Delite's voice annoyed him, at least she managed to stay in tune.

"Beautiful!" Pino shouted after Dolores' first take. "We got a regular star here. Listen to her. Look at her. I can see her in the movies, can't you, Gent?"

"Very nice," Gent said as, inside his head, he still heard Silky's original version. A masterpiece.

The copy prevailed. The next day Gent told the pressing plant to nix Eve's version and wait for a new one. By the time President Truman surprised the world by recognizing the state of Israel in mid-May of 1948, the new version sung by Dolores Delite reached number one on the hit parade. By then, Ruby was her full-time manager, and Eve Silk was living in London with a Britisher who was running her career. Ginzburg was crazy with jealousy. Dolores' success only made things worse.

The happier Pino was with Ruby's management of Miss Delite, the more miserable Ruby became. He found her thin voice increasingly irritating and disliked her personality. Dolores was no delight. In Detroit and Chicago, at singing engagements from Baltimore to St. Louis, she treated Gent like a lap dog, demanding Chinese food in the middle of the night or mink earmuffs in the morning. "Pino wouldn't want me to be unhappy," she would say. When Ruby suggested that someone could take better care of her than he could, Feldman wouldn't hear of it.

"Can't trust no one else," he said. "Anyone else would poke her the second I turned my back. You're the only one smart enough not to touch her. I know you want to—what guy wouldn't?—but I know you won't.

Besides, you know show business. Get her in the movies. Get her a part singing in a movie."

The movie was called *Mellow Love*. It starred Betty Grable and featured a five-minute segment of Dolores Delite singing Silky's song. Ginzburg had connected with a Hollywood producer, convincing him to use the title and Pino's girl. Despite the rich royalties she received for composing the tune, Silky was still furious with the white woman. Ruby was furious with himself. Pino had trapped him. Pino had a way of showing up on the road when Gent and Dolores least expected him. If anything happened to Dolores, Ruby knew what would happen to him. Gent was protecting and promoting a high-class hooker with a decent voice, a great body and a give-me attitude that drove him nuts.

When he drove her from Los Angeles to Palm Springs for a private party for a big-time director, she wouldn't stop talking about how great she was in *Mellow Love*. Ginzburg kept thinking of Silk, whom he hadn't seen in six months. Why should he be building the career of a woman he detested while the woman whose talent he loved was in Europe missing the opportunity of following up her first big hit, "Defend My Heart," in America? Gent missed Duchess, missed fighting for her, missed everything about her. He was so full of thinking about Duchess that in Palm Springs he almost missed his own golden opportunity. He almost didn't see Dolores Delite slip into a back bedroom with a young actor named Dick Rawfield.

NEW YORK CITY

RALPH CROSSMAN'S FIRST IMPRESSION of Mitchell Matson was that he looked like a middle-aged California surfer, an over-aged actor. He gave off good health, and at fifty-five Matson appeared a decade younger. Ralph suspected that the man's casually coiffed blond hair was dyed. Matson's tan and powerful chest gave him a confidence that Ralph Crossman did not trust. Matson's outfit also seemed inappropriate. If you are going to see the managing partner of Crossman, Croft and Snowden, wear a tie, not a double-breasted white blazer and lime-hued sport shirt, clothing more suitable to a yacht than a lawyer's office.

In fact, Ralph had been tempted to refuse to see Mitchell Matson. He had avoided clients in the entertainment business. On the other hand Matson was no ordinary mogul. He enjoyed a reputation for being very skilled, not only in complex business affairs but in reading the public pulse. Credit checks revealed his financial status comparable to a prosperous bank, with assets over a billion dollars. Such figures attracted Ralph, as they would any lawyer. After all, what harm could come from finding out what the man wanted?

Matson saw Crossman as a stuffed shirt. The lawyer dressed like an undertaker. Mitchell preferred the entertainment attorneys he retained in Los Angeles, wheeler-dealers who often doubled as agents and wore hip-suede baseball jackets to work. New York was too formal for Mitch Matson. He came there only out of necessity. The fact was that Ralph Crossman was one of the most sought-after counselors in the country, his establishment firm a symbol of responsibility.

"Let me explain my predicament," said Matson, his slow-mannered cool California accent irritating Ralph. "Friends have said things that concern me. People are looking into my business who have no right—"

"Who are these people?"

"Small people with small minds. People who have no idea what they are doing or why they are doing it. Not having achieved anything themselves, they seem to find pleasure in finding fault with anyone who has. You understand, Ralph?"

Crossman did not like being called "Ralph" by people he did not know well. "Please go on, Mr. Matson," he said, his annoyance under uneasy control.

"I don't have the details. But I'm concerned enough to retain a first-rate firm such as yours."

"If there's a specific problem it would be best to explain what it is."

"Let me explain, then, Ralph. My visibility is high, and for good reason. Not only do my entertainment products—my recording stars and my films—enjoy mass-market acceptance, but I myself am often in the press. You probably know that I'm the founder of the Players Foundation, an organization that recognizes and aids forgotten musicians and actors who have fallen in the cracks. We have benefit dinners, concerts, our own Hall of Fame and a retirement home being built in New Jersey that will, I'm proud to say, carry my name. I argued against it—I hardly need any more publicity—but the other directors, noting the size of my donation, insisted. At least they recognize my love of the music and film of the forties and fifties. Beyond this I'm on the board of another two-dozen charities for every imaginable disease and some that haven't yet been invented. In short, I'm a target for investigators who have nothing better to do than try to bring down a public figure. I want these bureaucrats to realize if they tangle with me, they're also tangling with some tough litigators. At least I want them wary."

"That's hardly the work of a law firm."

"I'm not sure, Ralph. Your own litigators have one hell of a reputation."

"Then you're anticipating litigation . . . ?"

"Not anticipating, not worrying," said Mitch, maintaining his cool, "just being cautious."

"I'm still not certain how we can help," said Ralph, clearing his throat.

"I'm certain enough to offer Crossman, Croft and Snowden a retainer of, say, fifty thousand a month. If that's not sufficient, just say so. I won't challenge you, Ralph. I want you on my side."

"I'll need to know more about your affairs, Mr. Matson. You see, the record and film business are areas I've avoided—"

"Another reason you seem right for me. You come into my life, frankly, wearing a white hat. Your reputation is spotless."

"As I said, this will require further consultation. I have partners."

"I don't, Ralph. All I have are resources. I'm not only willing to cooperate with whatever research into my affairs you feel necessary, Ralph, I'm willing to pay for it. Please accept this," he said, placing a check on the desk, "just to start things off on a reasonable basis."

Ralph wanted to kick him out, wanted to get him on the squash court and humiliate him, see him lunge for the ball and fall on his ass. Ralph wanted nothing to do with him. On the other hand, the check, he saw, was for one hundred thousand dollars. He also had to admit that Matson held a fascination for him. Even David would be impressed.

Later that week Ralph Crossman was still thinking of Mr. Mitch Matson—and of his son David—while he and Margo watched *Don Giovanni* from their patron's seats in the third row at the Met. Ralph loved the theme of intrigue and the artifices of eighteenth-century staging, the moving columns and painted backcloths, the fluid rhythms, bright costumes, the wit of the *dramma giocoso,* the sensuality of the singing. Afterward he felt renewed. He had finally gotten to the age where he understood, unlike Don Giovanni, the pleasures of fidelity. For a very long while now he had been faithful to Margo, who was especially attractive tonight in her Gianfranco Ferre black suit, draped and shaped to her figure.

Margo was a leading light of the Met, recently elected president of Friends of the Opera. But it was not all altruism. Her volunteer work also led to business. Divas were asking her to decorate their New York apartments and summer retreats. She had just returned from London, where she turned a Victorian mansion into a museum of modern art. Her fees now rivaled Ralph's. He was proud. When the New York Times Magazine ran a feature on the city's leading decorators and mentioned Margo Cunningham, he sent it to David. David hadn't responded.

"David is still so damn distant," he told Margo as they ate strawberries and cream at an after-opera bistro near Lincoln Center.

"He might say the same of you," replied Margo, who was planning a secret trip to Orange County, California, next week to help her parents set up a modest apartment in the Leisure World retirement community. Henrietta and Wilbur Smith had decided Orange County was preferable to Duluth.

"Why is he so secretive about his work?" asked Ralph. "He's had some success, I know, with this one group. Beyond that, he says nothing."

"Is Carla Bari with him?"

"I assume they're together, but even her own father doesn't know what's happening between those two—"

"You and David live in two different worlds."

"As a matter of fact, a man from David's world came to see me today. Have you heard of Mitchell Matson?"

"He was in *People* last week. He makes millions on trashy movies and rock and roll. I think he controls a record company too."

"He controls a great deal. He's anxious to retain me."

"I wouldn't think you'd be interested—"

"He intrigues me. My people have compiled a report on him that's fascinating. Apparently his father was in the film business in Los Angeles, a pornographer who failed when he tried to produce mainstream films. His pornography made money, enough to leave a considerable inheritance. The son, who had worked with the father, took the money and managed to build his own empire. Mitchell Matson started by making television commercials. He also owned a number of Manhattan dance clubs that prospered in the seventies. His trading instincts are very sharp. He sold his nightclubs just before disco crashed and invested in a Danish heavy-metal band that made a fortune in Europe and Japan. His first film, *Rock Murder,* did what none of his father's mainstream films were ever able to do—make money. In fact, it made a great deal of money, and ever since his entertainment products have succeeded, even if they are considered one thin line above pornography. Interesting, too, how Matson has always worked outside the Hollywood establishment. He lives all over the world, but his favorite home is in Hawaii. He's a maverick, yet judging from his behavior in my office this week I'd say he's anxious for respectability—though he'd be the last to admit it."

"He's probably on the verge of being indicted for God knows what. I say avoid him, Ralph."

"I've always resisted show business, but now that David's so active in Hollywood, perhaps I at least ought to learn more about that world. And Matson might be the perfect teacher. He's slick, he's done a superb job of covering over his father's shady past. I feel somewhat compelled to learn more about him. Moreover, he'll pay me a fortune to do so."

"And there's no risk for you?"

Ralph smiled. "Lawyers are hired guns, Margo. We do the shooting. And the good ones never get shot."

HONOLULU

"YOU'RE RELATED TO RALPH Crossman, aren't you?" Mitchell Matson asked Ira Crossman.

"He's my uncle but I've never even met him."

"He's an interesting man."

"He's a jerk. And he's got a jerky son who's trying to make it in the music business."

"I didn't know that. Ralph Crossman has a son? What's his name?"

"David."

"He isn't a lawyer?"

"He is, but he wants to be in records. Started up his own label. Calls it David Crossman Records but it's a joke. It ain't going nowhere."

"Fascinating," said Mitch. "Is he using his father's money?"

"He and his father don't exactly see eye to eye. He got some Italian dame to put in some dough."

"What's her name?"

"Something Bari."

"That's a name in European banking. I'd like to meet this David Crossman."

"No, you wouldn't. He's got tin ears."

"He hasn't placed any hits?"

"Maybe something on the black charts but no crossover acts. Doesn't know shit from shinola."

"I assume you and your cousin don't exactly work together."

"He wants to but I won't."

"And Ralph Crossman doesn't represent you?"

"I *told* you, the fucker doesn't know I exist. He hated my father and he hates me. Hell, he hated his own father."

"What did his father do?"

Realizing he was talking much too much, Ira stopped himself.

"If you'd like another taste," offered Mitch, nodding to a pile of fluffy white cocaine on the glass coffee table, "feel free."

The stick of Hawaiian grass, the Maui Wowee, had already loosened Ira's tongue. Rather than act as a soporific, pot sped up the promoter's rhythms. The heady mixture of coke and weed had Ira Crossman flying. His throat was dripping, his teeth on edge. As a veteran drug user, though, Ira knew that the stuff, especially in a business context, could be dangerous. He fought the temptation to chatter, realizing that, as Matson's guest, he was in a vulnerable position. He also couldn't deny that he was impressed. After all, Mitch Matson was a king in the record industry and one unusually cool individual. He had sent his private Gulfstream jet to fetch Ira from Los Angeles. A streamlined silver helicopter had brought him from the airport to Matson's Kahala spread.

This is living, Ira thought, looking around his host's glass-and-wood mansion perched on Oahu's most exclusive beach. Just beyond the den, sunlight glittered on clear green water, thunderous waves crashing on the ocean-swept bay.

For years Ira had chased after Matson. MM Records was the one account he could never land, the big fish that always seemed to elude him. Now, after his success with Jay Feldman and Sonsu, the legendary Mitch Matson had come to him. What could be sweeter?

"If you're hungry," Matson said with fatherly concern, "my cook has just made a batch of fresh brownies."

"Sure, great."

Mitch pressed a button, and minutes later a servant arrived with a platter of brownies.

"You put shit in these too?" asked a wired Ira.

Matson smiled. "Eat to your heart's content. You're my guest."

Ira bit into a brownie. It was moist and delicious, the best thing he had ever tasted.

"You were discussing Ralph Crossman," Mitch reminded Ira.

"Don't know much about him. Except he's an asshole."

"I get the idea you won't work with just anybody," said Matson, deciding to back off and not pressure the younger man—at least not now.

"I gotta be choosey, Mitch. This business is crawling with rats."

"You did a considerable job for the Japanese. Practically single-handedly you launched Sonsu. You placed Nightmare on the important playlists. I was convinced they'd bomb."

Ira felt the last blast of cocaine freezing his gums. He felt great. Confident. Went for another brownie. "I know what I'm doing, Mitch."

"No one comes into this house who doesn't. I'll be straight with you, Ira. You impress me. You really do. I've been resisting an independent promoter because, arrogantly enough, I didn't think I needed one. Up till now, I haven't. But things are changing. The marketplace is so crowded it's hard to tell up from down. But you're up, you've stayed up, and I, for one, respect that. I respect your independence."

"I got the right connections."

"Well, that's why I invited you here, Ira. You see, recently I made a new connection, a German connection."

"Heavy metal?"

"The heaviest you can imagine. A band called Shock Therapy. They're outstanding."

"When can I hear them?"

"Is two hours soon enough? I'm flying them in from Berlin to give you a private hearing. Naturally I've invited a few friends, a couple of the local ladies who are music lovers. The way you spend all your time taking care of program directors, I think it's time someone took care of you. This is your night, Ira. If you like Shock Therapy I'm giving you carte blanche in the promotion area. You merely have to get them on the major playlists. For me, it's worth a straight three million. That's cash. And that's payable up-front."

Drugs revving his brain, brownies sweetening his mouth, Ira got up to pour himself a glass of water.

"Let me do that for you," said his host.

He had arrived. He was being wined and dined by Mitchell Matson. Matson needed *him,* Matson was selling *him,* Matson was ready to make *him* rich.

"And this is only the beginning," said the older man, bringing Ira a tall refreshing glass of ice water and another platter of fresh brownies.

HIALEAH

NATHAN SILVER, GRANDFATHER OF Ira and David, hit the exacta.

In the fifth race, he picked two long-shots—Black Rage to win and Jamboree to place. On a five hundred dollar bet the old man won fifty thousand.

"You keep it," he told David.

"Why? You picked the horses."

"You helped me."

"All I did was read the racing sheets to you."

"You brought me luck, David. You always bring me luck. You're good for me. Since my little heart attack this is the best day I've had. Ever since you got here yesterday I've been feeling good. Maybe this time you'll stay a while. Maybe you'll make it a real visit."

With one hand Nathan took his cane and with the other hand his grandson's arm. The old man felt frail as David guided him to the clubhouse, feeling protective. To feel the old man's fingers pressing against his skin was somehow comforting. They sat at a table by the glass window overlooking the track. It was a cloudy, muggy early summer day. The fifty thousand dollars in cash bulged in David's pocket, convincing him, more than ever, that Nathan had certain magical powers.

"I'm glad," said his grandfather, "that you're using the Silver Printing Company. It's a good property. It gives me pleasure to see people working in there. I could never convince Ira to do anything with the place. You haven't mentioned anything about using the printing company to Ira, have you, David?"

"I never talk to him."

"That's bad, but I won't go into it now. Now we're enjoying our winnings, aren't we? You saw I was right. You print your own covers for your records and your cassettes and your compact discs—I know all about compact discs—and you get a break. You go through your distributor and they take a mark-up. You go through me and you save a pretty penny. How many acts have you signed so far?"

"Five."

"And how many are making money?"

"Tomorrow's News."

"A cute name. Back in my day, we didn't have names like that. Who would have understood? We kept it plain—Lord Lowell Foreman and his All-Star Band. Things like that. Today anything goes. You have any white acts?"

"One."

Nathan smiled. "I had one, and I hated her. All I could hear was the colored music. When it came to anything else I was deaf."

"You seem to know something about gambling."

"Don't be fooled. Today's the luckiest day of my life. You're here, David, and I'm not dead. God has given me a little more time. But no, I'm no gambler. I'm too smart. You see, my brother, he was a gambler. Did I tell you about my older brother Heshie?"

"I never knew you had one."

"So many stories to tell, so much I've forgotten. But Heshie is someone I could never forget. Sharp mind, strong body, four years older than me. I looked up to him. He looked after me. Anyone say anything bad to me, with one punch he'd let them have it. Heshie was my protector.

Maybe that's why it took me so long to leave Pino Feldman. Maybe Pino was like my brother. Anyway, Heshie had a problem. The way some guys like to drink booze or chase women, Heshie liked to gamble. Once in a while, that's alright. But if you do it all the time—the numbers, the nags, the prizefights, the ballgames—you lose. Heshie lost. He fell behind. He couldn't catch up. Certain parties were impatient. And one morning, coming back from school—this was when I was in the sixth, maybe the seventh grade, who can remember?—I saw something horrible in an empty lot and this horrible something turned out to be my brother. Even now I can see him. It wasn't pretty. After that, I wasn't a kid."

"Did you find out who did it?"

"I found out and I took care of it. That changed me. That's how I met Pino Feldman. He heard about me. He heard I had guts and he used me. But you see, David, I also used him."

"With Lowell Foreman and Eve Silk, you made him a fortune."

"That was after the trial, after the war. During the war there wasn't no shellac. All the shellac was being used for the war. So there was this demand for records. Plus, the major labels never understood the colored. They neglected their music. Not me. By 1947 I found a beautiful supply of shellac and there were all these newspaper articles on Silk and her trial and you could hear 'Defend My Heart' wherever you walked around in Harlem or the South Side of Chicago and that's when I had this plan for her to sing songs from *Porgy and Bess* with fiddlers from the New York Philharmonic, fiddlers Toscanini himself used. Pino ruined the plan but I did what I had to do. I don't want to talk about it now. All that business is over with. My business"—Silver paused and sighed—"my business is dead and gone—Ruby's gone, Bernie's gone, but your business is alive and you're young and I want to hear more about what you're doing, David. Tell me. I need to catch up. My little heart attack threw me off track."

"Why didn't you say anything when you were sick? The phone just rang and rang but no one answered."

"I didn't want you to worry. I don't like being fussed over. Besides, you had other things on your mind. You were just starting up your business. And talking about business, I want to go over to the printing company. Finish your dinner and take me over there. We need to have a business talk, man to man."

* * *

It was eight o'clock and the outlying industrial/warehouse section of Miami was deserted. The small crew at Silver Printing Company had gone home. As David led Nathan back to the old man's hideaway, the room filled with records, he saw that the main floor was filled with dozens and dozens of cartons piled to the ceiling. David poked inside one of the cartons and saw that they contained LP's.

"Jesus," said David, "there must be fifty thousand albums around here. What are you doing with them?"

"Take a look. Look them over. They're good product. You'll know the names."

They were cut-outs—remainders, discontinued discounted albums—by well-known artists like Joe Cocker, Fleetwood Mac, Diana Ross, the Bee Gees, Steve Miller, Boz Scaggs, Van Morrison, the Brothers Johnson, Elton John, all popular acts from another era.

"I still don't understand," said David.

"It's something I want to work out with you. It's product your cousin Ira found. Cut-out records are a goldmine. Especially now that they're not even making records anymore. You see, I keep up. Ira's paid less than a nickel a record—can you believe it?—and the market is strong out there. Some of these things are already collector items. Ira says some of them can retail for as much as ten dollars, others will go for a buck."

"I didn't know Ira did these kinds of things—"

"A good businessman sees an opportunity and grabs it. Ira's a good businessman."

"Then let Ira sell the records."

"He will. You see, a record mogul—a very important man—is doing Ira favors."

"I know, Jay Feldman."

"No, you don't know, David," said Nathan with some annoyance. "You'll listen and you'll learn. Ira is a very smart boy, and Feldman, that little bastard, isn't his only client. All the big-shots want Ira because Ira can get their records played. And one of these big-shots is courting Ira like Ira's a woman. Not just paying him top money to get his records played, but giving him perks—that's the beauty part—that no one else is getting. There aren't fifty thousand records here, there are one hundred thousand, plus another nine hundred thousand I got stashed in other warehouses."

"I'm not really interested—"

"You say that and you hurt my feelings."

"Look, I'm just getting started, Nathan, and I don't want to complicate things. I don't want to get over my head."

"Take me into my back room, David. I want to tell you a story."

More records, thousands of records, lined the walls of the old man's hideaway. Because he knew every inch of the sprawling room, he walked around as though he could see, going through his massive collection to find one record in particular.

"An instrumental," he said. "It's Lord playing ballads. He wouldn't sing that day. Said he only wanted to blow his horn. I never argued. That was my policy. So he played all afternoon and this is the best. This 'All the Things You Are.' Now you tell me about your artists. I want to know all about them."

David didn't really discuss his business with many people—certainly not his own father, from whom he felt increasingly estranged. Due to their pride, their calls were infrequent. Let *him* call me, each man thought to himself. Months passed without contact. When there was a conversation, it was cursory. "Doing fine out here, Dad. How's Margo?" "Margo's fine." "How's everything at the office?" "Everything is fine."

Carla had been a diversion, and a model silent partner. She was here and there, roaring into town for a night like a thunderstorm, exploding, then vanishing. The sex was always unpredictable, on the floor, against the wall, in the wake of waves on a moonless night when the Malibu coastline was desolate except for a few bonfires along the beach. And while she was wildly undependable on all personal matters—flying off for a movie in Tunisia or a secret rendezvous in the Caribbean—she had, after all, put up two hundred fifty thousand dollars of her (or her father's) money, allowing David, with the prudent use of his own capital, to sign and support enough acts to maintain his independence. With independent distribution, his small label was surviving.

David was somewhat surprised that he himself was surviving, surprised he was changing. He had proved to be kind of gutsy, ignoring everyone's advice except his grandfather's. He didn't need his father's firm and he didn't need a nine-to-five corporate job. He hadn't fallen apart. It had been scary and certainly the oddness of Carla's support had helped considerably—and he'd picked at least one winner. He'd gone with his own instincts, his own taste. In analyzing the record business it was clear that a strong-minded free-wheeling executive had to make only two or three good decisions to prosper. Clive Davis had done it with Whitney Houston and Milli Vanilli. David Geffen had done it with Aerosmith and Guns n' Roses. Jay Feldman was doing it with Nightmare. And if the trade papers were accurate, Mitch Matson was about to do it with Shock Therapy, still another heavy-metal blast from Germany. In a less spectacular way David Crossman had begun to do it with Tomorrow's News.

"You believe in this group, don't you?" asked Nathan.

"Their debut album," said David, picking up the CD package that had been printed by Silver's employees, "has sold nearly three hundred thousand copies."

"That's very good, but the other acts, they're moving a little slowly. Ira says he can help."

"Ira or you?"

"Both of us. We have projects together, just like you and me."

"You listen to heavy metal, you actually listen to the bands Ira promotes?"

"David, to tell you the truth, I listen to what I'm listening to now—the old things. Hear Lord Foreman? Hear the sound he gets out of that saxophone? It's like a man crying. I tried to listen to your group, your Tomorrow's News band, but the beat is different than what I'm used to and the words I can't understand. I trust you, though. If you say they're good, they're good."

"I have a saxophonist," said David, still looking for his grandfather's approval—not Ralph's. "I just signed him. Listen to this demo tape. He's influenced by the old masters. He's listened to Lord."

"What's his name?"

"Vince Viola."

"An Italian? I don't trust Italians. Just like the Italian girl you told me about, the one who put money in your company. You shouldn't have taken that money. It was a mistake. Italians are different than us. They think different."

"This Italian plays black. You wouldn't know he wasn't black."

"Like Charlie Ventura?"

"Saxophonists are becoming stars—Kenny G, David Sanborn, Gerald Albright. This Viola's a bodybuilder. Good-looking, sexy and a strong romantic sound. He'll sell records."

"Let me hear what you got."

Ironically, the song was "All the Things You Are" with a slightly funky rhythmic base. It was a sweet coincidence, and the old man and David were smiling together. Vince Viola's sound was intimate and heartfelt. He stuck with the melody.

"This," said Silver, "I understand. But in today's market, you really think it'll sell?"

"It's the only standard on the album. The others are all originals—the kind of romantic ballads women love."

"That's what I used to tell Lowell. I said, 'Play for the women. The women are romantic. The women spend money.' I like this Viola. Has Ira heard him?"

"I keep telling you, Nathan—I never call Ira and he never calls me."

"You did something I never did, David. You got your name on the records. You got your own David Crossman Records. I'll be honest with you, I hated seeing Pino's name on Duchess' records. 'Pino Records' it said, and meanwhile Pino didn't have nothing to do with the music. He didn't even *listen* to music. The schmuck didn't even *like* music. By 1950 Pino was leaving all the music to me. Know what he was doing? Cleaning up as a cigarette-machine vendor. He had that racket locked up in every major city. Made a fortune off cigarette machines. Later it was jukeboxes. But all that time he still had to have his name on the records, never mine. So having your name on the records is good, David, but it's also bad."

"Why?"

"You leave yourself open. You're exposed."

"Why should that bother me?"

"Maybe now it doesn't. Later it might."

"I still don't understand."

"I want you to understand this cut-out deal. There's money in those discounted records. You can make a pretty penny, you and Ira both. At least you'll think about it."

"Alright, I'll think about it."

"And I've been thinking about that colored girl you brought with you when you first came down here. You said she was a singer, a jazz singer. Then you never mentioned her again. Why aren't you playing me her records?"

"Rita Moses," said David, thinking how he'd dreamt of her only last night. "I don't know where Rita is."

But he found he cared.

NEW YORK CITY

RITA WASN'T HAPPY ABOUT taking Walter home to meet her parents. She and Gentry were planning her second album and didn't see eye to eye. She wanted to explore new approaches, which meant slipping in a few pop songs and easing away from unadulterated jazz. She had songs of her own that she wanted to record. Meanwhile, Walter had been honing his skills as a lyricist. He'd taken complex compositions by Charles Mingus and Thelonious Monk, gotten permission from their estates and put words to the melodic lines. Rita had to admit his lyrics were intriguing. They told stories about life in Harlem during an earlier era, the problems of jazz musicians, the journey of artists. Her own lyrics dealt with storybook romance, heartache and pain, love lost and found.

"If you're going to write a torch song," Walter said, "you're not going to do any better than the old masters."

"How do you know that?"

"Can you write another 'Lush Life?' Can you write like Billy Strayhorn?"

"I write like me. Besides, my love songs are the kind selling today."

"We're establishing a market—don't you see that?—a market of serious listeners. You appeal to people who know music."

Still, Walter, for all his talent, thought Rita, didn't know pop music. His songs had little commercial appeal. In spite of her Grammy nomination her debut album had earned her less than thirty thousand dollars. And even though she was working steadily and in better venues, including jazz festivals in Australia and Japan, certain singers she identified with—Anita Baker, for instance—were making millions singing their own material in the mass marketplace.

"It's been only a little over two years, Rita, and your reputation has gone international."

He was right about that, she had to admit. She was getting somewhere. She liked Walter, but she didn't like him trying to control her in what she wore. If she wanted to wear something flashy and not too dignified—Walter was big on dignity—that was up to her, not him. If she thought about money, that was her business, not his. And if she still thought of David Crossman, . . . well, what could she do about it? Sure, she'd been peeved seeing him with Carla Bari at the Grammys back in February.

Long ago she'd decided to forget about him. But she couldn't, and she couldn't help wondering how he really felt.

Now it was May. She *appreciated* Walter. She liked being treated seriously. But as she and Walter walked from her place to her parents' on St. Luke's Place, she also realized that passion had gone out of their relationship. They'd been wise to maintain separate apartments. He got up early, she slept late; he was neat, she was messy. And beyond stuff like that, the sex had definitely lost its sizzle. She guessed he had other women, but the thought didn't make her jealous. Business and art was their glue. He had produced a critically acclaimed Rita Moses album. He had brought her some fame. Which was why Rosy, Rita's mom, was so anxious to meet the man.

"Why didn't you tell me he was so fine?" asked Rosy the second she viewed the man she saw as her prospective son-in-law. "And so nicely dressed." He wore a dark blue Perry Ellis coat and light wool blue slacks. "Why, baby, this man looks like he just stepped out of a magazine."

Rita knew the evening would be embarrassing, which was why she had been putting it off for so long.

Hy Moses was sitting in the living room reading the New York *Daily News*. When he got up and smiled at his daughter, she was startled, then upset. He was reed thin.

"My God," said Rita, embracing her father. "What's wrong?"

"Nothing, honey. Just the diet the doctor put me on. It's working too well."

"You sure?"

"Sure I'm sure. Now introduce me to your friend."

"Walter Gentry, Hy Moses."

The two had little to talk about. The silences were especially uncomfortable. Hy liked to go to the track, play poker with his pals and plan his vacations with Rosy. He read murder mysteries.

"I hear you're a writer," he said to Walter. "You writing a book?"

Walter began describing his plan for a history of African-American music.

"Ain't that wonderful!" said Mama bringing in a plateful of roasted chicken and candied yams. "The more you get your name out there, the better it is for Rita. I love the way you two help each other. I'm so proud of both of you I could bust. When's the new album coming out? I was telling the girls at the beauty shop they each gotta buy at least three copies. They were thrilled when the TV camera caught Rita sitting there at the Grammys. They all saw it. Daddy taped it, didn't you, Hy?"

"Got it on tape. You looked beautiful, Rita."

"Didn't matter that she didn't win." said Rosy, passing a loaf of thinly-sliced crusty rye bread that she had brought from the Second Avenue Deli. "She'll win next time. You ought to hear how many of my steady customers bought the record. Anytime anyone new comes in the restaurant, first thing I do is tell 'em about Rita. I keep the tape playing most of the day."

"I bet you do," mumbled her daughter.

"And all the postcards from overseas, from France and Japan, I scotch-tape them on the pastry case. How's the chicken, Walter?"

"Delicious, Mrs. Moses."

Mama was non-stop chatter. "Are you a man who likes children, Walter?"

"Mama!"

"I didn't ask whether he wanted *your* children, darlin', I just asked whether he liked children. Some men take more to children than some women. Take Hy. He changed Rita's diapers. He bathed you, girl. Well, he was better with the baby than me. Till you have a baby, you just don't know if you gonna take to it or not. Ain't that the truth, Daddy?"

"Rita was a beautiful baby," said Hy. "No trouble at all."

"Walter is my *producer,* Mama."

"What part of the city do you live in, Walter?" asked Mama.

"Upper West Side, off the Park."

"One of those big ol' apartments?"

"Three bedrooms."

"Big enough for a family—"

"Mama, *enough.* We're not even discussing living together."

"These days," said Rosy, "everyone's living together before they get married. Far as I'm concerned, it's for the better. One thing to be going to bed with a man. Another thing to be waking up with him before he brushes his teeth. Living together is a test. I think it's a good idea. When's the lease up on your apartment over on Great Jones Street?"

"You're impossible," Rita said.

"I think your mother's charming," Walter put in.

"There you go," said Mama. "Not only is this boy fine and smart as a whip, he likes to please women. These days that's mighty unusual. I can't tell you how many of these sissies come swishing in and out of the deli with snooty attitudes, ordering me around like I wasn't nothing.

Some of 'em rich, but if you think they're good tippers, forget it, honey. Real men's a thing of the past. If you find one, you better hold on. And that's the truth."

For Walter the rest of dinner was grin and bear it. For Rita, it was worry about her father's weight. During dessert, a rich Russian coffeecake filled with cinnamon, nuts and dried dates, Rosy said, "Now I ain't one to criticize, and don't think I am, Walter, 'cause I thought my Rita's record was beautiful, just beautiful. It should've won that Grammy. And don't get me wrong because I'm the one who loves good jazz around here. Hy, he doesn't care too much about music. Not everyone appreciates good jazz but I do and, believe me, this is where Rita heard it, right here in my house I had the Sarah Vaughan and the Duchess Silk records, brought her up on that stuff, the good stuff. But I also hear all these things on the radio, on the stations they play at the deli, not the jazz stations. Now I know my baby. I know she could be singing anything she wants to sing—she got that kind of voice—and maybe the way that girl who sang 'Say a Little Prayer' was popular, that Dionne Warwick, or the way some of the girls are so popular now like Whitney Houston, making fortunes and living in mansions. Lot of those folks live in California. Sometimes me and Hy, we've thought about living in California. The way the houses cost out there and the rent, you need to be selling millions of records. But my baby, my Rita, I honestly think she can do it. What do you think, Walter?"

"I think she's your daughter, Mrs. Moses, through and through."

MIAMI BEACH

"DAVID!" SAID NATHAN, POINTING to the TV. "Look!"

David was looking out the window, not at the television. He was leaving the next morning. His week-long visit with his grandfather had been a break from the intensity of his work in Los Angeles. He was never exactly sure why he'd come to Miami—maybe for encouragement, reassurance. The old stories about Gent and Bernie still fascinated him. At the same time he was upset by Nathan's insistence that he sell Ira's huge inventory of cut-out records. Nathan was pressing for David's involvement harder than ever before. And David, still determined to stay clear of his cousin, nonetheless found resisting Nathan difficult. After all, Nathan had changed his life.

They were in the small living room of Nathan's apartment in the Atlantic Arms, Gertrude had gone to bed and the old man was seated in an easy chair in front of the TV.

"This old movie, it's with Dolores Delite."

"Who's she?"

"Please, David, don't ask questions, just describe what you see. I was there when they made the movie but I forgot. Help me see it. This is the opening scene. This is the whole thing."

"When was it done?"

"Who cares!" Nathan shouted, losing patience. "Nineteen forty-eight. Enough with your questions. Just describe."

"There's a girl on a camel-back sofa."

"That's Dolores."

"She has curly hair and a good figure—"

"*Gorgeous* figure."

"She's in a negligee . . ."

"The director's idea."

"The room's well furnished. Overstuffed wing chairs. Heavy damask curtains. Torch lamps. Silver cigarette lighter on the coffee table. She's lighting a cigarette."

"Watch what happens now," said Nathan.

"A man walks in the room."

"Dick Rawfield, one of the biggest actors of his day. A regular putz."

"You knew him?"

"Is he kissing her yet?"

"He's begun to . . ."

"A long kiss."

"Pretty risqué for those days."

"You should've seen Pino when he saw the picture for the first time. He went bat shit."

"Why should he have cared?"

"David, just describe what you see."

"He's holding her with one hand and with the other, Jesus, he's taking out a knife . . ."

"This is good, watch . . ."

"He's sticking the knife into her—"

"She falls on the floor, she drops dead."

"Right . . ."

"And she's out of the movie in the first five minutes. She threw a fit. Nearly died. For real. Said she'd have Pino break my balls if they didn't change the script. But I told her, 'Look, toots, you're lucky to be in the picture at all. You ain't singing this time, you're acting.' 'Acting?' she says. 'I'm kissing and I'm dying, that's all I'm doing. You call that acting?' So I called Pino before she did. See, when I saw that kiss you just saw, I knew she wasn't acting. Dolores was supposed to be Pino's girl, and I was supposed to be Dolores' manager, but I was dying to dump her and get back to my Duchess. I said, 'Pino, come to California so you can see the way your Dolores is acting in this movie. She's terrific. Surprise her and come out.' He liked the idea and he comes out on the Super Chief and sees the film and starts screaming, 'She's practically naked!' 'Boss,' I say, 'this is Hollywood. All the girls are naked out here.' 'Who the fuck is this guy she's naked with?' I act real surprised and say, 'That guy's Dick Rawfield. The girls are nuts about him. They say he's got a cock the size of a bazooka.' 'Where's Dolores?' he wants to know. 'She's at her hotel,' I tell him, and give him the address. I got everything set up perfect. He goes up to the Strip and who should be walking out of the lobby while he's walking in but big Dick Rawfield. Pino does a double-take and asks the actor if he knows Dolores Delite, and Dick, like it ain't nothing, smiles and says, 'Sure, she's in room 890.' That did it."

"Strange, I've never even heard of Delite or this Rawfield. You say he was a star?"

Nathan smiled. "Ain't nothing strange about it. For yours truly, it was just another day's work."

"Feldman had you . . . take care of them?"

"David, if you got a problem, you eliminate it. I had lots of problems with Pino, but this was one time it worked out beautiful. He thought I was doing him a favor, but meanwhile I was doing myself the favor. I got Silky back from England."

David never got used to Nathan's casual talk about eliminating people. "What was she doing over there?" he said quickly, trying to put it out of his mind.

"Let's say she was experimenting. There was this guy. He was supposed to be royalty but I think he was a fag. He talked like a fag and he had her singing songs she'd never heard of with a big orchestra. She hated it. I had the same idea, but with *Porgy and Bess* songs. She could relate to *Porgy and Bess*. He had her singing in Denmark and some other fucked-up frozen countries where they didn't even know what the hell she was singing about. I went over there and told her she was coming home. The fag screamed. He was weird, this guy, but I didn't pay no attention to him. I just put Silky on a plane and brought her back. Deep down she was glad. I knew she missed me. I told her that ever since 'Defend My Heart,' New York was more her city than Chicago or Detroit. New York had the people. I booked her in a club in Greenwich Village, Café Elite, where all the people that counted could discover her—the newspaper guys, the left-wingers, Socialists, Commies, college grads, poets, painters, God knows who they were. They thought they owned her, but they didn't. I found her, I molded her, I owned her—not Pino, not the Commies. The Commies didn't even know what the hell she was about. They thought she was a protest singer because of what happened in Charleston. They said she was part of the *Movement*, but, believe me, I knew better. She was a real artist, pure and simple. But I also knew how to keep my mouth shut and let them believe whatever the fuck they wanted to believe. See, these people turned her into a goddess. They changed her life. Before it was just the colored who loved Silk, but now it was the whites, and not just regular whites but whites with money, influence. Whites made her rich, 'nigger rich,' Eve called it, but rich enough where she had minks and a limousine and a new attitude that changed everything between me and her. Some things changed for the better. She was living up on Sugar Hill and I was in Chicago with Reba and my boys. I kept everything separate—a week in New York, a week in Chicago, back and forth like that. We were making so much money Pino couldn't complain. After what happened with Dolores Delite, he couldn't say shit. He just left me alone. But some things changed for the worse, see, because this is when Silk really became Duchess and if people are treating you like you hung the moon you start to believe it. You think you can walk on water. With Silky, it was always something. You never knew with this woman. She wasn't easy. But she became big business, David. Lowell too. In 1949 he had 'Whiskey Blue,' a very big song. The critics said it wasn't jazz, but fuck the critics. He sang like I told him to sing, from the heart, and the goddamn thing sold a half-million copies. He bought a Caddie and moved out to Long Island. Lord, he liked the country. He wanted Duchess to go along but she said she wasn't ready for no peace and quiet. You could say that again. Next thing I know, she's on the front page of all the New York papers. She got married. That wasn't bad, that was her own business. I could live with that. It wasn't just getting married, it was *who* she married. A white man, and not just any white man, but a rich Italian named Johnny Strazo."

"Didn't you once mention a Strazo guy from Buffalo who owned a nightclub?"

"This was Marty. Johnny was his first cousin."

"Why did Silky marry him?"

"To get my goat. See, I'd never leave my Reba—not ever. Duchess also wanted to get Pino's goat. Pino hated Strazo as much as me."

"Why?"

"I'm a little tired of talking," said Nathan, yawning. "It was all a long time ago. But sometimes it seems like it was just yesterday. I can still hear Pino going on and on about Strazo. He'd scream about Strazo for hours. Strazo made him crazy . . . But let's not worry about Pino; let's watch the picture. Describe it to me, David. Tell me what happens next. That Dick Rawfield was some good-looking fellow, wasn't he? After this, though, Dick Rawfield never made another picture. Never did anything. Dick Rawfield was another guy who made Pino crazy. Everyone made Pino crazy."

DETROIT

"IT ALL BEGAN IN Detroit," Mario Washington said to Kate Matson over the phone. She had just moved into her new office in a black glass skyscraper in midtown Manhattan, headquarters of "One Hour."

"What began here?"

"This record business connection. I keep finding historical threads. I pull one and another starts to unravel. This thing has a deep history. I need to keep digging."

"I'm surprised you're in Detroit, I thought you'd stay in L.A. for a while."

"Not a good idea. When I quit, Kalb said he wouldn't allow it, said I had too much sensitive information. He actually had my offices padlocked and my files carted away within five minutes."

"You duplicated everything, right?"

"Thet day before."

"And you didn't say anything about working with me?"

"No. In fact, I gave up my apartment, put my things in storage and got out of town fast as I could. I need to be invisible for a while."

"Good idea, as long as you get to New York soon." He was, after all, now her executive researcher.

It had been only a few days since they had been together, but they were already badly missing each other. He thought of their week-long lovemaking along with the openness about their past, and present. They shared the same frustrations, they came together in a perfect fit. They were an immediate team. Everything fit—goals, desires, passions, ambitions. Both their fathers loomed large in and out of their lives. They sought a kind of redress for past grievances. They wanted, needed results. They didn't mention it in so many words, it wasn't their style, but it was like destiny took over, was in charge. Until now, they'd played it all according to the rules. No more. The morning after their first night together at St. James's Club they told their respective offices they'd been hit with a powerful flu. They drove up to Santa Barbara, where they stayed locked in a hotel room, with time off on the beach for long slow walks. They stayed for seven days, not able to keep their hands off one another's bodies, to stop probing, pleasing. She opened herself as she had never done for any man. He dominated, submitted. They had been so hungry, lonely. Now they were discovering, revealing parts of themselves they hadn't known even existed. Their sexual exchange was a special revelation, an offering of trust. It was so good, and so sudden, they couldn't explain it.

It was Kate who had first seen the light just as the sun set on that first afternoon together on the California coast. Seagulls swooped from a cloudless sky, blue turning misty yellow, burnt orange, fiery pink. The sand was cool on their naked feet. They walked slowly, holding hands.

"There's no reason why you can't accomplish what you set out to do," she suddenly said, stopping in her tracks.

"What are you talking about?"

"Your work. Your investigation. It's perfect. You do it under the auspices of 'One Hour.' You head the research team. You can go after these people with *no* restrictions. The show has the budget, the surveillance techniques. Whatever you need."

"I have no background in journalism, Kate. I wouldn't know where to start—"

"You've already started. Look, my boss is a tiger, he'd love the idea. He was the one who found you. Paul Abel means business. He's not afraid of stepping on toes."

"Don't you already have a research staff?"

"Not assigned to my part in the show. That's what I'm supposed to be doing now—building a staff. Hey, the best investigative reporters are lawyers with backgrounds like yours. When it comes to investigating show business you've got a headstart on everyone."

"It's a wild thought—"

"No wilder than what's been happening to us."

He looked at her in jeans and sweatshirt, hair blown back by a brisk ocean breeze, her body's scent a mixture of salt water and perfume, her brown eyes on his. The "Ice Queen" was melting, she thought. Was it because his strength matched hers, or because they shared secrets and a vulnerability? Both? All?

He was wearing jogging shorts and an oversized tank top. He seemed so serious about staying in shape. She was the same. They ran back to the hotel room, where for the fifth or sixth time that day—they'd lost count—they devoured one another.

"I'm afraid you're going to say that you're married," she told him.

"We're both thinking it's too good," he said, his head between her breasts. "So here we are, trying to find something wrong."

"Can you find anything?"

"Not so far—not with you, not even with the job you're talking about."

"You'll move to New York?"

"And work for a woman I just met?"

"We'll be working *together*."

"If you can hire me, you can fire me."

"That worries you?"

"Not now. Nothing's worrying me now."

Remembering the week in Santa Barbara, looking out his window of Detroit's Pontchartrain Hotel across the river to Windsor, Canada, Mario asked Kate whether she was worried.

"About what? It's a legitimate program. It's legitimate work. If I understand things right, you need me, I need you.

"I miss you."

"Then come to New York for the weekend."

"I'll be there soon as I get through here."

"What are you after?"

"Two people from the past."

"Who?"

"Pino Feldman, for one. Ruby the Gent Ginzburg for the other."

HOLLYWOOD

"YOU GOT A MILLION cut-out records sitting around, and no one to sell 'em to," said Ira. He was on the speaker phone to his grandfather in Miami Beach.

"Pick up the receiver, goddamnit," said Nathan Silver. "I hate it when you talk on that fancy phone. It sounds like you're in a broom closet."

"Look, Bernie . . ." said Jay, picking up the receiver.

"*Nathan.*"

"Nathan, I'm crazy about you, I love you, but I got four other lines lit up. I'm doing twelve things at once. And in five minutes I'm on my way to New York to get some action for that Shock Therapy group."

"What's Shock Therapy?"

"Mitch Matson's boys. Remember I told you about Mitch Matson? He's the guy who sold me the cut-outs so cheap—"

"Don't talk down to me, Ira. Of course I know about Matson . . ."

"Well, Matson's doing favors. So now I gotta deliver for him, and to tell you the truth, I'm having problems. Right now I don't have time for the cut-outs. When you said you'd take care of it I wasn't sure but I went along. You said you'd get your David to handle it—"

"I got another idea. Sell the shit to Jay Feldman. He don't have to know what you paid for it. Do a side-deal with Feldman. Let *him* dump the merchandise. He knows distributors. If he's like his grandfather, he'll fuck his bosses and look to pocket the change himself. You'll see."

"Maybe, but more important is this Matson group . . ."

"Watch out for Matson. I'm beginning not to trust him."

"You don't even know the guy, Bernie."

"Nathan. I know the type. A big shot. A big fish. Him, he's the kind who's always stuffing little fish in his mouth. Can't eat enough little fish. Never satisfied."

"This guy's on the up and up—"

"Listen to me, Ira—*no one's on the up and up*."

"Why don't you have Gertrude take you on a walk around the pool?"

"That's how you talk to your grandfather?"

"I told you, I'm hassled. My brain is fried. I don't got time to play games with you now—"

Hearing that, Nathan slammed down the phone. He could take anything but disrespect. David was right—Ira was a punk, a crude kid. David had class, like the Gent, but why wouldn't David work a real deal with Nathan? Why was David, like his father Ralph before him, rejecting a man who loved him so deeply? Nathan's head ached. He kept thinking about those cut-outs. He'd begged for some responsibility, and now finally had gotten it. Okay, he had a job to do. And it felt good.

He wanted to do it with David but Ira was right about one thing—David was different. Ira was right about something else too—Nathan was out of touch. For the last forty years he'd been out of the business, hiding. For the past fifteen years he'd lived through Ira. He had no contacts, nowhere to sell the records. Without his grandsons, he was helpless. Without his grandsons, he might as well be dead. The thought made him weak. His head hurt even more. He lay down on the couch and slept for nearly three hours. When he woke up, Gertrude was there with a wet towel for his forehead and hot soup on the table.

Ira rode the exclusive MGM Grand jet from Los Angeles to New York. Next to him was his new secretary Kora, fresh from Hawaii, a twenty-two-year-old he had met through Mitchell Matson. The big plane was designed for only a small number of passengers, each of whom had a roomy seat, video-tape machine, private screen and large selection of cassettes. Ira had his own cassette—Shock Therapy in concert. Watching the tape, he couldn't see why they weren't selling. They sure as hell had the look—shaggy hair, tattoos up the ass, skin-tight black leather, screaming guitars, lewd lyrics, hoarse lead singer shouting like a demon possessed. Yet radio was resisting, and Matson was restless. He had paid big bucks and now wanted big results. Well, if his own reps couldn't get the group on the air, Ira was going to do it himself. He was going on the road to meet with program directors—contacts he himself had cultivated over the years, men he was sure respected, even feared him.

After his second Scotch his mind drifted from music to Miami. Maybe he'd been too hard on Grandpa Bernie on the phone, maybe he should've been more patient with him, but Bernie, goddamn him, Bernie had been driving him nuts. The old man was getting senile. Or stir-crazy. Or both. Ever since he became Nathan Silver he'd been itching for some action. He wanted back into the record world, but the record world of Gent Ginzburg was long dead and gone. Why couldn't he accept that?

Ira sighed. He'd thought that maybe, just maybe, he could appease Bernie by giving him something to do. Down in Miami Bernie could store the cut-out records Matson sold Ira. That would make the old man feel useful and even important. Let him and his hot-shit Ivy League cousin David put their brains together on this one. Let them find a buyer. The idea was to keep Nathan out of his hair for a while. Besides, there was probably a half-million dollars profit to be made.

But things didn't go that way. David didn't want in, and now Bernie was talking about Jay Feldman. What about Jay Feldman? Well, maybe the old man hadn't lost all his marbles. Maybe Jay wasn't a completely nutty idea, Ira thought as he looked over at Kora. She was asleep. He liked Kora . . . she was quiet, impressionable and gave good head. He could tell if a woman enjoyed giving blow jobs or just did it out of obligation. This one liked it. Sure . . . maybe Jay Feldman would like the idea of selling the cut-outs. Maybe Jay was the right person for the job. He'd have his own channels. He wouldn't mind making the money and would see it as a favor. Of course Ira could find his own buyer, but putting someone in the middle was always safer. The whole record business was structured around middle-men, multi-layers of executives separating labels from artists, producers from promoters, radio stations from retailers. The name of the game was protect your ass.

Ira asked a flight attendant for a phone.

"Jay," he said. "I'm at thirty-five thousand feet over Kansas and I'm thinking of you."

"Thanks, pal."

"Thinking of how you're always thinking of me. Thinking of the good fees you paid me last year and thinking how I owe you one."

"That's real good thinking. What's up?"

Ira explained it. "You interested?"

"I might know someone. A wholesaler in Detroit. I'll make a call. Check back with me tonight."

Thinking that Grandpa hadn't lost his touch after all, Ira poked his secretary on the arm, waking her up. Ira was excited. A few minutes later he was in the bathroom, sniffing from a vial of killer coke. There was a knock on the door. Kora floated in. He liked the way, without being told what to do, she kneeled before him.

Wearing steel-pointed boots under designer jeans, Ira kicked the program director's right knee and heard the break. The man tried to protect himself, but Ira was too quick, slamming his foot in the left knee. The executive collapsed on the floor face first. Ira hit him in the head with the butt end of a pistol. He would have liked to blow his brains out but that would have involved too many logistical problems. This was better, the lesson would be clear—no one should fuck with Ira Crossman.

The program director of WHIT, Geoffrey Wane, was new at his job. Ira saw him as a wimp and a fag. Ira believed there were too many fags creeping into the music business. Ira got along with most types, he liked to say, but not fags. And for him, Wane was the worst kind—uppity, bitchy, college-educated, hipper-than-thou. On the phone, back in Manhattan, he had told Ira he didn't have time to see him. It had been years since a program director had had the nerve to say something like that to Ira Crossman.

"Maybe you didn't get the name straight—Crossman, Ira Crossman of Crossman Communications."

"I don't take well to solicitations from indie promoters," said Wane in a voice that sounded English, feminine and uppity.

"You're new, right?"

"Just over from London—"

"Then maybe you ain't all that familiar with American radio."

"I'm familiar with business ethics, Mr. Crossman."

"I got product you can't refuse—it's too hot. MM Records. 'Downtown Demon' is a monster. It's Shock Therapy's new single. You know Shock Therapy?"

"They've been a disaster in Europe for years. Matson bought them for the States at a bargain price and now he's saddled poor you with getting them played. Sorry, Mr. Crossman, I just don't think so."

"Look, Wane, I don't work on the phone. I work in person. I'm coming to see you."

"Then you'll have to come to Fire Island, because that's where I'm heading this very instant."

It was on Fire Island, in Geoffrey Wane's rented beach house, that Ira confronted the thirty-five-year-old executive. Wane was Ira's height but reed thin with wheat-blond hair and outsized red-framed glasses. He wore a white fleece-lined Fila jogging suit with black-leather Italian sandals.

"My God," he said to Ira who stood in his doorway, "you really did come. Well, you're certainly persistent. At the least you deserve a cup of tea. Come in."

To Ira, the house smelled of tanning oil and petroleum jelly. He looked around, expecting to see another ballerina swirling about, but he and Wane were the only ones there. "Look, I got a girl waiting for me back in the city so we gotta make this fast."

They sat in the living room on small white sofas facing one another.

"What do you need to put Shock Therapy on the playlist?" asked Ira.

"A decent single," Wane said.

"'Downtown Demon' is a smash single."

"'Downtown Demon' is dismal. We gave it a shot; we even did call-out research on it but no one liked the bloody thing—that's all there is to it."

Ira had heard this before. In fact, he had heard it all week in New York. But his job was to get it on the playlist, to get it on the air. Exposure and repetition were the keys to pop radio. And Wane's station was critical. If they added it, others would follow.

"What do you need?" asked Ira bluntly. "What do you want?"

Wane smiled. "Not a thing."

"Everybody needs something. Everybody wants."

"Mr. Crossman, I've been courteous enough to allow you into my home. Now if you'll be courteous enough to leave—"

"I ain't going till I get some commitment."

"Surely you can get it through your thick skull that I am not in the least interested in favors, bribes *or* your company . . ."

Whether it was the cocaine Ira had been snorting during the week, whether it was his inability to sell Shock Therapy, whether it was the phone calls from Nathan bugging him to hurry and conclude the cut-out deal with Jay Feldman or the fact that Kora had caught cold and was out of commission, Ira was full up with too much frustration. When Geoffrey Wane snapped, something snapped inside Ira. He beat on the program director. Injuries resulted in a concussion, a broken rib and broken knee cap. Wane was hospitalized for two weeks. When he got out he was still unsteady, and frightened. But by the Fourth of July "Downtown Demon" was added to his playlist, and slowly began creeping up the charts.

ALBUQUERQUE

THE DIRT-BIKE RACES on the dusty track of the State Fair grounds on San Pedro Street did not interest Jay Feldman. The truck-stop crowd was loud and beer-buzzed, the August sun beating down so hard it was difficult to think.

"This thing's amazing," said the diminutive old man sitting next to Jay. "I seen a motorcycle wreck where five guys were thrown in the air. Two of 'em killed. If we're lucky, maybe we'll see something like that today."

"How long we gotta stay?" asked Jay, the heat baking his dark slicked-back hair. He wiped the sweat from his aviator glasses and smoothed his close-cut beard.

"I wanna see the big truck with the big tires crush those little Volkswagen bugs," said Pino Feldman. "He's gonna crush twenty of 'em. It's really something to see."

"My plane leaves at three."

"You got time. How often you visit?"

"You look good, Grandpa Pino. You're hanging in."

"I don't look in the mirror. I know better. But I'm still moving, and that's all that matters. Give me a sip of your soda and tell me more about the cut-out record deal."

Jay explained the details.

"I smell a rat," said Pino. "Smells like something the Gent would do. Sometimes I see a tall cocky guy strutting down the street and my heart stops 'cause I'm sure it's the Gent. Does his grandson look like him?"

"How would I know? I've never seen the Gent."

"I showed you pictures. I told you all the stories."

"That was back then. This is now. This is his grandson Ira."

"Sounds like this Ira's pawning off hot goods. I don't like it."

"The way I figure, I'll clear a clean half-mill."

"If you do it, do it on your own. The Japs don't need to know."

"The Japs don't need to know something else. I've been approached by Mitchell Matson."

"The guy with the record company?"

"And movies and concert tours and everything else you can think of. Mr. Big."

"So what does Mr. Big want?"

"Sonsu. He wants to buy the company from the Japs."

"Let him buy. What's in it for you?"

"A couple of million in stock, plus a forty percent raise in salary. He wants me to run Sonsu as an independent division of his record company."

"So what does he want from you? He needs you to get him a meeting with your Mr. Ohisto in Tokyo?"

"No, he can do that on his own. He's shrewd, this Matson. He says Sonsu is too hot. Business is too good. He wants business to be bad so he can buy at the right price. He wants me to cool off sales."

"It's the basketball league all over again. It ain't nothing but throwing a couple of games."

"So what do you think?"

"Tell Matson you want half-a-mill earnest money now, cash in advance. See what he says. Now I want to watch this truck with the big wheels crush the little cars. You'll hear all the noise it makes. It's an exciting thing to see. Believe me."

ROME

In an office in the shadow of St. Peter's majestic basilica, Carla Bari got up from her therapist's couch where she had brought him to a delayed and successful orgasm.

"See," she said. "You can do it."

Victor Susman, bald well-known Austrian sex therapist, was grateful. Since his disastrous coupling with Carla in Montreux, he had developed a pattern of premature ejaculation. Anxiety had led to a recurring nightmare in which his penis fell off, to be replaced by a small cherry tomato. Victor would wake up, grabbing his crotch and crying for mother. He also developed a complex about eating tomatoes. Too self-conscious to see another therapist, and unable to respond to the injunction physician-heal-thyself, he found his only solace in the arms of the woman who had triggered the crisis. Carla was gentle, understanding with Victor. Every month or so when *she* came to *him* as a patient—and in some matters he was actually quite skilled—she would wind up giving far more therapy than she got. Now, nearly two years after meeting the actress, the therapist at last found the control to prolong the penetrations.

"You've been very patient," he said to her, a large smile on his face.

"I think these sessions have come to a happy ending," she announced as she stepped into her yellow-silk summer dress, her legs long, tan and firm.

"We can keep seeing each other," he suggested. "I want to see you out of the office. I'd like to see our relationship evolve even further—"

"Dear Victor, I'd love to take you to Morocco for the weekend. We'd walk through the markets and Carla would tell you more about the mother she never had. But coming here and talking to you has already been so helpful, truly, and re-examining myself has resulted in such a change of heart, such a change within that I've decided to get married."

"We . . . we *could* do that . . ."

"I don't mean to you, sweet Victor, but to David. You see, I've decided to marry David Crossman. He has changed his life for me, and now I must change mine for him."

"The man in California?"

"With my help and a bit of my money he rejected his past and plunged into a future of uncertainty. David stood alone. Then foolish me did with him what I've done with all men. I flitted about like a butterfly, landing here, landing there, like an object of fleeting beauty. No longer is that satisfying. Europe depresses me. European men no longer interest me. Rome is tired. I'm through with tired old Rome."

"And your film career?"

"Will be better served from Malibu. Don't you see, Victor, Carla is settling down."

"David has agreed to all this?"

"I haven't told him yet. But I know David, and David will be thrilled. He is an adventurer, as I am. You see, David needs me. He doesn't know how much, but he desperately needs me."

"David and I, we will build up his record business together," Carla told her father Calvino on her final night in Rome before flying off to Los Angeles. They were dining on *penne alla carbonara* at a restaurant off Campo del Fiori, a statue of the shrouded monk-philosopher Giordano Bruno, burned at the stake during the Inquisition, hovering over the warm September evening.

"That means you want more money."

"Just a bit, sweet."

"And the first two hundred fifty thousand dollars?"

"He has had a successful record, nominated for an important prize—"

"I know, you told me. When do we get our investment back?"

"Tomorrow's News—that's the group. The critics loved them. And sales were not bad at all."

"But he still needs more capital."

"He isn't saying that, I am. I am taking over publicity for David Crossman Records. In America publicity is the key to selling records. Publicity is the key to everything."

Calvino sipped his wine. "It's been over a year since you accepted a film role, Carlina. If you went back to acting you'd have your own money, making discussions such as these unnecessary—"

"And then what would we talk about?"

"Your art, your acting."

"Through my psychoanalyst I have realized that my acting made me feel like a fraud. I'm like my father. Business is in my blood. Not the business of high finance but the business of the angels—music. Don't you understand, *babbo,* I want to manipulate the media, not be its pawn. I want to—"

"Why can't you just find someone and settle down?"

"*Appunto*! I have. I'm going to. *That's* what this discussion is really about."

"David Crossman?"

"He is the one."

Father sighed. He had eaten too many *penne* and felt bloated. "I continue doing business with Ralph Crossman. I'll be with him in Miami next week. Why don't you meet me there?"

"While you're with Ralph I'll be with David in California. Don't you understand, *babbo*? David is waiting for Carla."

Still asleep, David did not pick up the ringing phone. Helene, a red-haired pianist he had met a few weeks before, answered it. She had awakened early and was in his kitchen making coffee.

"Is this David Crossman's house in Malibu?" asked Carla, calling from the Los Angeles airport down the coast.

"Yes."

"Who is this?"

"This is David's friend. Helene. Who's this?"

"The nurse from Dr. Krakusin's office," said the actress after a brief pause. "The results from his AIDS test are in, and the doctor needs to see him. The doctor needs to see him *immediately*."

MIAMI BEACH

RALPH CROSSMAN PARKED HIS rental car a block away from the Atlantic Arms. As he approached the apartment building he was sick inside. He had been up all night with pains. In his suite at the Eden Roc Hotel he had studied the information on the yellow pad in front of him. Nathan Silver's address and phone number stared him in the face. This was information he had had for a very long while, information he could not get himself to act on. He did not want to think about it. David was out in L.A., was out of his life. David was making a life for himself and there was nothing he could do to deter him. Ralph told himself to stay clear. It was the wise course, the prudent course. Then what was he doing walking toward the Atlantic Arms?

Ralph disliked Miami Beach. He disliked seeing retired people play pinochle, sitting around on benches waiting to die. The place had an Old World Jewish ambience that made him feel uneasy. In the faces of the decrepit men and women he saw the faces of his own parents. He did not want to think of such things, did not want to be here, did not want to remember. But memories came flooding back, images from a life left long ago, doors he had slammed closed, shame he had shut out.

He crossed the street and stood before the Atlantic Arms, trying to steady himself, trying to think. He wasn't here on a whim. He wouldn't be in Florida, in fact, if it weren't for Calvino Bari. Bari was buying into a small bank in North Miami Beach and wanted Ralph to negotiate the deal. Ralph, the cool and rational one, couldn't help but take it as a sign. Being this close to Nathan Silver, he simply could not stay away—if only for the sake of his son. His responsibility as David's only guardian was to intervene before it was too late. Nathan *had* to leave David alone. But that meant getting involved with the man, the very thought of which made Ralph sick.

Ralph had developed other plans . . . he was going to write Silver a long letter but could never find the words. All he really wanted to say was "disappear." For a time he considered calling. As recently as last night he had picked up the phone and punched out Silver's number. He hung up before anyone answered. Now, the morning after, he was amazed to find himself in front of this building. He was actually there in person. Well, he had to do it in person. Had to see this Nathan Silver for himself. The question burning inside his brain was the same one he'd been asking himself over and over again—*was* this old man his father or not? He was sure it was. He was praying it wasn't.

Ten A.M. Silver should be up by now, probably eating breakfast. Just walk in the building, look for the directory. The lobby was dominated by a faded mural of pink flamingos drinking from a fountain. The place smelled medicinal. Ralph's throat was dry, his hands sweaty. He saw the name. *Nathan Silver*. Apartment 6C. Go to the elevator. Push the up-button. Stand there and wait for the elevator.

Suddenly Ralph looked to his left, to a glass door leading to the interior courtyard. His heartbeat quickened. There was an old man walking around a dirty swimming pool. He wore rumpled trousers, thick-soled shoes. He had on dark glasses. He was being led by a heavy-set black woman. The man was tall and thin. He looked frail. Was he blind? It seemed so. It also seemed he was Ruben Ginzburg, a.k.a. Bernard Crossman, a.k.a. Nathan Silver. Ralph froze. He couldn't move, couldn't approach the old man. Inside his head he heard a scream—*go, get out of here. Run.*

And he ran back to his car, got in, turned on the engine and tires screeching, drove away, never looking behind.

"You seem distracted, Ralph," said Calvino Bari a few hours later. "Is it your son?"

"Why would you say that?" asked Ralph, who had managed to negotiate the bank deal in near-shock. About to fly off in different directions, the men were having drinks in the Admiral's Club at the Miami airport.

"My Carla has gone to see your David. She makes it sound like he needs help."

"What kind of help?"

"I don't know. I presume you're not supporting his company, therefore I further presume that your son may need additional capital."

"You've given Carla more money to invest with David?"

"Carla, she is not what you would call reasonable. She is made for your David. She'll do anything to help him."

"I strongly suggest she leave him alone."

"These children of ours, they are no longer children."

"David doesn't need any more money. David shouldn't be in that business at all. Can't you control your own daughter?"

"About as well, *caro mio,* as you can control you son."

NIAGARA FALLS
1949

IF THE HOTELS WOULDN'T give him and his black bride a room, Johnny Strazo decided he'd buy his own hotel. Which is how he and Eve Silk came to be staying at the Honeymoon Hideaway. He had plunked down fifty thousand dollars in cold cash. And if the other Strazos—father Gito and brother Sam—disapproved of the marriage and swore never to talk to Johnny again, well, they could go fuck themselves. Johnny had his own family, his own partners, his own chain of saloons, gambling parlors and cathouses he'd inherited from cousin Marty Strazo, who had been blown away by the Feldman gang of Detroit. Fact is, it was in Marty's club, the Wander Inn, where Johnny first saw Silk eight years ago. That was where she'd attracted him, just like she'd attracted Marty. Johnny loved dark women. His own Sicilian mother had charcoal brown skin and was said to have had Negro blood.

In 1941 Eve Silk had been a teenager with a come-hither voice and full breasts that belied her age. Back then, the thought that cousin Marty was balling her drove Johnny nuts. He wanted her for himself. And after Marty's sudden end, Johnny would have taken her if it weren't for some problems of his own—a hijacking conviction that put him behind bars for six years. Even in jail, though, he had managed to get copies of Eve's records and follow her career. There in his cell, directly above his bed, hung a newspaper photo of Silk singing, her mouth open, a smokey light catching her misty half-closed eyes. Seeing how she had matured into a full-figured woman, hearing how she had grown into a sensational singer, he wanted her worse than ever.

In the Strazo family Johnny was the outcast. He did not give two shits that his family scorned the colored. He had dated Filipinos, Mexicans and an ebony beauty from Brazil. He had also had a long-time affair with the daughter of a crime boss from Cairo. Exotic women turned him on. And in jail, after years of deprivation, he decided to go after the most exotic of all—the Duchess.

And he got her. Now she was in his bed, asleep. He pulled back the sheet and examined his possession. She had put on some weight, but the tits, the hips, the thighs—it was all he'd ever wanted. And it had happened so fast it was still hard to believe. Only two weeks ago Silk was still a fantasy. Now this fine-looking broad was actually his wife. With that in mind, he went over and fondled her breasts, hardening her nipples, arousing her from a dream.

Duchess woke and looked up at this near-stranger. With his dark wavy hair and fine physique he was just about the best-looking white man she had ever seen. For a second there, in the twilight between sleep and consciousness, she had to remind herself that he was her husband. Eve couldn't help but laugh. *Serves Ginzy right,* she thought to herself. *Serves that skinny Jew right.* And that whole crazy time came back to her, the night she told Ginzy to shove it up his ass . . .

The Café Elite on Seventh Avenue was filled with Village types. The walls were covered with casually hung pieces of modern art—abstract, surreal, cubist. Pipe smoke permeated the air. The audience was predominantly white. Many of Bohemia's leading intellectuals were in attendance, young men with Trotskyite-looking eyeglasses and fresh-grown goatees. At one tiny table under the dim light of a flickering candle Columbia graduate students poured over the latest issue of Partisan Review with articles by Meyer Schapiro on Kandinsky, Mary McCarthy on Thomas Mann, Leslie Fielder on Simone Weil. At another, jazz buffs argued the comparative merits of Bud Powell and Thelonious Monk. In a back room, Gent Ginzburg was getting drunk.

Unusual for Ruben to be drinking like this, but Silky was driving him up a wall. Silky was being unreasonable. Just five minutes ago she'd kicked him out of her dressing room after calling him a "two-faced piece of shit." No one was going to talk like that to the Gent, especially some bitch he'd made rich. Ever since she'd become the darling of the hip bookworms Ruby had been having trouble with her. They were treating her like a goddess, a black saint symbolizing the noble suffering of her people, for Christ sake. Ginzburg saw the eggheads as jerk-off artists, but he also knew and had to remind himself that the eggheads had power. Some wrote for the New York newspapers, others for popular magazines. So let these writers fantasize about screwing his singer, at least they were helping him sell records. For Duchess, these people were also opening the door to white respectability.

The bookworms were out there in force tonight, but Ruby didn't want to deal with them. Instead he took another belt of rye, remembering how the fight had started.

"You don't like the picture," Silky had said while she was hooking up her bra—Ginzburg always moved by the size and shape of her breasts. "You don't like it 'cause it shows us holding hands. You're *ashamed* of me."

"It ain't that," Gent argued, looking at the photo from the New York *Journal American* of him leading Eve to his Cadillac after the show. She was wearing a diamond necklace—a gift from Gent—and smiling at the camera; he was looking the other way. "It's just lousy publicity, Silky."

"Why? You're the motherfucker who says there ain't no bad publicity."

"This is different."

"Why?"

" 'Cause people don't like to see that kind of stuff."

"Which people you talkin' 'bout, Ginzy?"

"Colored as well as white."

"You scared your old lady will see it. Ain't that it?"

"I'm scared it'll hurt business.

"Bullshit.

"Look, I'm your manager, Silky, and I'm telling you it could ruin you."

"You ain't worried about ruining me, you worried about ruining your precious little marriage—*that's* the shit you worried about."

"You don't think I care about your career?"

"Not more than saving your own ass, no."

"After all these years, after all I've done for—"

"I'm real tired of hearing that crap, Ginzy. Over in England I got hip to different attitudes. Cats wanted to marry me. *White* cats."

"Your manager was a fag."

"How you know that? He suck your dick?"

"Why do you gotta go talking like that, Silky. It ain't ladylike."

"You don't mind *me* sucking your dick, do you, Ginzy?"

"You're screaming," he whispered. "People can hear you screaming."

"Good. 'Cause the guys out there, they're writing poems about me and inviting me to supper at white dinner clubs and not looking over their shoulder or thinking twice about it. One of 'em took his mother to see me. This nice Jewish woman. Fat lady with a flowered hat and a pretty face. Said she knew everything I was singing about, said I reminded her of the old country when things were bad and life was sad. She invited me to her house. They're rich and they live in the country in Greenwich, Connecticut with green lawns and trees all around them and beautiful flowers. Jewish people, Ginzy, Jewish folks are having me over their house for dinner. Only time I was over your house was to fuck you on the couch when your old lady was out of town or laid up in the hospital."

"That was a long time ago, Silky."

"Nothing's changed. I'm your pussy, plain and simple. Piece of hot chocolate pussy."

"How can you say—"

"You got your sons, you got your wife. Me, I got a little cocker spaniel who pisses on my rug. I love the little fucker but I can't housetrain him, can't do nothing with him, he's so sweet, he hardly eats . . ."

When Eve started crying, Gent went over to put his arm around her.

"No," she said, pushing him back. "Don't need your pity. If I wanna have a baby I'll have a baby and it don't make no nevermind if I get me a fancy husband or not. I could get me a thousand fancy husbands, the kind that write poems or the kind that pimp bitches. Colored men, white men, even that Chinaman lawyer you hired had the hots for me. I swear he did."

Her tears turned to sobs, and Ruby didn't know what to do—the first set was to start, the trio had already played the warmup tunes—so he tried to reason. "Look, Silky, maybe it's that time of month, I don't know, but—"

"It's got nothing to do with no time of the month or nothing!" she yelled, furious at his insensitivity.

"I was down at the Jewelry Exchange on Canal Steet yesterday and I seen these genuine sapphire earrings," he told her, "and I know they'd look gorgeous on you, Silky . . ."

"It's ain't about *that* . . ." she yelled even louder, which was when she called him a "two-faced piece of shit" and kicked his ass out.

Gent sat at a back table, throwing back rye. He didn't even care that her set was starting an hour late. The crowd was anxious, and when she finally appeared, bathed in a blue light and dressed in a white gown, the packed room went wild. When she opened her mouth to sing, Gent's anger turned to mush.

Think it'll be easy
'Cause you fell so fast?
Well, let's see, sugar,
If this thing can last

Will last night's kisses
Just fade away
Or are we feeling feelings
That are here to stay?

I want a love that won't leave town
The kind of love that hangs around

Need a love long-lasting
A love that's true
A love from you that goes all the way through

All the way through, sugar,
All the way through
Give me a love that goes all the way through

"All the Way Through" wasn't fancy. Silk's songs were never fancy. But they reached Ruby and the rest of the audience with such poignancy and open-hearted candor that every male at Café Elite was convinced Duchess was singing just to him.

She's singing to me, Johnny Strazo thought to himself, his heart beating, his dick throbbing, his head dizzy with the freedom of his first night out of jail. *She's feeling what I'm feeling, she's giving it to me, she's staring me in the face, she's doing a whole show just for me.* All those years cooped up in his cell—nights of fantasy, days of listening to her records—and now he was here, listening to her live in a nightclub, sitting at a ringside table close enough to smell her perfumed body and follow the lines of sweat trickling from her neck to her bosom.

Ginzburg was lost in the music, too, caught up in her magic. The eggheads were right. She was a genius. She had something no one else had. She wasn't a singer, she was a truthteller. The truth went from her heart to her head straight out her mouth. Ruby brought another shot of rye to his mouth. He'd hurt her, he knew that. The song said so. The song was for him. He felt like crying.

"Felt like falling by," whispered Lowell Foreman, derbyless tonight, his hair slicked back, his coke-bottle-thick eyeglasses perched over his wide nose. "Duchess sounds sad."

"You're just in time, Lord. Go. Play. You'll be good for her. You'll make her happy."

Through Ruby's whiskey-haze, he watched the saxist approach the singer. Seeing Foreman, the fans applauded, delighted at their good fortune. Silky simply nodded as her friend stood next to her, taking his horn out of its case, adjusting the reed to the mouthpiece, blowing a few notes, tuning to the piano.

"Y'all know my partner?" she asked the audience.

A wave of jealousy passed over Johnny Strazo. He didn't like the way Eve looked at Foreman. But after a single song, the saxist was gone. The song, however, would stay in the memories of those in the audience.

Duchess sang and Lord blew behind her—it was that easy. They chose not to play one of their known recordings, but instead a tune linked to another artist, "When It's Sleepy Time Down South." Perhaps because of association with Silk's trial, or perhaps because Lowell had himself been raised in Alabama, there was something in this rendition, taken at an achingly slow tempo, that sounded very personal, shattering, sarcastic and sincere all at once. Duchess sang the lyrics—"pale moon shining on the fields below"—with a precision that painted a picture. But by the time she got to the chorus, syllables slurred and images blurred into an impressionistic dream. Behind her, Lord's sax sounded like charcoal-mellowed bourbon and branch water, breathy, lush, potent. Their conversation had an intimacy that made their listeners feel like eavesdroppers.

Lowell winked and was gone—without another song, without a word, without even waiting for the applause to die down. "Lord plays some shit, don't he?" was Duchess' only comment before ending the set with a house-on-fire "Miss Brown to You."

"Miss Silk," said the man in her dressing room a few minutes later, "I'm Johnny Strazo and I wanna marry you."

"What the fuck are you talking about?" asked a drunk Gent.

"He ain't talkin' to you, Jack," Duchess told Ruby as she gave the handsome Italian the once-over. "The gentleman's talking to me."

"The gentleman's a jailbird," said Ginzburg.

"I done served all my time, and I know all about you, Gent Ginzburg, I know how you wipe shit off Pino Feldman's ass . . ."

Ruby's inebriation made the fight unfair. His first and only swing missed Strazo by a mile. Johnny landed a solid right to Ginzburg's mid-section and a nasty left caught him on the chin. The Gent was out.

"Someone look after Ginzy," said Silk to the people in her dressing room who were standing in shock. "I'm going off to get married."

Eve looked around her suite in the Honeymoon Hideaway. It was the fanciest hotel room she had ever seen—red velvet curtains, gold carpeting, thick blue towels, a sunken bathtub. Even though they had been married in the drab office of a Justice of the Peace without guests or a party afterward, Johnny had given Eve a nice-sized diamond ring. She knew he wasn't much more than a handsome thug, yet he had managed to keep his business together from his jail cell. There was no doubt he was bonkers about her. Sure, he was boring, but look how pretty he was. Besides, this was one white man who put his money where his mouth was. He said he'd marry her and, goddamnit, that's just what he did—no hesitating, no double-talk, no guilty Jewish jive. Ginzy wouldn't marry her if Moses himself gave the go-ahead. She was sick and tired of being Ginzy's back-door hussy. Johnny was opening up the front door, and, with her head high, Duchess was walking right on through.

It had rained in the morning and the September afternoon was cool and pleasant as Eve and Johnny left their hotel to go see the Falls. She wore a wild flowery yellow dress, he a green suit and brown-and-white shoes, but it was the color of their skin, not their clothes, that caused the stares. Johnny didn't see the disapproving glances, but Duchess felt the heat. She glared back. To one old woman, she stuck our her tongue, wanting to say, *Fuck you, bitch. With those sagging tits of yours, no man—black, white or green—is gonna give your tired ass the time of day*. She took Johnny's arm and snuggled a bit closer to him.

Okay, she thought, maybe this Strazo wasn't a great lover—he was too fast and rough. Maybe he wasn't sensitive and maybe he was no Einstein, but he *was* a fan, her biggest fan, even bigger than Ginzy. His tool was bigger than Ginzy's which she was tempted to tell Gent just to get his goat. Men hated hearing that shit. *You see, Ruby,* she said to herself, *maybe you're scared to tell the world how you feel about me, but this guy ain't. This guy worships me like I'm the black madonna.*

They reached the promenade that followed the mighty Falls. The roar was tremendous, the spray refreshing in their faces. The bright sun and crystal-clear sky had Duchess feeling good. She felt respectable. She was a married lady.

A young woman pushing a baby carriage passed by. Eve looked at the infant, a sleeping angel.

"Want kids?" she asked Johnny.

"Can't have 'em."

"Why not?"

"The doc says my sperm don't got no tails. Can't swim. Me, I'm glad. Kids are always yelping. Pains in the ass. I hate fuckin' kids."

Eve was crestfallen. Johnny said it cheerfully, like he was relieved not to be having any black babies. While Silk was lost in thought, Strazo sat on a bench only a few feet from the very spot, just across the railing, where the Falls dropped down hundreds of feet below. Duchess sat down next to him, her heart broken by his news.

"This here says Truman thinks the Ruskies got the A-bomb." With difficulty he read from a discarded newspaper, having no idea how he had hurt her. "Truman should blast those fuckers the way he blasted the Japs, blast 'em before it's too late."

Duchess didn't reply. She didn't even hear him. Instead she stared at the rushing white water, the precipitous plunge. She looked at Johnny, the guy with whom she was supposed to be spending the rest of her life.

"Gonna take a little walk," she said, feeling the need to get away.

"Don't get lost," he called after her.

As she started her stroll, she felt like the world's biggest fool. She didn't love him. She didn't even care about him. She'd only married him to hurt Ginzy. Or just to have a baby. She wanted a baby so bad. She and Strazo had nothing in common besides the fact that they both liked the way she sang. She'd waited this long to get married, and now she'd blown it, running off with the wrong guy. Face it, Ginzy was the one she wanted. Ginzy was the cat who saved her and turned her black ass around. Sure, that Jew bastard loved her—he had to love her. But here she was, stuck, up here in jiveass honeymoon heaven with some crazy guinea, a boring, stupid, child-hating guinea.

Sighing at her own foolishness, she walked back to the bench. She felt she had to say something to Strazo, to let him know how she felt. As it turned out, she didn't have to say a word. Strazo wasn't there. Just as Eve looked around to see where he'd gone, she heard an elderly woman's frenzied cry shattering the afternoon calm. Duchess' eyes followed the finger of the screeching woman's hand. The finger pointed to the Falls. There, amid a shower of foam and spray, she caught a fleeting glimpse of a pair of brown-and-white shoes. In a second, the shoes, and the man to whom they were attached, washed over the edge and plummeted down, down, all the way down . . .

. . . Police came. Questions were asked. Strazo's dramatic demise made all the papers. The one eyewitness, an eighty-year-old Toronto woman, claimed a man had pushed him over, but she was hysterical, vision-impaired and considered unreliable. Some suspected suicide. Racist reports called it the guilt and/or the fate of a white man who married a black woman. But Duchess knew the truth. She knew it had to be Ginzy, that Ginzy had followed them up there to prove how much he loved her. Six months later she was pregnant with Ginzy's child.

NEW YORK CITY

MARGO ANSWERED THE DOOR to her Sutton Place penthouse, expecting the first guests to her dinner party to be either Ralph or Richard Humbolt, a rising young curator at the Museum of Modern Art. Instead she saw her own parents standing there, Henrietta in a pale blue pants suit, Wilbur wearing an "I Love New York" baseball cap.

"You said you'd be down to see us at Leisure World but you never came," said her mother. "We got tired of waiting and decided to surprise you. Aren't you even gonna give your folks a kiss?"

Margo froze.

This wasn't happening. This couldn't be true. God couldn't be that cruel. The problems she was having with Ralph were bad enough. She'd never seen him so sullen and preoccupied. At first she thought it was David, but now there was clearly something bothering him beyond his rebellious son. He would snap at her, cancel dates at the last minute, avoid sex, claim his work was overwhelming. Margo wondered whether another woman was involved. She even wondered about Carla Bari. But she knew Ralph well enough to see that the signs didn't point to a romantic distraction. When she probed, though, he became surly. Worst of all, their talk of marriage, begun only a few months earlier, had hit a snag. She'd been so patient, worked so many years to bring the relationship to the point where that delicate issue could even be discussed. Now for reasons she couldn't fathom, everything was changing.

"Everything is ready!" she cried to her parents. "I'm sorry but everything is ready!"

"What are you talking about, dear?" asked Mom.

"I swear," said Daddy, "this is fanciest place I ever laid eyes on. You own all this stuff?"

"I'm having a party . . ."

"Good," said Henrietta. "Will your Ralph be here? I want to meet your Ralph."

"No, he's—"

The doorbell rang.

"I'll get it," said Daddy.

"No . . ."

It was Ralph.

"Is this Ralph?" asked Henrietta.

"Ralph Crossman," said Ralph who, drained after an afternoon with Mitchell Matson, had nearly decided to skip the party.

"I'm Henrietta Smith and that's my husband Wilbur. We're mighty happy to meet you."

Ralph looked confused.

"We're Muriel's folks."

"Who's Muriel?" asked Ralph, looking for an explanation from Margo, who had run off to the kitchen.

The evening turned into a nightmare. Ralph left early. He said goodnight without even kissing Margo, barely acknowledging her parents and the other guests.

Riding in a cab to his brownstone, he thought about breaking off the relationship with Margo. He kept seeing her parents on the couch watching the guests as though they were watching a movie. At the dinner table Margo had acted as if they weren't there. When her parents finally spoke up, saying a word or two, she looked at them like they were Martians who happened to land on Sutton Place. Her half-dozen guests seemed to find Henrietta and Wilbur picturesque, maybe campy.

Not Ralph. Margo had lied to him. She was made-up. She was Muriel, not Margo. From Iowa, not Boston. She was a farmer's daughter. All these years she'd deceived him. And that thought, that word *deceit* woke him up. Because it wasn't Margo's deception that upset him tonight. *It was his own.* No wonder he had been attracted to her, and she to him. They'd *both* invented their pasts, and their frauds had been masterful. Sure, Margo had him fooled all the way. Only now, though, did he realize that he'd wanted it that way, that he had never challenged her because she had never challenged him. They had struck a deal, unconscious and unstated. What had gotten to him tonight wasn't so much the appearance of her down-home parents from Iowa but the threat of the appearance of someone else, namely, Mr. Nathan Silver of Miami Beach, Florida. If Wilbur and Henrietta could unexpectedly show up on the doorstep one fine evening, so could Nathan—or Ruby Ginzburg—or Bernie Crossman. And even more, the fact of his own life's deceit. He had run, run and hidden to deny his father. He was still running. Witness last week when he saw the old man at the Atlantic Arms. As a child he couldn't face down his father and claim himself. As an adult, nothing, it seemed, had changed.

Disgusted with himself, Ralph went to his study, poured a stiff Scotch. His thoughts went to Mitch Matson. Somehow Matson had prevailed on him to represent him. All afternoon this man, who also had reinvented himself in the face of a disreputable past, had discussed his plans to buy Sonsu Records. And the name Feldman had come up. Jay Feldman . . .

"He does business with your own relative," said Matson.

"What relative?"

"Ira Crossman. Your boy Ira."

"I have no contact with Ira Crossman. He's a distant relative—"

"Feldman recommended him highly. I've been doing business with him myself."

"There's a conflict of interest here, Mr. Matson. I can't possibly represent you—"

"What are you talking about, Ralph? You've already agreed to the retainer; you've accepted it—"

"That was before—"

"Ira's an indie promoter. He has nothing to do with my Sonsu buyout. That's Jay Feldman. Another smart boy. These are both smart boys. I'm surprised your own son isn't working with them."

At that moment Ralph would have asked Matson to leave his office except that Matson was his key to Hollywood—Matson could provide information and insight that just might help save David from the mess Nathan had made for him . . .

The Scotch had Ralph feeling a little better. He'd been right to avoid the old man in Miami. Nothing, after all, would have been gained from an ugly confrontation. The old man was his blood enemy, his life-long adversary. Silver knew that Ralph knew Bernie was not dead. That was part of the torture, part of the game. Well, Silver didn't have to know that Ralph had an advantage of his own . . . Mitchell Matson could be his ace in the hole. Ruby might be street-savvy, maybe he was wise in the ways of the back alleys of the music business, but things had changed since the days of Pino and the Gent. Now it was a corporate war in which financial sophistication backed by a highly developed sense of legal combat prevailed. As a kid, Ralph might have been intimidated by fists and baseball bats. No longer. He had grown up into one of the shrewdest, if gentlemanly, adversaries on Wall Street. Wasn't that, after all, why Mitchell Matson had sought out his help? Bernard Crossman didn't know that. Whether he knew it or not, his time was over. He'd be better off dead—.

The phone rang.

"Do you hate me?" Margo was trying to keep back tears, but there was panic in her voice.

"I . . ." The words wouldn't come. Thoughts of Margo and Ruby and David and Matson and Ira were fighting for space in his mind. He needed room to think or not to think . . .

"Can I come over?"

"Now?"

"Now."

"I'm not sure I'll know what to say—"

"I will."

But when she arrived she didn't. And Ralph, to his surprise, did. It had been building up inside him for too long. It had to come out, and if not to this woman, than to whom . . . ? He confessed . . . yes, confessed was the right word . . . the truth about his father. Margo's own secret was out, he felt safe in telling her his. She just sat there and listened. Afterward, profoundly relieved, he made love to her with more genuine passion than at any other time in their relationship.

And before she fell asleep in his arms, he had proposed marriage. And she had accepted.

Kate Matson entered the presidential suite at the Regency Hotel on Park Avenue a little late for her appointment with her father. It was a Monday morning, and neither the Russian ballet company nor the international tennis star in the lobby made an impression on her. Her mind was on Mitch.

"I'd rather you call me Mitch," he would tell her when, as a child, she would spend a rare and strained weekend with him. He hated the sound of "Dad" or "Daddy," saying it made him feel old.

Kate was nervous. She had wished that Mario could make this first approach, but that would have been impossible. Mario's former boss, Los Angeles D.A. Lawrence Kalb, was Mitch's longtime pal. For Mitch to discover the connection between Kate and Mario would only hurt "One Hour's" investigation into the record industry.

"Your first story is going to set the industry on its ear," predicted exec producer Paul Abel. "You're a wolf in sheep's clothing. Your soft-news rep with 'Show Business Today' should help you get anyone you want on camera."

She'd wondered whether "anyone" included her own father. She said nothing to Abel about targeting Mitch. Her boss might object to the father/daughter angle, and besides, she herself wasn't too sure she wanted to go through with it. When she finally did call Mitch, the sound of his voice put her off. She had forgotten, chosen to forget, how self-assured he always seemed.

"Honey, what kind of interview do you have in mind?" he said, speaking by phone from the Carlton Hotel in Cannes.

"Oh . . . well, something very simple. No cameras for now. I'll . . . we'll . . . just be looking for background information. The truth is, Mitch, I hardly know anything about my own father's business."

"So you're saying it'll be strictly a profile of me?"

"It may evolve into that. Right now I'm just exploring—"

"I'll send you some clippings," he said, struck by the idea of being featured on network television, but only and especially, of course, if it were a flattering piece. Though Larry Kalb had told him that the heat was off—the price, even for an old friend like Larry, had not been cheap—favorable publicity never hurt. With Ralph Crossman protecting his legal front, and now daughter Kate enhancing his image, things were going his way.

"I have a number of good clippings," he told his daughter. "*People*, *US*, the Wall Street *Journal*. The media's always been interested in me. I'll have my people send you everything you need."

"Thanks but I need to see you," she said, hoping not to sound like a daughter.

"My daughter can see me whenever she pleases. We'll meet in New York."

That was in July, a month ago. In fact, the timing had worked out to Kate's advantage, giving herself and Mario a chance to get situated.

Unsure about New York and still somewhat unsettled about his lightning-fast affair with Kate, Mario Washington still wanted to maintain some independence. He took a place on Fifteenth Street near Union Square. True, he was often at Kate's midtown apartment, but he also spent a good deal of time alone. Doubts remained about the affair. So did the passion. Going to concerts, jogging, talking in all-night diners, they opened levels of intimacy neither had ever known or acknowledged. At the same time, given their background, they couldn't help wondering if things seemed better than they were, distrustful of their own happiness and pleasure in each other. That ambivalence also showed in the office.

It wasn't that Mario hadn't impressed Paul Abel. In fact, the boss saw Kate's recruitment of Washington as a major coup, even if he were unaware that she and Mario were caught up in an affair.

"What's the point of telling?" Kate asked Mario as, earlier in the summer, they sat in a bistro by the Brooklyn Bridge, the moonlit East River reflecting the skyscrapers of lower Manhattan.

"No reason—other than to be honest."

"And to confuse him."

"Him or us?"

"Everyone. Business is business."

Mario laughed. "For you to say that . . ."

"You can say what you like."

"You're the boss."

"That's not fair."

It wasn't. It was.

Mario had his own office and own assistants. The salary was higher than his previous job and his mandate open-ended. He could go after his targets without restraint. Still, it was Kate who ran the unit. Kate was tough and demanding, but no more than he was. The two of them worked long hours after the rest of the staff had gone. During the days, though, when Kate was chairing a meeting, things could get tense. She tried to low-key her position, but there it was. She knew Mario was a proud man, the son of a proud cop . . . Well, she had some father problems of her own.

As she took the elevator to the penthouse of the Regency, Kate asked herself if maybe, just a little, was she using her lover to get to her father? She didn't think so, she hoped not. Did *he* think so . . . ?

A fifteen-year-old girl opened the door to Matson's suite, startling Kate. She wore a cream-colored blouse and faded jeans.

"Hi, there, I'm Melissa," she said, leading Kate to the large living room before disappearing. "You must be Mr. Matson's daughter. Mr. Matson will be right out." She smiled winningly. Not a hint of self-consciousness.

Kate entered the sitting room and sank into a sofa, taking a deep breath. She tried to concentrate on the financial news flashing across a big-screen TV set. She thought she heard a reporter say her father's name and she turned up the volume, catching the end of the story. "Industry insiders claim that Matson's interest in Sonsu Records, whose mega-groups include the heavy-metal band Nightmare, has cooled considerably . . ."

"Don't you believe it," her father said, entering the room wearing linen slacks and a short-sleeved sport shirt and looking very fit. Fresh from the shower, his hair glistened. It had been seven months since he had stood her up in Honolulu, nearly twenty months since she had seen him at all. She had to admit that he looked remarkably handsome. He walked over and kissed her on the cheek. His lips felt cold.

"Did you meet Melissa? She's my secretary. A delightful girl." He said it with a straight face.

"We met," said Kate.

"I hope you're not still angry with me about missing you in Kahala."

"I've come to talk to you about work," she said.

"You're so dedicated, Kate. You've always been dedicated. I want you to know that I'm very proud of you."

When he touched her hand, she wanted to pull it away. When he smiled, she had to force a smile of her own. She looked for her own eyes in his, looked for some resemblance but couldn't find it. If she didn't know better she'd think a mistake had been made, that he wasn't her father after all. She felt no connection.

"Let's discuss this profile, honey," he said.

Don't call me 'honey,' she restrained herself from saying. "I'm interested in your business, Mitch."

"My business often involves complex and delicate negotiations. Right now I'm up against a shrewd Japanese fellow named Oshito. He heads Sonsu and, as you just heard on television, I've been thinking about buying the company. Something tells me, though, that the timing may not be quite right. In business, patience is all. 'Patience is indeed that quality in man which most resembles the process which nature follows in her creations.' Balzac said that, honey. Not that I claim to read Balzac as a regular diet, but I did go with a lady who happened to be a professor of literature, and *she* quoted Balzac. In fact, she reminded me of you, Kate. She had a first-rate mind."

"I'm interested in the way record companies use independent promoters," said Kate, trying to bring it back to business.

"What do you know about independent promoters?"

"Very little. I'm here to learn." Her chest felt tight.

"I've just recently employed one," he said, "and he's doing me a world of good. In fact, he's largely responsible for the success of Shock Therapy, my newest group. I'm told they're breaking out big all across the country, and I suspect at the expense of groups like Nightmare, which, coincidentally, is one of Sonsu's most important acts. I wouldn't be too surprised if Nightmare's new album isn't a major disappointment, an album that Sonsu is expecting to sell nine or ten million copies worldwide. That's one of the reasons this may not be an especially good time to tender an offer to Sonsu. Naturally, honey, what I'm telling you is off the record. I just think it's important that I give you good background. I want you to see how your father's mind works. This business is not as simple as it may appear."

"The creation of a hit . . ."

". . . is an artform. Now I'm speaking on the record and you can quote me. To have ears," he said, pulling on his left lobe, "capable of reading the tastes of millions of people is a great gift. In that sense, you might say, I've been blessed."

"What about failures?" She could hardly breathe.

"Fortunately"—he smiled—"they've been few. But to get a real handle on the way I work, you'll need to spend more time with me, honey. I'd suggest, if I may, that your camera crew follow me around for a day, maybe a whole week. You'll see me evaluating tapes, chairing story conferences, board meetings, engaging in a wide range of charitable activities."

"That might work . . ." Her voice was cool. She felt cold.

"Whatever works for you will work for me," he said. Kate was a piece of work, all right. Well, she was his daughter . . .

Moments later, Melissa was serving them from a large pitcher of mint ice tea. Kate could take it no longer, ended the "interview" and went home.

Her head ached, her mind buzzed. She had to take two aspirins and lie down. It was early afternoon and she needed to take a nap. She hadn't taken a nap—a break from work in the middle of the day—in years. She couldn't remember the last time. She couldn't remember feeling this weak, helpless. She wanted to call Mario but what would she say? "My father has upset me. My father has a teenager he's screwing. My father has made me crazy . . ."

She closed her eyes, and in spite of the whirlwind inside her brain felt herself half-drifting off to sleep, half-dreaming of a time long ago, just before her father left her mother . . . She was barely a teenager, and she was in trouble—the house was being robbed, someone was after her, suddenly the door to her bedroom opened and her father, handsome, strong, protective, stood in front of her. He came to her bed and stroked her cheek and then he touched her, touched in a place even she hadn't touched herself. It made her feel different, funny, afraid, and then he told her to touch him down there, and afterward he smiled and whispered in her ear "Don't tell, don't ever tell, honey, it's our secret, our secret forever."

It had happened, not once but a number of times, it had really happened, no fooling, no dreaming. Kate Matson was awake now. She was awake then and she was awake now. And, thanks to a fifteen-year-old "secretary," damn her, she faced a truth she had been denying for fifteen years, along with her feelings of love, and hatred, over what this man, her father, had done.

WEST HOLLYWOOD

"IN ROME," CARLA TOLD David, "who would ever *think* to put duck sausage on pizza? For us, cheese, tomatoes and a thin crust is enough. Here at Spago you have pizza with Thai barbecue chicken, pizza with pesto and shrimp, pizza with goat cheese and walnuts. This is crazy pizza. Hollywood is crazy pizza. In Hollywood, everyone is cutting up the pizza pie and fighting over the biggest slice."

David looked at Carla. Her white lace outfit looked more like lingerie than an evening dress. The restaurant was crowded with stars. Near the entrance was a miniature statue under glass of Lucille Ball as Lucy Ricardo. Below on Sunset Strip traffic was reduced to a crawl—Silver Clouds, Testarossas, Turbo Carreras, vintage Thunderbirds in turquoise and white.

"So this is our *ultima cena.* Is that it?" asked Carla.

"Translate, please," requested David.

"Our last supper."

He smiled in spite of himself. For three weeks she had lived in his place in Malibu. For three weeks she had been trying to convince him that their marriage would be good for both of them. For three weeks she had alternately charmed him and driven him nuts.

"You liked me better as a silent partner, *non é vero?*"

"Well, you didn't scare off my female friends. You didn't scandalize my neighbors by parading around naked on the beach—"

"Your neighbors *love* me naked. They follow after me. Some invite me inside. I know more people in Malibu than you do."

"I don't want to play the numbers game with you."

"Then let us be serious. Americans are obsessed with duck-sausage pizza and, above all, *happiness.* But you are not happy. It is your father; it is my father. Our fathers are together, but they keep us from each other. We have a business that we believe in, but they are looking over our shoulders, they're wanting to know our business, and all we can say is that Tomorrow's News is making a little bit of money. What else can we say?"

"'Leave us alone,' is what we can say."

"You say 'us.' Then you are not dumping me in the Hollywood reservoir? I will not be forced to open Carla's Red Hot Chili Pepper Pizza Stand?"

"You had faith in me in the beginning; I appreciate that, you know that . . ."

"I had a sex therapist, a bald man with a beard who told me good sex depends on good dreams. Do you understand?"

"You're going to tell me anyway. Go ahead."

"Wish it into being. Isn't that what you have done with your business? In spite of the fathers, the children are surviving."

"I'm barely making it."

"You have your ears, your ears are fabulous. You found Tomorrow's News, and now you have found Vince Viola, the gorgeous muscleman saxman. You learn about distributors and program directors, you learn everything you need to know except the most important link is missing. Me. You think I am an actress. No. Carla never was an actress. A Brazilian director once called Carla a 'dramatic presence.' That is Carla. A presence, a promoter in American language. I promoted my presence. Now I dedicate myself to promoting your musicians. That is worth a million dollars and I charge you nothing. Vince Viola will be on two magazine covers next month because of editors I know. His saxophone will be in his mouth and his shirt will be off his back."

"You've talked to him?"

"He objected. He is an artist, he says, not a pinup, but I guaranteed him all in good taste, all in good fun, and record sales like he has never seen before. He said, 'Okay, Carla, I listen to you because you're a promoter. Clive Davis promoted Kenny G, now you promote me. Make me Kenny G.' 'Bigger than Kenny G,' I promised. 'You are the new Pied Piper.' "

"I admit that could be useful—"

"Useful? The difference between selling fifty thousand and five hundred thousand. This is something we do together. After the Grammy nominations, David Crossman Records had the opportunity of a lifetime with Tomorrow's News. Where was your promotion? You threw it away like cold pizza."

"The new album is going to be stronger than the first—"

"You are working on music, I on promotion. In two weeks I am taking News out of the studio and bringing them to the Hollywood sign. While they climb over the sign I have Matthew Ralston take photographs. He does Rolling Stone covers, he does Madonna. While he is photographing, Spike Lee will be shooting the video."

"You've arranged all this?"

"And the newspapers and the magazines and the television reporters from 'Show Business Today' will be there while it is all happening. An event. Like eating pizza in Hollywood is an event. Everything here must be an event—"

A gunshot rang out.

David ducked and brought Carla down with him under the table. A man groaned. People screamed, scrambled about confused. Another shot, another. Blood splattered on Carla's white lingerie top. The man sitting behind them had been shot in the ear. A fourth shot wounded a woman, piercing her side. A bullet hit a small child. A busboy fell, his right arm shattered muscle, bone and bloody tissue.

"From out there!" a waitress yelled, pointing to the plate-glass window facing Sunset, riddled now with bullet holes. Pizzas were dripping red, blood mingling with cheese and tomato sauce.

In an apartment a block below, a man with a telescopic rifle packed up his gear, including an ample supply of cocaine, and hurried out the back door. Later that night, when asked by Jay Feldman whether he had gotten his man, the gunman was not sure. "He didn't look like the picture of Crossman you gave me, and he might've ducked . . ."

"They said Ira Crossman had a reservation there," Jay told Pino the next day. "But maybe they read it wrong. Maybe it was David."

"Doesn't matter," said the old man in Albuquerque, looking out his trailer window at the mountains beyond. "I want both the grandsons dead."

CHICAGO

1950

"I THINK PINO WANTS me dead," said the Gent.

"You're crazy," said Silk as, between news of the Korean War, the radio played Nat Cole's 'Mona Lisa' and Louis Armstrong's 'C'est si Bon.' "

"I'm telling ya'," Ruby insisted. "I know this fucker. I can read his eyes. He's jealous I've made ten times he ever made making records. Pino's jealous over everything. Look what happened to Dolores Delite. Pino's jealousy, it's like cancer. It eats him up, it makes him nuts. If 'All the Way Through' wasn't such a big hit he'd rub us out like chalk on a blackboard. Only reason he ain't is 'cause of the money we're making for Pino Records."

"And how 'bout Lord? That 'Jukebox Jive' thing is selling, isn't it?"

"Selling good. The jazz magazines are saying he's selling out, but I'm saying thank God there's someone to sell to. Lord likes to see people dance to his stuff. What the hell's wrong with those writers?"

"Lord's reading the *Racing Form*, not no music rags. I wouldn't worry about the writers."

"My son, Miltie, he's only fifteen and already he's reading the great writers. He's very smart, this boy, but he'll have nothing to do with me. Nothing. He looks at me like I'm dirt, maybe because I don't read what he does. He looks at me like he knows everything there is to know about me, and he hates what he sees. I'm telling you, Silky, it's like he's not even my own son."

"This is the kid who walked in on us?"

"This is Miltie. The other boy, Irv, a regular *mensch*. He follows me wherever I go. All he wants is to be with his father."

Silk slowly walked to the brass bed in her well-appointed South Side apartment and stretched out on her back. For eight months her pregnancy had been difficult but she had managed to work anyway. She had wanted to work. She had also wanted to have the baby in Chicago, not New York, to be close to Ruben, to remind him that the child was his, not Johnny Strazo's.

"How can you be sure?" Gent had asked when she first told him.

"I can count, that's how."

"Maybe your counting's off."

"Maybe you want me to kill the kid."

"I didn't say that. I'd never say such a thing."

"But you'd think it."

"Look, Silky, I'm taking care of you like I said I would. What more you want from me?"

"I don't need taking care of."

"The hell you don't."

"I'm the one bringing in the bread, Ginzy, while you're the one giving it away. Feldman gets half of everything I make. And what about my songs? He owns those, too, don't he?"

"You get the writer's share. You get royalties. I see to it."

"But I'm talkin' 'bout who owns the songs—the *copyrights* of the songs."

"We've got a publishing company."

"*He's* got a publishing company. We don't got shit. And you're too scared of him—"

"You, of all people, should know why."

"Pino don't scare me none."

"Pino came within an inch of killing you."

"Fuck him. The cat's slime . . ."

"With a network like you wouldn't believe. I seen it when I was kid, and I seen it get bigger and bigger. He's got people all over the place, collecting on favors, taking care of problems, wiping his ass. If you don't wipe his ass right, he'll have yours, and laugh about it. There ain't no getting around Pino. You're either in or out."

"And you never thought of taking his ass out?"

"Sure I thought, which is why I've never done it. Thinking about it made me see I'd be doing myself in. I'd last a day, two at the most. Then there'd be no place far enough away on God's green earth to hide."

"You'd take over, that's what you'd do."

"Don't work that way, Silky."

"Hell it don't."

"Look, my own wife doesn't nag like this. She knows to leave me alone. My Reba, she keeps her nose out of my business. Business is something women don't understand."

"Your Reba lives in a dream world."

"You got no right to talk about her."

"*No right!*" Silk screamed as a sharp pain went through her abdomen. "Something's happening, Ginzy. Maybe you should get the car."

"I'll call an ambulance."

The pains sharpened. "No time for that. Go 'round and get the car."

He hesitated. "What's wrong?" she wanted to know. "You 'fraid the press will show up at the hospital? You 'fraid of seeing our picture in the paper again?"

"Stop screaming," he said. "Don't get yourself excited. I'll get the car."

Five minutes later he came back out of breath, his jacket off, his tie askew. "Something's wrong with the car. Engine won't turn. I gotta call an ambulance."

"No time," Eve spoke in spurts, her face grimaced. "My water broke. Pain's coming fast. Everything's happening at once. This child ain't waiting for no one. It done made up its mind to come on through."

Gent panicked. He considered running, leaving her there, taking off and forgetting the whole thing. He didn't want to deal with this. But there was Duchess on the bed, calling for his help, laying back, legs spread. What could he do?

The next half-hour was a nightmare for Ruby. In spite of the fact that blood had never fazed him before—he had done things that would cause most people to faint—Gent found himself at the point of passing out. Hearing Silk scream, seeing the great vaginal opening, the thick blood flowing, the sight of a full head of hair, the actual infant emerge, the mother in spasms of pain . . . it all nearly did him in. Were it not for the Duchess' orders "*Pull! Goddamnit, pull!*" . . . he wouldn't have, he couldn't have touched the baby, but he did, yanking and pulling until he saw it was a girl, his first daughter, with her eyes shut tight and her skin light brown, her mouth so tiny and everything so perfect, even her little fingernails, even her little eyelashes, a sweet angel of a baby.

"The cord," said Silk. "Get a knife. Get something. You gotta cut the cord."

Ginzburg took a deep breath, still on the verge of fainting.

"Just don't sit there, goddamnit!" shouted Eve. "*Do* it."

He did it with a knife from the kitchen. It wasn't easy, the struggle lasted minutes, the thing was so rubbery and strong, but he was finally able to separate child from mother.

"Give me my baby," ordered Duchess. "Hand her to me. Then find something in the bathroom to clean us off."

An hour later, the three were together in bed.

"It's a miracle," said Gent.

"Happened the way it's supposed to happen," said Silk. "The way God meant it to happen."

"You have a name?"

For the first time, the infant opened her eyes and Ruby saw himself.

"Sure I got a name," Eve answered. "I'm naming this baby after the sweet great-aunt who raised me. I'm calling this child Gertrude."

MIAMI BEACH

GERTRUDE SERVED THE TUNA fish.

"She makes it with chopped celery," said Nathan, telling David something he had heard many times before. "It's good with celery."

"Listen, Nathan . . ." David began, unable to eat.

"I know you're nervous. I can understand it. I been in your position many times. Who wouldn't be nervous?"

"I couldn't have made it any clearer that I wanted nothing to do with your business."

"It's this business with the cut-outs," said the blind man. "We've had a problem."

"What does that have to do with me?"

"You're my grandson. I been telling you that. Now you see it for yourself. Just like Ira's my grandson. We're in business together."

"The hell we are."

"Maybe you don't think so, David, but whoever went after you knows so."

"Who *did* go after me? That's what I came here to find out."

"What did that great writer say? If you don't learn from history, history comes back and bites your ass. You're getting bit in the ass now, David, but you're tough. I see that. You're tougher than your old man ever was. He'd pack up and run. Go crying to your grandmother, may she rest in peace."

"I want to know who did the shooting, Nathan."

"Don't ask me, ask Jay Feldman."

"Feldman's behind it?"

"The son is dead. But the grandson is alive. And so is the grandfather. Grandfathers and grandsons. Who would have thought?"

"Pino Feldman's alive?"

"Over ninety, but he refuses to die until he's sure I'm dead. And, believe me, he ain't sure."

"Where is he?"

"Ask Jay. Jay knows. Jay's working for him."

"I don't care who he's working for, he has to know I have nothing to do with your whole crazy business."

"He doesn't know about me. No one does."

"Well, I have nothing to do with Ira's business. I haven't seen Ira, haven't even talked to him. Doesn't Jay know that?"

"Call Jay and tell him what you're telling me. Say you have nothing to do with Ira. He just happens to be your cousin. You both just happen to be Crossmans who just happen to be in the music business. As far as the cut-out deal goes, you don't know nothing. Call. Tell him. This Jay, I'm sure he's an understanding fellow. The Feldmans are known for being understanding. Why shouldn't he believe you?"

"Cut the sarcasm, Nathan. Tell me what happened to those cut-outs."

"I'm telling ya'—Ira cut a deal with Jay Feldman. The records came through a man named Mitchell Matson. Matson fucked us."

"Fucked *you*."

"Fucked all of us. When we shipped the records to Feldman, it turned out Mitchell had slipped in mostly junk. Once you got past the first few records on top of each pile—the big-name artists—the rest was garbage. Instead of making a half-mill on the deal, Jay'd be lucky to make a dime. But more than the money, it made him look bad. It was an insult. Jay felt like a patsy. But it was Matson who fucked him, not us."

"So why is Jay after Ira?"

"Because he doesn't believe Ira."

"Let him check with Matson."

"He did, but Matson, Matson is slick. He denies it. He says Ira's the one who slipped in the junk fillers. I warned Ira, I told him months ago to watch out for this Matson, but Ira gets impressed too easy. That's why he needs you. I always knew that. Ira needs another set of eyes, Ira needs a head that thinks clear and won't get mixed up. Matson sold him a bill of goods. He hired Ira to promote some band that was so lousy Ira had fits promoting 'em. And, believe me, David, Ira can promote anything."

"Didn't Ira inventory the cut-outs before he sold them to Feldman?"

"It was a sloppy deal all the way around. That's why I wanted you to handle it, David. That's why—"

"*That's just why I stayed away, Nathan!*"

"You're shouting, David," said Nathan, standing up unsteadily, his voice starting to shake. "You come in here like you own the place. You show no respect. Just like your cousin Ira. I'd thought . . . I mean, I show you the music business, I set you up at the beach—"

"Now wait, goddamn you . . ."

"You use profanity with your grandfather? Like I'm a bum off the street?"

"You can have your place in Malibu back. Is that what you want?"

"I transferred the ownership to you in good faith. I put it in your name. It's a gift. I don't take back gifts. That's the kind of faith I had in you—"

"This is getting crazy . . ."

"This is logical, David. You and Ira get together, just like I've been telling you to do all along. The two of you, the team."

"This is your set-up, isn't it?"

"What set-up? You came along before Jay Feldman got back in the music business. Things have just happened. But things happen according to a plan, I'm convinced of that. I read some history books, I read history by James Michener. This Michener's a very great writer, he teaches . . ."

"You've told me before."

"Don't be so impatient because I'm going to tell you again. When you look at history you see things happen for a reason. Maybe when these things happen to you, you don't understand the reasons, not right away, but the reasons are there. Like with me and Pino. And the way I met Duchess. And the way I made her career. I made her into an international star. Pino tried to hurt, but he actually helped—at least until the end.

Did I tell you about the end of Duchess' career?" Nathan said, looking around to make sure Gertrude was gone.

"No."

"You don't sound like you want to hear."

"You're living with the past. And I'm living with a woman who was nearly shot to death two nights ago while she and I were minding our own business in West Hollywood."

"The colored girl?"

"No."

"Good. You listened to me, you dropped the colored girl. You made the right decision. I had the same decision to make. Is the one you're living with, is she a Jewish girl?"

"I don't know."

"How could you not know such a thing?"

"She's Italian."

"Then she's not Jewish."

"There are Italian Jews."

"Where I come from, the Italians, they worshipped saints, they went to confession. I don't know from Italian Jews."

"I don't care if she's Hindu, the point is that by being with me her life was put in real danger. By being with you I've put my own life—"

"David," said Nathan, "I never promised you a rose garden." He smiled, pleased with himself.

But the remark, the *tone*, chilled David. As the old man sat back down to eat his tuna sandwich, shafts of sunshine falling over his withered face, David saw Nathan in a different light.

He was, frankly, panicked by the Spago restaurant shooting; Nathan wasn't. Not at all. David could not conceive of himself dying in the crossfire of a time-worn feud. Nathan could. Nathan wasn't scared of what might happen to David. He didn't even seem worried. The truth was, the news had *excited* the old man. He probably felt rejuvenated by the old battle. You could tell that he relished the idea of David being under siege; it brought his grandson closer to him in a way his own son Ralph had never been close. Now David needed him. Needed his protection to go on living.

"I need to nap," said Nathan. "You'll go back to your hotel. Maybe you also need a nap. Come for dinner. Gertrude's making a pot roast. We'll talk at dinner. I've got some ideas. Feldman, Matson—they don't worry me. I've taken on worse and won. Ira's tough too. You come from a tough family. I'm going to take care of you. You'll see."

David sat by the pool at the Fontainebleau surrounded by sunbathing Long Island tourists and tried to consider his options. He *could* tell Ralph everything, ask his father's advice and admit he'd gotten in over his head. But, goddamnit, he hadn't. He didn't *need* Ralph to bail him out. He could just hear his old man: "I told you so." Besides, his small record firm *was* staying afloat; two acts were selling. With Carla's help he'd financed the enterprise by himself. David Crossman Records was working because David Crossman's ear for music was real, his business sense pretty good. Beyond that, his instincts about his cousin and, for that matter, Jay Feldman, had been right. He had avoided the crooks and he wasn't about to compromise his efforts or his artists through guilt by association.

On the other hand, the bullet had been live. At Spago a man and a child had been killed. Carla had barely escaped. He couldn't possibly ask her to go now. They were in this record business together, but he couldn't tell her the truth about his cousin, father or grandfather. He hadn't told anybody except Dr. Carlos, the New York psychotherapist. Carla had driven one therapist crazy. She would probably take the true history of the Crossmans to the press and use it for publicity. So who *could* he rely on?

"*Paging Mr. David Crossman . . .*" The announcement floated over the humid October afternoon.

He picked up the phone by the outdoor bar. Aside from her records, he had not heard Rita Moses' voice in months. Now it seemed full of pain.

"How did you find me?" Stupid question.

"Your office in L.A. I need to talk to someone . . . I need to talk to you . . ."

"What's wrong?"

"It's something I thought I could handle, but now . . ."

"What is it, Rita?"

". . . just needed to talk . . . needed a friend . . ."

". . . my father . . ."

"Is he sick?"

"Mama hid it. Didn't want anyone to know . . . I denied it, I guess . . . I saw but I wouldn't look at what I was seeing . . . I was out on the road . . . when I got home yesterday he . . . he weighs nothing . . . can barely speak . . . cancer's in his liver, his bone marrow, his blood . . . traveling all over his body . . . eating through him . . . oh, David . . ."

"I wish I were with you."

"It doesn't matter."

"It does."

"Too much time has passed . . . just like with Daddy . . ."

A little girl skipped by and tripped over the phone cord, pulling the plug, disconnecting David from Rita. The child was unhurt but frightened. By the time David called Rita back the line was busy. It stayed busy for the next hour.

Back in his room, showering, changing, ordering a beer from room service, David kept calling Rita until the line rang but no one answered. Was she with her father? He considered trying to locate the hospital, but finding Mr. Moses could prove impossible. Where was the great Walter Gentry in all this? David wanted to see Rita—just hearing her voice had brought to the surface emotions buried for months. She hadn't asked him to come, but she'd called. He didn't want her to think he'd hung up on her. He wanted to explain what had happened. He called again. No answer. He got her parents' number from information. No answer. No choice but to go back to Nathan's. For what? Pot roast? He didn't want pot roast. He was tired of that apartment in the Atlantic Arms, tired of the stories. The old man was vicariously living through him—that much was more than clear. But hadn't he done the same with Nathan? If it weren't for Nathan and Nathan's stories of Ruby and Bernie and Chicago and Detroit he would still be in New York running Ralph's errands. Nathan had at least freed him. Nathan had also trapped him. Nathan had him where he wanted him, in the thick of corruption, in cahoots with cousin Ira. Still, David refused to accept that collusion. It was a manipulation on the part of a blind man who could no longer see reality. In the here and now David was on is own.

The phone rang. David grabbed it, hoping it was Rita.

"Turn on the TV," said Carla. "Hurry."

David did. A leggy blonde on "Show Business Today" was saying, "Last week's shooting at Spago, which left two dead, is reportedly connected with executive David Crossman, owner of David Crossman Records, who was at the restaurant but escaped unharmed."

Suddenly an image of Carla, in a provocative pose from a French art film, appeared on the screen.

"Italian actress Carla Bari" reported the blonde, "who serves as publicity director for Crossman Records, has told us that underground figures have been vying for control of Crossman's rap-and-soul hip hop band

Tomorrow's News. The group's single—'It's all About Action'—hits the stores tomorrow. Bari claims that Crossman Records has been fighting these forces and that the song itself reflects that stand. The label will have more to say about the shooting at a later date. David Crossman could not be reached for comment."

"Are you *crazy*?"

"Yes! This is a crazy brainstorm! This is a million-dollar idea! After Spago I was so afraid, but while you have been gone, David, I listened to one of your records, this Marvin Gaye song called 'Ego-Tripping Out' and he sings, 'Turn the fear to energy.' I've turned it! I've done it! They are talking about you, they are talking about me, they are talking about Tomorrow's News. Tomorrow 'It's All About Action' will fly from the stores. Everyone will be looking for it, everyone will be buying it. It's as though it were written for this very purpose—the lyrics, the beat, everything—"

"You lied, fabricated this story—"

"Came to me in a dream. *Incredibile, ma vero, caro.* A dream like a gangster movie, you and me being chased, men in big hats, everyone after us but we were too quick, we got away. So many ideas come in dreams. I love my dreams. I use them, David. We made the show, we are on the air—"

"You'll get us killed."

"How? It's a dream, not real."

"The hell it's not."

"What are you talking about?"

"Things you don't know about."

"Now *you're* dreaming."

"Call up that show. Deny it. Say it was a foolish joke."

"Are *you* joking? You should have seen how long it took me to convince their reporter I had a real story. Anyway, the story is already out. The trades, the daily papers, everyone else will be picking it up—"

"You're turning this into a circus."

"Exactly, *carissimo*. Your American publicity *is* a circus. What I've been trying to show you."

"Stay out of this, Carla. Get out of my house and get out of my business—"

"*Our* business," she reminded him, sounding like Nathan Silver. "You and Carla are partners."

David slammed down the phone. What to do? Carla was right; the story was out. He would have to face the media. But how? With what story? What retraction would be plausible?

Driving to Nathan's, David knew enough not to mention this. If Nathan had not already heard the news on television, there was no reason to get him excited. It would only confuse the old man. David had enough problems dealing with his own confusion.

Ringing Nathan's doorbell, David decided to make this evening as brief as possible. The less said to Silver, the better. Eat and run. Maybe even take the red-eye to L.A.

The door was opened by his cousin Ira. His eyes were steely.

"What are you doing here?" David asked.

"Hell of a question for you to ask. Wouldn't be here except for Bernie."

"Nathan," Nathan corrected from the living-room couch.

"Nathan says we gotta talk," said Ira. "I don't think we got shit to say to each other but—"

"I don't either," said David, slamming the door in his cousin's face and walking away.

Ira opened the door and yelled at David, who kept walking. "*You think you're so high and mighty, don't you? Well, I got news for you, asshole . . .*"

"Lower your voice," Nathan was saying in the background. "Keep your voice down, let him go. He'll be back. I guarantee you, he'll be back.

David did not look back. He checked out of the Fontainebleau and drove to the airport, his heart hammering. His original plan was to head for L.A., but when he saw he could make an eight P.M. non-stop to New York he grabbed it. He wasn't sure why, he just felt he had to get to New York.

He still had the key to his father's East Side townhouse. Rita—and Carla and Ira and gunshots ripping through Spago—rattled in his mind.

NEW YORK CITY

PAUL ABEL WAS VERY angry. He had Kate Matson and Mario Washington in his office. Outside it was storming—winter thunderclouds cracking open over midtown—while inside Kate and Mario were on the defensive.

"Can't *believe* this," said the executive producer with the rumpled shirt and reddened skin. "Put you people in charge, give you *carte blanche* to get the goods, a backup staff, the works. And what happens? We get scooped by your old show, Kate, by those cockeyed lamebrained know-nothings at 'Show Business Today.' How could you let that happen, Kate?"

"They don't have anything," said Mario. "Their story doesn't check out."

"'Show Business Today'" was fed a press release—"

"They mentioned Crossman, didn't they? Crossman was your guy, Mario. You said—"

"Not *David* Crossman," said Mario, "Ira . . ."

"You said it was a whole family. You said there were old Mafia connections. Well, that's what 'Show Business Today' is implying—and they're scooping the hell out of us."

"This Carla Bari is a joke," argued Kate, "an actress turned publicist. Mario spent weeks checking—"

"The story's not ready, Mr. Abel. That's all I can say."

"That's not saying enough. How much goddamn time do you need? By the time you do get ready this stuff will be old news."

"I haven't run across anyone who's going into it in any depth," Mario told him. "There's an historic connection between Crossman and Feldman that goes back to the forties. If I'm right, Bernard Crossman was the name Ruben 'the Gent' Ginzburg assumed when he and his family disappeared into the Witness Protection Program in 1953. He staged his own death. He testified against his old boss Pino Feldman. Crossman died in 1986, but the circumstances are shady. He was living in Miami Beach. I'm scheduled to go down there next week—"

"And when are *we* scheduled to air this story?"

"When it's ready," said Kate.

"Unacceptable! With this shooting and killing at Spago, everyone's going to be snooping around. And what about the killings? How do they relate?"

"That's what I'm running down now," said Mario.

"And what have you come up with?"

"David Crossman has cross-connections. I'm following leads—"

"No one has the deep background on the story that Mario does," Kate said. "No one else is looking at the whole picture."

"And," said Mario, "no one else has Mitch Matson on the line."

"*Mario* . . ." Kate shook her head, indicating he'd made a major slip.

"Mitchell Matson?" Paul said. "The record guy? I never made the connection before. Is he related to you, Kate?"

"In a way."

"What *kind* of way?"

"He's my father."

"Your *father*? You mean your own father's involved in this business?"

"He's a major force in the industry," Mario said. "You must know that his MM Records is huge—"

"And you're willing to implicate your own father, Kate?"

"He's dealing with Ira Crossman and Jay Feldman," she said tonelessly.

"And," said Mario, "his lawyer is Ralph Crossman, David Crossman's father."

"Okay, okay, I admit this is starting to sound interesting, but, Kate, don't you have any reservations about going after your own father?"

"No," she said, not willing to tell him why.

"How are you going about it?" Paul asked, thinking this had to be the most cold-blooded female extant.

"He thinks I'm doing a puff piece; he's giving me full access."

"So you're ambushing him."

"If *you* have any compunctions about this, Paul . . ."

"Look, people, I have compunctions about two things and two things only—lousy ratings and stories that don't pan out. You two can bust the Pope and the Chief Justice of the Supreme Court, you can bust your own mothers, or fathers, if you want to—as long as you get the right goods on these jokers. As long as you get the facts. I want this music-corruption story on the air, and I want it on fast."

* * *

"You slipped up," said Kate when she and Mario were alone in her office.

"I don't want Abel to see the story as a personal vendetta—"

"Is it?" asked Mario.

"The truth is the truth." said Kate.

"The truth is that the whole goddamn record industry is rotten. Racist, too. If we were doing this thing right we'd look at the corruption of the whole institution before we focused on personalities. The majority of blacks have to make it to the top of the Black Chart before they can cross over to the Pop Chart. What's the difference between that and being sent to the back of the bus? These Black Music Departments set up by big corporations look like progress. They give you the idea that there's more promotional money for black music but the real purpose is to keep black music in its place. If you let the thing go—if success were based on talent and not restrictive categories—the music business would start looking like the National Basketball Association. *That's* the story we should be after."

"That's not a story," Kate countered, "that's an editorial. Besides, what about the black gangsters in the music business?"

"I give you that. But the Feldmans, the Ginzburgs—they led the way. They were there first."

Pause. "And Mitch Matson?"

"No one's ever been able to lay a glove on him, Kate. Too smart, too slick. You're the only one who has a chance of . . . getting him."

And, believe me, thought Kate, a strange excitement running through her, I want to get him, I want to get him in the worst way.

The night before, a Saturday, David Crossman had stayed at a hotel on Madison Avenue only a few blocks away from his father's brownstone. He'd arrived from Miami at one A.M. and had not slept at all. At one point he left the room to walk the streets of his childhood. The voices inside his head were unrelenting, voices competing for his attention: *See your father. Ignore your father. Call your father. Tell your father, don't tell your father. Protect your grandfather. Protect yourself. Call Rita, don't call Rita. Fly back to L.A., wait, think, stop thinking, stop worrying. Remember . . .*

As a private-school kid growing up on the Upper East Side, he remembered times when he thought his father was God, his all-powerful savior. Other times he saw Ralph as weak, frightened and insecure. Image was everything. He'd spent his youth and early adulthood switching back and forth between these two extremes. Father was there to run to. Father was there to run from. Father was everything he didn't want to be. Father could right anything that went wrong . . .

David stopped in front of an old-fashioned Lexington Avenue candy store left over from his childhood. He remembered stealing a yo-yo there and getting caught. Ralph had been furious. "If you don't know right from wrong," he had told his son, "you don't know anything, you won't be anything."

But who was Ralph? the son thought. A man in hiding. He had no idea of Ralph's coming to terms with himself, of his marriage plans with Margo. And who was Ralph's father? Another man in hiding. Who was David? Was *he* hiding? Was he afraid to go back to Los Angeles? Had he come running home to Daddy? Was he afraid of Ira, of Jay? Who did he fear most—his grandfather or father?

The sensible thing was to get a lawyer. David was a lawyer, but only a fool had himself for a lawyer, and besides, there could be no doubt that Ralph was the far better attorney. Ralph was a master at his craft. From working at Crossman, Croft and Snowden, David knew that the firm had superb back-up. It protected its clients, and right now David felt the need of protection. Did the shooting at Spago mean his undoing was already in the works? Because of his unwillingness to work with Ira, reinforced by storming out of the Atlantic Arms, hadn't he already antagonized the people against him? What people? Would Nathan kill his own grandson? Would Ira kill his own cousin? Would David, by confiding in his father, help destroy his own grandfather?

David longed for Rita. Up all night, he called her at nine, saying the truth. "I need you as much as you need me. Let's have breakfast."

She had been up all night, too, at the hospital by her father's side. When David saw her at a croissant-and-coffee shop in the morning light of MacDougal Street in Greenwich Village, he felt her strain. Saw it in her dark eyes. Somehow her pain brought him closer to his own. She had changed since he'd last seen her. So had he.

"You're different, David. You seem . . . steadier."

"It's a front.

"Tell me."

"You're the one who needs to talk."

"I'd rather listen. Tell me about that old man in Miami Beach. Doesn't it all go back to that old man you went to see when we spent the weekend at the Fontainebleau. God . . . that was three years ago, wasn't it?"

"You were there at the beginning."

"You never explained, but the way he affected you, the look on your face, it was like you'd seen a ghost."

"I saw my grandfather."

And saying the words, he felt a great relief.

"What? Why didn't you say anything to me? What's such a big deal about seeing your grandfather?"

David downed his espresso and ordered another. "You have anything to do this morning?" he asked Rita.

"Visiting hours don't start till one. And the hospital's not far from here. So go on, quit stalling."

The story that poured out touched Rita's heart. She was amazed to hear about Duchess Silk and the role she had played in the life of David's grandfather. The connection was bizarre. Who would have imagined? At the end Rita was shocked about the shooting and suspicious of Carla.

"A couple of years ago we ran into her in Montreux," Rita told David, who, at this moment, felt closer to Rita than he'd ever felt to any woman. In a way he felt he was trusting her with his life. "I didn't trust Carla," Rita went on. "She told Walter, practically promised, that she'd help us get a deal, and maybe she did have some connection with Sonsu and Jay Feldman, but I doubted it."

"I haven't mentioned Jay Feldman, but he's part of the whole picture," David said, going on to reveal the Pino-Ruby Ira-Jay connections.

"Then Sonsu is involved somehow?"

"I'm going to find out."

"My second album's coming out next week. Does Jay Feldman know that you and I are friends?"

"I mentioned you once to him but he was hardly listening. I doubt if he pays attention to jazz. He's interested in money, not music."

"Walter says the company's been acting funny."

"The trades claim Sonsu's in trouble. Business is off."

"They'll bury my record."

"Maybe not, maybe after your Grammy nomination . . ."

"My sales didn't reflect it. Anyway, we were talking about your career, not mine."

"I've talked enough; I want to hear about your new record."

"Walter produced it, wrote lyrics to classic jazz lines . . ."

"What about your own lyrics and songs?"

"What about your father, David?" she asked, uncomfortable talking about her album that wasn't her album. "I mean, does he know about Nathan?"

"He must. He's too smart not to. He's just staying away, trying to avoid his father and his past. That's the story of Ralph's life. No one can back to everything he's denied."

"What about you?"

"I haven't seen him in two years. In some ways that's made things easier for me."

"The 'Show Business Today' report must have reached him. He must be frantic."

"Frantic's not Ralph's style."

"I think you should go see him. You may have more of a handle on this thing than he does."

"You said you're going to see your father at one. Mind if I go with you?"

"I'd like that."

The weight of problems had shifted. By getting out of her own head and into David's, Rita got a little relief. She realized she'd missed him, his life. And he realized how much he had missed being close to her. They'd cut themselves off from one another just when their intimacy was deepening. At this point, on this misty Sunday, it didn't matter whose fault it had been. For whatever reasons, after having spent all morning talking, they both felt better. With David by her side, Rita was a little more confident about facing the day's ordeal.

"Will Walter be at the hospital?" David asked.

"He's still in Europe, arranging concert dates."

"And your mother?"

"Rosy never leaves Daddy's side."

Rosy's cot was next to her husband's bed. Hy was gaunt, ashen, tubes from his mouth, tubes piercing his veins. His eyes were shut. His head, contrasted to his emaciated body, appeared oversized.

Rosy was making oatmeal on a hot plate she had snuck into the room.

"This is David," said Rita after going to her father's bed and kissing him on the cheek.

"*The* David?" asked Rosy.

"*The* David."

"Strange time to bring this man 'round here, child," said Mama, shaking her head. "Strange time to introduce me, what with my hair not fixed up or nothing. Nice meetin' you, David. Feel like I already know you. Come pray with us. We're praying night and day. Praying every five, ten minutes. My husband's a Jew, just like you, but we pray in the name of Jesus because Jesus was a Jewish man, just like y'all. We pray in the name of Jesus because we believe in the Father. 'Dear God,' she began to pray, joining hands with Rita and David, 'we feel your strength this morning, yes we do, and we're just so grateful that we can speak Your name, that we can walk and talk, and that our minds are free to reach out to you and say thank you for letting me live with this good man and thank you for letting me have this good child, for giving us food and shelter and a life of so many blessings. We're not praying this morning for miracles. We're praying that our hearts stay close to yours, that you stay with Hy on his journey, stay right there with him, Lord, because he needs you, yes he does, he's never been alone and he's always had me to cook for him and look after him and I say, I pray, I ask you to let him feel you, let him see your light, Lord. Take him easy, take him careful, take him and give him peace because he's worked so hard, yes he has, worked and been good and loved us so long, Lord, and now he's yours, now he's . . .' "

Rita looked at her father. She walked over to the bed and put her head on his chest. He was gone.

"He waited for you to come," said Rosy, still in control. "I know he did. I was going to call you and tell you to hurry over, but I knew he'd wait."

The mother put her arm around her daughter's shoulder, then kissed her husband's forehead. "Good man," she said before turning to Rita. "Now it's just you and me, baby."

Tears were in both women's eyes. They held on to one another.

"Have your David take you on home," urged Rosy. I don't want you to worry after any of these details. I'll see to it all."

In Rita's small apartment on Great Jones Street, in the aftermath of her father's death, with the smell of lavender sachets and the light pouring through the lace curtains, David made love to Rita for the first time in over two years. She had taken his hand and led him to her bed. He was surprised, but he wasn't. He felt the same way. He had the same need. Tensions had built to the breaking point. Desire mixed with pain. Only shared passion could assuage loss, bring comfort and some escape. The sight of her naked body stirred him, her taut nipples, the sheen of her pubis, the taste of her tongue, her aching insistence, the way she took him in and tightened and held and squeezed his buttocks and demanded more, raising herself higher, moving on him, meeting his own rhythms, quickening the pace, full-tilt tight hard until they came, she crying, he whispering, "I love you, Rita, I've always loved you . . ."

An hour later they were seated at her butcher-block table, where they drank tea and searched for something to say.

"What now?" he finally asked.

"You're a friend, David," she said. "A wonderful special friend—"

"And that's it?"

"Much more," she told him, taking his hand. "I just don't want to mislead you—"

"What does *that* mean?"

She began to answer, but stopped herself. She rubbed his hand, caressed his cheek.

"What's wrong?"

"You've been here when I've needed you. No way I can't tell you how much that means to me, David. Today—"

"What are you trying to say?"

"I'm getting married."

"You're *what?*"

"Walter and I—"

"Why the hell didn't you tell me before?"

"I called you in Miami to talk . . ."

"Well, we talked and we screwed and now you're throwing my ass out the door? Is that it?"

"No, that's *not* it. I'm asking you to stay. I'm asking you to understand."

"Understand what? That you used me?"

He got up from the table and headed for the door.

"The thing with Walter," Rita said after him, "is right. It's strange, I admit, but it's right."

"You're in love with him like I'm in love with your goldfish."

"I'm just trying to be honest—"

"You talk honesty? Here's honesty. I think you're marrying your career, you're marrying the one man who got you a deal and put your voice on a record. I had a chance to be that man but I waited too long. You got tired of waiting. I guess I can understand that . . ."

"Oh, come on, David, you wouldn't have married me anyway."

"How can you say that?"

"Because I believe it. I was a diversion, a novelty. How many nice Jewish boys wind up with black wives?"

He almost exploded. How about a nice Jewish boy named Hy? he thought. But Hy had just died, and it was no time to bring it up to a grieving Rita, full of the pain of her mother's loss.

DETROIT

1951

"WHAT THE HELL'S WRONG with a Jewish man marrying a colored woman?" asked Eve Silk, nursing baby Gertrude in the dressing room of Morris Wasserman's Flame Show Bar at the corner of Canfield and John R.

"For Christ's sake, stop yelling," yelled Gent.

"Then you take care of this child," Duchess demanded. "She's yours."

After burping the infant, the singer handed her daughter to Ruby. Moments later, little Gertrude relieved herself on Ginzburg's custom-made double-breasted midnight-blue gabardine suit. The Gent was pissed. Looking at the light-skinned little baby, though, he couldn't help but be touched, couldn't even resist kissing her tiny forehead.

Standing at the back of the club, child in arms, Ruby listened to Duchess sing "Morning After," a thin blue spotlight illuminating her expressive face. Ginzburg remembered that the tune, by now a classic, was the first number he had ever heard Eve sing a decade ago at Marty Strazo's Wander Inn in Buffalo. She was great then—she'd always been great—but over the years the coyness of her style had been replaced by a breathtaking self-assurance. With notes and melodies, with syncopation and enunciation, she could do as she damn well pleased. She commanded. "The fussin' and fightin' lasted way too long," she sang, biting off the words with sly precision, "gee, baby, why couldn't we get along?" Her eyes were smiling, or laughing, or hurting—who could tell which? Rhythm was her slave. She sang with a subtle disdain, her annoyance at Gent evident, the husky pain in her voice accentuating the irony of her art. She was strong, so strong Gent worried how he was going to keep both his families together . . .

Back in Chicago, Reba knew—whether consciously or not. She had seen the picture in the paper, heard the rumors. The fact that Duchess and the baby lived in New York made no difference. Reba had to know what was happening.

She also knew her husband's business dealings with Pino Feldman were highly unusual. Still, no denying it. Ruben was a good provider. He cared for their two sons. He cared for her. Husbands had their ways about them—men could be a little wild—and women just had to understand. Ruben had given her a beautiful home. A woman from a frighteningly poor background, Reba was grateful she didn't have to scrub floors or wash windows. She never had to worry about money, and neither did her own mother and father, thanks to Ruby. Thanks to Ruby, Reba was secure from all harm. He'd never leave her. He promised that time and again. He'd never desert his family. What more could a woman want? Or expect . . . ?

"Pino wants to see ya'." Fingers Markowitz poked Ruby in the ribs so hard he almost dropped the child.

"What's wrong with you?" said Gent. "Can't you see I got a baby here."

"Pino wants to see ya'," Markowitz repeated. "He wants to see ya' now. He's out back."

Gent started worrying. Why was Feldman out back? Why didn't he just come into the club?

"I'll see him at the end of the set," said Ginzburg.

"*Now,*" insisted Fingers, who grabbed Ruby's elbow with enough force to crush a bone. The Gent winced and Gertrude started to bawl. Duchess looked up to see Ginzburg leaving the club through the front door, holding her baby.

Ruby followed Markowitz out back. Fingers looked fatter than ever, his great weight shifting from side to side. In the alley was a brand-new great-finned black Cadillac limousine. Markowitz squeezed behind the wheel. Ruby and his crying infant got in back, where Pino was smoking a cigar.

"What the hell's that?" he asked Gent.

"A baby."

"Why the hell are you holding a goddamn baby?"

"It's Silky's."

"Silky's?" Feldman was smiling. "It looks white. I can't believe you, Ginzy. I can't believe you're having kids with these niggers."

"It isn't—"

"Look, I don't care who the brat is, get it to stop crying."

"It don't work like that, boss."

"Fingers," ordered Pino, his slick hair shining in the moonlight. "Come get this baby."

"I ain't no good with babies," Markowitz protested. "The way they wiggle around and everything, they scare me."

Rocking the infant girl back and forth in his arms, Ruby managed to quiet her down.

"Now listen," said Feldman, "I got this very nasty problem and only one guy who can take care of it. You."

"Sorry, boss, but we're leaving for New York tomorrow, me and Duchess. We got the big show at Town Hall, then the Mosque in Newark, plus we're recording at the end of the week. Her and Lord together. You see how they're selling, boss, you understand—"

"Understand this, Gent, and understand it good—this here's a serious matter. This is a senator—understand me?—a fuckin' senator from California. Lindsay Kalb. Remember Kalb?"

"Years ago he was in Detroit. Wasn't he a judge or something?"

"And for years he's been in L.A. I been carrying the bum in my back pocket since 1938. Every month, without fail, I been taking care of his ass. Now what happens? He's on the committee, the committee looking into shit that ain't none of their business, ain't none of the goddamn government's business because this here is private business and what is this, communism or something? What are we coming to in this country? Uncle Sam should be worried about the army and not stickin' his nose into people like us who ain't doing nothing except trying to make a living. Am I right, Rube, or am I right?"

"You're right."

"Fuckin' A-straight I'm right. So Lindsay Kalb, I seen early on he's going places because of his brain and his personality—he's a friendly kind of guy—and I always look out for him and he looks out for me. I helped him set up in California when he went out there. Introduced him to a very big law firm. That's where he worked and that's where he started running for office, first up in Sacramento, then he becomes a U.S. Congressman in Washington. So I'm proud of the guy, I really am, and all of a sudden he's a senator, first term and all, and suddenly I hear this shit about the committee and I can't get the bum on the phone. Can you believe it? The papers are filled with investigate this and investigate that, and Kalb's giving me the cold shoulder. I'm telling you, him and me, we know stuff about each other no one knows. We got every reason in the world to help each other, except he's moving away from me like I got b.o. or something. He won't talk to me, which is why I need you to deal with him, Gent."

"I don't do that kind of work no more, boss. You know that."

"I don't know shit. And I ain't telling you what kind of work to do. I'm telling you just to talk to the bum and see what's what. First talk, then if you see he ain't being reasonable, you'll do what you gotta do."

"I gotta go with Duchess—"

"Fuck that bitch!" Pino's scream made the baby howl. "And get that kid to shut up."

"Boss . . ."

"Don't 'boss' me, Gent," said Pino, screaming over Gertrude. "This crime committee thing could fuck with all of us—you, me, every last one of us. Kalb can put the lid on it. Kalb can make it go away. Why do you think I been *shmearing* him all these years? I seen he was a winner and I was counting on him for something like this. That something's come up, just like I thought it might. So instead of being a genius I'm out in the cold. It don't make no sense. Look, Gent, just make goddamn sure this *schmuck* does a job for us. If not, you do a job on him."

"Where is he?" asked Ruben, resigned.

"He goes back and forth between California and Washington."

"Can it wait a week?"

"Hell no, it can't wait a week. Get on it tomorrow. And get that brat outta here. I hate brats."

LOS ANGELES

"CHRISTMAS IN CALIFORNIA IS always a little strange," Mitch Matson was telling District Attorney Lawrence Kalb.

Surveying Kalb's enormous den in Hancock Park, a stately residential neighborhood halfway between downtown and Beverly Hills, Matson noted the framed family pictures on the wall—of Lawrence Kalb, Senior, his friend's father and former governor of the state; and Lindsay Kalb, Larry's grandfather and prominent U.S. senator from the fifties.

The men sat in burgundy-leather wing-back chairs, a small perfect diamond in Matson's left ear, a gift from a South African film distributor and financier. Kalb was dressed for the golf course, his hairpiece short-cropped and discreetly gray. In large measure Lawrence Kalb had a discreet life—married, three grown and successful children, spotless record of service, the man pundits were predicting would be the city's next mayor. His loyalty, especially to close friends and generous contributors like Mitch, was constant. His public image, like his personal appearance, was that of a well-groomed, educated and ethical gentleman. Of medium height, Kalb's large brown eyes were encircled by gold-framed glasses, his baritone voice discreet and soft.

"You're always very generous at Christmastime," said Kalb, pouring Matson a stiff brandy.

"Not at all," Mitch Matson said. "Loyalty has no price. Which reminds me. Last time you mentioned one of your loyal employees giving you some trouble. He was intent on investigating the record business. What's his name?"

"Washington, Mario Washington."

"Is he still working for you?"

"He's gone."

"You fired him?"

"The boy quit. He could see he was getting nowhere."

"Where did he go?"

"Left the city. No matter. He never understood how things work."

"So I assume everything's quiet."

"You assume right, Mitchell. My department has far more to worry about than the alleged peccadilloes of the record industry. Let 'Show Business Today' chase down those stories."

"Or 'One Hour.' Did I tell you I was being profiled on that show? That's why I'm flying to New York in a couple of hours."

"Be careful, friend. 'One Hour' can be nasty. Paul Abel feeds off the junk legitimate law-enforcement agencies won't touch."

"I'm not worried, Larry," said Mitch, nodding after a quick sip of brandy." You see, my daughter is in charge. Beautiful girl. She worships me. Always has."

"I still say be careful."

"And I say you're a loyal and honorable friend, the best friend a man could have," Matson announced, getting up and approaching Kalb. "Merry Christmas, Lar."

"Have a wonderful new year, Mitch," said the D.A., accepting an envelope containing two hundred fifty thousand dollars in cash money.

David Crossman stood at the curb waiting for a cab at Los Angeles International Airport. He hardly noticed it was thirty degrees warmer here than in New York. Mini-buses from Hertz, Avis, Hilton and Sheraton shuffled by. Policemen ticketed illegally parked cars. Flight attendants with pretty legs and bright smiles walked right in front of him. David didn't care. He couldn't concentrate on where he was, couldn't get Manhattan out of his mind. First, Rita's rejection, then Sunday night at his father's townhouse. Both disasters.

He had left Rita's apartment on Great Jones Street and walked blocks and blocks to the hotel on upper Madison Avenue. Greenwich Village, lower Fifth Avenue, midtown—the island felt dead. David felt dead. *Someone* was trying to kill him; that much seemed certain. Rita wasn't interested in renewing their affair, another certainty. Nathan Silver was a crazy old man . . . all right, crazy like a fox. Cousin Ira was a low-life hustler; Jay Feldman a thug. And Carla? Eccentric, loyal, but her idea of p.r. and promotion was insane. Where to go, who to see? The pain of seeing Hy Moses die brought his own father to mind.

At the hotel he admitted he needed his father. His father's advice. He even dressed in an outfit he knew would please Ralph—blue blazer, gray slacks, blue-and-red rep tie. He called the house. The message machine picked up. In no mood to talk to a machine, he walked over to the house, figuring Ralph would be back by the time he got there.

Ralph was back. In fact, Ralph was by the door when David rang the bell. Ralph was in a dark formal suit, and Margo Cunningham wore a formal black evening dress. By the look on his father's face Ralph was not happy to see his son.

"The phone hasn't stopped ringing," Ralph said. "Apparently you're in trouble."

"That news report's a fraud—"

"I can't deal with it right now. It's come up at the wrong time."

"It was a public relations—"

"I don't care what the hell it was, I said I can't deal with it now."

"You're not going to ask why I'm here."

"I know why you're here. You're in trouble and you want me to bail you out—"

"Ralph . . ." Margo began.

"Okay, so you don't even want to talk about it—"

"Not on my wedding night, *no*."

"Your *what*?"

"It's a small affair," Margo put in. "At Judge Watkins' home. Only a very few friends. If we knew you were going to be in the city, David . . ."

"It wouldn't have made any difference."

Margo turned to Ralph. "Surely he can come along," she said.

"I don't give a damn what he does. Thirty years old and he still can't—"

"Fuck you, Ralph."

"This is how he talks to me. This is what he's learned from his grandfather, and his grandfather's sordid business."

"Then you know . . ."

"I know you're in over your head. I know you need a good lawyer. And mostly I know you don't know what you're doing—"

David turned around, went out and slammed the door behind him.

A day later as the cab crawled up crowded Interstate 405 from Inglewood to Santa Monica, David's anger had mostly changed to frustration. He'd wanted to be part of his father's wedding, to be part of *some* kind of a family. Well, he wasn't about to go back for help, not to Ralph, not to Nathan. He was cut off from both of them. He'd just have to do it his own way.

Even off the freeway the cab couldn't budge. At Ocean Boulevard, the location of the headquarters of David Crossman Records, traffic was backed up for miles.

"Something's wrong up there," said the Pakistani cabbie. "Police barricades. Something happened. Maybe a bomb. Who knows?"

David looked out the window and spotted a half-dozen squad cars parked near the building that housed his office. A *bomb*? Ira or Jay Feldman or one of their people had bombed his building! He paid the cabbie, grabbed his suitcase and ran the rest of the way. The closer he got, the clearer it became—his secretary—was she dead?—his files and records—were they destroyed?—it *was* his building that was surrounded, his building that had been hit. There were police barricades, hundreds of people gathered around, all noise and confusion—until he saw the band, until he heard the music . . .

Tomorrow's News were on the roof of the building—the funky drum intro, the rap refrain, little Gemini Star in his turned-around Dodger cap and wrap-around-shades, Plucky P popping his gold-glittered bass, Isaiah Z sending his sax sounds up to the sun, Summi on keyboards, Casey on drums, near-delirium on the streets as the chant turned to melody and the melody to dance:

Data information and the state of the nation
Computerized brains and mental invitations
Analyzin' fools ain't bringing satisfaction
Come on, y'all . . . it's all about action

It's all about action . . .
that's the name of the game
Living large, widening the frame
Forces of evil may be near
Until the action you take beats back the fear

It's all about action . . .
Can't you see?
It's positive action that makes you free
Outside world may be weird
But inside your head answers are clear

The minicams—Channel 2, Channel 4, Channel 7, "Show Business Today"—were recording it, monster loudspeakers blasting the sounds across the boulevard, across the ocean to China, a huge banner strung across the building in bold black letters: "TOMORROW'S NEWS HITS TODAY." Spike Lee and his crew filming from a chopper whirling overhead, hip-hoppers hopping, new jack-swingers and house-party dancers, balloons shot from cannons, the band wailing while in front of them Carla Bari, her tiny bikini visible beneath a sheer black mini-dress, undulating and frisbeeing copies of the single to the crowd below.

David just watched, stunned. Carla Bari strikes again.

A week later, "It's All About Action" hit the pop charts and did not stop until it reached the top.

And David Crossman wrongly decided he had been paranoid, after all.

NEW YORK

MARIO WASHINGTON LOOKED GEOFFREY Wane in the eye. He did not believe the Englishman, not for a minute.

"Are you saying," he asked the program director, "that you never met Ira Crossman?"

"I'm saying, Mr. Washington," said Wane seated behind his desk in his office at WHIT, "that you entered my office under false pretenses. You said you were researching a story on my radio station."

"I am."

"And that your story is focused on the ways in which this station promotes itself."

"That's right."

"Mr. Ira Crossman has nothing to do with that."

"Then you know him."

"I didn't say that."

"You mentioned him by name."

"*You* mentioned him first."

"Look, Mr. Wane, I'm just interested in the nature of your professional relationship with Ira Crossman."

"Do not take me for a fool, Mr. Washington. It's bloody well evident that you're digging for dirt."

Geoffrey Wane did not look the picture of health. Behind his red-framed glasses, his eyes were apprehensive. He tried to cover his nervousness with bluster, but Mario smelled the truth.

"I met the man once," Wane finally said.

"And that was just before your accident, wasn't it?"

"My accident? What does my accident have to do with it?"

"The following week, from the hospital, you gave instructions to add Shock Therapy's 'Downtown Demon' to the playlist. I'm looking for a possible connection."

"There is none. And I object to your snooping. How did you obtain this information? Have you a search warrant? Did you break into my office? I could have you arrested—"

"That would only bring more attention to a case that's going to see the light of day, I assure you."

"What *case* is that?"

"The case of independent promoters using cash, cocaine, sex and, in some cases, physical intimidation—violence—to make sure their products get airplay."

Wane sat expressionless.

"I'm asking you, Mr. Wane, off the record, if you have such knowledge."

"I'm British, Mr. Washington. I'm new to the system here."

"I think you're scared."

"And you, Mr. Washington, can you tell me if I'm right to be scared?"

"You have every right."

"Then you will not take offense if I ask you to leave my office."

"You're admitting that Ira Crossman put you in the hospital."

"I'm admitting nothing. I'm asking you to *leave*."

"I can put you on camera without compromising your identity. I can block out your face—"

"I can call our security guard and have you thrown out."

"Where was your security guard when Ira Crossman kicked your ass?"

"I have no security on Fire Island."

"It happened on Fire Island?"

"Look, Mr. Washington, I'm a viewer of 'One Hour.' I think it's an admirable program. I believe in investigative journalism. And I appreciate the fact that you must be persistent. On the other hand, there is nothing in this world—absolutely nothing—that I place above my own skin. Consequently, I will show you to the door, I will give you no information and I will ask you not to call me again."

Walking down Fifth Avenue, past sidewalk Santas from the Salvation Army, snowflakes falling on his face, Mario felt high. The meeting with Wane had gotten him what he wanted—confirmation that he was on the right trail. Ira Crossman was losing control. He was putting people in the hospital. Eventually someone would talk. Just a matter of time . . .

Back in the office, the latest Billboard, trade magazine for the music industry, was on top of his desk. The headline, circled in red by Kate, read: "MM Records Buys Sonsu/America for Surprisingly Low Figure—Feldman Fired as Pres." The story said Jay Feldman was ousted as head of the record division with no explanation. Feldman was not available for comment. In the margin Kate had written: "Will be with Mitch tonight. Will try for as much info as possible. Wait up for me."

"Where are the cameras?" Mitch Matson said, opening the door for his daughter. "Aren't we going to start filming?"

He was dressed for the part—blue blazer, white trousers, soft cotton shirt open at his throat. The very model of a modern movie mogul, she thought.

"I still need more background information before we start filming," she said. "I thought we could just talk for a while, the two of us."

He motioned her to sit beside him on the couch, which she did, then ever so slightly moved away from him. Smoldering inside, she fought down her anger, afraid she would show her distaste bordering on revulsion.

"We're dedicating the Players Foundation retirement home in Piscataway, New Jersey, for musicians and actors who have no savings or no retirement funds. It seems they want the main building to carry my name. I should think the cameras would be there for that, don't you, honey?"

"Yes."

"Now then, what is it, Kate, that your viewers will want most to know about me?"

For several minutes Kate verbally blew smoke in his face—asking about his widespread foreign dealings, his success with "adventure films" and "discovering popular heavy-metal talent"—before getting to the item in Billboard.

"Rumors have it you were going to retain Jay Feldman," Kate said.

"What rumors?"

"Research . . ."

"I wasn't aware you had researchers working on this story."

"It's standard procedure."

"Well, Kate, whatever I tell you must be off the record. Besides, it's something a smart daughter of mine must already know. The record business is filled with wiseguys. Listen to your father, your father's been around. Jay Feldman is nothing. He considers himself God's gift to the record business, but, believe me, he's already served my purpose."

"What was that?"

"When you deal as long as I've been dealing, honey, you learn who can buy and who can sell. I'm a buyer, Jay Feldman is a salesman. He helped me sell at the right price. But when it comes to buying he's out of his league."

My God, she thought, you could almost see the canary feathers sticking out of his mouth. "Buying cut-out records?" she said.

"Did your researchers tell you about that?"

"I heard something about it."

"I'm glad you're telling me this, honey, because none of it can go on the air. Yes, Feldman made a bad buy on those cut-outs."

"Which you sold to Ira Crossman?"

"Ira Crossman is another matter. Ira is skillful. He also won't take no for an answer. Without Ira Crossman, Shock Therapy, the number-one rock band right now, would be nowhere."

"And maybe Nightmare would still be on the charts. One theory says that because they were competing for the same market, Shock Therapy's rise coincided with Nightmare's fall—cutting into Sonsu's profits and reducing the company's worth."

Matson smiled, proud of his daughter. "We think alike, honey. Maybe you should be working with me instead of that TV show."

She tried to smile. "Will Ira Crossman be working with you?"

"I'm through with Crossman, just like I'm through with Feldman. They're both a bit too rough around the edges for my taste. I've got on board a team of corporate executives—Harvard and Yale people—to run the business. Let Crossman and Jay Feldman knock each other off."

"Literally?"

"Who knows with people like that. Did you happen to see that piece on your old show, 'Show Business Today?"

"I was going to ask you about that."

"The story is crazy."

"What's behind it?"

"I'm not sure. I asked my lawyer and he nearly had a heart attack."

"Who's your lawyer, Mitch?"

"Crossman, Croft and Snowden."

"Related to Ira and David Crossman?"

"Ira's uncle, David's father."

"Is there a business connection between all these Crossmans?"

"None that I know of or can imagine. Ralph's class, Ira's trash."

"And David?"

"He must be hot, because they were after him at Spago, weren't they?" Mitch laughed, shaking his head. "I never met him, but if he's anything like his father he's smart. I'm keeping an eye on him. If David Crossman's business takes off I just might wind up buying it. Those little labels can be profitable—if you know when to take them over."

"The shooting didn't make you nervous, didn't make you think that violent elements—"

"Let me stop you right there, honey. First of all, I don't scare. If I did, I wouldn't be in the record business. I go to sleep every night with both eyes closed. This cops-and-robbers baloney is something I avoid; I stay above it. That's what the Feldmans and Crossmans are for—they keep the dirt away." He looked at her, smiling now. "I'm sure you understand."

"Oh, I do, Mitch." She understood more than she could stomach about dirt and Mitch Matson. A few seconds passed before Kate added, "You know, the more I think about filming you at the Players' Foundation home, the more I like the idea."

"Now you're talking," said Mitch. "Now you're thinking like Mitchell Matson's daughter."

* * *

An hour later the lovemaking between Kate and Mario was ferocious, especially on Kate's end.

Mario was not complaining, but he still wondered a little. When they got around to work, he was very interested to hear from her that Ralph Crossman was her father's lawyer.

"That makes my trip to see David Crossman in L.A. that much more critical. This story is getting bigger every minute."

LOS ANGELES

JAY FELDMAN, DRIVING HIS Porsche at eighty mph on the Hollywood Freeway on New Year's Day, had just slipped a cassette into the tape player when a bullet ripped through one window and out the other, missing his head by a fraction of an inch. It did not miss the Korean woman driving the black Mercedes next to him, entering her ear and throwing her against her side window. Jay ducked as a second bullet hit the woman, sending her car swerving into Jay's Porsche, which sideswiped an old Mustang so that the Mustang jumped the divider, spun around and landed on the wrong side of the freeway. A trailer truck then plowed into the Mustang, crushing a teenage couple. Grabbing a revolver from the glove compartment, Jay stayed on the floorboard while cars—tires screeching, metal banging—crashed all around him. He was prepared to shoot the first person to appear at his window. That person, though, was a cop, to whom Feldman, of course, revealed none of his real concerns, which he voiced to his grandfather the minute he reached a pay phone.

"They're in it together," said Pino Feldman, who had just finished a bowl of hot soup in his Albuquerque trailer.

"How do you know that?"

"I know Ginzburg's mind. I know how it works. This David, this Ralph, they're in with Matson. To come up against the Feldmans, they needed a powerful partner. It wasn't Crossman who screwed you, it was

Matson who pulled the rug from under. He screwed you on your employment contract. That son-of-a-bitch was never going to pay you a penny. I told you that. I told you to get your money up front. He had this plan—to use you up and then dump you in the toilet. But he ain't working alone. He's got Gent Ginzburg with him. Just like back in '59 when Gent sent his son Irving to Detroit to fuck with me, he's got his grandkid to fuck with you. Well, we'll deal with this David the same way we dealt with Irving."

"You keep thinking of the old days," said a badly shaken Jay, "but this is something else. This isn't the old days—"

"I haven't lived this long for nothing, Jay. I swear on my mother's grave, Gent Ginzburg is walking this earth. He's looking to destroy you, the way he looked to destroy me. This time, though, we're waiting for him. I'm talking to my people in Detroit every day now."

"Your people missed Ira the first time and now they don't know where he is."

"We're going for David first. My people say he's changed his routine. He's giving them a run for their money. But don't worry, they'll get him. I'm paying them top dollar for Mr. Respectable David. There's an extra thirty K on his head. David's the Gent's favorite, I know. I can tell. It'll break Ruby's heart to see David go down. And it'll happen—today, tomorrow, any minute now. Anyone can be brought down. And we're bringing them down, every one of Ginzburg's people is going down. Now if they can only find Gent . . ."

"Someone came awfully goddamn close to finding *me* today. Maybe I should come out to New Mexico for a while."

"No! That's crazy. That's the worst thing you could do. You'd be followed. You'd lead them straight to me."

"Whatever you do, don't lead them to me," Nathan Silver told grandson Ira. "Don't come to Miami. You'll be signing my death certificate. Miami's the wrong spot for you."

"I don't feel safe any place."

"You'll feel safer when Jay's out of the way. My people from Chicago, are they in touch with you? What do they say? They're professionals, the best money can buy."

"Since your professionals missed Jay on the freeway he's gone into hiding."

"They'll find him. Who can hide forever?"

"And meanwhile, where the hell am I supposed to go?"

"Have you talked to David?"

"Are you kidding?"

"David's making money on this. David's on the news. He's smart, that boy. I need to talk to him."

"He's a slime bucket. I think he's in with Matson."

"You got it wrong, Ira. *Matson's* the slime. He's in with the Feldmans, believe me. He's in with Pino. Birds of a feather. I'll be in touch with David. David can be the key. He owes his life to me. David has to be loyal to me, I know the boy. Me and David, we'll take care of things. Meanwhile, lay low. Go to the desert, Ira. Palm Springs is nice. Get lost in Palm Springs."

WASHINGTON, D.C.

1951

GENT GINZBURG WAS LOST. The confusing plazas, the circular Monday morning traffic, the intersecting boulevards running parallel and perpendicular through four quadrants—the geometry of the city was driving Ruby crazy. Driving round and round, a map spread out in front of him, he couldn't find the Capitol Building. Downtown on Pennsylvania Avenue a blind man with long arms was waving the morning edition, crying out, "Truman Fires General MacArthur! Sterling Hayden Admits Commie Past! Get the news right here!" Ginzburg asked directions but the man just shrugged.

It was not only a long drive from Detroit but a far cry from New York—which was where Ruben wanted to be. The Duchess/Lord recording was happening without him, which he deeply resented. There was nothing Gent really enjoyed more than making records. The connection they gave him with his clients and their music was his great joy, and now, goddamnit to hell, he was missing the session. It was Feldman's fault. The whole thing was Pino Feldman's fault. Ginzburg also wanted a week alone with Duchess and little Gertrude. They needed something from him, at least being there with them. And he needed them too. The baby girl was growing on him.

Traffic was growing worse. So was Ruby's mood. The sky turned gray as a light April shower slicked the streets. Staying on Pennsylvania Avenue, he finally made his way to the Capitol. He wasn't thrilled about the job at hand. It had been years since he'd made a hit. Moreover, this was different. He'd have to talk to the senator first, somehow test his sincerity—was he protecting Pino or wasn't he?—and then make a quick decision. The operation was tricky and risky. Unlike underworld figures, senators were closely watched public people. Gent needed a foolproof plan. He couldn't afford slip-ups. The last thing in the world Ruby wanted was to wind up in jail—especially with Duchess's career going great guns, his boys growing up and good money rolling in. Sure, he resented Pino's cut, but Gent couldn't complain. Feldman had allowed him to become a rich man. Life was neatly compartmentalized: Reba and his sons loved their swanky South Side Chicago home, Pino would never leave Detroit—he owned the city—and Silky was happy in New York City. Everyone was in their proper place.

This place is unbelievable, Ruby thought as he reached the Capitol. *How am I suppose to case out this joint?* Ever since last year's attempt by Puerto Rican nationalists to assassinate President Truman, Washington security had turned super-tight. Guards were everywhere. Ginzburg saw his only chance was to latch onto a tourist group. Soon afterward, he managed to wander off alone down a long marble hallway, where he found the office of Lindsay Kalb, U.S. Senator from California. Fortunately the door was locked and the office deserted. Gent quickly jimmied the latch and soon had what he needed—the Senator's home address and week's schedule.

Ruby thought of driving up to New York for the night and dealing with Kalb later. Tonight Silky and Foreman were set to sing a duet of "Baby, It's Cold Outside," a tune he had suggested. He had heard it in an Esther Williams/Ricardo Montalban film *Neptune's Daughter*, a couple of years back. The song sounded corny in the film but Duchess and Lord would give it a sassy, sophisticated twist, turn it on its head. Gent knew it would be a hit. But he also knew his boss: Pino wanted *immediate* assurances that, one way or another, the Kalb threat was removed. At this point in his life—Ruben Ginzburg was forty—he was tired of being Feldman's errand boy. At the same time this particular errand paid a bonus of fifty thousand dollars. At least, thought Gent, Pino respected his skills as a problem solver. A pro.

The wallpaper in the little French restaurant off DuPont Circle displayed pen-and-ink scenes of Paris—the Eiffel Tower, Champs Elysées, Arc de Triomphe. Scratchy Edith Piaf records played through a small victrola. Sitting in a corner in the rear, Ruby was unhappy. He couldn't make out the menu. He told the waiter, "Cook me a steak and bake me a potato." Ruby hated French food. He checked his watch and figured at this very moment—a little past eight—Duchess and Lord were meandering into the studio. They'd be jiving around, having a taste, maybe a smoke, telling the rhythm section that this whole thing was going to be nice and relaxed, nothing to sweat. Relaxation, Gent had learned, was the key to great jazz. Don't anticipate, don't rush. You can't hit it too hard or too soon. "It comes over you," Lord would say, "when it wants to. Then it gets all up in your body and you can't do nothing but go with it." "It," Ruby came to realize, was the mystery, the moment of improvisational insight, the revelation, the mystical channel through which his singer and saxist told a story with straight-ahead sincerity, their mix of feelings—sensuous, jealous, joyful, pained—filtered through voices of total authority.

The man who now walked through the door had a regal air of authority himself. Lindsay Kalb had an abundance of light brown hair, a large handsome head, a slight paunch and a fine double-breasted spring wool suit. Gent admired his suit. He also admired the woman who was with him, a brunette whose cherry-red lipstick stressed her full lips and winning smile. Kalb was in his sixties, the woman in her twenties. Drinks were ordered and Ruby saw that the Senator did all the talking. It was clear what the politician was after. Finishing off his steak, his mind still playing with thoughts of music, Ginzburg decided he'd let Kalb have his fun. Like a good jazz solo, Ruby wouldn't rush it; he'd take his time.

Two hours later, when Kalb left the woman's apartment building on Wisconsin Avenue, Gent was waiting for him.

"That's a knife in your back," he told the Senator as they walked down the steps toward his car. "I don't mind killing you, but I'm not sure I have to. So let's talk first. What do you say?"

The reply was swift. "Pino Feldman is a fool. He uses people. He's obviously using you."

Gent was impressed. "You politicians are real good at figuring angles."

Kalb turned around to face him. "And you are not?"

It was three in the morning. The rains had come and gone, the whiskey bottle was drained, and Ginzburg was satisfied. Lindsay Kalb was a slime, no question. But he was also smart. Real smart. Gent recognized a good suit and a good mind. Kalb was a step ahead. Kalb had it figured out. From the moment he felt the steel of Gent's knife in his back he knew how to deal. A practiced manipulator himself, Ginzburg recognized a master. For the last several hours he'd seen the reports, read the confidential memos, heard the plan. There was no doubt. The committee investigating organized crime was just about to nab Pino. Ruby was shocked to see Feldman's network mapped out in black and white. Gent's boss had been sloppy, arrogant, his methods crude. To hear Kalb tell it, Feldman had done himself in. He was just too greedy to know when or where to stop.

"Years ago I tried to explain all this to your Mr. Feldman," said the Senator in a sincere voice reminding Ginzburg of Spencer Tracy at his best, "but he failed to realize his limitations. His inability to restrict himself to Detroit has caused any number of problems I'm afraid I can no longer control. It's fortunate you've come here, Mr. Ginzburg, because—and now I speak in all candor—you too are a target. Evidence links you to several racketeering charges, and even more seriously, several homicides, including Martin and Johnny Strazo of Buffalo, not to mention Nathan Aronstein and Leo and Harry Raminski of Chicago. You will certainly be indicted, and soon. But . . . how shall I put it? . . . providence has led you here. And ironically, the only man able to help you is the man you've come to silence. Doubly ironic is the fact that the only man who can insure that this committee bring Pino Feldman to justice is you. Beyond your own first-hand knowledge, you have access to his files, to the information which will bring a conviction."

"You're telling me to give up Pino? Just like you did—you're telling me to fuck over a guy who's been taking care of me since I was a kid?"

"You're very swift, Mr. Ginzburg?"

"And I'm supposed to go back and tell him the pressure's off—that the committee ain't gonna bother him?"

"Tell him whatever you like. Just bring me the documents we need.

I'll provide you a list. And, of course, you'll be required to cooperate with us in every way possible."

"And what do I get for doing all this?"

"Only what you're giving me at this very moment—a chance to go on living."

LOS ANGELES

AS THE PLANE LANDED at LAX, Nathan Silver was thinking of the years 1951 and 1952—several lifetimes ago, a difficult period. Figuring out angles was not so easy, yet absolutely necessary to survive in that world. In the fifties, Pino Feldman was going down. Gent had known it with absolutely certainty. The challenge was not to go down with him. Now it looked like Jay Feldman was going down. Four decades later, the same challenge: survival. This time, though, the terms were trickier. Back then, Ruben Ginzburg had enjoyed full control over his family—Reba and his little boys. Now, like his sight, control had slipped away. He had to reassume control. That was, in fact, the mission of his trip. As Gertrude led him from the plane through the airport to the limousine waiting by the curb, he remembered the last conversation he had with his people in Chicago.

"In the old days I'd have this Jay Feldman iced weeks ago. What are you guys running, a nursery school? Get him, and get him now."

As the limo sped up the coast, Nathan reviewed his plan. An hour later, he saw that it had accurately anticipated the first obstacle: when the limo reached David's Malibu beachhouse, two security men were stationed by the garage door, the only entrance from the road.

"Tell him Nathan is here," the old man told his driver to tell the guards.

"No one's home," said one of the guards. "No one's been home all day."

"Forget it," said Nathan. "We'll drive to Ira in Palm Springs. I'll nap on the way."

Besides, he thought, I'll be talking to David very soon. It should be an interesting conversation, very helpful for my proper young grandson, providing he gets the message . . .

David thought he was dreaming. It was World War II, but when he opened his eyes and the noise was still there—the explosions—he thought someone was setting off fireworks on the beach. He decided to look for himself.

By the beach entrance to the living room two guards were slumped over, a pool of fresh blood forming around them. By the garage two others had been shot in the head and chest. They were on their backs, blood draining from their stomachs. David wanted to run, but where? He looked around, waiting to feel the bullet piercing his skull.

Instead he heard the phone ring.

"You don't need to be scared," said Nathan, who knew how to make his point. "Nothing to be scared about, as long as you stay family. We're in control of the situation—you, me, Ira. I wanted you to understand, David, that those men were doing you no good. Your grandfather who loves you is the only one who can protect you. Do you understand? David, are you there? You listening to me? Now go ahead and call the police; let them round up the suspects. Tomorrow we'll have dinner, you and me. I feel like fish, but you'll have whatever you like. There'll be time to talk tomorrow. David . . . ?"

NEW YORK CITY

CALVINO AND CARLA BARI were sitting in Ralph Crossman's office, her mini-skirt so short that when she crossed her legs the flash of black panties was impossible to ignore.

The previous evening Calvino had told Ralph that his daughter was in the city promoting new records on the David Crossman label. When

Calvino indicated that he was not worried about the Mafia stories circulating around David, that, in fact, it was all a publicity stunt invented by his daughter, Ralph said he wanted to meet with Carla.

"It is a *divertimento,* an amusement for her, this record business," he told his lawyer, "something she has a knack for and learned from you Americans. Now it seems she is making money for your son. You should be pleased."

Ralph had just completed complex negotiations for Calvino in which the Italian purchased a major holding company in the Far East. Bari was about to return to Rome, delighted with Crossman's work. The deal, worth over a billion dollars, would net Ralph billings of five hundred thousand. Along with his work for Mitchell Matson, who only the previous month had used Crossman, Croft and Snowden to facilitate his buyout of a major French film production company, Ralph was having the most lucrative year of his career. Emotionally, though, he felt bankrupt.

If it weren't for Margo and the comfort of his new marriage, he might not have survived the pressure, the anxiety he felt. His father and son were somehow involved with each other, no question. To save his son from his father meant involving himself, shattering his so carefully cultivated image, ruining his reputation, even his firm. How could he risk everything he had spent a lifetime to establish? How could he not, though, protect David? Except what did protection mean? After their brief stormy encounter, David had gone back to California and wouldn't return his father's calls. He had no real idea of what was happening, but he had plenty of worrisome ideas. It was why he wanted to see Carla.

"Vince Viola is a major happening," she told Ralph.

"*Who* is Vince Viola?"

"A saxophonist *straordinario*. He has a big hit, bigger than Kenny G. 'Love Birds.' Do you know 'Love Birds'? A thousand white doves will fly from the roof of Rockefeller Center. Vince will play as they soar into the air. It will be a video and it will also be on the news. Already the song is in the top twenty. David found Vince. David has the ears of a wolf. David Crossman Records now has two hits at once. He is *caldissimo*—hot, hot, hot."

"But is he all right? I mean—"

"Better than all right. David is the best."

"And that business at Spago?"

"I am happy not acting. I am happy creating. I am a brilliant businesswoman. Finally my father sees that. Do you not, *babbo?*"

"I do," said Calvino.

"This was a creation. The press release, the coverage on 'Show Business Today.' I put Tomorrow's News in the news. Their music was always fabulous. David helps them with their songs. David is wonderful in the studio. David is a record man, but David is not a promoter. I am. I am his better half. Now he knows that. He cannot go on without me."

That evening when the national news came on Ralph was in the den leafing through the new Forbes. He heard something about "more bloodshed in the record industry." And then he heard the name Crossman.

"David Crossman, reputedly the target of underworld interests during a recent shooting at Spago restaurant, narrowly escaped when four bodyguards were shot to death at his Malibu home. Law-enforcement officials are making comparisons to the Chicago gangland wars of the twenties."

Paul Abel called Kate at home.

"I know Mario's out there somewhere in L.A.," he said, "and I know he's worked his ass off on this story. I also know he's having an affair with you. None of that means diddley squat to me—do you understand, Kate?—because I want this story on the air and I want it on in three weeks *period.* It's blown so big it will put our rating off the charts—*if* we can ever get it aired. Look, I know no one else has the background and no one else knows what's really going on. But that situation won't last forever. I want to go all-out with this thing. Even if we have to do a three-parter, even if we have to run a documentary mini series. I want to go public with what you've got—your old man, the Crossmans, this Jay Feldman, the back-story in Detroit, the whole nine yards. If your loverboy doesn't have the loose ends tied up by then, he never will. I'm paying you a small fortune, Kate. It's pay-back time. What do you say?"

"I say keep your shirt on, Paul. The goods will make the delivery date."

Ralph couldn't sleep. Several times he was tempted to fly to the coast. Or Miami. Margo stopped him.

"Why?" she asked. She was as motivated as Ralph—perhaps even more—to keep their world from crashing in around them. "What are you going to say to David? How can you really help him?"

"Matson can help him. Outside of business I haven't asked him for a thing. I haven't wanted to. But now's the time. Matson has connections in every part of the record world. He has to be able to help David. He has to know what's going on . . ."

"I'm on the Gulfstream and we're flying into Rome," said Mitch when Ralph reached him an hour later. "I have a ten A.M. in Rome."

"They're after David—"

"Who?"

"I think it must be Jay Feldman."

"Feldman's a nobody, Ralph."

"He's somebody who's after my son."

"Are you saying you'd like me to take care of the matter?"

"So long, of course, as you use entirely legal means."

Matson laughed, transatlantic. "You lawyers kill me, Ralph. You really do."

As long as David wasn't safe, Rita didn't feel safe. After her father's death she had mostly been living with her mother Rosy. The wedding was scheduled for the next week, but this news report was turning everything around in Rita's mind. Rosy had been driving her crazy, and Walter had been busy planning the ceremony in an art gallery/loft in Soho where a quintet of all-stars, including trumpeter Wynton Marsalis and pianist Marcus Roberts, two of his favorites, were going to play. Two hundred guests had been invited. What's more, work on Rita's third album was already under way. The second one had failed commercially but Walter considered this new effort, a jazz opera he'd written a libretto for, to be some kind of artistic breakthrough. She had to admit that kind of talk could make her squirm a little. Still, Walter was Walter and he *was* her biggest booster, wasn't he?

Watching the news with Rita, Rosy was quick to say, "Now you have every reason in the world to stay away from that David. Now you can see that you did the right thing, baby. Walter Gentry went to Harvard.

Walter Gentry is a gentleman. Walter Gentry is the right man for you. You listen to your mama."

At midnight as she boarded the red-eye for L.A. Rita was still thinking of what Rosy had said, and trying hard, without much luck, to convince herself that Mama was right.

DETROIT
1952

BASES LOADED, TWO OUT, bottom of the ninth, the Yankees up by three and Detroit at bat.

Everyone was on their feet at Briggs Stadium—kids, housewives, toughs, old folks screaming and suffering the summer heat for the sake of their much loved heroes. In seats directly behind home plate Gent Ginzburg was at Pino Feldman's elbow. One row directly above them Fingers Markowitz was chomping on a hot dog while signaling for another. Fingers was not a baseball fan. Neither was Ruby. Pino was a fanatic.

"Big Vic Wertz," Pino was saying, pointing to the Detroit outfielder in the batter's box, "bats lefthanded, throws rightie. Who can figure? Last year he hit twenty-seven big ones. Now he just needs one to win this goddamn game—clobber it, Vic!"

Behind them Fingers let loose a vicious fart. "Sorry, boss."

Pino, unmoved, did not take his eyes off the plate.

Wertz swung at and missed the first pitch. The crowd sighed.

"Allie Reynolds," said Pino, pointing to the Yankee pitcher. "Gonna win twenty this year. But not this one. Belt it, Vic, kill the fucker . . ."

Wertz fouled back a fast ball. No balls, two strikes. "Here comes a curve," Pino predicted. "Watch it, Vic. Slow curve!"

Reynolds' tantalizingly slow curve ball fooled Wertz, had him way out in front of the pitch. And that was the ballgame.

"Ready, boss?" asked Fingers, finishing off a box of popcorn.

"I don't wanna fight the crowds. Let's sit for a few minutes. Can you believe this shit, Gent? Did I tell him to watch for the curve or didn't I?"

"You called it, boss."

"So now you can tell me more about Kalb. Sounds like the putz threw *you* a fuckin' curve."

"I don't think so."

"Thinking and knowing are two different things."

"He's so scared of you, he pisses his pants when he hears your name."

"Then why hasn't he been in touch?"

"He's scared of the phone. Scared of wiretaps. Scared of someone opening his mail. He's scared of everything. Especially you."

"I don't like it. I don't like that you didn't eliminate the problem."

"I figure it this way—eliminating Kalb makes a bigger problem for you. It means the only guy who can help you ain't there to help you. So what good does it do?"

"Plenty, if he's after me."

"I say he isn't."

"What if he sold you a bill of goods?"

"Time will tell. If he did, I whack him."

"I don't got time—that's the whole point. My lawyer says that committee of his is meeting every day. My lawyer is even more nervous about this shit than me."

"Kalb swears he won't let 'em touch you."

"And he don't want nothing more?"

"He says you've always been good to him, boss. He says he owes you."

"Something's fishy."

"On my wife's life, I think Kalb's on the level."

"I want you to go back to Washington and bring me something, Gent."

"What's that, boss?"

"Senator Fuckin' Kalb's fuckin' liver."

"Pino, I'm trying to say—"

"I heard what you said, and the more I think about it, the more I don't buy it. I want you to *eliminate the problem*. No more discussions, no more nothing. This Kalb stinks to high heaven. I want you to take care of him. But this time, don't stop with Kalb. Go for the committee."

"The *whole* committee?"

"Every one of those bastards."

"That's pretty rough, boss."

"That's why I'm asking you. And that's why I'm tripling the bonus. You're the best I got."

"But I just got back, I got things to do. I haven't been back to Chicago to see the kids—"

"Then get to Chicago and get to Washington—one, two, three, just like that."

"That fast?"

"You can't do it fast enough. This is something that should've been done months ago. Do it this time, and do it right."

The next day when Gent arrived in Chicago, Eve played the song for him over the long-distance wire. She put the phone up to the speakers in the studio so he could hear her and Lord singing "Baby, It's Cold Outside."

"It's a hit! I know it's a hit. It's gorgeous. You sound terrific."

"Been feeling pretty good, Ginzy, 'cept for missing you. When you coming 'round here?"

"Gotta go back to Washington."

"Will you stop here first? Just for a night?"

Ruby felt his dick getting hard. He needed relief, a release. His stomach was churning from the decision he faced . . . who gets it—Pino or Kalb? Should Gent disappear forever, give up his identity and take his family into hiding, or should he follow the boss' order and blow away the senators, and life goes on as is?

At dinner Ruby couldn't eat Reba's beef flanken, couldn't touch the coffee cake, couldn't look at his boys as they slept in bed. How could he screw up their lives like this? But how would they feel if their father went off to jail for forty years? Besides, wiping out a whole committee of senators was plain crazy, a sure sign of Pino's desperation. But what about Silky? Silky needed him. In the Witness Protection Program he couldn't manage her, not for a minute. She wouldn't even know who or where he was. How could Gent ever give up Silky?

"I got to leave tomorrow," he told Reba as he started to pack his gear.

"Leave for where?" she asked. "You just got here."

"I'm going back to Washington."

"For Pino? Everything's for Pino. That's not fair, Rube."

"Life's not fair, ain't you heard, Reba? I gotta go to Washington."

Instead, he went to New York. He drove all day, all night and a good part of the next day. He was practically drunk on driving. But driving was an escape, an interlude between two lives closing in on him. Besides, at night the stars were bright, the moon full. On all roads, through Ohio and Pennsylvania, past the Burma Shave signs and Texaco stations, his vision was clear. Straight ahead, he just kept driving, the trunk filled with a small arsenal of weapons, his mind weighted by the decision—to betray his boss and desert his star, or carry out the orders he was being paid for. Gent had always obeyed orders, never mind the resentments, going along with a program that had made him rich. Help Kalb? Kalb was a worm. A slug. But what was Pino? Greedy, jealous, a user and a prick. Yet, in his own way, Pino had respected Ruby enough to let him carry on the management of Duchess and Lord. Pino allowed it because it was profitable, and also because he realized Gent's genius . . . for finding musical talent, and for killing people.

Ruby pulled up to an apartment building on Riverside Drive in early evening just as the sun was setting. Across the street the Hudson was bathed in hues of pink and soft blue. A pleasant breeze cooled the air. Children played in the park. The world seemed settled. Ruby hurried upstairs and knocked on the door. When it opened, Duchess was standing there in a light summer dress. She took him in her arms and kissed his weary eyes. In her bedroom they made love right up to exhaustion. When they heard Gertrude crying in the next room they went in to comfort her, bringing the baby back to bed with them. That evening Eve cooked turkey, candied yams and mustard greens. To Ruby, everything tasted fresh and delicious.

"You wanna talk about it?" she asked him when he was through eating.

"What's to talk about?"

"You're feeling crazy. *I* can feel it. You're going crazy."

"It's nothing."

"It's Pino, ain't it?"

"It's business. Man business."

"That man's never liked you."

"He made me."

"He made you believe his bullshit—that's what he made. He's jealous of you, jealous of what we have."

"It's not that simple."

"Tell me why not."

"This whole thing's getting bigger and bigger."

"Move to New York. Stay with me and your baby. That would make it simple, wouldn't it?"

"I want to make it simple, believe me. I want to make it right."

"Then do it. Follow your heart, Ginzy, 'cause your heart's leading you straight here."

After dinner, the apartment redolent with the aroma of Duchess' meal, they made love again, this time with a sweetness Ruby had never felt before. In the past he'd seen how Silky had done for him without getting too involved herself. This time it was different. When she came, she cried real tears.

"Nothing's wrong," he told her.

"Why do I feel like I'll never see you again?"

"Don't talk like that, Silky."

"I feel like once you walk out that door that's it."

"I swear—"

"*Shhh.* Don't make it worse by lying. Just leave it be. Just stay here for the night. But I know you. I know when I open my eyes in the morning you'll be long gone."

And he was.

Senator Lindsay Kalb was not afraid. He was alone in his house in suburban Virginia when he heard a knock at the back door and saw Gent standing outside.

Inside Ruby's suit pockets were two items—an envelope stuffed with incriminating documents he had taken from Feldman's Detroit office and a hand gun.

"It's good to see you," said Kalb.

Ginzburg was still of two minds. It all came down to the papers or the pistol.

He handed Kalb the papers.

"Excellent." The senator gave him a smile.

"Not so excellent," said Gent. "I ain't going down so easy. I know Pino, and as long as he thinks I'm alive, I'm good as dead. Understand?"

"I'm not sure."

"I am. I gotta be killed. Pino's gotta think I'm dead."

"You have some plan?"

"It'll happen in Chicago. I'll call Pino when I get back to Chicago. I'll tell him that I couldn't get close to you guys in Washington. When it happens, I'll be praying in synagogue. That'll make it seem real. Pino will think one of the wiseguys got me in Chicago. There are a dozen bums in Chicago that he knows would love to take me out. You can take care of me and Reba and the kids. You can put us somewhere where no one will ever know."

Saying it, Ruby felt dead already, knowing that, at this very moment, Gent Ginzburg was no more.

LOS ANGELES

"WHERE IS HE?"

"I can't find him."

"What do you mean you can't find him. He must be somewhere."

"He's not at home, not at the record company. David Crossman has disappeared."

"What are you going to do?" asked Kate Matson.

"Chase down another lead," Mario Washington said. "My surveillance people have indicated that Nathan Silver arrived here yesterday. We have a tail on him. He's saved me a trip to Miami Beach. What's happening back there?"

"Paul Abel's going crazy."

"Once I interview Silver we'll have everything we need for the first segment."

"We'll lead with the back-story."

"I agree. Where's your father in all this?"

"Rome. I'm meeting him there tomorrow but I'll be back by the weekend."

PALM SPRINGS

IT WAS PINO'S WORK . Nathan was sure of it as he and Gertrude
back of a limo speeding toward Los Angeles. Ira's body had
en discovered by anyone else. From the car phone he made
s for a four P.M. flight to Miami, then slumped over, his head
ds.
only boy, his grandson, was gone. Pino. Pino was alive. Just
n, Pino had contractors working for him. Pino was behind it.
he cause of his grief, just as he caused all the grief in the past.
would cause him grief as long as he was alive.
no genius, sometimes he didn't show respect, but he had balls.
e his mark. He was the best indie promoter this business had
He was still a young man, just like his father Irving was young
o got him. Back in 1952 when he turned against Pino it had
ke a smart move, the *only* move, except even then Ruby Ginz-
p down in his gut, knew it was a mistake.
no sped down the highway, Gertrude holding Nathan's hand.
was the only friend Nathan had, the only one he could rely
d was Ralph's son—Ira had been right about that. David was
wn; to hell with family. Well, Pino would find him. David
it. Let Pino get him. What difference did it make? Ralph never
ed anything, neither did David. His grandfather had gone soft,
tal. He cared too much. First he lost Irving, his one loyal son,
his one loyal grandson. Who was left? Gertrude. Silky's child.
would be there for him until the day he died, just like he had
re for her. Gertrude and he would go back to Miami Beach and
in quiet anonymity, just like he had lived before he'd found
n article about David Crossman's record collection nearly four
. He would sit by the pool, go to the printing plant, relax in
away office listening to the old records. What choice did he

first-class section of the plane, Nathan did not want to drink,
want to eat. All he could do was think of Pino. Decades had
more than half a century, if you thought about it, and he still
ree of Pino. Pino would never give up punishing the man who
n him up. Pino would not die until Nathan died.

"Good. By the weekend I'll have my answer about Ruben Ginzburg, Bernard Crossman and Nathan Silver."

"Sorry, Mr. Silver, Mr. Crossman is on vacation."

"Have you told him I've been calling?"

"I don't know where Mr. Crossman is."

Nathan slammed down the phone. Palm Springs was too dry. The arid air was rough on him. He worried about his health. He was used to the humidity of Florida and, besides, Ira was getting on his nerves.

"David's gone to the authorities," he had told Nathan. "You shouldn't have told him about you in the first place. I told you, I told you a hundred fuckin' million times that the kid was no good. I told you that when you first sent him to me and I'm telling you that now. You should never have gotten him involved . . ."

Nathan had tuned him out. Ira didn't understand family. How could he? When he was just a baby his father was killed, his mother left. All he ever had was his grandfather. Ira was just jealous of David. Sibling rivalry, the shrinks called it. Just like with Miltie and Irving. David would come for his help, his advice, his protection . . . it was just a matter of time. David had no choice. He had to see that he couldn't make it without Nathan. He needed Nathan to survive. Nathan had seen to it. Nathan had his Chicago people, the best people, running around Los Angeles doing anything he told them to do. Look how clean they dealt with the security guards. Only Nathan could protect David. They were partners, grandfather and grandson, they were family, they were in the record business together. The record business was too rough for one kid to handle alone. Who did David think he was kidding?

"Gert," said Nathan, calling her from the kitchen of the large two-bedroom condo they had rented on the outskirts of the city. "I'm a little hungry. Could you make a little borscht? And wave to Ira. I think he went for a swim. I want to talk to Ira."

Gertrude opened the sliding door and walked onto the small balcony. Three stories below, the blue of the kidney-shaped pool had turned a murky red. Ira's body was floating face up in the water, a huge gash across his throat.

* * *

Five minutes later Pino picked up the phone in his Albuquerque trailer.

"We got your Ira," his Detroit people reported in.

"David!" shouted Pino. "I want that fuckin' David. Why can't you find that fuckin' David?"

"He's next."

ROME

IT NEVER SNOWS IN the Eternal City, but as Mitchell Matson looked out the window from his suite at the Hassler-Villa Medici Hotel, he saw light flakes falling on the Spanish Steps. The tourists were snapping pictures, the natives shaking their heads in wonder, the phone next to Mitch's bed ringing softly.

"The local film crew should be there in an hour," Kate told her father. "I'm at the Cavalieri Hilton."

"Be best to hold them off until after lunch. This first meeting is private. The gentleman I'm meeting with is a little camera-shy. After lunch I'm due at the tailor. I like to have a couple of dozen suits made up at once. Perhaps your cameras can catch me over there. Have them here at one, honey, and I'll take all of you with me."

"Sure thing." Kate immediately called her surveillance people to make sure everything was in order. "I want to know who comes to his hotel, and if he leaves, where he goes."

Mitchell ate breakfast in bed, thinking how pleased he would be to have his shopping trip filmed. Later in the week one of his favorite ladies would be waiting for him in Geneva. Then he was off to France to survey his newly acquired production facilities. Everything was going great guns—if only the phone would stop ringing.

"*Are you mad?*" said Ralph Crossman over the transatlantic wire.

"What's wrong, Ralph?"

"NBC is reporting that they fished Jay Feldman out of the Hollywood reservoir. His head was severed from his body. My God . . ."

"Hell of a thing."

"Ira Crossman was found dead in

"Nasty business."

"Are you—"

"I'm just fine. And I'm happy you'
can help each other out when we nee
away. Have you spoken with your sor

"I can't find him."

"He's frightened. I can't say I blam
him, tell him he can come out from hi
Now I have to run. An important me

That evening, after the shopping tour a
which, with cameras still rolling, he e
global entertainment business, Kate we
the surveillance report slipped under th

10:15 AM: Matson leaves Villa Medi
10:30 AM: Matson arrived by limo at
Forum
10:32 AM: Matson enters office of Sign
11:15 AM: Bari and Matson exit Bari's
11:32 AM: Matson arrives back at Vill

Kate, excited, scared, tried calling Lo
morning, but Mario had already checked

When the jet reached cruising altitude, Gertrude went to the bathroom. Still obsessed with Pino, Nathan felt someone taking Gertrude's seat.

"Mr. Silver," said the man. "My name is Mario Washington. I'd like to ask you a few questions about Pino Feldman."

DALLAS

1953

PINO FELDMAN WAS IN jail. The prosecutors swore he would be there for the rest of his life, but Bernard Crossman, who had put him there, knew better. Pino had his ways. He always had, always would. He crept into Bernie's dreams at night . . . "I know you ain't dead, I know where you are, it don't matter where you are, I ain't forgetting—ever." As a kid, Ruby Ginzburg feared Pino. As a middle-aged man, Bernie's fears were just as strong.

The Witness Protection Program was a wonder. It brought him deep into the suburbs of Dallas, a city virtually without organized crime. It gave him, his wife and two sons new identities. And even though Miltie—now Ralph—was very unhappy, Bernie was sure the boy would come around. His wife Reba and other son Irving, now Lillian and Steven, cooperated beautifully. Their style of living was changed, but at least they had each other and security. So why was Bernie so miserable?

It was the nights that he couldn't control. On the nights he didn't dream of Pino he dreamt of Silky. During the days, working in his liquor store in South Dallas, he'd sometimes hear her songs on the radio. Her voice made him crazy. If it were an old recording, he remembered every detail about the session—how the smoke from her cigarette curled from her nose, how she'd sit on a stool and cross her legs, how Lord, in his derby and thick-lensed glasses, blew notes over and around her regal head, tilted to the side, half-smiling, eyes half-closed, singing, "Don't know when it happened, didn't check the time, but love came up and winked at me, your love's so sublime." As Bernie, he would be selling a fifth of Jack Daniels or a six-pack of Lone Star Beer when suddenly his mind would drift into the music and the customer would say, "Something wrong with you?" "Nothing at all," Bernie Crossman would reply, snapping himself back to reality.

Good sense said stay away from Duchess. She's better off thinking you're dead. Stay away from Eve's music. Don't even keep her records in the house. He didn't. Now when her songs came on the radio, he'd switch them off. If it was a new song he hadn't heard, he didn't even want to hear it. If it was bad, he'd be angry; if it was good, he'd be jealous. Either way, pain. He couldn't control the pain. He couldn't control his dreams. In his dreams, Duchess came and sang, the baby on her lap, the baby in her arms, sometimes in Carnegie Hall, sometimes in small dives, sometimes calling out to "my friend and manager and father of my baby, Ruben Ginzburg . . ." And sometimes Ruben would come to the stage and sometimes he'd run from the place and sometimes there'd be shooting, and he'd be hit in the heart and wake up with a start, forgetting that he was living in Dallas, Texas, the lower middle-class owner of a small liquor store on the wrong side of the tracks.

For the first five months the conflict raged like a live thing inside him. *I'm alive and I'm not behind bars*, he'd tell himself over and over again, justifying what he'd done to Pino and Eve. He thought he'd been putting a lid on his feelings, thought he could lose himself in his new surroundings, concentrating on his wife, the most loyal woman any man could ever hope for. The devotion was there, but not the sex. Reba . . . Lillian . . . would snuggle next to him at night for comfort, and nothing more. In his mind, he saw pictures of Eve Silk, singing or moaning or pleasing him with her mouth and tongue in the ways no other woman had ever pleased him before. The pictures would haunt him when he drove to work, or stopped at the market, or drank coffee in the afternoon.

Then, one blistering 102-degree Dallas Monday in August, he saw her picture in the paper. Eve Silk and Lowell Foreman were coming to Fort Worth, only thirty miles west of Dallas. They were appearing on Saturday in a new nightclub, the Black Parrot. Duchess and Lord were touring behind the strength of "Baby, It's Cold Outside," an even bigger hit than Ruby had predicted.

The photo cut him like a knife. He could hardly work that day, hardly concentrate for the rest of the week. He was jittery and short with his family, nervous with his customers, unable to sleep.

On Wednesday night he actually drove to Fort Worth just to see the nightclub, to make certain it was real. Seated in his Nash Rambler in front of the place, he felt foolish. What was he doing here? Was he hoping she'd arrive in the city two days early so he could yell out to her—*I'm still alive, I'm here, I'll do anything in the world for you?* If she had shown up he would have turned his head and sped off. Anything else could result in death, for real. But there were so many things he wanted to ask her. With Pino in jail, the government had sold off his record label to a major firm in California. Did Silky get a fair contract? Was she receiving her royalties? Who was looking after the details of her career, details Gent had so painstakingly poured over for so many years? He was sure unscrupulous managers or lawyers or booking agents were cheating her. He understood the business better than anyone, knowing how these musicians, these geniuses, were continually exploited by tin-eared thieves.

But the ride to Fort Worth had been in vain, and there was no way he would ever go back again—at least that's what he told himself. Thursday was rough, Friday rougher, and Saturday . . . all day Saturday he barked at whomever came in sight. The pressure was getting to him. He broke out in hives; he felt himself falling apart. He called his wife to make sure she had dinner on time.

"Dinner's always on time," she said. "You know that."

"I gotta see a movie tonight," he told her. "Can we go to a movie?"

"Sure we can go to a movie. Whatever you want."

After dinner, though, he cracked.

"I can't take it!"

"Take what?" she asked.

"This life, this hiding, this goddamn city . . ."

He was out of the house with the last words, into the car, and his heart pounding, fuck the consequences. He floored it all the way to Fort Worth.

LOS ANGELES

"IF YOU CAN'T FIND him, come home," Rosy told Rita over the phone. "Come home right now. Walter's beside himself but I think he'll still listen to reason. Walter's a very smart man but no man's gonna put up with a woman who skips out on her wedding the week before without saying why. No one does that, not even my sweet Rita. Besides, baby, I don't think you meant to do it, I really don't."

"Look, Mama, if you're so worried about Walter, *you* deal with him."

"And what am I supposed to tell him?"

"That I'm tired of singing his songs, that I've gone to California to write and sing my own damn songs."

"Why, that's ridiculous—"

"You've never understood; *he's* never understood."

"You are finally getting married—*that's* what I understand."

"Marrying's the last thing on my mind."

"So this thing with David—"

"I have to find him. That's all there is to it. He's in trouble and I have to find him."

"So the marriage is off?"

"It wasn't even a marriage, it was a career move." Like David had said.

"And what about your David? What was your interest in him? Wasn't it about what he could do for you?"

"Maybe at one point. But it went deeper. I realize that now."

"You're talking crazy and you're acting crazy. You're getting in hot water. If he's in trouble, I don't want you burned. That's what your father would say if he was here, and that's what I'm saying. Get your butt back to New York—now!"

"Don't worry about Walter. I'll call him when I have a chance. First I have to find David."

But all Rita's efforts to find him had run into dead ends. The office of Crossman Records on Ocean Avenue had been sealed off. Police were all over. When she drove out to Malibu—David had sent her the address some months before—the situation was the same, police at the door wanting to know who she was and what she wanted. Quickly, she drove back down the coast. A call to David's father had confused matters even more.

"Why are you calling me?" he asked. "What do you know that I don't?"

"I don't know a thing, Mr. Crossman. I'm calling you for information."

"Had you been working with him?" asked Ralph, himself reduced to raw nerves.

"No."

"Are you involved with him? Personally?"

"No . . . I mean yes."

"Which is it?"

"I'm very worried about him—"

"How much do you know about him?"

"What are you talking about?"

"How much has David told you?"

"About what?"

"His family, his story . . ."

"Very little," she lied.

"Well, no one knows where he is. How do I know this call isn't some kind of trick?"

"For what?"

"To get information out of me, young lady."

"I asked you straight-up, I didn't hide what I wanted."

"But you must have some notion of why David is hiding. What dealings have you had with him recently?"

God . . . even at a time like this David's father talked like a lawyer . . . "I saw him briefly in New York—"

"When was that?"

"Around Christmas."

"Was that before or after I got married?"

"Mr. Crossman, I had no idea that you *were* married, so please, stop questioning me and let me go out and try to find David."

"What can you do to help him?" asked Ralph, who had been swamped with requests for an interview from a reporter at "One Hour," a man looking into mob connections in the record industry. Ralph had told his secretary to turn down that and all other requests relating to his son.

"I can be with him—that's what I can do," Rita told Ralph. "Right now I'm sure he badly needs somebody."

Somebody had to know where he was, Rita thought as she drove aimlessly around the city, feeling helpless, uncertain of where she was going or why. Only when she passed by the supermarket-sized Tower Records on Sunset Boulevard, just across the street from Spago, did she suddenly have an idea.

She knew David. Now she thought she knew where to look. Inside the store, she went to the bins and found the two Tomorrow's News' albums. She bought them and hurried to the phone, reading the personnel off the back of the record and calling the local musicians' union for telephone numbers for the group's members. Because Gemini Star, Plucky P and Isaiah Z did not use their real names, no numbers were available. But Dale Summi did have a number, and an address.

It took her a while to negotiate the freeways, but she finally arrived at a modest home in middle-class Pasadena. Summi's grandmother was home alone, an elderly Japanese woman who led Rita to Dale's desk, where she found the addresses of all the members of Tomorrow's News.

Now, her map of the sprawling L.A. landscape spread over the front seat, Rita hit the freeways again—thinking of the story David had told her about his grandfather and his blood-soaked history—past Dodger Stadium, past downtown, past USC and the Coliseum, further down into the black neighborhoods of South Central L.A., then west to Ingelwood.

ROME

"RALPH, GET HOLD OF yourself. You're the counselor. I'm the client. It's not like you. Calm down."

"'One Hour' is breaking a story. You're in the business my son is, I'm your lawyer, David's father . . ."

Mitchell Matson smiled and carried the phone over to the window. The church spires and rooftops of Rome were bathed in sunshine, the winter storm having passed. "All true, Ralph, and I'm on top of things. They're over here right now; they've been filming me all week. My daughter's in charge, Ralph."

"It's going to be an exposé of the record business, they're looking into—"

"Ralph, you'll go into cardiac arrest if you don't watch it. I *said* things are under control. This is my own daughter and she's focusing the story on me, her father, not on any so-called exposé. I've steered her clear of anything dangerous—"

"Are you certain?"

"I am. I'm also rather adept at public relations. If I weren't I wouldn't be where I am today."

"This Mario Washington won't stop calling me."

"Mario who?"

"Mario Washington."

"Mario Washington . . ." Mitch repeated the name, trying to remember where he'd heard it before.

Matson thought about the name off and on during that afternoon. Something about it, something he didn't like. It kept gnawing at him. His well-honed survival instincts had surfaced.

He fought to remember. He recalled his brief stayover in L.A. at Christmas . . . He was at Larry Kalb's home in Hancock Park. He tried to recall details of that conversation, picture the den, recall his friend the D.A. talking to him. Kalb was smart. Another one with developed instincts for survival. He had warned Mitch about "One Hour." But Mario Washington . . . Mario Washington . . . what, if anything, had Larry said about Mario Washington?

And then Matson remembered . . . *Mario Washington was the guy investigating his alleged underworld connections in the record industry . . .*

"He still working for you?" Mitch remembered he had asked Kalb.

"He's gone."

"Did you fire him?"

"The boy quit, he could see he was getting nowhere."

"Where'd he go?"

"Left the city. Disappeared. It hardly matters. He was a lightweight."

Sweet Jesus. Mario Washington was calling Ralph Crossman. Mario Washington was working for "One Hour." *Mario Washington was working with his daughter.*

"Your daughter is downstairs," said the hotel operator in accented English. "Should I send her up?"

Professor Victor Susman, whose sex-therapy practice was flourishing, did not hesitate. "Come immediately," he told Carla. "Come over as soon as you can."

He told his secretary to cancel all appointments and take the afternoon off. "I have concentrated research to do," he told her.

It had been five months since he had seen Carla, and not a day had passed when he did not fantasize about her. In fact, whether making love to another woman or making love to himself, his compulsive behavior was getting rather out of hand—the healer could think of no one except the actress-turned-publicist. Now in a very few minutes she would be in his office, in his arms, his fantasies turning to reality.

"I'm going *crazy*," she said, walking through the door to his private office. Her eyes were bloodshot, her body tense, her fabled energy shot.

"I've not been happy myself," he told her, taking her hand, sitting on the couch next to her.

"I need someone to talk to, Victor. You always understand."

"Count on me," he said, putting his arm around her shoulder, brushing back her hair.

"This is the crisis of my life."

"Your relationship with the man in California, it failed?"

"Worse, my father has failed."

"How so?"

"He's not who I thought he was."

"Tell me about him."

"He's a no-good bastard, a crook."

"Why all of a sudden have you—?"

"He is a devil, a hypocrite who has used me, fooled me. Now he tells me that he himself is in the music business, but he is more; he owns a large and important piece of it, owns it secretly, through another man, another crook who came to my father long ago for money and connections. They are dangerous, my father the most dangerous because he is most powerful. I loved him for that power—how many times have I told you that?—but now that power has turned against David."

"Why?"

"Because David stands alone. David has gone his own way. Did I not tell you David was brave? That is why Carla was drawn to him. Bravery is exciting to me. But now they are at work against him, and David doesn't know, or perhaps he does, but I don't know where he is, no one does, he's hiding, he's right to hide. My father and this man who works for him, this Matson . . ."

"An American?"

"An American gangster, a smooth man with no conscience, no heart. Why has it taken me so long to see the truth about my father?"

"It's the most difficult truth of all to face," said Susman, going professional for the moment.

"He let me play as long as my play was harmless, as long as I was acting, or play-acting, playing like a child in his dirty music business. He sees me as a child. But now he says this Matson has called off the games. I am forbidden, forbidden from returning to America, forbidden to see David. He swears to me that David won't be harmed, but how can I believe him? And this at the very moment when I have helped turn David's business into a success. His records go to the top. How is that, dear Victor, for irony?"

"You are badly upset and frustrated."

"Very."

He took her in his arms. "I, too . . ."

She pushed him away. "But to resist him is to endanger my own life—that's what my own father says. It seems no exaggeration. Turning the killings at Spago into self-serving publicity—incredibly stupid. And dangerous. And now to go against my own father, he claims, is also to endanger *his* very life. He says it will kill him. Why suddenly is he sharing all these secrets with me? Why?"

"He uses secrets as a way to bond with you and insure your loyalty."

"Oh, Victor, I feel like such a fool. Silly and naive and, as you have said, desperate for my father's love and approval. Sickening! I thought I was strong, clever, but I was weak enough to believe his lies. While I was working so hard for his attention, he was able to fool me, pretend his enterprises were legitimate, act so respectable, beyond reproach. Oh, such a great man! *He* was the actor, not Carla. He has been fooling Carla, fooling his own lawyer, fooling the world. He has secret networks . . . God only knows how deep his criminal connections go. I am angry, yes, I am furious with this liar, this charlatan. I despise him. And I told him that. But what do I do? Am I, after all, ready to disregard his warning and destroy my own father?"

"To save yourself . . ."

"That is why I came here, Victor, to hear those words."

"And?"

"And nothing else, dear Victor," she said, her last words before leaving his office and hailing a cab for Leonardo Da Vinci Airport outside Rome.

Fifteen miles southeast of the city, in a Renaissance villa near Castel Gandolfo, seat of the Pope's palatial summer home, Mitchell Matson sat next to Calvino Bari on a balcony overlooking Lake Albano.

"The lake, *caro mio*," said Calvino, invigorated by a fifteen-minute stay in his sauna, "seems so calm, it is easy to forget that it lies in the crater of a volcano that was once active. They say the volcano is extinct but I wonder—will it erupt one day and fool us all, much like these problems facing us today? I ask you, Mitchell, are these problems out of control?"

"I'm putting a lid on those problems," Matson said, feeling less sure at the moment than he hoped he sounded.

"Are you? The two of us, we've worked so hard for control of our affairs. And we have maintained that control. Yet when it came to our daughters—"

"She's a spoiled bitch." Matson, despite his appearance in comfortable tennis whites, was losing his cool.

"Your daughter or mine?" asked Calvino wryly.

"I never met your daughter, Bari, and mine, I guess I never knew her—not really. She lied to me. The little cunt pretended she was someone she wasn't."

"Precisely my daughter's accusation of me." Calvino took a bite from a ripe pear, cleaning the juice from the corners of his mouth with a white linen napkin. "Let's examine the situation, Mitchell. This Jay Feldman, he has been dispensed with, is that correct?"

"I got word yesterday."

"And Ira Crossman . . ."

"Someone else's work, I'm not sure whose."

"It doesn't matter. He had contact with you. He had information that could prove harmful. I presume your political contacts are still secure?"

"I talked to Larry Kalb only an hour ago. He has huge influence with the media. He assures me he'll get this thing quashed."

"*Ottimo*. Then that leaves only the matter of David Crossman."

"I've had no contact with him."

"You were protecting him for a while."

"You were the one, Bari, who had that idea. Because he's Ralph Crossman's son, you felt it was important to protect him."

"I no longer think so. It's now clear that David Crossman is, as you say, the wild card in this deck. He makes me uncomfortable."

"He does, or his thing with your daughter?"

"Both. We need him out of the picture. If he were in Europe it would be a matter of a phone call for me. As matters stand, however, he is in your territory."

Matson downed his glass of San Pellegrino mineral water and reached for the phone.

MIAMI BEACH

THE PLANE RIDE HAD been a nightmare. This man, this Mario Washington, had been impossible.

"Who are you?" Nathan had asked him. "What are you talking about?"

"I'm working on a television story, Mr. Silver. I'm talking about a man named Pino Feldman. I'm also talking about a man named Ruben Gent Ginzburg. I think you know them both."

"Are you crazy? I've no idea what you're talking about."

"I think you do know, Mr. Silver."

"How do you know my name?"

"I've been interested in you for a long time."

"Why?"

"Your past, your present."

"I have a printing company in Miami. What's interesting about a printing company?"

"Aren't you coming back from a visit to your grandsons in Los Angeles?"

"What grandsons? I have no grandsons."

Gertrude came back then, surprised to see someone in her seat.

"Excuse me," said Mario, who got up only to move to the empty seat directly behind Nathan. For the next several minutes, Washington intoned names into the old man's ear—Lowell Lord Foreman, Eve Duchess Silk—"

"Stop it," Nathan finally said, his voice raised.

An attendant came over and asked what was wrong. "This man," said Nathan, "he's a pervert; he's out of his mind."

Washington concentrated on his Wall Street *Journal.* He was silent for the rest of the trip, letting the silence and his questions do their work.

And they were getting to Nathan—this man behind him seemed to know . . . But how was it possible? And was it going on television? Ira was gone, and now Bernard Crossman's elimination of Nathan Silver would come out. Instead of living out his life in peace, he'd be sent to prison, maybe executed. Who knew? Lawyers, trials, appeals—either way his life would be hell. This man behind him, maybe he wasn't from television. Maybe he was from Pino. Whichever, this man was dangerous. The man behind him did not speak for the rest of the five-hour trip, and Nathan tried to pretend that he wasn't there, that the man meant nothing to him.

It did not work. Nathan's breath was short, he felt the sweat pouring. Was he having another heart attack? He tried to nap, no use. He tried to figure what had gone wrong—who was talking to the press? Not Ralph. Never. Ralph had everything to lose. David? Why should David—? Wait. Why not. David had nothing to lose. David wasn't hiding who he was, his past life . . . lives . . . like his father and grandfather. David was a loose canon; *David was the one who had to be stopped.* Like his father, David was a betrayer, turned against his own. As soon as the plane landed he would arrange with his contractors. The same who had taken care of the security guards at David's place. David. Could he do that to his grandson? Yes. Why not? His grandson had done it to him, hadn't he?

Or was it Pino? Pino was alive, he knew. Pino never stopped punishing. All this was Pino's pay-back. Now, as before—Pino was the root of all his pain.

FORT WORTH

1953

STANDING IN THE BACK of the crowded Black Parrot club, Bernie found himself looking around for Pino. He knew that was crazy—Pino was locked up in a prison hundreds of miles away. But Bernie checked out the joint anyway. A wide-brimmed hat tilted over his face, he also knew he had no business here, no business in the world. He promised himself he would stay only for the first set. Silky would never see him, never know he was here. She couldn't. Letting anybody know he was alive would be dangerous for everyone—especially himself, his wife and sons. But he had to see his Silky one last time, had to hear her and Lord perform "Morning After" and "Defend My Heart," "Silk Web" and "All the Way Through." He was a junkie looking for one last fix, swearing to God Almighty that he'd never ever go near the stuff again.

The crowd was excited. It was a special occasion; jazz artists of national stature came to Fort Worth infrequently. Champagne bottles were popping, fans buzzing. Bernie did not recognize the rhythm section—local guys picked up only for this gig—but as they played their fourth number, still waiting for the arrival of the stars, Bernie began to feel nervous. He flashed back to the Regal Theater in Chicago, to 1945 and the concert that featured Gene Krupa and Coleman Hawkins and Tiny Bradshaw's big band, to the night the Raminskis had kidnapped his artists to get to him. Just like tonight, he had waited and waited until it was plain that his artists weren't coming, those same artists who were late tonight. The Raminskis knew how to hurt Gent, and so did Pino. The Raminskis were dead, but Pino wasn't. Pino's arm reached around the country . . .

But this was only sick imagining, thought Bernie. A week of too much stress, days and nights obsessed with thoughts of Silk and this club date. Now that he was here, he couldn't help but be a little crazy. He couldn't help but worry about Pino. Hadn't Pino put Eve in the hospital the first time he saw her? Wasn't that how this whole thing had started—by saving the singer from a guy who didn't give two shits about music, a guy who'd sooner wipe you out than brush a piece of lint off his sleeve?

An hour passed and Bernie was feeling worse. What was happening? Why did he keep flashing back to Chicago? Outside he heard noises from the streets. Another fifteen minutes. The crowd started whistling, stomping, carrying on so that the manager had to come out and announce that Duchess and Lord were on their way. Another fifteen minutes, and still no Silk, no Lord, and Bernie imagining things, Bernie feeling sick until he finally went to the dressing room and, mumbling in a phony voice, asked the musicians where Eve and Lowell were staying.

"The Jackson Hotel," he was told, "two blocks over toward the stockyards."

Fort Worth smelled like cow shit no matter where you went, he thought as he more and more worried, fear reaching his legs, making him start to run, run past cowboy bars and boot shops, past the stink of slaughtered cattle, the twang of honky-tonk music, past rednecks riding 'round in pickup trucks, out of breath, stumbling, nearly falling, finding himself following a firetruck around the corner to where the green neon light flashed "Jackson Hotel . . . Jackson Hotel . . . Jackson Hotel" and a squad of cop cars and fire engines parked in front, smoke rising from the second story, a crowd gathered around, people pointing to the second story, Bernie asking questions, getting vague answers, something about an explosion, a bomb, no one knew, no one knew who was up there, but Bernie, he'd known all along, known all week, sensed it, now saw it, ran around back, up the fire escape into the second story and down the smoke-filled hall toward the room with the door blown off, and inside found her body, all limp and lifeless, her eyes without expression, and Lord on the other side of the room, his face mutilated beyond recognition, his thick glasses shattered on the floor and the sound, the small sound of a crying three-year old, a toddler, miraculously alive, under a smoking mattress, somehow cushioned, saved by the mattress, a little brown girl picked up finally by Bernie and carried out the same back way, off into the night so no one could see him or stop him or make him leave his little baby, this traumatized baby who would never utter a word, this baby whom he would take care of, one way or another, for the rest of his life.

MIAMI

"I'M CALLING FROM A phone booth at the airport. The New York office said you've been trying to reach me—"

"He slipped out," said Kate Matson from Rome. "He must know something. I was waiting down in the lobby for over an hour when I finally went up there. By then he was gone."

"What did you learn before he left?"

"That's why I was calling. He's in with Calvino Bari—"

"Carla Bari's father?"

"And Ralph Crossman's client. From what I've found out here, Bari has secretly underwritten Mitch for years. Bari's his bankroller. They have these dealings in records and music publishing. Their holdings go beyond the United States into France, Germany, Switzerland, South America, Japan. Mitch is the front man, the star-entrepreneur. Bari's the squeaky-clean behind-the-scenes conservative old world financier. But his connections go straight to the most prominent mob families of Palermo."

"Kate—you're fantastic. But what about your old man? Why did he take off? Could he know?"

"Last night he was still playing the starring role in my version of 'Lifestyles of the Rich and Famous.' His ego helped him buy into the whole thing. I don't know what happened to change things for him."

"Obviously something. Be careful."

"Of my own father?"

"Especially your own father."

"*How does a father come to murder a son?*"

The words haunted Ralph Crossman as he got into a cab at the airport and gave the driver the address of the Atlantic Arms. He felt out of control, as though he were on some drug. On the plane to Miami he only knew his life had turned into a nightmare. Margo was wonderful, but Margo couldn't understand. Not really. How could she? Yes, she had denied her parents like he had denied his father. But he was the son of a hit man. The anxiety, the fear, the hatred . . . no one could understand. No one knew what it took for him to get on the plane to finally confront his father.

"If it's so terrible for you, why are you going?" Margo had asked.

"I have to. I think he's the only one who can save David. He holds the cards . . ."

"*What* cards, Ralph? You aren't making sense."

"He can expose everything—"

"Why should he? He'd be hurting himself."

"I don't know, maybe to get back at me."

"You just said he could save David. You're confused; you're not yourself. Don't go, Ralph. Stay away from him—"

"I've tried, but things have gone too far . . ."

Deep into old Miami Beach now, the cabbie dropped Ralph in front of the Atlantic Arms. Ralph remembered the musty Tropical Deco lobby, the seafoam green mural of pink flamingos drinking from a Byzantine fountain. It was the moment, during his last attempted visit, that he had run. He could no longer do that. He had to go into the elevator, had to push the button, had to ride to the sixth floor, walk down the hallway to Apartment 6C, ring the doorbell and wait . . .

Gertrude half-opened the door, saw this man in a distinguished suit, then opened it all the way. Ralph's half-sister looked as calm and placid as ever, her face turned into a partial smile. She had, he remembered, come to live with his father the year he had gone off to college. He knew, though, by the character of her eyes, by the way she was treated, that she was his father's child. He had also guessed that she was the child of the woman he had seen his father with on the couch that gun-shattering night back in Chicago. Beyond that, he had never wanted to think about her, never wanted to consider what she meant or who she was. She was mute; he had blocked her out.

"If it's someone named Washington," he heard his father say, "tell him to go away."

Gertrude stepped aside to let Ralph move into the apartment. "It's me," he said. "Ralph . . ."

Silver sat on the couch in the living room listening to "Wheel of Fortune" on the television. Someone had just won a G.E. refrigerator. Nathan was wearing dark glasses, an Hawaiian shirt and blue trousers. When he heard the name, his body twitched. For a long while he just sat there. Finally a single word fell softly from his mouth. "Miltie."

"We need to talk."

"I'm an old man, Miltie. I've lived a long life, but this is the first time I've heard you say those words. 'We need to talk.' Fine. But first, tell me what you look like."

He took a deep breath. "A little gray but mostly the same."

"Good, good. Tell me, Miltie, what do we have to talk about?"

"David."

"David is your son. I have nothing to do with him."

"You have everything to do with him." Ralph was pacing back and forth now, too worked up to sit. "You got him into this."

"You've come to tell me that?"

"I've come to ask you to save his life."

"I have such power?"

"You know you do."

Nathan smiled. "You confuse me with God, Miltie." He was beginning to enjoy this.

"This is no time for games; people are being killed—"

"People are always being killed."

"And you—"

"Me what? What have you come to say? You, Miltie, you of all people have no right to point a finger. Whatever you've done with your life, you've done it on your own. You never wanted to have anything to do with me. Me, your father, I wasn't good enough, I—"

"Irving was, look what happened to Irving, look what happened to Ira, look what happened to everyone else you've touched . . ."

"If I didn't know better, Miltie, I'd think you were here to kill me. Maybe that is why you came. Except my little Miltie is afraid of guns. My little Miltie is afraid of his own shadow—"

"I came because of my son."

"I don't know where he is, and I don't care."

"You're not in touch with him?"

"I'm in touch with no one. If it wasn't for your son, Miltie, you'd still have the pleasure of thinking your father was dead."

"You're responsible for what's happened to him. You're going to kill him the way you killed your own wife—"

"You're saying things you don't mean, things—"

"The doctors called it a heart attack but that attack was by you. If you put a knife through her heart you couldn't have done a better job— the years of cheating on her, running, hiding, bringing home a baby you had with another woman . . . it killed her—"

"And you, turning your back on her, you did nothing?"

"It was *you* I left, not her."

"Me and Reba, we were one."

"What about your mistress . . . your lying—"

"What about you, high and mighty Miltie? You didn't lie to your son? You didn't lie to the world? Your lies were worse because you didn't need them. Mine were lies to protect my family. *Family*, Miltie . . . but you couldn't understand—"

"I understand, damn you. Your lies were to save your own skin, lies of a man who wouldn't know right from wrong if—"

"Why are you yelling, Miltie? Is it making you feel good to yell? Why don't you just walk out like you walked out forty years ago?"

Ralph forced himself to quiet down, at least to try . . . "There's this television show, 'One Hour.' You must not talk to them. At least you must deny—"

"Listen to the lawyer. 'You must do this . . . you must do that . . . ' Do you think you're talking to a child? Do you think because I didn't go to a fancy school like you I can't figure these things out? Do you think I have anything to talk about on television? If anyone's not thinking, Miltie, it's you. Because if you were thinking you'd know not to come here. The TV people, they probably have cameras on everyone who comes in and out of this building. By coming here, you've hurt yourself more than I could ever hurt you. But that's my Miltie. You thought you could get away from me, but you never could. You were never as smart as you thought you were, Miltie. Never."

Outside the Atlantic Arms, Mario Washington and a three-person camera crew were waiting for him. Ralph's first reaction was to cover his face, which he quickly realized would only make it worse.

"Why would you be visiting Nathan Silver?" asked Washington, putting a microphone in Ralph Crossman's face.

Ralph didn't answer.

"Is it true that you represent Mitchell Matson and Calvino Bari, both with alleged connections to the underworld of the music business . . . ?"

Mario trailed after Ralph, following him back to the car. His questions also trailed on—questions about Matson and Bari. Ralph said nothing, showed nothing.

Driving back to the airport, he felt as though he had been shot. Stunned, he held a single thought: had Matson and Bari used him for their legitimate transactions while hiding their dirty ones? Had they used him and his firm to cover themselves? Of course, they had.

Covers. Everyone had a cover, starting with his father, starting in 1953. Hidden agendas, false fronts. And now they were all crashing down at once.

NEW YORK

PAUL ABEL SAT IN the top-floor office of Mark Costein, the thin, intense forty-five-year-old chief executive officer of the parent broadcast company that controlled the television network and owned "One Hour." On the speaker phone, his voice booming from one side of the enormous room to the other, was Lawrence Kalb.

"I want to be very straight with you, Mr. Costein. This program you're about to run is not only exposing you to legal repercussions, it's also destructive of what we're trying to do here."

"How would you know that, Mr. Kalb? You haven't seen it."

"My contacts are very good, very reliable. Look, the point is, I've been investigating the record industry now for over five years—"

"And with what results?"

"Results that I guarantee will be undermined—drastically undermined—if this thing goes public now. You'll be compromising our progress that's going to lead to the arrest of major felons. Good arrests that can stick. Not to mention, Mr. Costein, that your information, such as it is, is seriously tainted. A former employee of mine, and now of yours, Mario Washington, improperly obtained confidential department records for which he may well be indicted."

"That could be a serious problem for Mr. Washington. You should take it up with him."

"He's *your* employee."

"And from what I understand, a damn good one."

"I'm telling you, Costein, this thing cannot be aired. You'll be tied up in courts for years. Your stockholders will be all over you. And you'll be compromising real law-enforcement—"

"Your interest in the story is appreciated, Mr. Kalb, but I suggest you take up the matter with Paul Abel, the show's executive producer. Paul's sitting right here."

"I know about Abel, he's not reasonable. I thought you ran the show there."

Abel spoke up then. "Mr. Kalb, I don't know what's 'reasonable' with you. Mostly I'd guess it's going along with Lawrence Kalb. Forget it. Two weeks ago I said this story was wrapped up, that nothing new was going to develop, that we had to go with what we had. Then they started showing me stuff, *evidence*, linking *you*, Mr. Kalb, to the likes of Mitch Matson. I'd say your calling today only confirms that. For sure, you sound pretty worried to me, sir."

"Good try, Abel, but that's bullshit. My job is to make cases. I called to tell your boss that this so-called news program was going to undermine my work. *Period.*"

The executive producer looked at the C.E.O. He got an abrupt nod and a finger across the throat—signal for him to cut it off. He did, by switching off the speaker phone and leaving Lawrence Kalb with nothing but dead air to talk into.

The bomb was defused minutes before it was set to explode. The mail clerks had been alerted and security was tight in the network studios where tapes were stored and edited. The attempt was reported on the nightly news, thereby raising interest in Sunday night's presentation of the first part of Kate Matson's three-segment series on the underworld of the record business.

* * *

Back from Los Angeles, Mario didn't let Kate out of his sight that whole week.

The day she was set to tape the first segment, the day before the actual broadcast, she fell sick with the flu. She insisted that the doctors give her shots and went on camera anyway. She looked stunning in a navy-blue suit and short-collared white silk blouse as she began to narrate the story with authoritative intensity.

ALBUQUERQUE

"BEING OLD," PINO FELDMAN remembered Bette Davis remarking on some talk show just before she died, "isn't for sissies." Pino Feldman was no sissy. At the same time, he hadn't been feeling so good. Well, did a man in his nineties ever feel terrific? Especially on Sunday nights. Sunday nights were rough. Another week stared him in the face, another week of small errands and dumb tasks, the arrival of the physical therapist on Tuesday, the housecleaner on Thursday. Pino walked with excruciating slowness, every joint a source of pain. Where was there to walk to? What did he have to look forward to? When Jay was alive, Pino spoke to him every day; he lived through his grandson and his grandson's adventures. His grandson had spirit, smarts. But that was all over, and Pino wasn't sure he could deal with the mourning much longer.

To see this television show, then, to watch this segment of "One Hour," brought him a peculiarly strong pleasure. What difference did it matter that his past was revealed? He liked seeing photographs of himself as a young man, his hair slicked back, his eyes handsome and clear. He liked being called a "kingpin." It gave satisfaction to know that fifty million Americans were learning about Pino's successes, his power, his great days in Detroit and Chicago when Pino Feldman's name got instant respect. The reporters had done a job, reminding him of things he himself had forgotten. He appreciated that. But mostly, after all the history between him and Ruby Ginzburg was laid out, he appreciated the fact that the program had been able to do something Pino himself had failed to do for so long—locate Gent.

His suspicions were confirmed. He felt vindicated and alive. Because Gent was alive. "One Hour" speculated that Bernard Crossman might have disposed of Nathan Silver and assumed the man's identity. Pino *knew* it. Suddenly his life had new meaning. He had calls to make, people to contact. His strength was returning. He had unfinished business.

MIAMI

NATHAN STILL FELT SECURE in the backroom of his printing plant, his womblike hideaway. With Gertrude, as usual, calmly knitting close by, he would spend every afternoon here, running his fingers over his thousands of records, stopping at this song or that, pulling out a record, usually one of Duchess', placing it on the phonograph, settling back into his easy chair and listening. That's all that was left. Just like all those years before David came into his life.

After the "One Hour" broadcast, he told Gertrude to disconnect the phone in his apartment. He knew the police would soon start investigating the real Nathan Silver's death. Soon he would need lawyers. He figured he had at least a few days of peace before the process began. He thought, too, of running, taking Gertrude and flying off somewhere far away. But he was too tired, too old, and, besides, they'd find him. They'd find him wherever he went. In the meantime only Silky provided peace. Silky sang about summertime and lost love, about the man who did her wrong and the man who did her right, men she could trust and those with hardened hearts, moonless nights alone along the waterfront, waiting for love to turn hurt to joy, to live happily-ever-after in the arms of a true man, a good man, her man forever. Soothed by the smoothness of her pain, Nathan would float away from his suffering, sleep for a while, lose himself in dreams of when Silky took him deep into her, shutting out everything except the tastes and flavors of her warm body. Sometimes the dream would be interrupted by violence—a break-in, a murder—but the music always returned, the music made everything all right...

At first, he thought he was still dreaming. It sounded like a buzz saw. Was someone severing the steel bolt that guarded the door to his inner-sanctum?

"Gertrude!" he called out.

But by then he heard footsteps. The door opened. It sounded like two men. He heard one of them grabbing Gertrude. Someone else was walking slowly, unsteadily, walking with the steps of a very old man. Nathan knew.

"Pino."

"Gent."

The younger man searched Nathan. "You think I carry a gun?" asked Nathan. "What good would a gun do a blind man?"

"With you, Ruby," said Pino, "I never knew. I didn't know you was blind. I wouldn't even know it was you—you look like an old piece of shit—if it wasn't for that mole on your chin."

"You got here faster than I thought you would, boss. All I ask is that you leave Gertrude—"

A single gun shot. Nathan heard Gertrude's body slump to the floor.

"My baby..." he whispered to himself.

"My *son*," said Pino in a trembling voice. "My grandson... my business... you took it all."

Nathan's eyes had gone dead. Gertrude was dead. On the phonograph Duchess and Lord were singing "Southside Velvet."

"That nigger music," said Pino. "You ain't ever changed."

"They were artists, they were geniuses, but you were too stupid to ever understand it."

"You were the genius, right? You sang and you ran, but look what happened. You can never run from Pino Feldman, didn't you know that, Gent? Why didn't a man with a brain like yours know that?"

Nathan listened as Duchess sang:

Look here, Southside Velvet
If what I hear is true
You ain't taking care of business
Like you oughta do

The humor in her voice, the lightness of tone, the easy swing . . .

"You listening to me, Gent? You got nothing left except your grandson. David. Where is he? You gotta know. And even if you don't, I'll find him just like I found you . . ."

Lord sang the second verse:

Southside's Velvet sure to win
I'm your lucky charm
Southside's Velvet coming in
Straight into your arms

The blind man remembered how he talked Lowell Foreman into singing, how he changed his career and turned him into a star. The critics said this and that, but screw the critics. The people loved Lord, they understood his sincerity, he had style like no one else . . . him and Duchess, the way they sounded together . . .

"You ain't all there, Gent. I wish you was. I wish to hell you could see. The funny thing is, I ain't hardly strong enough to pull this trigger. But I got someone else to do it for me. Remember Fingers? Fingers is dead, but this here is his little brother's son. We keep it all in the family."

The music stopped. "You haven't changed either, Pino," the Gent said. "You always had to have someone else to do it for you." For the first time in his life, he wasn't afraid of Pino. For the first time, he felt free.

The blast hit Gent in the chest. He gasped for breath. "You'll never get out . . . never get out of Miami . . . you're stupid, Pino . . . you always needed me to—"

The second shot penetrated his skull just above the eyes.

FBI surveillance, a bit slow, caught up with Pino Feldman and Gerald Markowitz when they got off the plane in New Mexico.

The Gent had had the last word.

TULARE, CALIFORNIA

DURING WINTER, THE IMMENSE San Joaquin Valley, spread over central California, can be shrouded in fog for weeks at a time, fog thick enough to close highways and schools. In springtime, though, the rich agricultural region has its own sort of beauty. The distant mountains of the Sequoia National Forest frame the flatness of the land. The crops—cotton, oranges, alfalfa—are plentiful, the fields cultivated with a geometric symmetry that many a landscape painter would find irresistible.

On the outskirts of Tulare, a small city in the midst of this valley, beyond orchards of walnuts, almonds and peaches, David Crossman and Rita Moses sat by the edge of a man-made lake, its mirror-surface eerily still, a seventy-five-degree sun reflecting golden light on the face of the lovers as they held hands, relishing the hush of the afternoon.

Two weeks earlier Rita had made the 175-mile drive from Los Angeles. Her instincts about the members of Tomorrow's News had been right. Since the murder of the four security guards in Malibu, they had been hiding David. At first he had lived in the black neighborhoods of Inglewood and Compton, at the home of cousins of Gemini Star and Isaiah Z. When things got hotter, though, no place in the city seemed safe. Plucky P, the bassist, had been raised in Tulare, where his parents had bought farm land in the early fifties. That was where David had been living. That was where he had been thinking through his life, looking at his relationships with his grandfather and father, accepting that the circumstances—his survival—had estranged him from them probably forever. Still, in spite of the dangers and the violence of his dreams, his days had been almost tranquil. He surprised himself with a new sense of confidence.

Rita's arrival was part of it. She was the only one who knew him well enough to understand where he would go and who would help protect him, the only one those people trusted enough to tell where he was. At a time when he could trust no one, her being with him won his deepest trust. They talked about her music, wondering about the creative possibilities of her collaborating with Tomorrow's News. The blending of their funk and her jazz intrigued. The unspoken, possibilities about the two of them being together were even more intriguing.

The first shock prompted by the violence of Ira's and Jay's deaths had faded. But his grandfather's death was different. He had assumed the old man would fool them all. Live to be one hundred ten.

"He was a murderer, a hired gun," David had told Rita, yet how did you square that with the other side of him . . . his love of music, of the Duchess, Gertrude . . . ? Maybe you didn't.

The third segment of "One Hour" reported the news of his father. It came after the interview in which Geoffrey Wane told of his beating at the hands of Ira Crossman and the footage of Mitchell Matson speaking at the dedication of the Players Foundation retirement home named in his honor in Piscataway, New Jersey.

"She's got ice water in her veins," said Rita, watching Kate Matson narrate the story with chill precision. "Listen to how she talks about her own father."

"Reliable sources say," Kate Matson told the viewing audience, "that Mitchell Matson is negotiating with several Central and South American politicos. Reportedly he has offered over one hundred million dollars to any government willing to grant him asylum. Calvino Bari was last seen in Sicily. Courts in Italy, France and the United States are actively seeking his extradition. In Los Angeles, District Attorney Lawrence Kalb, facing bribery charges, has resigned his office. 'One Hour' has also learned that Ralph Crossman has entered a private hospital in Stamford, Connecticut, where a staff member said he was suffering from, and I quote, 'a mental breakdown.' His wife Margo would not comment, nor would any senior members of Crossman's prestigious law firm.

"The story, then, is complete," said Kate, "except for the whereabouts of David Crossman, missing now for over three weeks . . ."

A week went by before David surfaced. He had discussed it with Rita, who reluctantly agreed.

At first, Carla was furious that David was back with his former lover, but how angry could Carla be? The day she had arrived in California she had started a torrid affair with Vince Viola, the saxist whose songs were selling so well. Besides, she was grateful that dear David was alive and well.

"Of course it's good publicity," she said. "It's the kind of publicity money can't buy. Just don't do anything. Let Carla do it all."

Two days later, Kate Matson, Mario Washington and a crew of camera and sound technicians traveled to Tulare, California, where, as the sun fell behind the faraway mountains, they filmed David Crossman giving his detailed narrative of exactly what had happened, from the time he met his grandfather until the present.

The next Sunday night Paul Abel, along with some sixty million fascinated Americans, watched the additional fourth and final segment—an hour long—of the story of a family too long soaked in treachery and blood.